GW00994394

The Great Affair

VICTOR CANNING

HEINEMANN : LONDON

William Heinemann Ltd
LONDON MELBOURNE TORONTO
JOHANNESBURG AUCKLAND

First published 1970
© Victor Canning 1970

434 10768 9

MADE AND PRINTED IN GREAT BRITAIN BY
MORRISON AND GIBB LTD, LONDON AND EDINBURGH

For my part, I travel not to go anywhere, but to go. I travel for travel's sake. The great affair is to move.

Robert Louis Stevenson

CHAPTER ONE

THE GENERAL HAD sent a car for me. It was 18 June, the
anniversary of the battle of Waterloo. In our family you knew
all the principal battle dates in British history because my father
had insisted on it but, despite Waterloo, I wasn't likely to forget
this one because only a few hours previously I had finished a
three-year prison sentence. The car was a gun-metal coloured
Rolls and was driven by the General's chauffeur, Anderson.
Anderson and the General had spent most of their life together.
It was a fine morning, full of warmth and colour. In the circumstances I suppose most men would have filled their lungs with
the bland air and given a glad welcome to freedom. The fresh
air I welcomed, free of prison smells. But freedom is always
around us. True freedom is lodged somewhere under a man's
vest, and once he has it nothing can take it away.

I hadn't been unhappy in prison. How can a man—particularly an ex-priest like myself—be unhappy simply because
he has to make a justifiable payment for his failure? In a good
cause you win or lose, and if you lose you hand over your sword
with dignity and submit without bitterness. (My father had many
sayings about honour. But this was a subject over which we
never agreed. Men can only be honourable after their own
fashion. Prison was full of such men, and I enjoyed their
company.)

We drove to Petersfield in Hampshire, a detour on my
journey farther westwards on which my brother had insisted.
My elder by two years and only brother—Edward Leno
Sangster, barrister and Member of Parliament (Conservative),

I

a just but hard man, full of love for me and no small portion of despair either—lived in a grey-stone substantial country house to the west of Petersfield. (I should explain that my father, born on Christmas Day 1884, had been christened James Noel and, because he was given to such quirks, had decided that all his children should have second names which were anagrams of Noel. My elder brother became Edward Leno, which particularly delighted my father because he was a great admirer of Dan Leno from the moment he had first seen him playing the Baroness in *The Babes in the Woods* in a Drury Lane pantomime. I became, not Leon as might have been expected, but Nelo—Charles Nelo Sangster—and my sister was called Onel.)

My brother's house stood on a tree-ringed knoll approached by a gravel drive that at the foot of the knoll crossed an ornamental lake by way of a rustic stone bridge. There were swans on the lake this morning and a scurry of coots and dishevelled dabchicks. Three chestnut hunters grazed in a paddock beyond the lake and from the top of the flagpole which stood to one side of the gravel circle before the house flew a Union Jack. That, I knew, was for Waterloo and out of respect for my dead father, beloved, irascible and unpredictable, who always flew a Union Jack—sometimes at half-mast—to mark the battle anniversaries he loved. My brother was a man with a strong sense of duty which led him to actions of which he did not necessarily approve.

He was waiting for me in the library. Most of the books had come from Stonebridge Park and had belonged to my father. Stonebridge Park now belonged to Uniprods Limited and was used for staff training courses and conferences. A silver tray with a sherry decanter and glasses stood within reach of his hand and he faced me in his rough tweeds with a false Churchillian pout to his lips and thrust to his chin which served him well in the House. In appearance we were remarkably alike—a fact which we had sometimes used to advantage as boys.

2

He shook me by the hand and said, "Welcome back, Nelo."

"Thank you, Teddie." He always called me Nelo, but I would never have called him Leno. He hated it and had made it clear to me from a boy.

"Sherry?"

"Thank you."

He poured sherry for us. We drank silently.

He put his glass down and said, "Let us not muck around with sentiment and regrets. What are you going to do?"

"The General has kindly lent me a small house near his and I'm going down there. It has all modern conveniences and there is quite a nice little garden."

"I'm talking about your future. How do you see it?"

"I don't. I'm Nelo, not Cassandra. But if I could I doubt whether I would want to."

He groaned. "Oh, Christ—you're just the same."

"More or less."

"What are your assets, your plans? Nelo, you've had three years to think things over."

"Oh, I did a lot of thinking but nothing conclusive. I've no plans—"

"I hope you're going to go straight."

"I always have. It's just that ethically we don't all see eye to eye."

He finished his sherry quickly and helped himself to another. I finished mine and went over and helped myself. It was good sherry, a warm, flexible-bodied Amontillado and all the more delicious after three years of abstinence. Not that I'm a steady drinking man and had missed it. But it was before me now, and suddenly I wanted more of it.

"Well," he said, "I have a suggestion to make. In this country—no matter what affection I have for you—you are an embarrassment to me and a small shadow on my career. You have nothing. The whole of Father's estate came to me under the family entail. True, he could have left you something but he didn't, so great was his shock—"

3

"He wasn't shocked. He was confused. The first year I was in he visited me twice and he'd got it all wrong. He thought I was in for rape and you know what he was like once he'd got an idea in his head—it was a waste of time trying to correct him. Not that I minded. Mind you I met one or two rapists inside and it seemed to me that they were sad victims of their own fantasies and it's a form of fantasy far more common than—"

"Nelo!"

"Teddie?"

"I'm going to make you an offer. You're penniless—"

"That's not so, Teddie. I have a villa, let furnished in the South of France. You remember, Aunt Tillie left it to me. And also I have Mother's diamond necklace. That must be worth many thousands of pounds."

"You have the villa, that's true. But precious little you make out of it. That caretaker out there robs you."

"How is he robbing me if the little he takes I never miss?"

"Cut that out. You're not in the pulpit here and, thank God, you never will be anywhere else."

Unfrocked, prison-stained, the unwelcome prodigal, an embarrassment to his career, I stood before him and understood his point of view perfectly and had great sympathy because I loved him as he loved me and no one wishes to hurt a loved one. But sometimes it can't be helped.

"All right, Teddie. The villa, true, brings me very little because I have an unfaithful servant. But I have Mother's diamonds. I thought of selling them and going in with La Guicha and enlarging that place she runs in—"

"Nelo!" Even as a boy it had been his way of bringing me to heel. The sergeant-major bark.

"Teddie?"

"La Guicha is a crook. She runs a racket."

"I disagree."

"Then disagree."

He was getting cross and if it went on I knew that he would

4

begin throwing things. He always had. We were bathing together once, both stark naked, when some idiocy of mine had annoyed him and he had thrown a dustbin lid at me. The edge was jagged and cut me, leaving me for the rest of my life with a long, slightly puckered scar on my left side just below the ribs. The memory came back now, sharp and clear; blood coiling from my belly into the water, moving like idle trails of red smoke, and the scared look on his face. It was the only time I ever saw him scared.

I said, "What was the offer you were going to make me?"

He smiled suddenly at the beginning of reasonableness in me. "I am prepared to pay your passage to Australia . . . no, no, wait . . . to settle on you three thousand pounds a year for life since I think Father was hard towards you in his will. In fact, as a legal man, I would go so far as to say that he wasn't quite sane at the time that he cut you out and you could contest it. Though if you did—for your own good—I would fight it and win. So don't let's have any talk about that."

"I wasn't talking about it."

"You will in a minute. Anyway, that's my offer—with the condition that you promise not to come back to this country for at least ten years. And a very generous offer I think it is."

"So do I. But I don't want it. I shall sell the villa and Mother's diamonds and give the money to La Guicha. I have decided that the future of this world lies with its children not its adults—for the moment that is. La Guicha—"

"Is a crook. You can sell the villa and give her the money. I can't stop that. But you can't have Mother's diamonds."

"Why not?"

"Because they don't belong to you."

"But she gave them to me."

"She promised them to you. But she left them to Father."

"But he said they were to be mine. He'd made a point of it in his will."

"He made six wills in his life. The sixth and last, as you know, in the first year of your prison sentence. He died within

5

six months of making it and the diamonds were left to me with the rest of the estate."

"Well, there's no problem is there?"

"Why not?"

"Mother always said you could have the emeralds and me the diamonds. That was because she knew you would inherit more than me anyway under the entail. Well, you have the emeralds and the diamonds are morally mine. All you have to do is to give them to me."

He shook his head. "Only in a few and extreme cases has the law ever recognised a moral right. Legally the diamonds are mine and I mean to keep them."

"Why?"

"Largely because I am not putting one hundred thousand pounds' worth of precious stones into your hands to be dissipated by you and La Guicha in some hare-brained, altruistic non-sense about needy children."

Suffer the little children to come unto me, and forbid them not: for such is the Kingdom of God. I didn't quote it to him because I knew he would have some legal answer to St. Mark. Instead I said, "You're a bloody thief, Teddie."

He shook his head, and smiled. I knew the smile. It was full of the rectitude he felt when he thought that he was doing good by denying someone else the right to do ill.

He said, "Your moral right I acknowledge. The diamonds are morally, sentimentally by the wish of our Mother, yours. And you shall have them the moment that I consider you have reshaped your life along solid, acceptable lines and have become a worthy citizen. Nelo, it is for your own good that I do this. An elder brother has duties."

I stood up to go. "Morally," I said, "you're still a bloody thief. But don't think I don't understand the admirable sentiments that have made you one. I understand them but don't agree with them. Well, well, I mustn't keep Anderson waiting."

I made for the door.

6

He called, "Nelo."

"Yes?" I turned.

"What about Australia?"

"What about it? So far as I'm concerned it's still where it was. One day I hope I may visit it, but for the moment it doesn't come into my plans. Thank you for the sherry. It was excellent."

Back at the car Anderson opened the door for me and said, "How was Master Edward, sir?"

I said, "He is rejoicing because he has found the sheep which was lost."

"If he kept proper fences, sir, he wouldn't lose any."

An hour and a half later I met her. Sarah Minihane.

*   *   *   *

Somewhere before we reached Alresford, it began to rain and blow. Clear out of the June sky the storm came and with a wrecker's fury. So hard was the rain that the wipers could not deal with it and the windscreen looked as though the glass were melting, blurring the outside world. The wind struck great paranoiac blows at all that stood or moved. Blossoms, twigs, branches and leaves were hurled high. Slates took wing and came slicing through the swamped air like furies. Even the Rolls, which was a solid enough thing, responded reluctantly now and then to the manic gusts.

Anderson said, "Tunis 1944."

I said, "Why?"

"Last time I seen anything like it, Master Nelo."

Anderson had known both my brother and me since we were boys. He was a man who vigorously opposed change so we had always been Master Nelo and Master Edward. In some ways I think we were still boys to him. On meeting me that morning he had said, "They feed you well, Master Nelo?" and when I told him they had (which was more or less true) he had said, "Good." From that moment, for him, the whole prison episode was closed.

7

I said, " 'He blew with his winds and they were scattered', " thinking of the Armada, which in the past had meant flags flying for many days at Stonebridge Park, and it was at this moment that dimly, distortedly through the windscreen, I saw something ahead of us on the road. It was twenty or so yards ahead and to our left. Then there came an exceptionally violent gust of wind and the thing disappeared from the road.

I said, "Anderson, what was that?"

"Girl on a bike. Wind took her clean through the hedge. She must have been daft, trying to ride in this."

I made him stop. He wouldn't have done so willingly because for him if you dropped out of the march that was your fault for not keeping your feet in good order and you could take your chances with the harrying marauders behind.

"You'll get soaked, Master Nelo. I ain't got no mack in the car."

I got out and the wind obligingly slammed the door shut for me. There was a small gap in the roadside beech hedge. (Hampshire is beech, hawthorn and a permanent draping of old man's beard.) I went through it and down a steep grass slope to a small pond, green with wild watercress. The rear wheel of what I learned later was a Lambretta scooter was sticking out of the water. A girl, who had clearly once been fully immersed, stood by it up to her knees in cress and was unstrapping a small suitcase from the carrier.

She gave me a glance and said through a curtain of wind and rain, "You from the Rolls?"

"Yes."

"I saw you for a moment in my mirror as I was skyborne. I said to myself coming down the slope, it'll be a bloody miracle if those bastards stop. Here." She slung the now freed suitcase across to me and I caught it.

"Are you hurt?"

"No. Just wet."

I waded into the water and said, "Let's see if we can get this machine out."

8

"Why?"

"Well, you'll want it, won't you, eventually?"

"I don't want it. It's served its purpose." She held out a hand for me to help her out.

"Which was?"

"To start me moving from where I was to wherever it is I'm going."

I said, "I've a curious feeling that we might talk something like the same language."

She said, "I'm wet and beginning to be cold. Is it the kind of Rolls that has a built-in bar?"

"I think it is."

"Don't you know?"

"It isn't mine."

"Maybe not—but any normally curious person would have checked after the first five minutes' riding. Here you are, doing a kind Samaritan act and not even knowing whether you can top it off by giving me a brandy as we go along."

It did have a bar and she had her brandy as we rode along and by the time she had finished it the storm was gone as suddenly as it had come and June had slotted itself back into place in the calendar, and the girl began to undress in order to wrap herself in the two big car rugs. After she had got to the stage of removing her dress and stockings and shoes, she said, "Do you intend to watch the whole operation?"

I said, "There's nothing prurient about my regard. I was just admiring what I had seen. I was, in fact, about to turn my head."

"Fair enough, if a little stiltedly put. Now turn."

I turned away and saw Winchester sprawled in its hollow far below us. It was appropriate that Winchester should have been there at this moment, for much of my life had been connected with it. It was there that I had spent three years at the Theological College studying for my General Ordination Examination. But the past was only intermittently in my thoughts.

9

Chiefly they were with the girl at my side. Woman, rather. She was probably nearer thirty than twenty. Her voice had something a little Irish about it. She had dark coppery hair, darker now because it was wet, a nice face full of self-assurance and a well proportioned body. In fact she was very rewarding to look at. But at this moment I was not concerned with her, personally, but with the fact that she was a woman—the first I had touched or sat close to for three years. Throughout my life, desire for the sexual act had not bothered me overmuch and now, after three years' abstinence, her presence had not raised any desire in me. I found this interesting, because in the case of my brother's excellent sherry I had helped myself to a second glass, not out of pique that he hadn't offered it—but from a sudden desire to have it because it was there after the deprivation of so many years. In actual fact, most of my sexual activity had been the result of women finding in me something which compelled them to desire, so that, out of politeness and sociability, I usually complied with their wishes. At such times I enjoyed the congress although I do not rate it as high as many other pleasures. Paradoxically now, I think I was a little disappointed that three years' abstinence should work so positively for sherry and not for a woman. It seemed not quite natural.

She said, "All right now."

I turned. She was wrapped in the rugs with her feet drawn up under her on the seat and was smoking a cigarette from the General's bar.

I said, "What would you like us to do for you? I mean, about getting to wherever you were going."

"I wasn't going anywhere specific."

"I see."

"Do you?"

"Yes, of course. It applies to a lot of people."

She laughed and it was a very pleasant sound, and said, "What's your name?"

I told her.

"Nelo. I like that. I'm Sarah Minihane. My father was a Colonel in the Seventeenth-Twentyfirst Lancers. He now trains polo ponies in Pakistan. My mother died when I was twelve. She was never very strong. I was trained once as a nurse, once as a secretary and once as a dancer. I never did any good at any of them."

Later I was to hear different stories from her since she was very forgetful of what she had already put on record. I never did have the truth, but then it didn't matter. For some people fantasy is more fitting than truth.

I said, "Where have you come from? At least that must be well established."

"A boys' preparatory school in Kent. I was the matron for eighteen months. Yesterday I decided that I had been there long enough. The little boys were nice, but in their spare time the masters were vultures. Where are you from?"

"Prison. Three years."

"Really?" She sat forward and stubbed out her cigarette. "And where are you going?"

"Eventually abroad, but first of all I have to recover some property which morally belongs to me. Immediately, I'm on my way to a small cottage which is being loaned to me by the owner of this car. It's quite a nice cottage and there is plenty of room. And I'm not a vulture."

"You should be after three years. Anyway, thank you for the invitation. I'm a reasonable cook."

"It wouldn't matter. I'm an excellent one."

So she rode with us, into my life, though I didn't know what it was going to mean to me then; and up ahead Anderson sat without a word, though he could hear everything and I knew that a detailed and probably embellished report would be given to the General. Not that that worried me. He had been my father's best friend, and was now mine, and his life, not by a long way beyond reproach, had given him a tolerance and understanding which I envied.

She said, "What did you do before you went to prison?"

11

I said, "I was a Minister of the Anglican Communion with a small living near Barnstaple."

"Defrocked now?"

"Yes."

She giggled. "That makes two of us."

CHAPTER TWO

THE GENERAL HAD a large estate some way north of Salisbury and most of it was given over to the stud farm which he ran. The house itself was Palladian in design and the large, circular entrance hall had a painted ceiling by some minor Italian artist who had covered it with scenes from English rustic life of the early nineteenth century. (One of the pleasures of my father and the General after they had taken their port of an evening was to lie on their backs in the hall and run a score against each other for the mistakes they could find in the paintings. In fact one of the earliest recollections of the General I have was walking in one night—having been driven over by my mother to pick up my father—and hearing him bellow, "Huntsman's horse by duck pond—standing martingale twice as long as it should be. Two points!" They accorded their own points, following some intuitive agreement. And my father answering, "Girl bathing. Anatomically impossible for paps to ride so high out of water. Two and a half points!" He always called breasts paps, and whenever he used the word, for I used to read the Bible for pleasure long before I went to Theological College, I would recall the revelation of St. John. Clothed with a garment down to the foot, and girt about the paps with a golden girdle. I don't think they ever exhausted the game, so prolific of mistakes had the artist been. The last time I heard them play it they were down to noting the wrong number and colour of the primary feathers of the assortment of birds.) In addition to his own estate the General owned considerable property in the district. The house which he had loaned me,

13

completely furnished and provisioned—there was a long typed list of supplies and where they were stored and services and their modes of operation on the kitchen table—was some miles north of Salisbury in the valley of the River Avon, close to a village called Upper Woodford. It stood with its back to a wooded escarpment and there was a thin strip of green lawn between it and the river. You could stand in the bedroom window of a morning and watch the trout and grayling nymphing or taking fly and the housemartins swooping low to cool their breasts in the glass clear water. Seeing it would have made my father or my brother turn for their rods. But not me. Though I was brought up in the country where field and river sports were considered essential adjuncts of life I had always been content to stand and stare or walk and watch. My father never understood it, and if ever the solemn tablet of truth should be laid before me saying that that was the reason he had cut me out of his will there would be no surprise in me. A big, strong, healthy young man with no desire to shoot or fish, to kill or gaff was an oddity to my family. In the manly sports the only good marks I got were for riding and boxing. Though I never rode to hounds. However, they accepted my oddness and made a good-natured joke of it, which is as good a way of dealing with oddness as any.

That first evening with Sarah, I sent her upstairs to bath. She had a change of clothes, fortunately dry, in her small case. I took the General's list of supplies and checked them in cupboard, pantry and refrigerator. It was no surprise to me that he had made a good job of provisioning. Among many other things there was a pair of fresh Torbay soles in the refrigerator and some packets of frozen spinach, so while Sarah was bathing I made the basis of a *sole Florentine*, just leaving myself the *sauce mornay* to do when we should be ready for it.

When she came down she was wearing a very short-lengthed black velvet dress and she had piled her hair—which now seemed more red than coppery—at the top and back of her head. She looked quite beautiful, and her eyes, I saw now—

14

normally I'm rather unobservant about such things—were a pleasing striation or marbling of green and brown, not hazel, which reminded me of a stone in one of the rings my mother used to wear.

It was a warm evening and we sat outside on a small paved terrace in white painted wicker chairs and had our drinks. Over her second whisky, she said, "Were you a good parson?"

I like directness, and curiosity is no crime. It had always seemed odd to me that so many people considered too open a show of them bad manners.

I said, "I thought I was, but I suppose now I must have been wrong. Were you a good matron?"

"Christ, no—but I tried hard. Anyway, it made no difference if one boy got another boy's pants and socks. Whether their shirts were too tight or too big they seemed to like me. Your friend the General must be stinking bloody rich."

Her use of the words "Christ" and "bloody" didn't disturb me. I often used them and others myself. Blasphemy and lewdness lie in the intent not in the sound, and a thing so alive and protean as language can absorb and refine over the years a spate of blasphemies and obscenities. (I well remember my father once overhearing me as a boy call another a "dirty bugger". Later he asked me whether I was using the phrase parrot-fashion because I had heard other boys use it or whether it was meant to be a sexually accurate description of the boy's habits. When I said I didn't know, he explained to me what the word meant and added the rider, "I should prefer a son of mine to use words accurately. In the heat of the moment it is not always possible, but it is possible more often than people think.")

"Because he has a Rolls?" I asked.

"No. Because all the fittings in the bathroom are silver—they really are. And all the toilet stuff in there and on my dressing table is Lalique, and he's got an Etty hanging in the loo. The painting in the lounge is a Munnings and I've seen at least two gold cigarette boxes hanging about."

15

"Yes, he is wealthy, very. I believe that until recently one of his mistresses lived here."

"One of?"

"Ever since I've understood about that kind of thing—I think I was about eleven when my brother explained it to me—he's had at least two around."

"You approve of that?"

"Well, he's a bachelor. You could say that keeping two women happy is, if only on a quantitative basis, more to be commended than just keeping one."

"You've got some odd ideas, even for an ex-parson."

"I've been told so, but they don't seem odd to me."

"Well, well, Nelo—you don't mind if I call you that?"

"I'm delighted."

"Well, I'd like to hear more from you on that subject. I begin to get some idea why, perhaps, it was always on the cards that you'd land up in prison."

"We can talk about it later. I'm now going to finish off the dinner. If you want to help you can lay the table. All the cutlery is silver."

"He'll have this place knocked off one day. When we leave he'd better get another mistress in here quickly to look after it."

"When we leave?"

"Well, we shall do some time, shan't we?"

"You mean together?"

"I have that feeling."

"How could you?"

"Because I have second sight. My mother was Irish. I can read hands, too. Mind you, we shan't stay together long."

"Why not?"

"Because we're that kind."

"What kind?"

"The going on kind. The always wanting to look around the next corner kind. It's not altogether a good thing and I try to fight it sometimes. That's why I get myself a job and stick it for months and months hoping to break myself of the habit

16

of wandering. But always it gets too much for me. I suppose I get it from my father. He was an oil geologist always moving off to where the next lot of rocks or green sand or whatever was."

"You said he was a Colonel in the Army."

"This was before that. When he was young."

I said, "When you give up a job and start wandering, how do you manage for money?"

"Money?" She looked at me in genuine surprise. "Good Lord, I've never had any trouble about that. Have you?"

Truthfully, and completely understanding her, I said, "No, I haven't—not personally."

Finishing off the *sole Florentine* in the kitchen I thought about her. I liked her self-assurance, the way she was completely mistress of herself and the way she clearly accepted whatever situation the day brought forth and adapted herself to it without tedious questions.

Nothing, except a stupid question, like mine about money, seemed to surprise her. I'd picked her out of a pond and driven her off and she'd considered our destination the least matter of concern. She inhabited this house now as though she had always known she was going to and, in some odd way, as though she knew it with the familiarity of years. And she gave me the same feeling about myself . . . that already she had known me for years, that we were taking up again some long forgotten relationship, memory and knowledge melding gently back into place. I found it most intriguing and refreshing.

Over dinner, she said, "Did you miss women much when you were in prison, Nelo?"

"Occasionally."

"Don't you like women—sexually, I mean?"

"Of course—at intervals."

"Three years is a long interval."

"I suppose it is—but you don't have to lock your bedroom door."

"Oh, Nelo, that's the last thing I would do with you."

"Why?"

17

"Because clearly you're the kind of man who waits to be asked, or asks nicely when the interval becomes too long."

"Are you inviting me to sleep with you?"

"Not at all. I know quite well that between us it's something that will just happen. No asking on either side. Mind you, I don't want you to have the wrong idea. I'm not a virgin by many years, but neither am I promiscuous. The last time I was with a man was a year ago. It was the school sports day—June like this—and I was bored with it and walked down to a meadow by the school lake. They'd been cutting and stooking the hay and this man came along—he was one of the boy's parents who'd wandered away from the sports, not bored, he told me, but attracted by the lake. And it just happened, almost without words. Because he was the kind—almost at the time I thought he was the one I was looking for. But he wasn't."

"How do you tell?"

"Ah, Nelo—if we only understood that. You know it in here"—she touched her heart and rolled her eyes comically, "but you can't explain it up here." She put her fingers on her forehead.

After that I wasn't surprised—and that is said without arrogance—that after I'd been in bed about an hour she came into my room. If she hadn't come the truth is that in another five minutes I should have gone into hers. Three years, I had decided, was too long an interval.

She switched the bedside light on, finding it instinctively in the dark as though she had done it a hundred times before, and said, "There's a nightingale singing like crazy outside. Listen."

She stood there in a very short nightdress, her long, beautiful legs shining like ivory, her hair, now tawny with red-gold gleams in it from the light, loose around her neck, and we listened to the bird . . . the notes, dark and vibrant across the river.

"Lovely," she said and got into bed with me.

Naked on the covers in the warm night we made love joyfully and robustly and without haste and I was happy to find that three years in prison had neither improved nor impaired my ability. When we were finished, Sarah stretched her arms and legs wide, hair tangled over the pillow and sighed, "Delicious . . ." A word fitly spoken is like apples of gold in pictures of silver. I turned and took her gently in my arms. Within a few minutes she was asleep.

And then I lay there and thought that it was a good homecoming, but that it was neither a beginning nor an ending, but a drawing together that might stay sweet or turn sour because it was done with affection and desire, yes, but not with love. The woman whom Thou gavest to be with me, she gave me of the tree, and I did eat. So far back, was there not a note even then that it was the woman's fault? That had been my trouble, of course, all through Theological College—not the truth and beauty behind the words, but the stumbling blocks and trips for the tongue and thoughts that the words themselves were, because no man interprets a single word the way another does. It was this which often got me into trouble with my tutors at college, particularly on the subject of the Christian doctrine. Knowledge of the Christian faith is one thing, but an understanding of it in relation to human life and an ability to present it effectively to the contemporary world is another. It gave me trouble until I decided that where my interpretation differed from the orthodox it was better for me to stick to my own but make no great show of it until after I was ordained and, even then, not to display it unnecessarily though I would always be guided by it. Nor did I ever seek to excuse myself by saying that God could choose strange messengers. God didn't choose me. I chose God and was happy to do so. If He at any time found me unworthy, I told myself, he could always sack me. Which, of course, He did. Examine me, O Lord, and prove me; try out my reins and heart. He did—and I was discharged, at least from wearing His uniform. Not that I was ever forced to put it on. (My father when I told him of my intention bellowed, "There's only one kind of dog collar allowed here— and that's in the stables!" Not that he was an irreligious man.

But apart from bellowing, he did nothing active to stop me—though he had very much wanted me to go into the Army or Navy, principally I think because he thought that one day he might fly a flag for some battle in which I had been engaged. His elder brother by five years had served in the Relief of Mafeking and the hoisting of the flag on 17 May was always accompanied by a slow roll of the drums. The brother had been thrown from his horse three weeks later and died of a broken neck. My own father—again because of a horse, an animal which has accounted for a considerable decimation of the landed classes—suffered a leg injury at the age of seventeen which had left him with a pronounced limp and no chance of serving.) However, go into the church I did. At the time I did it because I had decided that I wanted to help people and it seemed the most convenient way, and also because I had—after leaving public school—just spent two years abroad in mild dissipation and idleness making a gentleman of myself and studying languages, and was suddenly overcome—apart from the languages—by the waste I was making of my life. We are very serious and very sudden about these things when we are young. After ordination, I was a curate in two London parishes and finally, when I was a little over thirty, got my own living near Barnstaple. I almost didn't get it, one because I was not married and still rather young, and, two, because there were certain aspects of my curacies which were not entirely sympathised with by the Bishop of the Diocese and the elders of the church. However, since the living was in the gift of a dear friend of the General, the matter was arranged. I lasted some years and then went to prison, and out of the kindness of their hearts my parishioners and others concerned excused my conduct as the result of a brainstorm—which it was not—and appointed another priest. My father, as I have said, always thought I had raped someone. In some way, I think, he linked this with my being a bachelor, which he regarded as an unhealthy state after the age of thirty, unless one was practical about it like the General. No, I was sent to prison because I wanted to help La Guicha and carried out a deliberate fraud with share certificates.

Lying with Sarah in my arms, but far distant from her in the scented darkness of the night, I was content that I had been punished by the law, but in my heart I was quite unrepentant. Christ took a whip to the money-changers. I was a little more subtle, and thoroughly enjoyed what I did because I did it for a good cause and with an equally good conscience.

Of course, I could not have carried out this particular fraud without help, but that had not been difficult to find among the variety of men I had met as a curate in London. I remembered with pleasure the beautiful job which James Jago had done for me in forging a certificate for two thousand ordinary shares of five shillings each in the Imperial Tobacco Group Limited. He had done quite a few others also, all at the modest price of five pounds each. At my trial and before, there were many attempts to make me disclose his name—since I clearly was no expert forger—but, of course, nothing would have made me disclose it. However, now, in order to acquire that which belonged to me by moral right, I saw that I would also have to have help. What I wanted was a good safebreaker able to handle either jelly or a peter cane to liberate my mother's diamonds from Teddie's safe. Although I didn't know one personally from my London days I knew that I should have no difficulty in finding one through some of my contacts. Peter, of course, among some of my London friends, referred to a prison, a police cell, or a safe and was derived from St. Peter who was regarded as perfectly secure and unbreakable. Thou art Peter, and upon this rock I will build my church; and the gates of hell shall not prevail against it. My brother Edward's safe would have no such invulnerability. James Jago if I could trace him would put me on to the right man. I fell asleep well content with my first day of freedom.

*　　*　　*　　*

The General woke us both at six o'clock the next morning

by thundering up the stairs and bursting into the bedroom, calling, "Wake up and welcome back!"

I sat up in bed, and Sarah sat up beside me. Outside the birds were singing and there was the music of river water over the hatches. From the end of the bed Major-General Lewis John Blandon, C.B., C.M.G., D.S.O. and bar, late the Black Watch, earlier Eton and Sandhurst, holder of the Order of Leopold and the Croix de Guerre, born 1897, regarded us from his pale blue eyes. White-haired, red-faced, wearing riding breeches and a black cossack shirt buttoned tightly to one side of his neck, he stood in silence enjoying the scene for a moment or two and then shouted, "By God, Nelo—celebrating freedom and the loss of the cloth with a vengeance. Bonnie lad! Bonnie lad! Introduce me to the lady."

I said, "This is Miss Sarah Minihane. Sarah—Major-General Lewis John Blandon."

Sarah, naked to the waist, but now raising the cover a little, said, "Good morning, General. You keep a very good brandy in your Rolls."

"The best, the best! If you can afford it, insist on it. The best. Do you ride, lass?"

"My father put me on a pony when I was three."

"Good. Downstairs in ten minutes. We'll go up to the gallops. Got a mare that will soon let you know whether your arse is in the right place still—you I'm referring to, Nelo. And welcome back, boy. Welcome back!" He reached across Sarah and shook me by the hand vigorously and, withdrawing, patted Sarah's smooth shoulder, and left the room.

Getting out of bed, Sarah said, "He's not true."

Watching her walk naked to the window and stretch her arms to the sun, I said, "When he was born God filled him full of love for living and seventy years have only lowered the level a little."

He took us in his Land-Rover up to the gallops where the horses waited, and we rode across the wind-sifted grass with the sun in our eyes and the wind in our faces like the sweet breath of saints and the horse beneath me moved like a miracle and my arse was in the right place and my hands almost as sure as though three years of absence had never been and I was wondering where Sarah had found jodhpurs and shirt and boots until I realised that the previous mistress of the General must have walked out suddenly and left part of her wardrobe, and the larks above gave praise and a cock pheasant, bright lacquered in the sun, exploded away from our path and rocketed into a field of wheat which made me think of my father and make a promise to myself that on my way to London the next day I would visit his grave and put some flowers on it, though, as his grave was a thirty-acre field over which his ashes had been scattered, the gesture would at the best be only an approximate one.

After our ride the General took us over to his house for breakfast and a tour of the stables and then, instead of driving us back, made me the loan for as long as I wished to keep it of a small car in which Sarah and I drove back to our house by the river. That afternoon she went off by herself to Winchester to do some shopping and I went through a box of my private papers and correspondence which had been lodged in the house before my arrival. I was looking for a card which had been sent to me on the Christmas prior to my going to prison. It didn't take me long to find it. It was a very expensive, privately printed card, with a Cranach reproduction on the cover of the "Rest of the Virgin during the flight into Egypt". Inside was printed a straightforward greeting from Miss Sylvia Dupont with an address in Curzon Street. Scrawled in purple ink and an atrocious hand across the lower corner of the card was— "God bless you, Nelo. Angles round your bed! Via." Seeing the misspelling of angels again made me smile. Although Via had come from humble beginnings and had made more handicaps than most of us meet mere stepping stones to success, the one thing she had never refined much was her spelling. When I had first met her she had been close to her sixteenth birthday. Her parents had brought her to me—then a young curate—

23

to see if I could talk any sense into her. Even at sixteen she was a well-built, generous-natured blonde who seemed to have little capacity for saying no, particularly to the youths of the neighbourhood. Her real name was Emma Spot and she was an intelligent, if misguided, girl. It was clear from a few minutes' conversation with her that it would be a monumental task to bring her into the fold. The seedling hawthorn reaching up to throw its first leaves and branches on the clifftop is doomed to be misshapen by the wild ocean winds. The fear of the Lord is the beginning of wisdom. But some come late and some come early to the Lord, and there is no hurrying the matter of when you first know fear. So I advised Emma—later for good economic reasons to become Sylvia Dupont because in some trades a name with a hint of ribaldry is no help—along those lines which would soonest bring her to fear (in her case the acquisition of wealth and stability which are very powerful impellers of grace). By the time she was forty I was sure that she would be rich, comfortably and faithfully married, and begin to store up good works at more than average rate to make up for lost time. No bell is ever rung for closing time in the parks of Paradise. At this moment, however, I was not concerned with Via's soul—only the fact that she would be able to help me to find a good safecracker or at least put me on to James Jago who would. High though she had risen Via had no real snobbery and had kept in touch with her old friends.

Sarah came back at five o'clock and brought me a beautiful melon, golden and faintly green striped, which I decided to serve with dinner, steeped in brandy, then iced with a coating of soft white sugar like hoar frost. For herself she carried five or six expensive looking parcels.

I said, "You must have spent a lot of money?"

"I did, Nelo. But then I've got a lot at the moment. Savings from eighteen months of forcing myself to stay in one place." She unwrapped a pair of crocodile leather shoes from a box and began to put them on. "This place is lovely. But my feet are restless. When do we go?"

"And what did he contribute?"

"Oh, nothing here. But he's my investment counsellor. He's bloody marvellous. He just knows everything there is to know about making money. I'm getting to be a very rich woman."

"And when you are?"

For a moment her handsome, happy face was serious. "Like you once said. I'm going to be really respectable. My own place, my own man, and, if it ain't too late, my own kids. This is business and I'd be a liar to say that I don't enjoy it. But one day I'm going to kick it. However, don't let's pull long faces over that now. Come and have a drink and tell me what you want—none of that, I'll bet, though you'd be welcome." She nodded at the bed.

"No, thank you, Via."

"Pity, I rather fancy you."

We went back to the drawing-room and a maid served us China tea and Barmouth biscuits and I told her what I wanted, a good safebreaker who would do a job for me not for a cut of the proceeds but on a cash basis—and not an exorbitant cash basis because I did not have all that much money to spend.

"Well, Nelo—" she said, "you know as well as I do none of the top hands like working on a cash basis. Profit sharing's their angle. But there are one or two who would, second-raters but handy. How much were you thinking of?"

"Three hundred, maybe four hundred pounds. No more."

"I see. Is it a difficult setup?"

"No. My brother's house in the country and quite an old safe."

"You, robbing your brother? Is that Christian?"

"Eminently—in this instance."

"What is it? Cash or tomfoolery?"

"Jewellery."

She shook her head. "All the good boys like a cut on that. You won't get the best just for cash."

"Do you know someone? Or perhaps James Jago does?"

"Haven't you heard? James went inside six months ago. Something to do with false passports."

"I'm sorry to hear it."

"Don't be. He was getting nostalgic for the life. Anyway, I'll do what I can for you. Just leave me your address and I'll send someone. But it may be a few days."

She got up and went to a small bureau. She came back and held out a slip of paper to me. It was a cheque, made out to me for five hundred pounds.

"What's this for?"

She smiled and said, "'Suffer the little children to come unto me, and forbid them not: for of such is the kingdom of God.' See, I remember a few things."

Not many of course, but I had managed to get her to attend half a dozen Bible classes before deciding on my final advice to her. She had been a very disruptive influence in the class, not only because of her beauty and bounty but also because she had a sharp, logical mind and would argue. For in the resurrection they neither marry, nor are given in marriage. She'd wanted to know why one should have to wait for this reform. Surely, if it were good enough for Paradise it was good enough here below? I think the dispute crystalised my final advice to her.

I said, "What children?"

She said, "I had a chat with James Jago before he went in. He told me why you worked that share deal. I'm all for kids, particularly since I'm taking a risk I may never have any. That's for La Guicha. A tithe on part of my earnings."

I thanked her and stood up. "Tell whoever you find that it is not a difficult safe and I can almost certainly promise that my brother will make no report to the police."

"All right, Nelo." She kissed me on the cheek, and then said, "You're sure you wouldn't like to try the bed? My friends wouldn't mind. They'd consider it an act of courtesy. And I wouldn't be embarrassed because you're an ex-reverend. I've had gentlemen of the cloth in there before."

"Some other time, perhaps."

I tucked the cheque in my pocket and went out to find a taxi.

* * *

The following evening Sarah and I drove over to the General's house to have dinner with him. On the way, I said to her, "Have you a valid British passport?"

"Yes."

"I'm thinking of leaving England some time within the next two weeks. I have to go to France to sell a house I have there and then on to Switzerland. I'd be happy to have your company."

"Delicious!" Then she added, "What about after Switzerland?"

"You're welcome for as long as you wish to be with me."

"That sounds a bit starchy, but I wasn't thinking of me. What are you going to do?"

"I don't know. I may stay and work with La Guicha—not for long though because we always quarrel, although I love her dearly. After my mother died, she became a great friend of my father's. She regards herself as one of the family, so she treats me as though I were her son and has no hesitation about throwing a plate at me or kicking me in the leg when she loses her temper. She has very decided views about the bringing up of children."

(She had very decided views about everything. My father had first met her at the Folies Bergères—I fancy, just after my mother died—and he used to visit her in France twice a year regularly. I'm sure that he loved her as much as it was possible for him to love anyone after my mother and he would un-

31

doubtedly have married her except that he had obstinate ideas about mixed blood and La Guicha was a beautiful light coffee-coloured, fiery angel with a silver and brass voice that could draw tears or laughter from the coldest of souls.)

The only other guests at dinner with the General were a Portuguese Count and Countess who had large estates in the north-east of Portugal and were over here buying bloodstock for their racing establishment. Count and Countess Padilla. Their full names and titles I soon forgot, though the General sounded them off at our introduction as though he were blowing a fanfare. After that they became Antonio and Leonora. The Count was a tall beanpole of a man, sixty, with a very bald head, black bushy eye-brows like Groucho Marx and with a long beaked nose. He looked like a crude child's drawing, but a fortunate one because somehow the child had from pure chance endowed him with the most enchanting smile. He drank little and was extremely polite. The Countess was much younger, still in her thirties, a dark-haired, small-framed woman with a beautifully tanned skin of which she showed a great deal; she was a ripe, polished hazelnut of a woman with a laugh like a donkey's welcome bray, vivacious, very beautiful and quite extraordinarily drunk in a contained way. At least it was contained until about half-way through dinner when sitting next to her became an embarrassment, not so much for what she said but from what she did, mostly under the cover of the tablecloth. She made it clear that she had taken a fancy to me. Raising a wine glass to my lips became a positive hazard and dealing with a particularly fine piece of sea-trout —a six pounder which a friend of the General's had sent home from the Torridge—almost impossible if one wished to concentrate on the fine flavour, which I, being fond of fish and a good Epicurean, wished to do. I became quite angry inwardly and, because of her behaviour, lacked charity in thought and deed. As a jewel of gold in a swine's snout, so is a fair woman which is without discretion. I kicked her hard twice under the table and saw the silver centrepiece on the

32

table tremble a little. It was a nineteenth-century piece of the famous racehorse *Eclipse* which had been presented to the General by his regiment on retirement. After that I had no more than minor trouble from her and about this I detected something of a conciliatory touch.

Later, when I was washing my hands with the Count, he very graciously apologised for his wife by saying, "Senhor Nelo, please make no hasty judgment on my wife. There is much in-breeding in her lines which has resulted in increased excitability. She is a sprinter not a stayer. She has a vivid imagination and her mind is half fantasy so that on being confronted with something or someone unusual she is over stimulated. But there is no vice in her that a good pair of hands can't control." He up-palmed his own big, soapy hands.

I said, "What could there be unusual in me? By the way I took the liberty of kicking her twice hard under the table. She'll be bruised on her right cannon bone, but a few cold compresses will bring it out."

He nodded approvingly and said, "You don't think you're unusual? The General has told her your history."

I said, "Somewhere, every day, a priest is defrocked, and many men go to prison. The Governor of my prison told me on wishing me goodbye that he calculated that the population of our prisons will be around forty thousand within the next few years. And such prisons! Pentonville was built by a major in the Royal Engineers in 1842. Very shortly men will be housed three to a cell designed originally for one. So you see, there is nothing unusual in my record."

The Count increased the power of his smile and said, "From my wife's point of view it is not just your record—but you yourself. Ex-priests (we have many in Portugal, our economy promotes it) and criminals are two a penny, but few of them come—as the Americans say—packaged as you do." He nodded at my reflection in the glass. "Six feet tall with, I think I say right, the physique of an international Rugby lock forward, a

33

face like a prize-fighter and ginger hair. Add to this your blue eyes and you are expecting too much of my wife."

The party games the General always insisted on playing after dinner didn't help. If we could just have lain on the hall floor and spotted mistakes in the ceiling it might have been all right, but with the passing of my father the games had become less intellectual and more boisterous and included a great deal of chasing up and down stairs and hiding in cupboards and small rooms. There were one or two unavoidable incidents with the Countess. Excitable she certainly was, but she had, too, the tenacity of a Jack Russell terrier down a rabbit hole or flushing granary rats.

As we left, the General boomed at me on the drive steps, "Splendid evening, Nelo. Splendid. Pity your father couldn't be here. He wouldn't have been half as bashful with the Countess as you. Nice filly but not the kind I'd like to put my colours on. Now cut along. Sarah's waiting for you. I'll have the horses waiting for you at the gallops tomorrow morning. See you then."

I drove home, recovering slowly.

At my side, Sarah leaned over after a while and kissed me gently on the cheek. "Did she worry you, Nelo?"

"A bit."

"Poor dear."

"Me?"

"No, her. She's got everything in the world she wants. The Count is a millionaire some times over. What she wants she can have."

"Then why be sorry for her?"

"Because it's healthy to have some things out of reach no matter how high you go up on your toes."

"Well, I'm out of reach."

"If she wants you enough, she'll find a way to you." She kissed me again.

I said, "Would you be jealous?"

"I don't know. It's something I've been considering all the evening."

34

That night we slept together again, and although we were so close that there was an affection in me for her which was different from any I had known before, filling me with rare thought and a strong happiness, I tried to still both thought and happiness because I sensed that in the naked touch of our bodies there was a pulse of sorrow and confusion that moved from her into me so that at times I felt that I held and comforted a frightened child whose fear has no form yet pursues it into sleep with nightmare shadows.

When I woke early in the morning she was not with me. Pinned to my dressing-gown that lay over the foot of the bed was a note:

I have gone to see my mother for a few days.
                                                              Sarah.

Had she forgotten that she had told me that her mother was dead? I began to see then that, probably for her own protection, there were some parts of her life that she peopled with fantasies.

She had gone on foot because the car was still parked outside. I breakfasted and drove up to the gallops.

The General and the Count and Countess were there and I made some apology for Sarah. The Countess, to my surprise, was riding a big, black stallion called—I never knew why—Furnace Fork. He was a big brute of a horse who when he got bored kicked down the walls of his stall and bit stable boys and showed his joy in high and boastful neighs. When he was put to a brood mare it was like thunder on the mountain tops and he had sired many a famous winner and there was no sign yet of his seed withering. He was fast, powerful, clumsy and without fear. If a fence could not be jumped he crashed it down and to hold him one needed iron wrists. To my surprise the Countess did hold him and also encouraged him. They went like a gale of wind scattering the Hampshire countryside before them. It was the first time I had seen her ride and I was full of admiration for her. I kept close to her, taking advantage of the hedge gaps that Furnace made. When we finally drew up to wait for the others she drew alongside me and said with unexpected demureness, "I apologise for my behaviour last night—though I thoroughly enjoyed it. If at any time you're in Portugal I do hope—and I know Tonio would, too—that you will come and stay with us."

"That's very nice of you. However, I'm afraid I don't have Portugal on my list at this moment."

"Who knows? Anyway, I thank you for the corrective bruises and for the few minutes' wrestling match in the butler's pantry." She smiled and rode off, taking a high wire fence like a bird and I felt the ground shake as Furnace landed. I rode on after her, but not thinking about her. I was wondering if, in fact, Sarah meant to come back. She had left most of her stuff but that meant nothing. Some people are avid packers and carry their possessions around with them. Sarah was the walking out with scallop shell and staff type and the roadways lined with almsgivers to sustain her. She had only been with me a few days, true, but that seemed to me merely as though we were taking up again from some distant point in time where we had left off. I wasn't in love with her. The good Lord hadn't so far granted me that grace, but I did have a strong sense of communion with her though, if asked why, I would have been hard put to analyse it. But I did feel much as though I had looked at the night sky and seen there revealed for the first time the bright star of promise.

When I got back to our house by the river there was a motorcycle propped against the garden hedge and a man in the sitting-room holding one of the gold cigarette boxes. He gave me a little nod and said, "The Reverend Sangster?"

"Mister."

"Sorry, of course. Nice box. Nice lot of stuff here. I particularly like the Etty nearer the door in the upstairs loo. The other one isn't so fine. In fact it could be a fake. Miss Dupont sent me. Would there be any coffee about?"

36

I said, "Come into the kitchen. I was going to make some for myself."

As we went into the kitchen, he said, "My name is Dorsmo. Horace Dorsmo. Don't ask me the origin of the name. Even my father didn't know. I was called Dormouse at Wellington."

"Wellington?"

"College. My father was a great believer in middle-class *mores*. He was Herbert Dorsmo, a great safebreaker who made crime pay—which, of course, is not so difficult as a lot of people, except the police, think. I'm afraid I was a disappointment to him. Maxwell House coffee, I see. Personally I prefer to grind my own beans. Never mind, it'll do. Yes, a great disappointment. I ran away after a year. I couldn't bear the unbelievable squalor of the little cubicles we boys had to live in. Anyway, I wanted to be an artist. By the way, if I run on too much just flag me down. All my friends do and I'm used to it."

I said, "You've come about the safe job?"

"Yes. Dear Miss Dupont begged me to help. But I must warn you I can't tackle anything really difficult. I only do this on the side, and sort of mildly carrying on the family tradition, so that I can keep my studio going. Five hundred, she said you would pay?"

"Three hundred."

"Oh, dear. Perhaps four hundred?"

"Three-fifty."

"Very well."

He sat down on a kitchen chair over which were already draped his black motor-cycling coat and a crash-helmet painted mauve with spirals of gold and white running round it. Anyone less like a safebreaker it would have been hard for most people to imagine, but not for me. Prison had taught me that most of its inhabitants looked nothing like the kind of men they were. I shared a cell for three months once with a fence who looked exactly like the Duke of Wellington and he had the same forthright and acute kind of mind and mannerisms and his favourite saying was, "If you believe that you'll believe any damned

37

thing". Only he didn't say damned! Mr. Horace Dorsmo looked anything but like the Iron Duke. He was a small fragile man in his thirties with fat, baby hands and a thin starved face. He looked, in fact, like a grown-up baby so that his head, limbs and body were all out of proportion with one another. I was particularly intrigued by his red riding boots, black cycling breeches and a multi-hued Fair Isle sweater.

I said, "Do you wear that gear when you're on a job?"

"Oh, no. This is for visits to the country. I'm passionate about the great out of doors and speed. It's something I've been trying to get on canvas for years." He smiled, and added, "Not with any success. When there isn't a safe around I do technical drawings for the motor and motor-cycling trade magazines. When do you want this job done?"

"Well, it could be, say, within the week, maybe a little later." I was thinking of Sarah, wondering if she were going to come back and wanting to give her time.

"What kind of safe is it?"

"Quite an old one. It came with the house when my brother bought it ten years ago. It could be twenty years old."

"Then it's either a straight blowing job, or oxy-acetylene. Depends on the noise level which can be tolerated."

"You can make all the noise in the world."

"Good. Then I'll blow it. I love blowing. I suppose because that's how my father used to do it. I shall never forget the first time he took me with him. He was a genius, absolute touch, absolute instinct for just how much jelly a door needed. Not too much, not too little. That first time—I think he was showing off a little to me—when he was ready, he covered the safe with the room carpet, put a cushion on top and sat on it and then fired it. It was miraculous. There was just a gentle *whoomph* and the door swung open. I've never been as good. Forgive me if I run on, but I had a great admiration and affection for my father."

We sat with our coffee over the kitchen table and I explained the layout of my brother's house with diagrams and made all

38

my arrangements with him, except the date of the operation. I would be going with him, of course. And it would have to be when my brother and his wife were away. This presented no great problem because while the House was sitting they spent the bulk of the week in London at their flat.

Before he went Horace said, "Your brother must be an imprudent man to leave a diamond necklace of this value in an old safe."

I said, "My brother is a curious combination of rectitude and recklessness, and also a very conventional man. The safe has the name Chubb on the door and that is enough for him. 'The shield of faith wherewith ye shall be able to quench all the fiery darts of the wicked.'"

"He's in for a big surprise. I wonder whether it would be convenient for you to let me have fifty pounds now on account? The rest on completion?"

I paid him fifty pounds and accompanied him to his motor-cycle. It was a Japanese Honda, painted by himself to match his crash helmet, and he went away up the river valley in a psychedelic blur of speed, and I went back and finished up the rest of the coffee.

At four o'clock Sarah returned. She walked in carrying a small wooden box which held a white ferret with pink eyes.

I said, "Does your mother live locally, then?"

"No—" she came and kissed me on the ear. "I got the bus down the road this morning to Salisbury. But just before the train went I thought I ought to phone to make sure she would be at home. Her maid told me that she had gone on a cruise to the Canaries. She loves it there, particularly the botanical gardens at Oratava. So there was no point in my going. I did some shopping instead."

She opened the box and took the ferret out, handling it, I noticed, expertly.

"What is he called?"

"She. Nipper. So the man in the shop said. I've got some nets in my bag."

39

"For what?"

"There are rabbits all along the bank above the garden."

"We don't want rabbits and they don't do any harm."

"I like ferreting and so does Nipper." She sounded slightly belligerent, upset even.

"You told me your mother was dead."

"So she is. My real mother. This is my step-mother. Daddy married again—but they separated. She's very wealthy and very bored."

I said, smiling, "I'm glad she went to the Canaries. I should have missed you, even for a few days."

She looked at me, about to say something I felt, then shook her head and walked through to the kitchen to give Nipper some bread and milk. She might have been telling the truth about her step-mother, but I had a feeling that truth or not she had been glad to find an excuse for coming back but would rather that I were not aware of her gladness. It was all very confusing.

Half an hour later she went out with Nipper and her nets. She was back in time for a drink before dinner and when I asked how she had got on she said, "Not at all, I think Nipper is anti-blood sports."

* * * *

Now that Sarah was back there would have seemed nothing to stop Horace and me from carrying out the safe business at the first opportunity—except for the advent of two considerations. The first was the question of the diamonds themselves.

When I woke the next morning Sarah was sitting on the cushions of the bedroom window-seat in black pyjamas, looking out at the sunlight on the river. Without saying good morning to me and as though we had already been talking about it for some time—there was always this feeling with her when we met or started to talk that a lot had already gone on before—

40

she said, "Have you really thought carefully about these diamonds?"

"In what sense?"

"You're going to take them abroad and sell them?"

"Yes."

"And you don't think your brother will make a fuss . . . tell the police?"

"I'm gambling on that."

"Then you mustn't. People don't always act the way you feel sure they will. You've got to get those diamonds through Customs. Here and abroad. You won't do that if he tells the police. The moment you show your nose at Heathrow you'll be picked up. All right, when he gets the diamonds back he may drop charges—but that doesn't do you any good, Nelo. You've got to think about that."

"You could take them out for me—then I could follow."

"You wouldn't. He'd have you held until they found out where they were."

There was sense in what she said and I realised that I hadn't given this aspect enough thought. I decided to do so and was helped in the problem by the second consideration.

Two days later while we were having lunch with the General he told us that he had sold Furnace Fork and a brown mare called Policy Princess to Count Padilla and that he was arranging to have them flown out to Lisbon by British Air Ferries. Would I like to fly out on the plane and keep an eye on the horses?

I said, "Is this your idea?" Sarah was watching me from across the table.

"Of course," said the General. "Thought you'd like the trip. Take Sarah with you, too. It's a free trip, round ticket or one way just as you like. You know Furnace, he's a hellion, and I'd like to have someone with him that understands him. There'll be a horse box waiting at Lisbon and, if you want to, you can go on in it and spend a few days with the Count until the horses settle down. He'd appreciate that."

41

"And it would be nice to see the Countess again," said Sarah. I asked her, "You'll come?"

"Delicious, yes."

To the General I said, "I've got a few bits of family business to clear up here. Is it all right if I let you know a convenient date, say, next week some time?"

"As long as you give me time to fix up the transport, my boy."

That evening I telephoned my brother for a friendly chat and learned that he would not be at his country house the whole of the next week. Then I telephoned the General and fixed a date, and after that I spoke to Horace Dorsmo and fixed a time and a rendezvous with him.

As I put the phone down, Sarah came and sat on the arm of my chair and said, "You have a clear conscience about the diamonds?"

"Yes. But if I hadn't?"

"It wouldn't be quite so much fun."

Thinking of the Countess, I said, "We needn't go beyond Lisbon. The Count's man can drive the horse box without us."

"But it would be rude not to accept their hospitality. We must go."

So all was arranged and we were booked to leave from Gatwick Airfield on 11 July which was the anniversary of the battle of Oudenarde in 1708. (A flag for that, of course, at Stonebridge Park in the old days.) In the meantime I wrote a letter to La Guicha saying that I was soon to be on my way to see her and would she write me a note, care of Count Antonio Padilla, Castelo dos Montes, Mirandela, Portugal, giving me the name and address of someone in the South of France—where I should go first to dispose of my villa—who would help me to market my mother's diamonds. I had no doubts about La Guicha being able to help. She had walked in so many ways of life and had known so many people that if the request had been to dispose of my mother in a semi-illegal fashion she would have riffled the pages of her memory and come up with a name.

It was fanciful but pleasant to consider that, if my father had met her before my mother, then he might have found his racial bigotry about marriage swept away and I could have been the son of La Guicha . . . black but comely, O ye daughters of Jerusalem, as the tents of Kedar, as the curtains of Solomon. My brother would have hated the idea.

CHAPTER FOUR

THE CARGO PLANE with Furnace Fork and Policy Princess was due to take off from Gatwick just before mid-day on 11 July. The plan for Sarah, Horace and myself was a simple one. Sarah would drive to Gatwick in the horse box with the General's man—who was to bring the horse box back—taking our little luggage with her. I was to drive up ahead of them, much earlier, in the car the General had lent me and meet Horace, at five o'clock in the morning, at a crossroads near my brother's house. Here, he would leave the car he was borrowing for the trip—there was a certain amount of equipment to be carried which he could not accommodate on a motor-cycle— and we would proceed together to the house and deal with the safe. Afterwards I was to take him back to his car and he would go off on his own and I would drive on to Gatwick, to leave my car in the car park with instructions for a car delivery firm to take it back to the General. I would then wait for the arrival of the horse box and conceal the diamonds in a small bag of oats before we went through the Customs and exporting formalities at the airport. Sarah was to make sure that the bag of oats was loaded—ostensibly for the comfort of the horses during the flight—before leaving the General's stud farm. Like all good plans it was simple and I had no fears for its success.

The dawn was just beginning to break as Sarah said a sleepy goodbye to me from her bed before I left. I drove with a light heart, singing to myself now and again, through the developing July dawn, watching the world come awake on the heels of the

44

morning. It was, naturally, quite some years since I had gone abroad and there was excitement in me at the thought. The sun came up royally scattering his gold and silver and blue, and the birds greeted him with their matins and for a hundred yards along the main road, just the other side of Winchester, a soft-winged barn owl, tardy from night revels, flew ahead of me and then swung away across a field to be mobbed by a bevy of finches.

Horace was waiting for me at the wheel of his borrowed car, soberly attired in a black track suit and a woollen helmet of the same colour but sporting a white pom-pom on the top. He greeted me warmly, transferring his working case to my car and, as we drove off, said, "I've got some new jelly I want to try. A lot of the boys are using it now so I must keep up to date. You've brought the rest of the money with you?"

"Naturally."

"I forgot to ask you this before. Do I get paid if it doesn't come off?"

"Honest, conscientious effort will be rewarded."

"I take it that means maybe?"

"There is no question of failure. Success is in the morning air."

He gave me an odd look but said no more.

We turned through the park gates, the gravel crunching like brown sugar under our wheels, and the grass was hoared with a faint dew. As we crossed the lake bridge the water below was ringed by my brother's trout rising to a hatch of flies and for a moment I had a memory of my father at his bench tying flies, remembering the miracle of his big, normally ungainly hands manipulating feather and ribbing, silk and wool with a delicacy and precision granted seldom to women. If I forget thee, O Jerusalem, let my right hand forget her cunning.

Drawing up below the stone steps of the main door, Horace and I got out; he with his working case and me with a small grip in which I was carrying a few essentials.

I rang the bell and waited. When my brother and his wife

45

went to London, she took her maid with her and he took his valet. The only people left in the country house were the butler and his wife, who was cook-housekeeper. In addition there was a village woman who came in to work of a morning arriving at nine o'clock. I had calculated and timed our arrival so that I knew I could deal with her just as our work was done and she arrived.

After some delay the door was opened by Rodmer, the butler. He was a slow-moving, impressive man of nearly sixty, bland and benevolently faced, with the alert eyes of a terrier. He gave me a smile of surprise and said, "Why, it's Mister Nelo. How are you, sir?"

"I am well, Rodmer," I said as he let us in.

He said, "If you have come to see Mister Leno, sir, I am afraid he is not at home."

"I know he isn't, Rodmer. Come into the library, I want to talk to you." I turned to Horace. "You wait here for a moment."

Rodmer and I went into the library. In a far corner by the window squatted my brother's antiquated safe, wedged diagonally into the angle of the walls, with one of his old school photographs perched on top of it.

"Rodmer," I said, "I am about to take you into my confidence and ask for your co-operation."

"Well, Mister Nelo, it wouldn't be the first occasion. Can I get you some coffee first?"

"No, thank you, Rodmer. My time is somewhat limited. I suppose my brother hasn't left the keys of his safe here, has he?"

"No, sir. He takes them with him." Then, his smile twinkling, he said, "Would it be the matter of your mother's diamonds?"

"Yes, it is, Rodmer."

"Ah, sir, I was only saying recently to Mrs. Rodmer that there would be trouble about them; knowing Mister Nelo, I said, and how he felt about his mother and, of course, your indubitable moral right to them. Is that what the other gentleman is for? To open the safe?"

"He is indeed, Rodmer."

He favoured me with a frank, broad grin of pleasure. "I

46

shall be happy to see him at work, sir. I have read of such operations often. As you know, sir, my reading is confined almost entirely to works of detection, espionage and criminal activities and—"

"Rodmer—" I cut in—"you shall have the pleasure. But first listen to the conditions."

I began to tell him what I was going to do and what I wanted from him.

Rodmer had been my father's butler and had known me for years. (My father had first met him when he, Rodmer, had been working as a barber's assistant in Salisbury. I sometimes thought that this—apart from Rodmer's character —was a strong motive for his employment since my father hated all hair-dressing saloons and knew that henceforth he could be served at home. Rodmer had cut my hair all the time I had been at Stonebridge Park. Mine, Leno's, my father's and that of every man and boy about the place. My father had taught him his new trade, made him an excellent judge of wines—though later they disagreed with polite but unbending conviction about vintages—and coached him in the degrees of order and precedence, and opened up the labyrinthian delights of Debrett to him so that for the short while that my father was Deputy Lieutenant of the County he had been invaluable in the matter of place settings and protocol. Between them, too, they had established a secret code of phrases and signs that enabled them to deal with, dispose of, dis-countenance or—it must be said—deceive any guest, visitor, charity worker, farm tenant or tradesman who offered some problem or tedium to my father. When my father died, Rodmer had descended to my brother Leno and served him loyally in all matters except in the rare disputes between Leno and myself and then Rodmer reserved the right to sit in judg-ment and there was no appeal from the verdict. It was Rodmer, I may say, who had beat the slow drum roll for the Relief of Mafeking and my uncle's death each year. As my father often said, if anyone deserved to be Deputy Lieutenant of the County and take the knighthood that went with it, it should have been Rodmer.)

I was not surprised now to find that Rodmer was on my side and ready to co-operate. At the end of my explanation, he said, "For the record, of course, Mister Nelo, I am doing this under duress."

"Of course."

"Very well, sir. I will go and lock my wife in her bedroom. She won't mind because usually at this time of the morning she is giving it a good turn out. But you, sir, will have to deal with the cleaning person."

"I will."

He went off and I brought Horace Dorsmo into the room. He stood in the doorway, case in hand, and looked round approvingly which was no more than I had expected. Two sides were lined with bookshelves, holding many rare editions, chiefly of sporting books. Stone mullioned windows looked out over the park, the three chestnuts were still grazing in the paddock and made me think of Sarah, now on her way in the horse box, and in the far wall was a large and richly carved marble fireplace which my brother had imported from some Venetian *palazzo*. Personally I had never liked it. It was over-ornamented and vulgar, but my brother doted on it. Above it was a large Whistler painting looking out of place. However, overall, it was a richly furnished room and most of it in good taste.

Horace said, "Your brother is obviously wealthy but his taste is erratic. How can he bear that fireplace, particularly after the Grinling Gibbons in the hall?"

I said, "Concentrate on the safe. Time is passing."

Horace examined the safe, and then opened his case and took out his tools and drills.

Rodmer came back, eager not to miss anything, and said, "My wife is quite happy and understands and she sends you her kind regards, sir. Also I've cut the telephone wires as you directed. Are we to blow the safe, sir, or cut it open with oxy-acetylene?"

"Blow it, Rodmer."

"I think that's wise, sir. I understand from a most informative thriller I've just read that some years ago for protection against oxygen cutting Chubb's introduced a new alloy in the making of their safes—called I think Chubb TDR—which gives a very high degree of immunity from oxygen cutting. Though, I think this one could well be dated before that happened."

His eyes on every move that Horace was making, he allowed me to sit him in a wingbacked arm chair near the door and tie his ankles to the chair legs and bind a rope around his body, trapping his arms at the elbows. I fastened the rope at the back of the chair, so that he sat, unable to reach any of the holding knots at chair back or chair legs but had his hands and forearms free to move and reach the sherry decanter and glass which I placed on a table at his side. He made no use of the refreshment now, but I knew that he would when we left. In fact, in our preliminary discussions, he had stipulated which sherry he would prefer to have left, a light amontillado that drunk in quantity was not over severe on the liver.

Rodmer, securely but comfortably fixed, and Horace saying that it would be some time before he was ready to blow, I went out into the hall and found in a cupboard my father's flags which Leno had inherited and took a Union Jack which I hoisted on Leno's flagstaff, for Oudenarde but perhaps more for some kind of spiritual excess which the early morning drive and the thought that I would soon be able to help La Guicha substantially in her work had wrought in me. Like as the arrows in the hand of the giant: even so are the young children . . . an heritage and gift that cometh of the Lord. My mother would be glad to see from above how her diamonds were to be used and in the fullness of time, too, I was sure that Leno would understand; but for the first few days, of course, he would be hopping mad and possibly only his wife would stop him from picking up the telephone and calling the police.

I took a stroll round the gardens and some time later went back into the library and found that Horace was almost ready.

49

He had drilled holes around the lock and door fittings and packed them with his new jelly and completed all the other technical acts which were a mystery to me and was now fixing a detonator and running a plug on wires to a wall socket so that the safe could be fired at the press of a switch. Rodmer was still watching him with keen interest and trying not to disturb his work by asking too many questions. When all was ready he took the heavy pile Passavant carpet from the floor and draped it over the safe, added a smaller Ispahan rug for extra thickness and then topped the lot off with a thick window-seat cushion.

Turning, he said to me, "You stand by the wall switch and press it when I give the word. You remember I told you about my father? I will show you exactly what he did."

He went over, hoisted himself on to the safe top and sat cross-legged on the cushion.

Alarmed, Rodmer asked, "Is that wise?"

Horace waved his fears away. "My father held a glass of beer in his hand and not a drop was spilled."

Personally I wondered whether perhaps something of my morning exhilaration had not also entered Horace, but I was never one to question the judgment of a craftsman. I went to the wall switch and awaited Horace's command.

Rodmer, fascinated but mindful of his master's minor possessions, said, "What about the china and stuff on the mantelpiece? Won't the shock of the explosion dislodge them?"

"Nothing will move," said Horace and he smiled and nodded to me to press the wall switch.

I did.

There was the most tremendous roaring explosion that flattened me against the wall as though some invisible arm had pinned me there. Hast thou an arm like God? Or canst thou thunder with a voice like him?—Horace had come near to producing it. In the break between two eye blinks I saw many things and they were all wonderful, awe-inspiring and one, I thought, prophetic.

The safe door was blown, violently, clean off its hinges, and propelled across the room like a manhole cover. It smashed right into the front of the Italian marble fireplace, pulverising vulgar fruit and bird sculptings, shattering sirens and satyrs, mashing the stone into milky shards. The ornaments on the mantelshelf were swept into oblivion by a fiery wind. Every pane in the mullioned windows was blown outwards, seen from the corner of an eye to fly fast and crowded through the bright air like birds of lustre and silver. The chair in which Rodmer was sat toppled backwards to the floor and all I could see of him was the soles of his shoes. The two carpets—so eccentric sometimes are the dispositions of disaster—were back on the floor, almost in their original positions each with a large, neat hole in them the shape of the safe door. Dispensations of grace there were, too. Rodmer's table with his sherry decanter and glass stood intact; the Whistler and other pictures held firm to the walls not a degree out of true, and providentially (since clearly no selfish pride had motivated him, rather a desire to honour his father) Horace sat untouched on his cushion on top of the safe, the explosion having whipped the carpets from under him as a skilled waiter can whip a cloth from a table and leave everything in its place even to the slim silver-plated vase of flowers.

As the smoke and sound of battle died, Horace, from his perch, said a little shakily, "That's exactly how my father did it . . . almost."

And then, as I moved to rescue and restore Rodmer, I saw at my feet a long, wide, red leather case. I picked it up and opened it. Inside, channelled in an oval velvet bed, were my mother's diamonds. The backwash or vortex of the explosion inside the safe had—prophetically I liked to think—rendered them up to my feet. As I bent and picked them up the words of St. Matthew 7.7 were diamond bright in my mind. The rest of the contents of the safe, mostly papers, were scattered about the room like autumn leaves.

I went over and righted Rodmer. He was unharmed and

51

very little shaken for he was a man of almost imperturbable phlegm. However, he allowed himself to give me a reproachful look and said, "Mister Nelo, you brought an amateur. It was never this way in any of the books I've read."

Horace descended from the safe and came to us.

"Thank God,' he said, "it was only that ghastly fireplace. No doubt your brother will be glad of the opportunity to replace it." He began to search around the room for his scattered pieces of equipment.

After that events moved smoothly. The cleaning person appeared within the next ten minutes and I brought her in and lodged her in another chair, roped as Rodmer was, and placed the sherry table between them. She was a plump, cottage-loaf shaped woman and a little nervous until Rodmer said, "Just settle down, Mrs. Lloyd. An anonymous call is being made to the village constable just after eleven to release us. That means we shan't be free until one o'clock because his wife won't give him the message until he returns from the Horse and Hounds at half-past twelve."

Driving Horace back to his car, although I was naturally a little distressed at the damage which had been caused to my brother's room, I had to chide myself for the uncharitable thought that while he considered the antiquated safe a sure depository for my diamonds he clearly had not seen fit to keep his emeralds there. But on second thoughts I decided that his wife must have taken them to London with her to wear at some function that week.

At his car I paid Horace off and he said, "It's been a pleasure to work with you, Reverend. I shall never forget it."

I said, "The sentiment is common to us both."

* * * *

I drove on to Gatwick, which was not a long journey, left my car and made arrangements for its return and then walked round to meet Sarah and the horse box at the cargo entrance of the airport.

52

She jumped down and kissed me, and then she raised a finger and touched a dried cut on my chin.

"You cut yourself shaving this morning."

"Yes," I said, "it happened this morning."

"You've got them?"

I handed the diamonds, free of their case, to her, and she went back to the cab of the horse box and put them in the small sack of oats that sat by her seat. We drove into the airport and began to go through the formalities of shipping the horses. When this was done we were checked by Customs, and cleared for the flight. Remembering Rodmer, I slipped away and made a telephone call to the number of the village policeman so that Rodmer and his wife and Mrs. Lloyd might be duly freed.

As I came out of the cargo and dispatching office, where I had been given the use of a telephone, and began to walk back across the tarmac to the plane which was now ready to taxi out to its runway and await take-off, I was joined by a man who had been sitting on a crate outside the office. He was wearing a navy-blue serge jacket and trousers, the jacket rather shiny but bright with brass buttons. On his head was a peaked cap, like a chauffeur's, with some monogram device over the brim, and in his left hand he carried a clipboard with a piece of paper attached to it.

He said, "Mr. Sangster?"

"Yes."

"I'm an inspector of the Royal Society for the Prevention of Cruelty to Animals."

"Indeed."

"Import and Export of Animals division. We work with the airport authorities and the Customs people and now and again carry out spot checks on transport facilities and conditions. You're taking two horses to Lisbon, I think?" He consulted his clipboard.

"Yes."

"May I come and just have a formal look around?" He smiled. "Purely routine. I'm sure everything is in order."

53

"Certainly."

We walked across to the waiting plane. It was a Bristol Super Freighter. The car bay had been converted into a two-stall compartment for the horses with a runway down the side. This cargo hold was now closed up and we entered the plane through the starboard passenger door. Sarah and the steward were in the small passenger compartment, the captain and his first officer were out of sight in the cockpit waiting for their clearance from the control tower to move out to the runway.

I explained who the man was to Sarah and the steward and then took him aft to look at the horses. He went down the side of the stalls, patted Princess Policy on the rump and got a baleful stare from Furnace Fork, checked the water supply, the stall fittings, and then made a few notes on his clipboard. Then he gave me a friendly nod and said, "Everything seems in order."

I said, "Are you sure?"

"Quite."

"It doesn't seem so to me. What does R.S.Y.C. stand for? Surely not the Royal Society for the Prevention of Cruelty to Animals?"

He said, "Oh, dear," and his face fell a little as he took off his hat and looked at the badge. Then with a little beam of commendation for me, he went on, "I must congratulate you on your powers of observation. You're well above average. Actually the letters stand for the Royal Southampton Yacht Club, I think."

"So?"

"Well . . . usually I like to pace things my own way, but you've hurried me a little. Not that it makes any difference." He took a gun from his back trouser pocket.

I said, "Are you a hi-or-skijacker?"

Almost offended, he said, "Good Lord, no. I just want a free trip, unimpeded by formalities either end, to Lisbon. No, no—" he waved me down with a gentle movement of the gun as I started to say something—"I know you're full of curiosity

54

and I'll do my best to satisfy it later. For the moment I'm just anxious to get us off the ground and safely into the air. Let us go back to the cabin and arrange that."

Since it would have been idle to argue with a determined—no matter how polite—man with a gun we did that. And I wasn't at all surprised to find that Sarah and the steward adopted the same policy. The steward carried out his instructions meticulously. He ordered the ground staff to take away the shallow flight of boarding steps, closed the door and phoned through to the cockpit to tell the captain that all was well.

As we taxied out to the runway, our friend with the gun asked us to sit in the seats forward of him so that he could see us comfortably and then sat down himself and adjusted his safety belt. He sat there, beaming at us, not flushed, but mildly happy with his success so far. He was a man of about forty-five with a round, Pickwickian face, a plump, little capon of a man who reminded me very much of the vicar of my first parish. (He had been called Trimble, was a devoted model airplane maker—which doubly recalled him to me at this moment—and at every Christmas church party for the children dressed himself as Santa Claus and was a great favourite with them, because he, too, was a child at heart and to be that after thirty is granted to few of us.) I had a feeling as we waited for take-off that this man might, too, be a child at heart, but not a normal child.

He said now, "On the whole Chesterton was right about uniforms . . . people either don't notice you or they accept you. Disguise, too, is a matter of confidence—inner and outer. That is, it's no good putting on a sailor's dress unless you become a sailor. I should know, of course, since I have been many things in my time, too many things. That is the trouble. I have been, like water, poured into so many differently shaped receptacles that I have long forgotten the shape of my original bottle."

Sarah said, "What was the label on it?"

He smiled. "François Xavier Mabluto."

"But that's not an English name," said Sarah.

55

"Did I say I was English? My mother was a San Fernando octoroon and my father a Maori from Wellington, New Zealand. But I am white, you say? Meaning I have that blanched veal complexion which all Anglo-Saxons look upon as a special gift from God. God has his gentle jokes, you know. The whites may be all powerful but in the eyes of three-quarters of the world they are really quite unpleasant to look at. He had his joke with me, too, because I am genetically a freak, but I bear Him no grudge."

"Which San Fernando?" I asked.

"Ah, my mother, yes. Well, it was either the one in the Philippines or the one in Trinidad. My mother was never sure. As for my father, I never asked him, since he deserted the family when I was four. I see that you are a man of a sharp and enquiring mind. I shall have to watch my words with you, Mr. Sangster."

At this moment the plane started to take off and in a few moments we were airborne above Sussex and the plane turned southwards towards the English Channel. Not that we could see much; since man took to the air, travel has become a tedious vacuum.

When we had reached our cruising height Mr. Mabluto unfastened his belt and said to the steward, "Now take me forward to the captain."

The steward, a young craggy man of considerable phlegm, said, "You speak polite to him or you're in trouble."

"Except when it is professionally necessary I am always polite. The captain and I will understand each other. He is going to Lisbon and so am I."

They went forward through the cargo bay to see the captain. Sarah said, "Nelo, is this what happens to you when you move around?"

"I don't understand you."

"Oh yes, you do. I thought you might be one of those—in fact I wouldn't have come with you after the pond if I hadn't had a strong feeling about it."

"About what?"

"Some people are magnets for trouble. The iron filings of broken and bewildered lives fly to them through the air. It happens to me a little, but I am only a toy magnet."

"There is nothing broken or bewildered about François Xavier Mabluto."

"No?" She was holding his clipboard in her hand which she had picked up from his seat. "Then why did he write this?" She handed it to me.

Instead of making comments about the safe and proper stalling of the horses on the plane he had written—"I have run out of countries and almost of personalities. For my part, I travel not to go anywhere, but to go. The great affair is to move."

I handed the board back to her. I said, "The last two sentences are quoted—maybe subconsciously—from a man who might have known his father as a boy."

She put her arms around me, kissed me and said, "The great affair is to move. I like that."

"To move with me?"

"Why do you say that?"

"It came naturally."

"Are you falling in love with me?"

"I doubt it."

"Good. Love has nothing to offer us that we would be happy to endure. The great affair is to move. Let's be content with that."

The wind bloweth where it listeth, and thou hearest the sound thereof, but canst not tell whence it cometh, and whither it goeth. She could hear the wind and I had a feeling that she was afraid of it for some reason.

After a while Xavier and the steward came back, Xavier smiling and quite composed. He had, he said, arranged things amicably with the captain, for whom in a few moments he had formed a great respect and liking. When the plane landed at Lisbon, the captain would pull up at the end of the landing

57

runway before turning and taxiing into the airport disembarkation point and Xavier would drop overboard and make his way to the perimeter fence, cut a hole in the wire—he had, he said, wire cutters in his pocket—and disappear. In addition the captain had promised that he would make no report ahead to Lisbon of his unauthorised passenger. (Conventionally Xavier had pointed out that if there were any signs of a reception party on the field he would not be responsible for his actions. Sensibly, the captain in order to avoid invoking the real dangers of duress had been content to act them rather than suffer them.)

I asked, "Why haven't you a passport? Why couldn't you travel normally to Lisbon?"

Xavier said, "The British authorities have confiscated it. And I didn't have enough money to buy a false one—my money is in Lisbon. Also, until seven o'clock this morning I have been under constant watch by the British authorities. They still think I am sleeping late at an East Grinstead hotel, no doubt. It is a long story and I am reluctant to bore you with it. Briefly I am, or rather was, in the Secret Service."

Nevertheless he did tell us his story, as we flew across France, over St. Nazaire and the mouth of the Loire to meet the Bay of Biscay and headed south-west for Gijon, Vigo, Porto, Coimbra and finally Lisbon. The world turned under our wings and the steward, after having served our tray lunches—he fortunately had a spare for Xavier who ate with a steady appetite—lay back in a seat and went to sleep, while forward Furnace occasionally gave the padded side of his stall a bad-tempered kick. We sat there in our little capsule, sustained by the monotonous miracle of flight.

At one point in his story he took off his peaked cap, removed the band which held the yacht club badge (he never did explain that) and also slipped out the black Perspex from the peak which gave it a chauffeur's cap appearance, and then put the cap back on, now a crumpled any sort of cap. He also took off his jacket and reversed it so that it became a rather cheap looking worsted sports coat. (He told us that, had he considered it necessary, he could have reversed his trousers into plain grey flannel.)

He was the first secret agent that I had ever, knowingly, met. He had gone into the profession as a free-lance at the age of twenty-one and had done very well for himself. He had a gift for languages, absorbing them like a sponge. Unfortunately—maybe it stemmed from his patronymic background—he was a man who could not, try as he often did, muster up any loyalty or patriotism towards any specific country and, although he had—when free-lancing became unprofitable—joined in turn the secret service organisations of many countries, he could never remain faithful to them. Not for any of them could he find the least point of extra favour. He that is faithful in that which is least is faithful also in much, never could be said for Xavier. In his time he became a double, triple, quadruple and maybe far-more agent, until the time arrived—not so long before this day—when he was a nuisance and a doubt, a sore in the side and an anxiety in the mind of every organisation from M.I.17 through the C.I.A. and the K.G.B. (and even to some extent the Mafia) right down to the smallest and latest of Indonesian and emerging African countries who had set up their own rudimentary intelligence services. He was unwanted and by common assent—for he assured us that there was a high level of communication between all these organisations where mutual problems were discussed —a danger, and it had been decided that he was to be eliminated. In England his passport had been withdrawn and he put under surveillance while the technical matter of his elimination went forward to the next co-ordination committee for settlement. There was not, as you might expect, a reluctance on any country's part to be landed with the job, but, on the contrary, such an eagerness in each country for the pleasure that, Xavier assured us, it would take a twelve-hour meeting and probably four ballots to decide his exact fate. Meantime he had temporarily joined the R.S.P.C.A. and the R.S.Y.C.

without either organisation's knowledge and made his escape.

He sat, beaming with pleasure that sprang from his own resourcefulness. A most likeable man and with the natural good manners of a gentleman, as my father would have been the first to acknowledge. (My father had always maintained that a gentleman, no matter his colour or his language, was always immediately recognisable by any other gentleman no matter what his colour or language. It was a free-masonry—a sect for which my father had no time—that needed no more than a look to be established.)

Sarah, full of sympathy, said, "Surely you must be very worried? How can you escape all these people? Is there a country in the world that doesn't want to see you dead?"

"I doubt it," said Xavier cheerfully. "I have run out of countries and—temporarily until Lisbon—passports and money. But I have money and friends. And, understand, it is useless having the latter without the former. I shall survive. Somewhere there is for me, as for my father's journeying ancestors in the past, a Rarotonga, a port of call, a haven of rest for a while. Settled permanently I do not wish to be until the day of my death, when I shall happily abide with half of my ancestors in Te Reinga—unless, of course, there is a colour bar there."

"What," asked Sarah, "is Te Reinga?"

"The Maori heaven—only it is located under the sea which seems a far more feasible and interesting location than somewhere up here where there is little to see but clouds and bits of discarded ironmongery from space machines."

I said, "My father would have preferred it. As a keen fisherman the thought of heaven used to drive him to distraction and as a first-class game shot he was sure there would be a year round out-of-season ban on angels. To cheer him up I would sometimes recite him Ecclesiastes 3.4, always omitting the last three words."

Xavier gave me a keen look and said, "You are of the cloth?"

"Was."

"Interesting. We had quite a few like that in the various organisations I served."

So we sat and talked while the hills and valleys of first France and then Spain and Portugal rolled steadily away beneath us. It was while we were over Coimbra (a name my father would immediately have associated with Marshal Massena, the greatest of Bonaparte's marshals, his *enfant chéri de la victoire*, born to begin life as a cabin boy, who bloodily sacked the place in 1810) that the captain of the aircraft, leaving his first officer in charge, came down to us.

He was a big man, almost as tall as myself, with the mournful, red-rimmed eyes of a bloodhound and a sleepy manner as though he had already flown round the world non-stop and was, without emotion, setting out to do it again because he had forgotten to pick something up in Tokyo. He came into our midst and enquired after our health and comfort.

Assured by us on these scores, he said, "You can fly for bloody months and nothing happens and then like a happy marriage breaking up you run on the rocks and you can bet your month's pay that trouble's picked you out for a long visit. I don't like it because I don't like trouble. I want trouble, I take myself out on the golf course and get it out of my system. Up here, different tactics. No smashing your way out of it as though you were in a bunker. First we have Mr. Mabluto, here, hitching a free lift and I'm nice to him because nice you have to be when you're eight thousand feet up from terra firma. If you knew the number of forms I'm going to have to fill out over him and the reports in triplicate I'm going to have to write, you'd be sorry for me."

"I'm sure we all are," I said.

He turned his big head towards me. "Nice of you to say so, Mr. Sangster, and nice of you to break up my monologue. It's a habit that comes from talking to oneself while flying, and sitting up there in that damned little cockpit that looks like and isn't much bigger than the inside of a television set. One

61

should drive a bus, there is more to occupy the mind and, at least, you see people. I like people, especially girls in mini-skirts, women pushing prams, old ladies and gents taking the air, city workers beating their soles off to get there and open the post and check whether the firm is still solvent and—"

"You were on the subject of trouble, Captain," said Sarah.

"Ah, so I was. Thank you. As the sparks fly upwards, man is born into trouble."

"It's the other way round, Captain," I said. "Man is born unto trouble, as the sparks fly upwards."

"That you should correct me is hard, but I take no offence, Mr. Sangster, because if I have trouble so have you."

"Me?"

"Yes. You couldn't know it, but the sunny skies around here have been full of your name for the last half hour. From London and from Lisbon and even some half-wit from Paris who said he was speaking for Interpol. The names they have these days. They all begin with Inter. Personally I take that to be a contraction for Interference. By and large, you will have gathered that I am a man who likes to be left alone to fly in peace. All trouble should be kept strictly at ground level. And that is where it is waiting for you, Mr. Sangster. At Lisbon. A police escort and then no doubt police interrogation. Information has been laid against you in connection with a diamond robbery. Have you stolen diamonds, Mr. Sangster?"

"I recovered some diamonds which were morally mine."

"That is for you to argue at ground level. You don't leave this plane until the police take you off."

Before I could say anything, Mr. Mabluto gave a little cough and said, "Unless he likes to get off with me at the end of the landing runway, Captain."

"You would apply *force majeure* on his behalf, too?"

"Why not, Captain—if he wishes it? And, anyway, isn't that what you intended? Otherwise you had only to keep this information to yourself until Lisbon."

The captain pushed his peaked cap back, hesitated, and then

62

admitted, "Well, in a way, it was at the back of my mind."

"But why?" I asked. "You don't know me, though I'll admit that the Good Samaritan had no personal knowledge—"

"Skip that one, Mr. Sangster. I don't know you or care about you but I don't like the police, particularly foreign police, and I don't like trouble. I'm going to have some, but by ditching you with Mr. Mabluto I shall avoid a great deal more. These damned Portuguese would probably hold me for a couple of days, giving evidence and all that nonsense if they got their hands on you. But if you're not aboard they'll just shrug their shoulders and let me go. Could I have done other with your friend here holding a gun on me and my crew?"

"I think you're quite right, Captain," said Sarah. "Anyway the horses will be all right. I can handle them."

"Thank you, miss." He looked at me. "You've got these diamonds aboard?"

"Yes, Captain."

"Well, take 'em with you when you go. I don't want this ship turned upside down by police searching for them." He looked sharply at the steward. "You have heard nothing of this conversation, Steward. All you heard was Mr. Mabluto here threatening me if I didn't let Mr. Sangster off as well."

"Yes, Captain."

In all fairness to the captain, I felt I had to say, "But surely the Lisbon police will realise that you came and told me that they would be waiting for me?"

"Not at all, Mr. Sangster. Your friend here—uncomfortable as it would have been for him—has spent the entire trip in the cockpit monitoring all messages, in and out, to make sure that I couldn't inform the Lisbon people of his presence aboard. I may say that I understand that it is your brother who has laid this complaint against you. I never got on with my brother either. Brothers should be separated at birth and only meet years later in happy and convenient Gilbert and Sullivan situations."

He went back to his cockpit. Sarah gave me a look and

63

enquired quietly, "Why should your brother have done this?"

"I think because of his marble fireplace and the two carpets. Possibly even the window glass. Rodmer probably was forced over the phone to itemise the damage caused when the safe door blew off."

Xavier asked, "Was it a valuable fireplace?"

"Costly, but vulgarly carved in three varieties of Italian marble; breche rose, Loredo chiaro and veined piastraccia. It was lucky for me, Mr. Mabluto, that you were aboard."

"Not luck, Mr. Sangster, but fate."

"Neither," said Sarah. "Just iron filings being attracted to the magnet."

"Fasten your seat belts, please," said the steward. "We are going down."

Out of the starboard little window I saw the Atlantic shining below; that was marble, too; green and white veined. Neither luck, nor fate, nor attraction, I thought, but just part of the monologue that God recited as he piloted the world and the universe through space. . . . By every word that proceedeth out of the mouth of the Lord doth man live.

*   *   *   *

So it was arranged that I should leave with Xavier, and that Sarah should take the horses on to the Count. I was sure that in a few days my brother's anger would subside and that he would withdraw charges against me. For the moment he was just throwing the dustbin lid. As soon as I could, I told Sarah, I would join her at the Count's castle and then we would go on to France to my villa.

The plane flew in to Lisbon and landed with the gentlest of bumps. I went forward and collected my diamonds and Furnace rolled the whites of his eyes at me.

Back in the cabin I held Sarah in my arms and kissed her while the steward got ready to open the door and said, "Just watch out for the back draught from the props when you get out."

The plane taxied to the end of the runway, slowed and turned and then stopped. The door was opened and Xavier dropped out and I followed. The wind from the propellers wrapped a small gale around us and we ran through it to the tall-grassed, wide stretch of ground beyond the runway. Two hundred yards away was a chain link fence. For all his dumpiness Xavier ran fast, reached it ahead of me and pulled wire clippers from his pocket.

I said, "Do you always carry those?"

"No. I bought them in East Grinstead for this particular operation."

Behind us the plane was now taxiing towards the main airport block and I could see the usual crowd of people waiting on the open-air platform above the building. It was a beautiful afternoon, little puffs of white cloud sailing across the blue sky, the air beating warmly up from the ground. I was in Portugal, the traditional ally of the British. (I had a vivid memory of my father at the dinner table, disposing salt cellars, wine glasses, and anything that came handy to demonstrate the phases of the campaign around Torres Vedras and then going on—despite the restlessness of Leno and myself—to illustrate how damned lucky Wellington had been to get away with it at Fuentes d'Onoro. I wondered what he would have said had he known that I would come here, a man wanted on a criminal, though not moral, charge laid against him by his own brother. He would have got it all muddled, of course.)

We went through the hole in the fence on to a narrow, chalky white road and five minutes later had flagged a passing taxi and were on our way to Lisbon. Leaning back in the car Xavier pulled off his cap, turned back the lining inside and drew out a variety of currency notes, dollars, pesetas, francs, dirhams and others.

"I always," he said, "like to have an emergency supply—enough for the odd taxi or two—of the world's currencies."

"Where are we going?"

"At the moment, down to the railway station at the docks.

65

Then we shall take a charming little train that runs up the coast to Estoril, and then we shall walk up to my house and have a bath, a drink and a meal."

"You have a house in Estoril?"

"I have houses—mostly rented furnished—in many places and I try always never to fall far behind with the rent. Lately it has been difficult."

"And from Estoril where do you propose to go?"

"I am not sure, but I am considering Addis Ababa. It is one of the few places left to me. But everything depends on my being able to transfer my money there from Lisbon."

"You are a wealthy man?"

"To some extent. Most of my life I have served at least two, sometimes three or four masters. Combined with a natural thrift it has made me a reasonably rich man. The problem now is to find a place where I can enjoy it. Tell me now, why should you have to steal these from your brother?"

From his pocket he produced my necklace of diamonds which until then I had thought were in my own pocket. Seeing my astonishment, he went on, "You are a man of too open a nature to be trusted with valuables. Learn to be suspicious." He handed them back to me.

"They are mine," I said. "I was recovering them."

"You mean to sell them?"

"Eventually, yes."

"And then?"

"I shall give the money away."

"You are either a fool or a saint or deceptively unhinged. Whichever, you are storing up trouble for yourself. The world takes unkindly to mutations. Birds peck their albino brothers to death. Two-headed calves are slaughtered as abominations or, much the same thing, exhibited in freak shows. I knew a man once who committed suicide because he had webbed fingers. People don't give money away unless they have so much it won't be missed. Normal people, that is."

I said, "The debate on poverty and charity is endless. Just

66

as the Holy Bible is full of contradictions so are the different goodnesses of man. I preached a sermon on it once and was reported to the Bishop. So far as I remember my main point was that the giving of charity to any able-bodied person in full possession of his or her faculties between the ages of twenty-one and seventy-one was a sin. Looking back on it now I see that I was guilty of some exaggerations."

We took the train from Lisbon to Estoril and now and then had charming glimpses of the sea and gaily painted fishing boats, and from Estoril walked up through the public gardens and past the Casino to Xavier's house. Before we entered he warned me that I must no longer call him Xavier or Mr. Mabluto in public, since his name here was Senhor Luigi Prades, a wealthy bachelor and an importer of radio components from France.

The villa he rented was hung with purple bougainvillaea, the garden studded with date palms and the little verandah on the first floor overgrown with a climbing Madame Barbier rose, blooming wantonly and filling the air with scent. He was greeted effusively by his resident housekeeper, a tall, dark-haired, good-looking but large-faced woman with a Junoesque figure, whom he called Tita and with whom he moved in for the night for he insisted on giving me his own and best bedroom since it had a view of the sea. It was difficult for me to have much conversation with Tita. She had little English and I had no Portuguese and after a time Xavier got tired of translating.

It was quite clear that Xavier considered himself safe from the police, sure that they would never connect the wanted Mr. Mabluto of the plane with Senhor Luigi Prades of Estoril, now back from a business trip abroad. And, indeed, when he came down to breakfast the next morning he was a different man; dapper, smartly dressed in an Italian silk suit, hair pomaded and even, it seemed to me, his complexion sun or lotion tanned. He was in high spirits when he went off to attend to his money affairs. I sat in the garden and wrote a letter, conciliatory but occasionally chiding, to my brother, offering, naturally, to pay for the damage I had caused.

When Xavier came back, late in the afternoon, it was clear from his manner that things had not gone well with him at the various banks he had visited. He offered no explanations and I did not ask him for any, but he was manifestly preoccupied and retired early to bed with Tita which, in the circumstances, struck me as a sensible thing to do. At heart there is something of the child left in all men and the comfort of a woman is a solacing spring that never dries.

I went up to my own bedroom just before midnight. I tend not to be an early retirer. I had no luggage of my own—Sarah had taken charge of that—and as Xavier's pyjamas were much too small for me I slept in the raw. I had been asleep a couple of hours when I was rudely awakened by all the clothes being ripped off the bed and the room light being switched on. I came sluggishly out of a dream-laden sleep, blinking my eyes against the sudden blaze of light, to hear a voice say, "Good. It's just a personal foible, but I could never bring myself to kill a man while he slept. I hope the same courtesy is accorded to me some day." The voice had an American accent and there was a smell of cigar in the room.

CHAPTER FIVE

Whoso sheddeth man's blood, by man shall his blood
be shed—a contradiction of other Christian dicta, but a strong
argument used by some for the retention of hanging. Coming
awake, eyes and mind clearing slowly, I sat up, stretched and
yawned, shook my head to clear it and said, "What did you
say?"

The voice said, "Shake the sleep dust from your eyes, you
Maori misfit, and take what's coming to you."

I saw and understood then perfectly the man who was standing at the side of the bed. He was a big fellow wearing light
green overalls with the words "Hotel Atlantico" embroidered
in red over his left breast. He had a big Teutonic head, his hair
en brosse, and its darkness was echoed by the blue-black stubble
of his badly shaven face. He wore thick lensed glasses, held a
cigar in his even, nicotine-brown teeth and a gun of some
kind in his left hand. There was a curious swelling at the end
of it.

I said, "You're left-handed?"

"Ambidextrous." He tossed the gun into his right hand and,
without removing the cigar, blew a cloud of pearl-grey smoke
towards me.

I said, "Why should a porter from the Hotel Atlantico wish
to kill me?"

"Heating engineer—temporary, and a sinecure, Maori boy,
since it's summer, but there is a certain party at the hotel who
rates twenty-four-hour watch. I check him in and out of the
garage. Monotonous work as you must know so when they call

me and say that Mr. Mabluto, alias Senhor Prades, is definitely on the D list—"

"D is for death?"

"As you know well. The co-ordinating committee put you there at half-past two yesterday, *nemine contradicente*."

"You could have the wrong man."

"Not a hope. And don't start quibbling. There's nothing personal in this. Just stand up and take it. You have outlived your usefulness, exhausted your goodwill, and come to the end of the line."

I could see that there was little point in arguing with him. Even if I could persuade him that Xavier was in the next room which, just for a moment (so strong is the instinct for self-preservation in us all), I considered but immediately rejected, I felt that he would shoot me anyway just to dispose of an eye-witness. So I stood up, naked, and pulled from behind me with my right hand the pillow and swung it, knocking the gun from his hand. He might have made some protest, probably about unfair tactics, but I gave him no opportunity. I hit him hard under the jaw with my left fist so that he bit off the end of the cigar and the body of it fell to the carpet. He took the blow well and now, without indulging himself in the luxury of words, rocked back from his heels and came for me. In prison I had kept fit. He was fit, too, and not far short of my size, and certainly not lacking in courage. But of the noble art he had only the crudest conception and some tactics which are not listed in the Queensberry rules. Feinting with his right to distract me, he raised his foot and kicked at my groin. I went back, bringing him a little off balance and took him with a right hook on the side of his head so that he reeled caterwise across the room and smashed into the fireplace, bringing all the ornaments off the mantelshelf, including a rather nice French ormulu clock. He came back without much delay and tried to close, his arms outstretched now, seeking for a wrestling hold; gouging, boring and kneeing clearly his intention. So I let him come and took his wrists and threw him over my shoulders. He landed on the bed behind me, broke one of its legs and slid off with a thud against the far wall just missing the window or he would have found himself cradled in the top hamper of one of the date palms in the garden. Even then, to his credit, he was full of fight, threw everything that came to his hand, tried to retrieve the gun from the floor (the swelling on the end, Xavier later told me, was a silencer), and would not admit defeat until I had battered and bruised him, thrown and floored him, and finally like Abner with Asahel—though without a spear—smote him under the fifth rib and he went to the carpet and remained. I reached for the carafe on the bedside table and poured some water on his face.

From the door Xavier said, "Save a little for the cigar. It's burning the carpet."

Xavier was standing in the doorway with Tita at his side. I jerked a sheet from the bed, wrapped it around myself and then poured the rest of the water over the cigar.

Xavier said, "He came for me?"

I nodded.

Tita said something to him in Portuguese and when I looked questioningly at him, he said, "She wishes to know whether we would like omelettes. She is a simple soul. When men are in trouble she thinks feeding them is a remedy." He turned and said something in her language to her and then interpreted to me. "I have told her to make two big ham omelettes right away. We must leave as soon as possible. All journeys should be begun on a full stomach. Meanwhile, let us take this person down to the cellar."

We carried the man down to the cellar and tied his hands and feet with lengths of lamp wire and made him comfortable on an old *chaise longue*.

Xavier said, "For an ex-man of God, you are strong in battle but rash. It amazes me he didn't make a pepper pot of your body before you could move."

I said, "When he's missed they'll send someone else for you. No matter where you are."

71

"No. If I can go on avoiding them long enough my file will be lost, heads of departments will change and the obscurant dust of bureaucracy will settle over my memory. But we must go from here quickly."

So we had a three o'clock in the morning breakfast of ham omelettes, prepared by Tita who, with a large, sad face, watched us eat for a while and then went up to pack a case for Xavier. Xavier told me that he had expected trouble, though not so soon, because all the banks he had visited had immediately gone into polite but long-winded explanations of the difficulties of transferring money to Ethiopia and that he had had the impression from each bank manager as he talked that the man was inwardly measuring him for a shroud and calculating the minimum which should be spent on a wreath.

"They knew, each one, what was in the wind for between the worlds of Mammon and Politics the air is full of signals," he said, and went upstairs to say goodbye to Tita and to give her instructions to release the prisoner before the following mid-day.

We left, Xavier at the wheel of a Lancia Flavia saloon which he produced from the garage at the side of the house, changing the number plates and the licence details in the driveway, and we took the coast road north under a fine moon that made the sea look as though a limitless shoal of fish were breaking surface as far as the eye could see and turned the pines and oaks into black, iron cutouts. As we left Estoril and Cascais behind us I asked Xavier where we were going.

He said, "To Mirandella and Count Antonio Padilla."

"You know him?"

"I have heard something of him, and your Sarah was telling me something of him, too. He sounds a man of understanding. Also he lives in a part of this country where the rule of law instead of running has never been able to muster more than a hobble. You are content, Nelo?"

"I wish I knew."

"Because of seeing Sarah again?"

72

"I've an idea that's the reason."

"Would my observations on love and the attractions of the sexes, the alchemy of male and female and the metaphysics of natural selection help?"

"In no way. There are some things a man must learn for himself."

"Or suffer."

"Sometimes I think I chose the wrong communion. I should have taken the vows of celibacy."

"You say that without sincerity. It is not your body you fear but your mind. Your body you give freely, yourself you wish to hold back, a little treasure so unique that you are frightened of sharing it. Sarah feels the same. Sharing a bed is an easy and natural thing. It calls for no great talent or sacrifice. Sharing yourself with another is anathema to those who love their own loneliness like you, Sarah and myself. Thank God, the temptation has never sincerely come my way or I should not be alive today. Do I make sense?"

"Something like it."

"She is a copper-headed beauty and her heart is unflawed. Like you she is in love with her own completeness which is an illusion from which she, as you do, draws strength. How are you off for money?"

"I have very little."

"Perhaps I could raise a loan from the Count. Enough to get me through France to Switzerland. I have money there."

"You could always sell this car."

He laughed. "Nelo, you are too simple and direct. You want the pilgrim to put his staff in hock? In this world the last things to sell are status symbols. Sell the television set but not the aerial on the roof. Sell the bed you lie on but not the velvet curtains from the window. Realise on your life policy, cash in on the silver tea service your father gave to your mother but go on travelling first-class and keep the electric mower on the lawn, the garden dwarfs on their pedestals and your shirt cuffs unfrayed. . . ."

73

I went to sleep. When I woke the car was drawn up at the side of the road. Below us was a dried-up river gorge, above us were myrtle and pine-coated hills and ten yards away was an old woman in black, knitting and keeping an eye on three sheep. Xavier was at my side drinking coffee from a flask which Tita had provided. He poured me a cup and we sat and drank and smoked in the early morning sunlight and after a while the old woman got up and moved her sheep and herself down towards us and from a large wicker basket sold us early grapes which were sour enough to set the teeth on edge and Xavier began to talk to her and she began to laugh and the laugh was gay and young enough to belie her wrinkled face by about twenty years, and for some reason which I felt she knew she could never make clear to me she reached out and patted my arm and winked with a sudden lascivity that made me laugh, too. So we all laughed and then hard-up, hunted Xavier gave her a hundred pesetas and we drove on.

*   *   *   *

The Castello dos Montes was like a castle from a fairy tale but with all modern conveniences; hot and cold running water, flush toilets fed to the latest in septic tanks, oil-fired central heating from a Potterton boiler for the winter, television, an electric lift to take one from the lowest of the wine cellars to the highest of the slate-roofed, conical shaped towers, its own electric plant, Aga oil-fired stoves in the kitchens, infra-red grills, a heated swimming pool twice the size of a tennis court with a little islanded Greek temple in the centre that sheltered a marble of the Aphrodite of Cnidus (a copy from the original in the Vatican), a home-farm with pedigree Herefordshire cattle, stables and training gallops for the horses, thousands of hectares of mountains and woods full of partridge, quail, deer and boar, and in an office off the main hall a telephone exchange and telex manned by two girls, multi-lingual and pleasant to the eye; and it sat on its lofty tumulus, bow-shaped, yellow-stoned, slate-roofed and towered, nursing in its shallow crescent formal gardens that fell away in grottos to a river that flowed—little more than a trickle at this time of the year—through a broad valley, bowl-shaped, mountain-encircled, hawk, kite and buzzard-surveyed, which as far as the eye could reach held not a square metre of ground that did not belong to Count Padilla. The castle was fixed dead centre in the valley, the hub of the Count's domain.

We reached it late in the evening—Xavier had mistaken a road and we had made an unnecessary detour of about eighty kilometres—and were welcomed with every hospitality and kindness by the Count and Countess. There was no need for explanations about Xavier because Sarah had already told them about him and I, briefly, brought them up to date on his latest position.

The Count said, "As long as he is here he is safe and I never greet a guest by asking him how long he intends to stay. Make yourself at home, ring for anything you want and, if it is not here, I will send my private plane to Lisbon or Madrid for it." He said it without a shade of extravagance, rather with the shyness of a man who knows that there is nothing in life of material significance which he cannot command. I have often felt that it is a position of perpetual penance for a man to be so endowed, to be so singled out beyond his neighbours and thus never certain of their love. Wrath is cruel, and anger is outrageous, but who is able to stand before envy?

The Countess's welcome, to my relief, was restrained and correct, even when she showed me my room. I decided that she was one of those people who only let their hair down when they are away from home.

Sarah welcomed me with outstretched arms, put them round me and held me in a long hug and then stepped back and said, "Xavier tells me you had a fight."

I said, "It wasn't a situation in which to turn the other cheek." I reached and kissed her, and went on, "You look beautiful. You are beautiful. I can't imagine why once or twice I thought I never wanted to see you again."

She smiled and said, "Give it some thought. There must be an answer somewhere."

That night I slept like a child and dreamt of my mother who had died when I was fifteen years old. We were walking in the walled vegetable garden at Stonebridge and she was picking early peas, shucking them as we strolled and feeding them to me and herself. (She often did that in real life. Not only peas. She would pull a clutch of young French radishes, clean them on a spittle-wetted cambric handkerchief and feed me like a young bird.) It was no surprise to me when she took me by the hand and said, "Let's go and have a look at the river." We just took off like a couple of birds and flew up over the high, plaster wall with its capping of thatch where wrens and bluetits nested and then planed down to the river valley. Looking across at her in the morning sunlight I saw that her hair which was normally as black as jet, so black that it always looked wet, was now turned to a fine copper colour that trapped and held the soft sunlight. We flew low over the water, hovering sometimes so that we could see the trout and grayling against the gravel beds and the multi-greens of the weed patches and once a huge perch, striped like a zebra, motionless and bored in the gentle back-eddy of an old tree stump, until we came to a pool where my father stood in the shallow runout fishing and as our shadows crossed the water the feeding trout scattered in panic and my father looked up and shouted, "You damn fools. You've put 'em down for a week!" and my mother laughed, swooped, and took his fishing cap, and we flew on laughing and she said to me, "The anger of love is music."

I woke, to find a manservant putting an early morning tea-tray by my bed, wondering what on earth she had meant. I didn't wonder for long because there was a letter from La Guicha on the tray.

She wrote in French, which was one of two languages apart from my own, which I had painfully acquired. (My father employed a French governess for Leno and myself for two years. He sacked her in the end, not because she was a rabid Bonapartiste, but because she finally corrected him—or rather contradicted him—over the order of the French fleet at the Battle of the Nile. They quarrelled loudly and she, goaded beyond endurance, made disparaging remarks of Lord Nelson, chiefly concerning his morals, so that my father rang furiously for the car—which was a 1928 8-litre "Boulogne" Hispano-Suiza—to take her to the station and, while she packed, wrote her a cheque for a year's wages in lieu of notice.)

La Guicha, translated, wrote: Every day until you come has a hole in it. Bring plenty of money. Rob, pillage and plunder in the name of the Lord. The necks of the unheeding should be twisted until they can see their own backsides in the mirror. The children greet you with one voice. The person you need for the diamonds is a Monsieur Crozette, a herpetologist—ask him to show you his Arizona coral snake, a most beautiful creature—who lives in the Villa Pontois (he was born there, Pontois, not the villa) on the road to the golf course at Beauvallon. Name of road escapes me—my mind has no attics for rubbish. Ask him also whether he could find a market for a superb Monet which a well-wisher has just presented to me. I cannot send it to Christie's or Sotheby's for legal reasons. He will understand. Photograph and details enclosed. Come soon, and come happy. Love. Guicha.

The letter was written on the back of an unreceipted account rendered from a Geneva garage for 2000 Swiss francs. The photograph of the Monet was a winter scene of the Cathedral at Rouen. I had no doubt that it had been stolen. La Guicha's system of morals was unconventional—chiefly concerning the laws of property.

I went riding with Sarah that morning through the sun-dried, rocky-soiled meadows along the rain-starved river. She was riding Furnace and the stallion at one point in a gallop, full of oats, lordly and arrogant in his new surroundings, pulled away from her hands and was master. He went with the un-

77

caring madness of arrogance and while it lasted, good a rider as she was, I knew that Sarah was in danger for she had no control over him. A horse is a vain thing for safety: neither shall he deliver any by his great strength. So I went after her, slowly caught them and shouldered Furnace round in a wide circle until he was suddenly bored and Sarah took control again.

She said, "You needn't have done that."

"He could have broken your neck on this ground."

"Then it would have been broken."

I realised then that she was angry, as she had been angry once before over the ferret. And now, as then, I had no idea why. But in a few moments when we pulled up in the shade of a clump of eucalyptus trees for a cigarette her anger was gone and before we remounted she kissed me and said, "Don't take any notice when I fly off the handle. It's just me. Could the Countess have held him?"

"Yes."

"Did she come to your room last night?"

"No."

"You didn't come to mine."

Before I could answer she got up on Furnace and trotted away, and following her I remembered something that Xavier had said about loneliness.

Back at the castle, Xavier came into my room before lunch—which was to be served at the side of the swimming pool—and said happily, "The Count, while not willing to lend me money, has sent a telex to Lisbon for my money to be transferred. He is the chairman of two of the banks and the thing will be done discreetly. I shall stay here safely until the transfer is completed."

Without thought, I said, "I shall leave tomorrow."

He looked surprised and said, "With Sarah?"

"If she wishes to come."

I should have known better than to have said, "I shall". The absolute is in the hands of Fate, and Fate likes nothing better than to masquerade as a woman.

* * * *

That afternoon, about five o'clock, I was in my room, writing a reply to La Guicha's letter, though strictly speaking it didn't need a reply but it was always a pleasure to write to her and, anyway, I thought she might be interested in hearing how I had obtained the diamonds and the incidents of the air flight to Lisbon, when one of the castle's manservants—they all wore white gloves and a green livery with silver buttons with the Padilla crest on them—came into my room and said, "The compliments of Madame the Countess, sir, and she would be happy if you could attend upon her now."

As a guest I had no option but to say that I would be delighted and to follow him. He took me down the vast corridor, the floor black-and-white tiled against the summer heat, the windows, now open, double-glazed against the winter's cold, and every five yards a suit of armour, some of which had been used at Roncesvalles, until we came to the central lift. The inside of the lift was lined with rose-coloured silk and decorated with hand-finished coloured lithographs of birds and I contemplated—not without inner sadness for the greed and stupidity of man—a noble drawing of a Great Auk as we went up three floors.

The manservant took me along another corridor to the door of the Countess's apartments, opened it and announced me as he motioned me in and shut the door behind me. It was a large sitting-room decorated in green and pale cream, but before I could make much examination of it the Countess's voice came to me, calling, "Nelo—come right in here."

I followed the voice through a side door and found myself in a large bedroom whose windows looked west to the far slopes of the valley. The walls were mostly lined with mirrors, an immense crystal chandelier hung from the ceiling catching the rays of the lowering sun in an explosion of rainbow lights, and the bed reminded me of an illustration I had seen somewhere of Cleopatra's barge. On it, curled up on a red blanket, which had been spread over the yellow silk cover, lay a Rhodesian ridgeback dog. It opened one eye, quickly vetted me, and then went back to sleep.

79

The Countess's voice called, "In here, Nelo."

I went through a far door, down three steps—a fleeting memory of Via surfacing briefly in my mind—into a bathroom. The windows looked south and on the balcony outside were three dark green, fruit-studded lemon plants in pots. The walls were of green and agate coloured onyx marble, two niches each held a seven-branched silver candlestick with electric light bulbs for flames and along one wall was a comfortable banquette in black velvet in front of which stood a round, marble table on silver legs. On the table was a silver tray with bottles and glasses and an ice-bucket. The bath was egg-shaped and low to the ground and in it, as though awaiting hatching, the moment of release to the world's delights and terrors, lay the Countess, her knees drawn up to her chin in a foetal position which was far from elegant. Her dark hair was piled up at the nape of her neck, though the water of the almost full bath teased at a few wanton strands, and from the water itself arose a perfume, erotic and secular, and far removed in origin from the golden vials full of odour, which are the prayers of saints, of the revelation of the blessed St. John the Divine. Actually, the need for prayer at that moment was strong in me. A captain stripped of his insignia, drummed from the ranks, does not lose his martial instincts and habits in an hour. One lapse of honour (no matter how curiously intentioned) does not necessarily presage another. Adultery in its true sense was not in my nature, though like most men the temptation had now and then been with me. That a woman chose to show her body willingly to a man caused me no moral qualms. Why should we not have moments that recall the pastoral innocence of Adam and Eve before the fall? (King David forfeited much in my esteem when he played the peeping Tom with Bath-sheba and put her husband, Uriah the Hittite, in the forefront of battle to be slain.)

The Countess straightened her legs, floated a little in the deep water, adjusted her balance and said, "Help yourself to a drink, Nelo. I've got one."

80

Her drink, champagne, I thought, rested at the end of the bath on the flattened head of a silver tiger whose panting jaws provided hot and cold water.

I sat down on the banquette and helped myself to a whisky and soda, and said, "You wanted me?"

She laughed and said, "That is the understatement of the year, but you don't necessarily get what you want just by announcing it." She lay back, putting her hands behind her head and managed to look remarkably like La Maia. Her skin was an even milky coffee tan, unlike Sarah's warm creaminess. They were both much the same size, but I noticed with interest that the nipples of the Countess's breasts were surrounded by large, dark purple aureoles whereas Sarah's were small and the colour of dried hazel nuts.

I said, "You wanted my company? I give it gladly."

"Thank you, Nelo." She raised a leg and began to soap it idly. "But I want more than that. I want to know about you and some of your friends. For instance, who is La Guicha? The real La Guicha?"

"Yes. How do you know she is a friend of mine?"

"I went into your room this morning when you were out and read your correspondence. Tony has often tried to break me of the habit. But as I've pointed out it has sometimes been of help to him. Is she the one with the children?"

"Yes. She has a family which is God's delight. But she has trouble feeding them."

"So I gathered. Before you go I will give you a cheque for her."

"Thank you, Countess."

"Nelo, my name is Leonora, and I like to be called Nora."

"Nora."

"Good. And you went to prison for her?"

"I went to prison because I broke the law."

"Pouff! It's done every day and men get away with it. Tony should be in prison for life. You forged share certificates, the General told me."

"A friend did that for me. I merely lodged them with my bank—which had never handled my few small investments—as security for a large overdraft. I drew the money and sent it promptly to La Guicha. Then I began to pay back the overdraft in such amounts as I could manage. I calculated that in ten years I could clear the loan. The bank manager had known me and my family for the last twenty years. It never occurred to him that the certificates were not genuine. He was of the old school who believed in trust. I'm happy to say that he died two years after granting the overdraft without ever being disillusioned. And in heaven now, since he has no head office to worry about, I am sure he forgives me."

"But the new manager was a different cup of tea?" She stood up, reached for her glass and sipped a little, the water running from her shoulders that the glow from the seven-branched candles behind her dewed with a soft gold lacquering of light. Her legs were the smallest shade short for her body but she was very beautiful and very desirable.

"Indeed he was. A young man with a future to make and hearts to break. He noticed that none of the dividends on the shares had been paid by the companies direct to the bank and that neither had they been paid into the bank by me. It has always been difficult for me to deny the straight truth to a straight answer, though lately I have cured myself of the habit somewhat. So you see . . ."

"Indeed I do. So that was that." She picked up a large towel from a stool by the bath, stepped out and began to towel herself as she walked about the room, and added, "You must have known that you would be caught out eventually."

"No. I had hoped that I might be given ten years' grace. How can we tell how the mind of God will work? Personally, I think He himself just overlooked the dividend aspect."

"Oh, Nelo!" She laughed and came over and bent to kiss me on the forehead, stumbled a little so that just for a moment I had to put my hands under her breasts and support her. Then she stepped back from me and shook her head and said, "You

82

look like a heavyweight bruiser, you've got a nose like a squashed pimento and blue eyes that I could fall through into space, and your theology, I'd say, is mostly from the Old Testament."

"I don't think so."

But whoso shall offend one of these little ones which believe in me, it were better for him that a millstone were hanged about his neck, and that he were drowned in the midst of the sea. How many offences, and for how long must they continue?

She said, "Were you unhappy when they threw you out of the church? The idiots."

"Well, yes. But I'm beginning to see that there is much to be said for being a franc-tireur, a guerrilla. I'm learning the rules."

She tossed the towel to the ground and began to powder herself and said, "And what about Sarah? Do you love her?"

"No."

"Does she love you?"

"No."

"Would you like to have love for her?"

"No."

"Why not?"

"I can't find words for an answer, but I know it."

"The day you couldn't find words for things has long gone, from the moment you first burped in your cot and said 'Mama'. Do you love me?"

"No."

"Do you desire me?"

"Yes."

"But you don't intend to do anything about it?"

"That is correct."

She slipped into a large Japanese kimono and shook her hair over her shoulders and turned towards the window. A scaly red dragon sprawled the length of the back of the kimono. He had a weary, terror-tired face as he hung, head downwards, watching the smooth, brown ankles of the Countess. Hiding

83

her face from me as she stared over the valley, she said, "Well, I know someone that will please."

"Who?"

"Tamba."

"Who's Tamba?"

"My dog on the bed in there. He hates to be disturbed before I'm dressed for dinner."

She stayed, looking out of the window and I got up, my whisky finished, and said, "It was nice of you to ask me up for a talk. I've enjoyed it."

I walked out, past the dog in the other room, on my way to the lift. There are some moments when a woman doesn't want her face to be seen.

*　　*　　*　　*

We had a very pleasant dinner that evening, and the Countess was particularly gay and charming, but even though she did more than justice to the various wines as she sat alongside me she was a model of propriety compared with the evening at the General's house.

After dinner she and Tony and Sarah and Xavier made up a bridge four while I sat and leafed through a novel—the Count was an omnivorous reader and there were piles of new books about the place—about two homosexual barbers who shared a flat. Not only was it badly written but badly observed. In prison I had known quite a few homosexuals. Skipping through it in many ways I wished I had been playing bridge but, although I enjoy card games, bridge was the one game I had never bothered with.

Going up to bed much later, Sarah and I stopped outside her bedroom door and she put her arms around me and kissed me goodnight. Then she stepped back from me and looked at me and said, "Nelo . . ."

"Yes?"

"We're leaving tomorrow, is that right?"

"Yes. The Count has offered me the loan of a car."

"If I said, 'Go now. This moment. By yourself', what would you say?"

"If it were something you wished with good reason, why yes. But I would want you to come with me."

"Just you—not me."

"I'm not fond of night driving. But if you say the word . . . well, yes. You can tell me the reason some other time."

"Some other time. Why do you bring the future into the present?"

"All right. If you want me to go, say so."

For a moment she looked forlorn and unhappy, then she came to me and buried her head in my neck and I heard her say, "No, it would do no good, Nelo . . . no good." I felt her body tremble under my hands and then she moved quickly away from me into her room.

I lay in bed for an hour, thinking about her, and about us. Xavier had asked if I loved her, and so had the Countess. Why should they even ask? Was there something about us, apparent only to other people, that prompted the question? Some sign we carried unknowingly? She was lying in her own bed now, unhappy I felt, maybe asking herself the same question and wondering, perhaps as I was, why we should be burdened with it? The moment I loved her I would know. Of this I was sure. But there was something in me, a fear, instinct-born, word-escaping, that urged me not to wish even that it would happen. I lay there thinking of her with affection and tenderness and also with, I couldn't hide this from myself, a beginning of desire which made me consider whether there wasn't a wisdom and knowledge lodged more securely and strongly in the body than the head which signalled truth; truth through a man's muscles and movements. I saw the Countess rising like Venus from her bath and she was Sarah, the water filming her creamy shoulders, her breasts pink-nippled and hazel-haloed and there was an undeniable but rare tumescence in me of spirit and flesh which I decided it was better not to question, so I got out of bed and walked quietly down the tiled corridor to her room.

She had drawn the curtains but left the windows open so that, as I entered, the curtains billowed in the draught, flapping with a sound like night roosting pheasants disturbed into clumsy flight. Either the noise awoke her or she was already awake for I heard her turn in the bed.

I said, "It's all right. It's me."

The curtains subsided as I shut the door and I went gladly across the darkness to her. Standing by the bed, shedding my pyjamas I spoke as though I were a dictating machine, mouthing words from some record made long ago, and unknown to me.

"Nobody," I said, "is going away from anybody. Nobody is asking questions which have no answer. There is only one road and it must be followed. So let it be followed without words."

I got into bed with her, felt her arms reach and draw me to her, and there was no surprise in me to find that she was naked and awaiting me with a hunger that matched my own, a famine of passion in us both that demanded immediate, silent and almost brutal appeasement. I entered her like a leopard leaping, flesh and muscle arched and arrowed, to its prey, and it was no entering because in the moment of possession I was received and possessed and we became one; mute flesh, one body, exalted beyond personality, translated beyond thought, engulfed beyond all sensation except sensation's sensation itself.

When it was done I rolled from her and lay on my side in the darkness and I felt the bed shake gently and thought she was sobbing. And because this was no moment for sobbing, but for a laggardly ebbing back to life and individuality, I put out my hand and felt her face and her eyes were dry, and suddenly I knew that she was laughing and my hand, leaving her face and moving down her body, touching and moulding her breasts and the long length of her thighs and the knolls of her knees, knew the truth before even it came to me for it drew back sharply as though a hot coal had seared it.

I got up without a word and walked to the door, and found

86

my own room and my own bed and lay, numb with a coldness and misery greater than any I had ever known before or—though it would pass and the sun would shine the next morning and I would be myself to the world—I would ever wish again to know or be known by any other man. And the Lord said unto Abraham, Wherefore did Sarah laugh . . .? But my Sarah had not laughed. Somewhere in another room she had lain, knowing my moment of betrayal, cradled in the cold comfort of her own beloved loneliness.

CHAPTER SIX

IT WAS NO surprise to me when my tea tray was brought the next morning to find on it a note from the Count saying that he hoped I would not mind deferring my departure for a day since something had gone wrong with the car he had promised to lend me. I could, of course, have made my own arrangements and gone, but there has always been an instinct in me which forces me to meet the wounding throws of Fate with another throw myself in the hope—so clearly vain—of recuperating that which is irrevocably lost. Farce is Fate's brother and when the two go on a rampage one has to put up with the ensuing saturnalia. Besides which, curiosity in me has always been stronger than caution. I was wounded, but wondering. A healthy body cures its own cuts, but a questing mind carries no remedy of its own.

Neither was there any surprise in me that I did not see either Sarah or the Countess. Nor did I seek them out. Such is the way of an adulterous woman; she eateth, and wipeth her mouth, and saith, I have done no wickedness.

I went for a ride on Furnace during the morning and gave him his head and his freedom, pushing him to the stone walls and the dried water gullies and felt, first, the surprise in him and then the added surge of power from him as he took up the challenge. I could have broken my neck and he his but I knew that the grotesque brothers were watching us.

Coming away from the stables afterwards, I was met by the Count, bushy eye-browed, beaked of nose, a tall, elegant figure in a paisley neck scarf, blue silk shirt and immaculate grey linen trousers.

He said, "Let us go for a walk down to the grotto."

We went around to the front of the castle, down through the parterres and terraces to the grey, craggy body of rocks and ravines through which ran clear streams and waterfalls fed by an artesian well a mile away. We sat on a stone bench opposite a grilled gateway that led into the underground tunnels and caves of the grotto.

The Count said, "There are two entrances to the grotto. That one and another a few hundred yards away. Both are kept locked and each has its own individual key." He handed me a key. "Tonight you will enter by this gate. At midnight precisely. I shall enter by the far gate. One of my manservants will be on guard at this gate. He has strict orders to shoot you if you try to come out by this gate. The only way out for you safely is by the gate through which I shall have entered, and it will be locked and I shall have the key with me in the grotto. Does it explain itself?"

"Clearly."

"You will be provided with a torch and a gun. So shall I."

"I am a poor hand with a gun."

"I am not."

"Then you must make arrangements for my burial."

"That will be done in the grotto."

"I have no complaint. The precedent was well established by the early Christians in the catacombs of Rome. But the law might become curious."

"There is no law in this country which cannot be satisfied by me. You left at midnight at your own wish—and disappeared. It happens every midnight all over the world to men and women. By the way, I should add that you are completely free to leave the Castle, this country, to go where you will, at any time up until midnight and become just a pathetic memory to me."

"Have many men availed themselves of the choice?"

"A few."

"My name won't be added to theirs."

"I never thought it would."

I lit a cigarette and saw that my hand was steady, which only proved the arrogance of the body's strength over the weakling mind.

I said, "From what does her madness stem? Not secret lust because that would be practised with deceit."

He smiled gently, "From what does Sarah's madness stem?"

I said, "I know now, but it would take too long to tell in detail. Briefly the wrong gods demanded a sacrifice from her. What of the Countess?"

"She is mad in her genes. Her family have conserved madness for generations, even been proud of it as other families are of honour. Her pride is wanton and heeds no rules; but since I love her I have to follow the rules of my own pride, or she would think me nothing."

I stood up and said, "Perhaps you would kindly make the gun available to me after lunch with some practice ammunition. I presume, if chance should be so, that if I kill you the law will have no concern with me?"

"Of course. I often practise revolver shooting in the grotto at night. How many competent men have been killed in their own gun rooms at their own hands?"

"Too many."

(Far too many according to my father who, eccentric though he had been over many things, forced a draconian law in the gun room and in the field. No man ever came twice on his shoot if he observed the slightest infringement of the safety rules. He had slippered the bare bottom of my sister—who had a passion for firearms as most of the statuary in the garden proclaimed —from the age of six until twelve when she finally learnt wisdom through that sensitive part of the anatomy. I should say that my sister, although she loved us all dearly, ran away from home at the age of twenty-one, and we had postcards from her from all over the world for three years, and then she was killed in an air crash in Mexico.)

After lunch, which Xavier and I took alone, the others having made some excuse, I took the gun which had been provided with ammunition down to the dried river bed. I don't like guns. In the hand they breed their own evil. But then the same could be said of club, staff, spear, bow and arrow and cross-bow, so I am no abolitionist because even the bare hand itself will turn to evil if evil is given a place in the heart. The thought of death was an annoyance, because there were so many things I still wanted to do. The fear of death meant nothing since it was merely the opening of another door and, I hoped, a chance to put some pertinent theological questions to a higher authority than any available here below.

My practice shooting didn't impress me. At ten yards I never once hit a beer can off the rock. I hit the rock in various places, but after half an hour I gave the whole thing up as an idleness of effort, and sat down and smoked a cigarette in the shade. I went to sleep. When I woke up Sarah was standing looking down at me.

For a while I said nothing. I was content to look at her, wondering why, since I now knew that she loved me so much, there was no answering love in me, wondering, too, whether she was prepared to admit the truth of her love. I doubted it. Loneliness still shone like a star for her and dazzled her sight with a luminous blindness.

She said, "Nelo, you must leave here before midnight."

I said, "The Countess is an extraordinary woman. Have you learnt this since last night—or did she tell you before then what the consequences would be?"

"Since."

"A small point in your favour, but not hers."

"You must leave . . . now."

"I can't."

"Why not?"

"You know already."

She dropped down on her knees beside me. "I was a damned fool . . . a stupid, selfish—"

"No. You did what you did out of your wisdom. The only wisdom you know at the moment. If I didn't understand that I would leave here before midnight."

She stood up, turning her back to me, the sun touching her hair made the thinnest of haloes, and her shadow reaching back to my feet along the sandy soil was a jet pillar.

She said, "Do you hate me?"

"For wanting to rid yourself of me? No. There is no injury you can do me which will make me hate you."

She swung round and snapped, "Oh, you bloody impossible man!"

"That I know and regret and of a certainty inherit from my father. If I come out of the grotto tonight, the Count has said his car will be waiting for me. You can come with me if you want to."

She said, "If you come out, you will travel without me. Don't you understand that? Don't you see that that was what it was all about?"

"Perfectly. But I think there is a lot more which you don't see. Unfortunately I can't make up my mind yet whether it would be a Christian act to pray that you come soon to clearer sight."

"For God's sake—not a bloody sermon!"

"I said prayer. There's a great difference."

Her anger, so characteristic of her, was like the brush of a bramble across the face at night as one walks, sharp pain for a second, then dead before it can lodge a lasting wound in the flesh. She stooped and picked up the gun from my feet.

"How good are you with this?"

"Abysmal. My shooting has always been approximate."

"Would it matter? You'd never kill a man would you?"

"I most certainly would. Life has no inviolable sanctity for me. God put the hawk in the air and the shark in the water. A son is not always a good bearer of his father's message. Turn

92

the other cheek was not the original message I like to think. There is a moment for killing and a moment for mercy. God paid us the great compliment of thinking we were capable of telling one moment from another. Few of us can."

"Sometimes I can't tell when you're joking or blaspheming."

"Frequently the first but, never, I like to think, the latter; and at the moment neither. Anyway, you're making too much of the matter. It's very simple. You want to kill your love for me, before you find yourself admitting it openly; and the Count wants to kill me for a moment of farce with his mad wife which would have delighted Boccaccio. Actually, since we are being serious, the moment delighted me too. And, anyway, the whole thing is such a tangle that I'm content to let time unravel it. I've never considered myself a fool but maybe I am and this night my soul shall be required of me."

"You're bloody hopeless."

As she stamped away, I said to myself, surely not that, not with my training and belief? And I smiled to myself for it brought back my father to me, for the only time he had ever beaten me—I was more tractable than my sister—was when he had caught me in a rare moment of pubescent curiosity indulging in some mild sexual play with a maid at Stonebridge, willing and some years my senior, and as his switch (slippers were for girls) fell he recited to the beats, "Chasten thy son while there is hope, and let not thy soul spare for his crying." It was almost a complete cure.

*   *   *   *

The only personal possessions of any importance that I had on me when I went to the grotto were my mother's diamonds, wrapped in a handkerchief in my pocket, and an envelope—in the same pocket—which contained a cheque from the Countess for La Guicha for a thousand pounds, and a note from me to the Count asking that diamonds and cheque might be forwarded. A proud and hasty man might, I suppose, have torn up the cheque—delivered by a manservant—but whether

93

it was to be conscience or blood money made no difference to me or La Guicha. To talk of tainted money is to talk of guilty water. They both flow and men use and abuse them.

Out of long habit, I am always early for appointments. I had ten minutes to wait for midnight, so I sat on the stone bench, listening to the sound of the waterfalls and watched the pale wings of a crowd of moths hovering over a near-by bush. A few lights showed from a hamlet at the head of the valley. There were no stars, no moon. From late evening the clouds had gathered, hanging low, bulging over the mountain tops and the air had turned cooler as though in the darkness above rain storms were gathering to cool the parched earth. As I sat there, a few odd, fat drops of storm rain began to fall. Then, as from beyond the house in the stable clock tower I heard the bell begin to toll midnight, the rain thickened and the warm ground, slaked by the fall, gave up a sweet breath of gladness. I took torch, gun and key and went to the locked grill. As I turned the key and opened the gate, the sky was seared with lightning, lacquering the wet rocks and foliage with yellow and blue for a vivid fraction of time, and the rain roared down, striking at the earth with a hissing of serpents. I moved into the grotto a few feet and turned as another flare of lightning slashed across the sky, thunder bursting on its heels, and saw a man come into the shelter of the grotto arch. It was my keeper who would deny all escape from that gate. I switched on the torch and moved into the grotto, the rolling artillery of thunder following me. And they shall go into the holes of the rocks, and into the caves of the earth, for fear of the Lord, and for the glory of his majesty, when he arises to shake terribly the earth.

It was then, as I saw the smooth sandy path of the tunnel stretching ahead that I knew that it was no time for stupid self-sacrifices—they are an embarrassment on earth and in heaven. When I met the Count I would shoot to kill and leave the Lord to make any necessary corrections to my aim if He were in the mood.

After ten yards the tunnel forked. I took the left fork, flicking

94

the light briefly ahead to mark the route in my mind and then moving in darkness until I felt it was time to show the torch again. The Count might ambush me in dark or light, or he might show himself openly before firing, giving me the grace of a few moments and himself the dignity of some personal hazard which would satisfy his honour. After a few minutes I heard the sound of running water. I switched on the torch. A few feet in front of me was a stream of water about eight feet wide and beyond it a smooth rock face. The water was rushing down in a fast spate, already swollen a little, I guessed, from the heavy rainfall outside.

I went back to the fork and took the right-hand tunnel, and for the next five or ten minutes I moved on, meeting further forks, sometimes taking the wrong one to find myself at a dead end. Finally, in a quick flashing of the torch, I saw the tunnel roof slope upwards to form a large opening with three shallow steps at its base. As the light went I had the impression of a large cavern beyond.

Keeping to the side of the tunnel, I went up the steps and eased myself as silently as I could to the right, my back against the hard smooth rock. There was a cool, strong draught in my face now, and away to my right I could hear the loud sound of turbulent water. Somewhere through this cavern flowed the stream which I had met before. I stood in the darkness, waiting, and I had the strong conviction that somewhere in the darkness ahead, also, the Count would be waiting. The whole thing, I thought, was ridiculous, but that was little comfort because so much of life is ridiculous. I remembered once discussing with a Bishop at my club when the port had gone around three or four times the proposition that the whole Universe was no more than a joke in the mind of God, and his admitting that there was no evidence to the contrary and then confiding in me that one of his earlier preoccupations in the study of the Holy Writs had been with the lack of humour and true gaiety they manifested. Of joy and rejoicing there was much, but seldom over simple, ordinary things, and so often with a look cast back over the shoulder. Serve the Lord with fear, and rejoice with trembling. No one, he said, ever got together and had a pleasant evening, a secular sing-song, and the bandying of innocent jokes. He had a theory that it had once all been there but Time and man's pomposity had written it out. There was no true heaven, he said, unless it had place for a good belly-laugh, puns and limericks and the warm, relaxed gaiety of old boys' reunions. I hoped he was right and had the comforting thought that if I were killed this night at least it would make a good story when I arrived.

I moved a little more to my right and felt water around my ankles. Not wanting to step into the stream, and not wanting to be shot the moment I flicked on the torch, I squatted down on my heels and held the torch high above me and out to my left. I switched it on to get my bearings. Before I could see anything, there was a shot from the middle of the cavern and the torch was sent spinning from my upraised hand and I fell over backwards on my heels and cracked my head against the rock wall. I lay in the darkness, listening to the dying thunder echoes of the shot, full of admiration for the Count's marksmanship, and aware that I was resting in three inches of water and that there was a rain swollen torrent a few feet from me. My left hand was numb from the shock of the torch being shot from it. In fact, for a moment or two I thought I had lost my hand.

I lay there until the echoes of the shot had died and there was only the sound of rushing water. Then I crawled, gun in my right hand, a few feet to my left, away from the water, and slowly stood up. As I did so, the cavern suddenly blazed with light.

High in the roof a galaxy of electric bulbs had come to life, and from various niches and rock ledges spotlights flooded the place. It was some seconds before I could adjust my eyes to the light and see the Count. He was standing some yards from me, across the sandy floor of the cavern, one hand still on a main light switch in the rock, a gun in the other. Behind him and to his left a great waterfall spouted from a hole in the rock to fall into a wide, dark pool from which the stream swept away to my end of the cavern to disappear through a shallow archway.

Although I realised that he was having the courtesy to allow me a few seconds' grace for my eyes to clear, I fired wildly while my sight was still hazed. I shattered a spotlight five feet above him and to his right.

He nodded his head, almost as though he approved, and then fired at me. He hit me somewhere in the left arm just below my shoulder and I was spun round like a top, lost momentum and my gun, and staggered forward and fell flat on my face, almost at his feet which was fortunate for me because as he stepped forward to administer the *coup de grâce* I swung with my right leg and knocked him off his feet. He fell on top of me and since I discovered that I still had the use of my left arm, I grappled him to me and pinned his gun hand hard between us so that if he shot there was as much danger to him as there was to me. He lay perfectly still in my arms, knowing he had not the strength to break my hold; and so we lay there on the damp sand, face to face, and I said, "This is ridiculous. Why don't we just call it a day and go our ways peacefully?"

"It would not," he said, "be consistent with honour."

"Yours, not mine. But if you insist I shall just crush the wind out of you and then take your gun and key."

"Do that."

But I couldn't because I suddenly felt my left arm going numb and the strength ebbing from it, and I had a feeling that he was aware of it.

"In the old days," I said, "there was a tradition in duels that a flesh wound satisfied honour."

"Not in my family. All duels were fought to the death."

"Tradition," I said, "is an ass. I'm not going to kill you and I'm not going to let you kill me."

"We cannot," he said, "lie here in an eternal embrace. One way or another it will come to an end and then one of us will die."

"You are set on this?"

97

"It is inevitable."

"Inevitable is a word that makes God cock His ears when it comes from the mouths of men."

Which, of course, it is, and which is why dead certs are neither dead nor certain, and infallibility a will-o'-the-wisp and a prayer for intercession a daily necessity. I offered mine then silently, and modestly make no claim that what happened next was an answer to it. There has been more loose talk about miracles in this world than there has been about morals.

The roar of noise from the waterfall suddenly, like a cage of lions breaking into voice, rose to a thunder peak and over the Count's shoulder I saw the volume of water rushing through the great hole in the rock increase until it filled the whole aperture and spouted forward in a great jet, smashing into the pool, filling it and flooding over us, a wild mass of undeniable power, herald of some flash flood in the stream above ground. Still locked together we were taken up by it, eddied like bound twigs, sucked and swung and tumbled and finally shouldered up and borne away by it into the main stream and swept, rolling and curvetting, into the darkness of the underground labyrinth; tumbled over small falls, moved easily along wide reaches and finally spilled out under a rain and storm filled night into the small lake which graced the bottom of the grotto system.

Swept into the fringing reeds, we broke our embrace and rose, our feet sinking slowly into the mud, lightning and thunder flashing and booming away in the distance as the storm passed. The Count's gun had long gone. He had a nasty cut on the side of his face, and I was feeling dizzy from the battering of our ride and the loss of some blood from my arm. We stood there, the pull of the flood waters tugging at our legs, and looked at one another without words. Deep calleth unto deep at the noise of Thy waterspouts; all Thy waves and billows are gone over me.

We waded to the bank and I checked that I still had my mother's diamonds with me. Then I said to the Count, "My dear Antonio. A family tradition has been broken. In its place

plant another. The next time that your wife sleeps with a man
—beat her. I think you will find that that is what she is waiting
for."

He said, "You are so knowledgeable about women?"

"No. But when a sickness won't respond to one remedy it
makes sense to try another. And let's face it there are a lot of
happy and faithful wives whose husbands beat them once a
month on principle."

He gave me a wan smile from under his beaky nose. I left
him there and walked away, up to the castle forecourt, holding
my arm. Xavier was sitting at the wheel of his Lancia waiting
for me.

He said, "There was never any doubt in my mind."

"About what?"

"Your coming."

I climbed into the back of the car and found Sarah sitting
there.

"Why are you here?"

She smiled. "Firstly to do something about your arm." She
tilted me forward as the car moved away and began to ease
off my wet jacket. The movement made my head swim and I
fainted. A thing I had never done in my life before.

*   *   *   *

We drove through Portugal into Spain and then across
Spain to the coast and into France, staying one night at a small
hotel near Palafrugell. The roof of Xavier's car had a secret
compartment into which we put the diamonds to avoid Customs
trouble. The bullet had gone right through the soft underflesh
of my left arm near the shoulder. The wound had been cleaned
and bandaged by Sarah using the first aid kit which Xavier
carried in the car. It throbbed and ached a little for the first
day, but on the second it was no more than a dull, painful
reminder of the grotto. Xavier was going to drop us at my
villa and then motor on to Switzerland, where he also had funds
banked. He explained that the Count had withdrawn his offer

to get his funds transferred from Lisbon since he, Xavier, dwelt in the shadow of my opprobrium. However, he was quite cheerful about it. Similar setbacks were so common in his life that they had become old friends. Sarah was cheerful and gay, enjoying the ride and the company, and I knew that from the moment we had turned out of the castle grounds the whole place and its memories had passed from her mind. As she moved along the corridors of time she shut each door carefully after her. Her only regret or joy or both was that at this moment I was moving with her. She had conspired with the Countess to deceive me, I knew, in order to test a love for me which she was not ready to admit. The act done, she had to be left with remorse, indifference or jealousy and of this trinity surely hoped for the second. However, on our journey, she gave no indication of her response and I did not question her because I realised by now that truth seldom came from her as a reply to a direct question. And, anyway, I was mildly engaged in considering my own feelings towards her.

On the way along the coast to my villa we stopped at Beauvallon and I visited Monsieur Crozette. His villa overlooked one of the fairways of the golf course and the front garden was full of fig trees on which the fruits were beginning to purple. The house was large and untidy and so was Monsieur Crozette, a warm, mildly sweating mountain of a man with small bright brown button eyes and a drooping Viking moustache. His crumpled shirt was unbuttoned to the navel. There were paint stains on his linen trousers and he was wearing odd sandals. He could have been any age from forty-five to fifty-five and he welcomed me effusively as though I had come at last to fulfil a long pressed invitation, and the welcome was made in a mixture of French and English which it would be tedious to reproduce.

"La Guicha has written about you. A friend of La Guicha's is a friend of mine. And one day, if she is not more discreet she will need all her friends and, of course, not one of them will be found wanting. What is she? I often ask myself. A new kind of sub-celestial being? She hangs between heaven and hell, between saint and sinner and she goes her way like a wandering storm of charity."

I said, "When she dies she will go to heaven, without doubt. But they will have trouble with her because she is not bureaucratically minded."

He led me through the house. There were unopened crates everywhere, uncurtained windows, bare boards, and pictures piled against skirtings as though he had only moved in the day before, though I later learned that he had been there ten years. He took me through a kitchen whose disorder was monstrous, as though two chefs had recently fought a throwing battle there, and out into a large glass-roofed conservatory, part of which was shaded with green blinds so that one stepped from the confusion of the kitchen into the bland, green warmth of a semi-tropical glade. Three sides of the conservatory were glassed off vertically to the roof and in this space grew a proliferation of plants and creepers and small trees. One corner was taken up by a large, rock-edged pool and there were patches of sand and moss and small grottos and caves running right round the three sides of the conservatory. The three-sided enclosure was full of snakes, though at first because of their colouring against the vegetation they were not quickly seen; snakes coiled and sleeping by the pool, snakes twined the length of branches; snakes idly and torpidly hanging in loops from the creepers, and snakes moving gently along the back of the restraining glass, bodies half raised, their tongues delicately flicking and probing.

I said, "La Guicha said I should see the Arizona rock snake."

"Alas—she is shedding her skin in the grotto. Most of them, they like to do it in the open, but she, she is modest."

"Why do you keep them—for sale?"

"No. Though sometimes I oblige a zoo or a private customer. Many years ago I used to practise as a veterinary surgeon— but I gave it up for a more profitable occupation. No. These are my pets. I like to sit here and watch them and talk to them.

I have tried everything—dogs, cats, mice, rabbits and tropical birds. Oh, never have tropical birds—they are so noisy, so restless and so small-minded. And dogs and cats are so demanding. They have been domesticated so long they think they are human and demand human rights—and mice and rabbits have nothing but copulation on their minds. But snakes, so dignified, so clean, so self-contained . . . aloof and with malice to none although the world has so maligned them."

We sat down at an iron table and, as he poured wine, I watched a snake slide gently into the water of the pool and swim in slow, immaculate esses to the far side, all grace and beauty. And the Lord said unto the serpent, Because thou hast done this, thou art cursed above all cattle, and above every beast of the field; upon thy belly shalt thou go, and dust shalt thou eat all the days of thy life. Either the reporting was wrong or the good Lord had been overhasty. I remember preaching a sermon on original sin at my church in Devon a week before I was arrested—a sermon in which I invited some sympathy for the serpent since it had been, after all, one of God's chosen instruments—and afterwards a farmer from the congregation had said to me, "Parson, you should have preached that sermon first to the bloody little adders up on my top fields."

As we drank wine, I gave my mother's diamonds to Monsieur Crozette. He pulled out a jeweller's optic and began to examine them.

He said, "They are very fine stones. Very fine. Do they belong to you—legally?"

"Morally. They were once my mother's."

"You want them disposed of, quietly?"

"Yes."

"I can find a buyer. My commission will be five per cent. What do you intend to do with the money?"

"Give it to La Guicha."

"My commission will be one per cent." He handed them back to me. "Keep them. I will let you know when it is arranged."

"But don't you want to show them to people . . . possible buyers?"

He laughed. "No. They will take my word."

He picked up the photograph of the Monet and examined it, and then sighed, "Beautiful."

"Someone, I fancy, stole it and gave it to La Guicha."

"Naturally. Actually I know the legal owner. A man of great taste. He will be heartbroken. But then that will do him good. He has broken many other people's hearts in his time. Tell La Guicha I will arrange it for her. All she will have to do is to deliver the painting and collect the money."

"And your commission?"

"None. She paid it long ago. In Vichy during the war, when I was a young man, the Germans thought I would be better out of the way."

I put the photograph and the jewels into my pocket and said, "I imagine the police might feel the same about you today."

He laughed. "Possibly. Though I have my uses for them sometimes. Contrary to most people's beliefs, the police are very broadminded and sophisticated. I make a living arranging things for my friends or those recommended to me by my friends. And the arranging is not always a matter of dealing and selling. What do you intend to do after you have paid over your money from the diamonds to La Guicha?"

"I don't know. I might help her for a little while, but that won't last. We always quarrel in the end. At the moment my plans for the future lack definition."

"I thought they might."

"Why should you think that?"

"Because it is always in a man's eyes. That look of one who searches for something and is not even sure what it is he looks for." He smiled. "Until you find out what it is and where you want to go, I might be able to put you in the way of temporary employment."

"That's very kind of you."

103

"Not at all. If something comes up I will get in touch with you."

"How? I shall be moving around."

He smiled more broadly, his big face glossed with perspiration. "Don't worry about the how. That is part of my profession."

I left him, leaving the address and telephone number of my villa, and went back to Xavier and Sarah.

The villa which my Aunt Tilly had left me was not far from Beauvallon. It lay between Fréjus and St. Raphael and about a mile inland. It was called the Villa Laren—but not so named by my aunt. She had bought it from a wealthy Dutchman who had named it after his birthplace in the north of Holland and, since my aunt never believed in change unless change produced improvement, she had left it so. My aunt had been my father's elder sister and she had never let him forget it. She was a formidable, but good-hearted woman, who favoured Edwardian dress for most of her adult life. My abiding impression of her was feathered hats, lorgnettes, high, hard, lace-covered bosoms, violet face powders, cachou scent, a long, mannish face and a voice which could drown my father's at any time. They loved each other dearly but did their best to disguise the fact from the outer world. Wherever she went there was always some olive-skinned, willowy young man in her company right up until the day she died in a boating accident on Lac Leman. The young man had courageously tried to save her but had failed and only just managed to save himself. She had left him four thousand pounds and her villa in Switzerland. The Villa Laren came to me, my brother had her Paris house which he promptly sold, and the bulk of her fortune came to my father. She visited Stonebridge Park twice a year and each time brought one of her young friends, which meant that my father would go about the place muttering about "damned gigolos". To me she was always very kind and when she knew that I was going into the church she wrote to me and said, "It is of course the greatest mistake of your life, but let us not forget that the greatest lives are the ones that have held the greatest mistakes—

e.g. Lord Nelson, but do not say this to your father. However, I wish you well and am only sorry you have chosen the wrong church." She had turned Roman Catholic at the age of twenty —to my father's fury. Love her as he might he could not forgive her for that. He also—though this was not her fault—found it hard to take that she had been born on 15 July but whether this was because it was St. Swithin's Day or the anniversary of the massacre at Cawnpore none of us ever found out. Anyway, he gave half the money he received under her will to the Bible and Medical Missionary Fellowship, invested the rest and put up a plaque to her memory in Stonebridge church. And the Villa Laren came to me, with all its furniture and fittings, and a caretaker called Ernst Daubel who lived in a flat over the garage.

The villa sat on a little knoll at the end of a stone-walled lane. It was fronted by terraces of vines and flanked by rough fields of olive trees. The garden was small and overrun with oleanders, geraniums, cactus and hibiscus. Ernst was no gardener. The front of the house was smothered in bougainvillaea and its wide terrace looked south to the sea. At the back of the villa was a wired-in hard tennis court that had not been used for years.

When we arrived there was a note pinned to Ernst's flat door which said—*En vacances*. However, this did not worry me. The front-door key was always kept under a loose tile in the doorway so that we could let ourselves in. Among a few letters in the mail box I found one I had written from England warning Ernst that I would be coming out to the villa soon. Ernst was clearly on a long vacation, but that was not unusual.

It was late when we arrived. Fortunately we had stopped for dinner on the way. Sarah found the linen cupboard and made up beds for us and then we sat and had a brandy each before going to bed.

Xavier went up first and I was left alone with Sarah. We sat on the terrace and the warm air was full of the dying sun-scents of the past day. Moths circuited the terrace lamps like stacked planes waiting orders to land, and three lizards sat on the stone balustrade and waited for them to fall. We sat with our feet up and there was perfect peace between us because we both knew that we were the kind that took each day as it came, suffered or enjoyed it, and greeted each new dawn as though it were a miraculous egg of hope and freshness waiting to be cracked and tasted with a palate untouched by the past. That's how we were and, as far as I was concerned, I knew I must wait patiently to grow out of such childish euphoria. For Sarah I could not speak, but I suspected that she was growing out of it faster than I was and resenting it. Meanwhile there was a curiosity in me that prompted me to break our silence.

I said, "You are afraid that you have fallen in love with me."

"Christ, Nelo." She flicked her cigarette end away over the balustrade in a fire-fly parabola.

"Why try to kill it?" I asked.

"There should be a law against it. It leads to unhappiness for some people."

"Through marriage?"

"Of course. For some people love and marriage don't mix."

I smiled. "That's a stupid remark."

"It happens to be true. At least, for me."

"You've been married before?"

She hesitated, and I knew that the hesitation was temporarily cradling the twins, truth and falsehood, and she was wondering which to kick out of the bed to face the world first.

She said, "As a matter of fact, yes. And it was so disastrous I don't even like to think about it."

What she meant was that she wanted more time to invent the details and I made a small bet with myself that I would get them, tuppence coloured, before long. I contented myself, however, with saying, "Before marriage there must be love. Don't overlook the fact that I don't love you."

"And don't you overlook the fact that you might very soon. You must have considered that."

"It's been in my mind."

106

"Then kick it out. It only leads to a making of contracts. And neither of us are contract keepers. We can't avoid being the falling in love kind, but we should avoid being the marrying kind."

"St. Paul said, 'It is better to marry than to burn.'"

"St. Paul needed his head examined. And don't quote scripture at me. The church should be barred to all burly athletic types. They never sound sincere. Religion comes best from people who look half dead and out of touch with the world."

I said, "I don't quote scripture aloud very often. Usually to myself. It's like touching wood secretly. And I agree that St. Paul needed his head examined. His seventh chapter of his first epistle to the Corinthians gave me a lot of trouble at Theological College—still does. However, I don't want you to be troubled on my account. I like being with you and sleeping with you, and I agree there's a probability that I might fall in love with you and then want to marry you. So to avoid stupid stratagems on your part like the Countess episode, I suggest you go away. It will make things much easier and less complicated for you."

"You want me to go?"

"I'm advising you to go."

"Absence makes the heart grow fonder."

"Now you're quoting to me and out of context. The author was referring to a place. The next line is—'Isle of Beauty, Fare thee well!'"

"Oh, go to hell." She stood up and I sensed that one of her flashes of anger might be coming. At her movement the lizards on the balustrade scampered for cover.

I laughed and said, "What on earth are you worrying about? So you're the child of an unhappy marriage, and your own marriage didn't go well, but—"

"It was perfect!"

"I see. Forgive me. But you told me once that you'd never met the one you were looking for."

"I've told you a lot of things and some of them lies. That's because I take a pleasure in lying sometimes. But this is true. I don't want to be in love with you and I don't want you to fall in love with me. Here below, you get Paradise once. There's no second entry because you've got too much excess baggage."

"Nonsense. Now you are talking like St. Paul."

But I didn't quote it to her. *I say therefore to the unmarried and widows, it is good for them if they abide even as I.* And for the first time I really had a better understanding of her. She was just a stupid, frightened girl. Which, of course, at her age and with her experience made her an unintelligent one. Not that that, of course, would have any effect on whether I was going to fall in love with her. These matters are out of our hands.

She came over to me and said, "Nonsense or not, that's how I feel." She bent and kissed me briefly and then drawing back went on, "I've been lucky so far—but this time it happens to be you. What I want is someone comfortable and undemanding about the things that matter."

I said, "When I fall in love with you I shall want to marry you."

In the terrace light I saw her mouth tighten and then she ran a hand characteristically through her hair. She turned away from me and said, "Oh, Nelo—you should have said 'If' not 'When'."

Without looking back, she went into the house, without a goodnight or a goodbye, but I knew that she was going, knew that in the morning when I woke she would be gone and that I was going to do nothing to stop her.

What I couldn't know then was that she had decided that her going should be made painful not only for her, but for myself and Xavier. She took with her Xavier's car and also my mother's diamonds, and she left a note for me which I never showed Xavier. It read:

The day I read the announcement of your marriage in The Times,

I will return the diamonds. If you make any attempt to find me and I hear of it, I shall sell them. Please think badly of me, because that is what I am.

The note raised no emotion in me at all, except for a slight displeasure at the bad syntax of the last sentence.

CHAPTER SEVEN

XAVIER TOOK THE news with his usual calm. No day was complete for him without some disappointment to test his resilient faith in himself. He was rewarded a little at mid-day when a telegram arrived from Nice, unsigned, but stating that his car had been left in a garage there for him to pick up. He telephoned for a car to St. Raphael and left that afternoon for Nice. Before he left he handed me a slip of paper with an address on it.

"If you want me, or there is anything I can do, you can always get in touch with me through that address in Switzerland. Of course, I may be a little time in answering or arriving. As for Sarah, I give you my advice for your peace of mind. Employ some agency to find her and when found—marry her. Don't take no for an answer. Just marry her. Or—as an alternative, and far more difficult—forget about her."

"I'm far more concerned about my diamonds."

"Concerned. But not far more. We all cover our emotional losses by substituting some material counter-balance. When my first mistress ran off with a pizza cook in Naples she took with her a gold watch which had been given to me by a Swedish cabinet minister. Much though I loved her, I made myself so angry about the loss of the watch that I forgot her in a fortnight. So, find Sarah and marry her or build up a nice anger about the diamonds."

When he had gone I telephoned Monsieur Crozette and told him that temporarily I should not be wanting a market for the diamonds, and explained why. Of his own accord he said, "Do you want to trace this woman?"

I said, "I would like my diamonds back."

"She may have sold them."

"She won't do that."

"Extraordinary woman. I will make some enquiries. Something may turn up."

I gave him some details and he promised to telephone me if he heard anything. I then telephoned an agent in St. Raphael and told him that I wished to sell the villa. Maybe, as some compensation for the loss of the diamonds, luck was accorded to me by whatever power it is that dispenses such favours. Two days later a man drove up to the villa in an open Mercedes car, introduced himself as Monsieur Caesar Cazar, was shown round the house and gardens by me and then, over a glass of Amer Picon, said that the villa was just what he wanted and wrote me a cheque for it there and then, saying as he handed it to me, "I'd like possession in two weeks. My lawyers will fix up the legal details with your agent, but I like each day's business to be cleared from my mind before I sleep. The purchase price is to include all the furniture and fittings except for any sentimental pieces—but no photographs—you might wish to take within reason."

I said, "That suits me, Monsieur Cazar, and I hope you will be very happy here."

He said, "I shan't be here often. Business keeps me moving. But when I am, I am sure I shall be happy."

"Because the house has happy memories for you?"

He jerked his head up, gave me a cold stare, and then smiled delightfully.

"You have a good memory?"

"I seldom forget faces."

"Even when Time has retouched them again and again?"

"You once taught two boys how to rhumba in an English country house. Neither of us was a good pupil and I don't think I've danced it since."

He nodded. "Your aunt was good to me—and also I was good to her, but in the end there was not enough I could do for her. I had to see her drown because I could support her no longer. She was a brave and splendid woman. Her last words to me were, 'Caesar, such a vulgar way to die.' "

"And since?"

"What she left me, I have made multiply many thousand times. And I have always wanted this villa and left my instructions with all the agents around here."

I said, "I shall take nothing with me."

"You are kind, monsieur. And your father? He is still alive and well?"

"No. He is dead."

"Ah, sad. Such a gentleman. He did not understand your aunt, of course. And he did not like me until I taught him a few card tricks and how to shave the sides of a pack to make dealing at poker easier. You are the one who went into the church or became a member of Parliament?"

"I went into the church. But I have left it now."

"Ah, that would have made dear Tilly so happy to know."

I saw him back to his car; olive-skinned still, dark-eyed and tall, but no longer willowy, and as he drove away I liked to think that he would possibly stop at the next church and light a candle for my aunt. I went back into the villa and, from her portrait in the hallway, my aunt smiled graciously down at me, splendidly coiffeured, a great osprey feather waving in her hat and one long, finely veined hand resting lightly on the ebony and gold handle of a silk sunshade, her dress a cascade of blue and white silk.

I cashed Monsieur Cazar's cheque the next day, and the ones from the Countess and Via. The bank wouldn't take the one from Via because of sterling currency regulations but the manager sent me to a café a few doors away with a note of hand from him and I had no trouble. La Guicha would be pleased with the money, but angry with me when she learnt of the loss of the diamonds. Carelessness with valuables was not something to be tolerated. Money lost was food or treatment denied to some small body. I packed the francs in a small case and decided, for economy's sake, to go to Switzerland by train the next day. I should have remembered my St. James. Go to now, ye that say, today or tomorrow we will go into such a city . . . Whereas ye know not what *shall be* on the morrow.

*   *   *   *

The next morning as I was sitting at the window of the lounge having my breakfast coffee, two cars turned into the villa driveway and stopped outside. One was a gunmetal coloured Rolls, which reminded me of the General's car, and the other was a small open truck. The Rolls was chauffeur-driven by a coloured man in a pale blue livery. He opened the rear door and two other coloured men got out. One was a man of about fifty, large and bulky, dressed in clerical clothes and gaiters and wearing a black-banded panama hat, and the other was a tall, slim man in a grey silk suit, black and white shoes, and he was carrying a cane and wearing a monocle. They all went back to the small truck and there was a discussion between them which ended with the chauffeur dropping the tailboard of the truck. Then, with the assistance of the truck driver, he began to unload it. I watched with interest. They unshipped two trusses of hay, then a couple of boxes of cabbages, and finally two long stems of bananas. They then started to carry the lot around to the back of the villa while the two other men came up to the front door which I had not yet unlocked from the night.

However, there was no need to go and open it for them because I heard a key turn in the lock and then their voices in the hall. They came into the room and stopped in surprise when they saw me. Then the man in the grey suit, who must have been in his mid-thirties, tugged at the top of his cane and with a little flourish revealed a sword-stick. He had a lean, intelligent face, sported a little dash of a moustache, and he was wearing a Guards' tie.

113

I said, "You won't have any need for that."

The other, hot and perspiring, took off his panama and wiped his face with a large blue silk handkerchief, and said, "Who are you, man? Some French official?" He was smoking a large cigar.

I said, "My name is Charles Nelo Sangster and I own this villa. At least I did until yesterday. I've now sold it. Who are you?"

Both of them smiled and relaxed and the younger man put the sword back into its cane with a little awkwardness.

"Allow me," said the elder of the two, "to introduce to you His Royal Highness the Bakata of Bakata, at the moment cruelly exiled from his own country."

His Royal Highness said, "Alfred Sequimango. My friends call me Alfy. I was at Sandhurst and in the Brigade."

"And I," said the other, "am Dr. Bomokandi, Archbishop First Christian Church of Bakata, B.A. Hons., London University . . . a long time ago by correspondence. It is good of you to greet us here, Mr. Sangster."

Alfy said, "Very decent, old chap. But you shouldn't have put yourself out. We've already been shown round the place by your caretaker when we hired it."

I said, "I didn't know he'd let it. But then this was just a flying visit on my part to sell it. Have you taken it for long?"

"A week, maybe less," said Dr. Bomokandi.

I said, "That's all right then. You'll be gone long before the new owner wants it. And don't worry about me. I'm leaving today."

"No need, old chap," said His Royal Highness. "Plenty of room. In fact we insist."

"In fact we'd rather," said Dr. Bomokandi. "You see His Highness is here incognito." He moved to the sideboard and began to examine the bottles and then poured himself a brandy, sipped it, and turned and beamed at me. "Nobody, my son, is going to suggest you could be guilty of loose talk but delicate negotiations are in hand and it would be better for us if you stayed."

I said, "What negotiations?"

Alfy said, "We are guests in this country of the French government. But you know how it is . . . some things have to be done delicately. Present them with a *fait accompli* and they don't mind. But let them get wind of it first and they say no."

"But nothing criminal," said the Archbishop.

"I'm glad to hear that."

"So you should be, man. By the way, if you are the owner, Mr. Sangster, then from what the caretaker told me you were once in the Ministry. Correct?"

"Correct, Archbishop."

"What you do, son, to be kicked out?"

"I was a little unorthodox in my charity work."

"Man, you got to be those days sometimes. However, I don't sit in judgment. That's for my brother Canterbury."

I said, "Why have you brought hay and bananas and cabbages?"

Alfy said, "Don't press the point, old man. But you'll see in time. But it would be damned decent of you if you would stay on until it's all over."

I said, "I assure you I'm not given to loose talk and I'd rather go. I have business to attend to."

They both looked unhappy about this and there was a short conversation between them in their own language. I sat there and tried to remember what I could about Bakata. So far as I could recall it had once been a British possession but on achieving independence had changed its name. I vaguely recollected that there had been trouble there in the last year.

Their conversation finished, the Archbishop turned to me and said, "You got a choice, my son. You stay here as our guest with your given word not to leave the house, or you stay here locked up in some room—which is a damned nuisance for us and you—until we leave. Furthermore, by willing co-operation, you are helping the Lord's work which is to overthrow evil and deliver the suffering ones from oppression."

"Just give your word, old chap," said His Royal Highness, "and that's an end of the matter."

I said, "You really would lock me up?"

"Reluctantly, yes," said the Archbishop. "This is an important matter for us. Can't take any chances."

Since I didn't want to spend three or four days locked up, I gave my word, and so took my place in the complicated design which was to affect the lives of thousands of people in distant Bakata and to give a direction and purpose to mine which I was later glad I could not have foreseen. Also it brought about my acquaintance with the Bakatsi of Bakata.

The Archbishop and His Royal Highness and their chauffeur moved into the villa. The truck driver departed. The hay, cabbages and bananas were stored in the small pavilion behind the tennis court and two days passed very quietly. The Archbishop smoked his cigars and drank his brandy and talked to me about church affairs in general and my affair with the church in particular and, when he knew the details, was very sympathetic and said that had it happened in Bakata he would have exercised his discretion in my favour, and His Royal Highness, Alfy, either sat and read Wild West paperbacks or spent long periods on the telephone talking in his own language, and the chauffeur, Tombo Thompson, looked after us and cooked highly spiced Bakatan dishes and made a fourth in the evenings when we all sat and played Monopoly at which the Archbishop always seemed to win.

On the third evening at ten o'clock, the Bakatsi of Bakata arrived. There was a phone call for Alfy at eight and at ten we all went out into the night on to the tennis court and Tombo placed a large torch in the centre of it, its beam spearing skywards, attracting a cloud of moths.

After five minutes I heard the beat of an engine to the south and suddenly the sky was noisy with the clatter and whirr of a helicopter. It came low over the villa and then hovered some fifty feet above the tennis court and I thought it odd that it wasn't showing any navigation lights. It dropped a little lower and then I saw a hatch in its belly open and a dark shape was lowered on a winch rope to the tennis court. Tombo ran forward and released whatever it was from the winch cable and the helicopter lifted swiftly and beat away westwards into the night. As it went, the Archbishop embraced Alfy on either cheek and then stood back and in a loud voice declaimed, "Where the Bakatsi is, there is the Bakata; where the Bakata is there is Bakatsi; and where the Bakata and Bakatsi are there is the Royal State of Bakata and let all its enemies fear and tremble." Then he turned to me and said, "Son, I speak it in English for your benefit. Come and meet Bakatsi."

I went forward with them to Tombo in the centre of the court and there with a neat little silver diadem strapped to his forehead and a pale blue mantle over his back was Bakatsi, three foot high, a small African elephant, looking a little unsteady on his feet after the air lift but not apparently bereft of a sense of the occasion for as His Royal Highness made a little bow of welcome, Bakatsi raised his trunk and gave a thin trumpet of greeting, and Alfy said, "Now the people of Bakata will know that the only true king is where Bakatsi is. . . . Now they will arise and throw out all usurpers and call for the return of their true king."

"Take a little time, maybe," said Dr. Bomokandi, "but it will happen."

Alfy grinned at me, fixing his monocle tight, and said, "Royal elephant. Always one in Bakata from ancient times and same blood lines."

I said, "He's very small."

"Very young. He's the last of his line. Got to wait for him to grow and then find a mate for him."

I said, "How did he get here?"

The Archbishop said, "Good friends in Bakata stole him and shipped him. The helicopter picked him up at sea. As I told you, son, the French wouldn't give official permit for importing

117

him. Too much politics involved, but now he's here they won't bother. They look at him and they pretend not to see him." He peeled a banana and handed it to Bakatsi, who curved it into his mouth with his trunk and munched happily.

So, we left Bakatsi on the tennis court to be fed and watered by Tombo, who was to sleep in the pavilion to keep an eye on him, and we went back into the house where the Archbishop poured large brandies and we drank a toast to the speedy return of the Bakata to his country. Over the drinks the Archbishop explained some of the recent history of Bakata to me and said, "You a rich man, son? You like to put money in movement for the return of the Bakata?"

I shook my head. All the money I had was earmarked for La Guicha.

"Never mind," said Alfy. "One day Bakatsi and I will go back in triumph—and we'll have you over for a visit."

"For, say, ten thousand pounds," persisted the Archbishop, "you not only get your three-hundred-per-cent return, but I'll re-ordain you into the First Church of Bakata."

I said, "I've no money to spare."

The Archbishop consoled himself with another brandy and I went to bed, leaving them talking.

The next morning I was up at dawn and, still being curious about Bakatsi, I went down to the tennis court to have a look at him. When I got there the animal was lying on his side close to an old tin bath of drinking water which had been provided for him. He opened one eye, flapped his trunk feebly and gave a long groan. I'd had a lot of experience with sick animals at Stonebridge, and Bakatsi looked a very sick little elephant. I ran across to the pavilion to wake Tombo and found him lying on a pile of old tennis netting, his mouth gagged and his hands and legs tied. I untied him and he rose shakily to his feet, saying, "Somebody come in night, boss, and grab me. They put stuff in Bakatsi's drinking water. That animal die then Archbishop have me shot."

He was a small, anxious man, and very much afraid.

I said, "Go and tell His Royal Highness what has happened."
I ran back into the villa and, standing under the portrait of
my aunt, who looked fresh and cool, I telephoned Monsieur
Crozette and explained things to him and he said he would
be over as fast as he could. As I finished the Archbishop
came rumbling and panting down the stairs in his dressing-
gown.

He said, "That Bakatsi die then Alfy never go back."

I said, "I've phoned for a vet. Not an official one. I thought
you wouldn't want that. This is a friend of mine. He's on his
way."

"Man, bless you. That damned Tombo went to sleep on the
job and let someone jump him. Plenty of bad people want to
do harm to Bakatsi. He know that. If Bakatsi die then Tombo
dies. If Bakatsi lives then Tombo lucky man and get a good
beating till he can't stand or sit for days. Now I must go and
make special prayers for Bakatsi."

He went off into the main room and, while I had no
doubt that he would pray hard and fervently, I heard the
clink of a glass against a bottle as he fortified himself for the
ordeal.

Tombo was lucky for Bakatsi lived and I interceded with
Alfy to spare him the beating. Monsieur Crozette arrived with
his professional bag, took the situation in his stride with great
aplomb and injected three powerful pig drenches into Bakatsi
and bedded him down in the pavilion on a litter of hay. There
is no need to go into the clinical details of the small animal's
recovery, but recover he did within forty-eight hours to the
great joy of everyone and, when he was on his feet again, the
Archbishop led us all down to the tennis court and he conducted
a little service of thanksgiving for the elephant's recovery,
finishing with a very fine rendering of *In te, Domine, speravi*,
which Bakatsi topped with a thin little trumpet of approval,
and that afternoon Bakatsi was driven off in a horse box and
the Archbishop and Alfy followed in the Rolls Royce, leaving
Monsieur Crozette and myself with their thanks.

I shut the villa up and left a note for my caretaker, explaining about the sale of the villa, and then Monsieur Crozette kindly drove me into Nice to get a train for Geneva and, although I wasn't bringing La Guicha all the money I wanted to, I was glad at the thought of seeing her again.

CHAPTER EIGHT

LA GUICHA HAD a château a few miles from Lac Leman, in the hills above Evian. It was turreted and towered, the roofs blue slated, and stood on a small eminence in its parklands like an illustration from a fairy tale. Inside it was full of bustle and people like a railway hall on a Bank Holiday. People never did anything quietly and smoothly at the Château La Guicha. They might for the first few days of their work there, but then they were caught up in the race against time and want and distress which were La Guicha's enemies in her work for children. In the grounds around the château were a variety of modern buildings beautifully laid out and constructed—a famous German architect had planned them for her free of charge, thinking it his contribution to her work, but found himself sent back to Germany as her chief organiser for fund collecting. This—unless one were extraordinarily strong-minded— was what happened to everyone who made some offer of help to her. The offer, gladly accepted, was merely an introduction to more work, more demands. She bullied State officials and private citizens and never did more than pretend to take no for an answer while she planned a fresh assault on their charity or their power to help. Around the château she had a school, a clinic, a hospital, a recreation centre . . . a whole complex of buildings where her children were housed, fed, taught, healed or helped to learn to live on terms with their handicaps. She had a first-class staff of nurses, doctors, teachers, and welfare workers, all of them grossly underpaid but happy in their work. She never refused a child in want who was brought to her, and she didn't just sit down and wait for them to be brought. She and her friends went out and found them, children of all nationalities. She was intolerable and irresistible, a bully and a bore when she met those qualities in other people, an enchantress who could entrance a millionaire so that his hand itched for his cheque book. She had no principles except where children were concerned, and she cut through regulations and cant with a knifelike directness. People hated her and loved her and she didn't care so long as they did something for her; an angel for one, a pest for another, but always demanding . . . always hard up, always full of hope . . . if she could have got at God in His heaven she would have criticised his provision for her children and blarneyed Him into something extra. She was an impossible woman, and she did and made others do the impossible. My father spent a fortnight with her once at the château, helping her, and he came back and went to bed for three solid days' sleep, announcing that charity work with La Guicha was the best training he could suggest for anyone dreaming of laurels in the pentathlon. The day after my arrival I was assigned without any choice to a voluntary gang digging out the foundations for an extension to her clinic for autistic children.

However, when I arrived she kept her plans for me hidden. Her room was large and untidy, the walls covered with photographs of her past children, now grown up and many of them successful. She came from behind her disordered desk and threw her arms around me and kissed me on the cheek and said, "That's something I could never do to your father without bending and putting a crick in my back. How did such a jockey spawn a Hercules like you? Welcome, dear Nelo—but only if you come bearing gifts."

Her manner of speech was always an amazement to me. She was protean with languages. She could be grave with a Senator, sly with a politician and bawdy with a music hall artist. She was tall, leggy—dressed now in green velvet tights and a plain white shirt—dark-eyed, with a skin the colour of polished

122

walnut wood, and a wide generous mouth which spoiled the lines of a long, oval face. She wore her dark hair piled on top of her head carelessly but attractively and there was a white hen's feather stuck in it at an odd angle. Wherever she went she had the unthinking habit of picking things up and adorning her person with them.

I opened my case and handed the money I had brought over to her, saying, "It should have been more but I haven't been able to realise my mother's diamonds yet."

"Why not? Your mother would be far happier for me to have the money than you the diamonds."

"Temporarily they are not in my possession."

She said, "The church—from which you are now happily free—has taught you the habit of indirect speech. Lost or stolen?"

"It's a long story."

"Then I've no time to listen to it."

I said, "A girl took them."

She said, smiling suddenly, "A girl? Oh, Nelo! Then you must tell me. But keep it short."

I told her briefly and when I had finished she said, "She loves you?"

"Yes."

"And you?"

"I like her."

She shook her head. "I don't like the way you say that. You sound as though you were sickening for something. However, it's none of my business—except for the diamonds. You'd better go and find her."

"But I don't want to particularly."

"You will after a week here. I'm putting you on foundation digging. We've no vacancy here for brains or pious sermons. Brawn is our need at the moment. You'll get free lodging, but pay for your own meals in the canteen." (Later I discovered that my free lodging was a share of a marquee tent pitched in the woods behind the château.)

I said, "I shall be happy to do that."

"I'm sure you will, Nelo. And don't think I'm not grateful for this." She put her hand on the pile of money. "I know I sound awful at times. A dragon. But people just won't respond these days if you're polite or send out an illustrated pamphlet on glossy paper. They've lost the faculty for hearing or seeing properly. Newspapers, films and television have made the real world remote for them. They see a crowd of pot-bellied starving Biafran children on the television and it's just a series of pictures only briefly touching them. Newspapers and newsreels are paper and celluloid walls that shut out reality. You have to shout and scream at them to wake them up and open their eyes. Now, you put in some useful work here for a few days and then go and get those diamonds. That's what she wants you to do. By the way, what about the Monet painting?"

"Monsieur Crozette is going to telephone you about it."

"Good. What I really want, of course, is someone to steal the Mona Lisa for me. Just think of the money I could get for that pudding-faced Italian!"

So I went to work for La Guicha on the foundations of the clinic extension, filling a wheelbarrow with soil and trundling it away, stripped to the waist in the sun with a dozen students and volunteers, some of them much older than I was, aged men sound in charity, and young men noisy and happy in it, joking and teasing the children who came to watch us. Sometimes La Guicha came and pretended to be disgusted with our progress so that the students would down their picks and shovels and refuse to do another stroke of work until she sang for them. And then her strong, husky voice would ring out under the blue sky, sometimes sentimental, sometimes devout, sometimes suggestive according to her mood but always un-stinting, and the effect was so electric that it divorced us all for a little while from ourselves. Children and nurses would move in to listen, men and youths would relax and dream, the birds seemed to halt in their flight, the bees to cease their humming and the boats on the distant lake, the moving trails of cloud, all freeze into a motionless moment of time centred on La Guicha. She wasn't real because she refused to recognise the impossible, because all was possible under God; and sometimes I felt that all her giving and working and fighting for children might slowly be destroying her, and that she knew it and it was her happiness because her desire to give and fight was a divine compulsion, and I liked to believe that when the day came that the Lord would gather his saints together with him, those that had made a covenant with him by sacrifice, then she would be among them, and at ease with them, and be called on for song.

*   *   *   *

On the morning of my fourth day there Sarah appeared. The date was the anniversary of Bosworth in 1485—and my father had a flag for that, not so much because the battle established the Tudor dynasty as because of the death in it, at the hands of King Richard, of Sir William Blandon, the standard bearer of Richmond, just before King Richard himself had his head split open and his brains scattered; a misplaced mark of respect to the General, who had long given up any hope of convincing my father that there was no family connection; but you couldn't make my father waver once he had an idea in his head. Anyway, on this morning with a fierce August sun tanning my back and shoulders, I sat down on my loaded barrow and lit a cigarette for five minutes breathing space and looked up to see framed against the distant pines and the red, raw piles of soil the slim figure of Sarah standing at the edge of the foundation diggings. Her hair was beaten, shining copper, her face beautiful with mild regard and the light breeze took the edges of her flared white skirt and flirted with them wantonly, and I stared at her like an idiot while one or two of the students gave low whistles of approval, and a lump came into my throat.

I got up, threw my shirt loose over my shoulders and went to her and, as the diggers behind us gave a low, concerted moan of dismay, I took her hand and led her away to the pines where

125

we sat each on a dead anthill tumulus, and I said, "Why are you here?"

She picked up my shirt from the ground and took my cigarettes and matches from the pocket and lit herself a cigarette.

"To see you," she said.

"You never wanted to see me again. Only a marriage announcement in *The Times*."

"That was then, back there at the villa. I've changed my mind."

"How would a man ever know where he was with you, since you are always changing your mind, changing the truth, changing even yourself to fit each newly-born moment?"

"Even a whirlwind dies away sometimes to a steady breeze."

"But the trail of destruction is only just over the horizon behind. Anyway, I'm delighted to see you."

The mild seriousness of her face changed to a smile and I sensed the mood of self-chastisement sliding from her.

"You mean that, Nelo? You feel it?"

"Of course. I looked at you standing on the edge of the pit and a lump came into my throat. You were so beautiful and I thought to myself, 'So, she's come to give me my diamonds back.'"

"Which was more important? To see me, or the diamonds?" She blew blue smoke into the summer air and it trailed and coiled like a genie and vanished.

"How would I know? One was spiritual and the other material, yet both pleasurable."

"Like having two birthday presents, both wonderful, and not knowing which to play with first? For a girl, if it's a doll and a pram, it's easy. They fit. But nothing fits this morning."

"Beauty and diamonds do."

"Except that I haven't any diamonds. Oh, don't get me wrong, Nelo. I took them. I do wild, stupid things, but even when I took them I knew I wouldn't keep them for long because I knew what all this meant to you." She waved a hand

126

and a few children, stumbling and halting in a ragged but happy crocodile down a near-by path with their charge nurse, waved back at her, legs in irons, armpits moist with crutch-pad sweat, small bodies that had known and still testified to famine, disease and cruelty.

"No diamonds?"

"No. Does it make the beauty fade?"

"No. What happened?"

"Xavier took them." She picked up a pine cone and balanced it in her left palm and I was suddenly reminded of my sister. She would gather pine cones and range them on the kitchen garden wall and shoot at them but the memory was only a spur for the sharp, new awareness that Sarah and my sister were much alike. You never knew where you were with them. They never settled, could never be defined for long, they were like fresh sprung springs, spilling down a hillside and never constant enough to scour out a permanent bed. My mother said that my sister was touched by the fairies at birth so that they always had a claim on her. It was a long time before I knew what she meant. But I understood now that Sarah had been touched too. There is no sense or stability in fairies. They have a few tricks, a few magic moments to dispense but they have no discretion and are never on hand when you want them.

I said, "Tell me what happened?"

"Can you spare the time from work? I watched you working, you know, for a bit, before you saw me. All your movements had a rhythm. A man must be happy to have a body that moves so smoothly to his command."

"Just tell me what happened."

"Are you going to hate me?"

"No, but I might be angry if you don't get on with it."

So she told me, not without prompting on my side and digressions on hers. When she had got to Nice with the car, without any reason that she could pinpoint, she had decided to send a telegram to Xavier about the car and then wait for him to arrive so that she could drive up to Geneva with him.

"You wanted to go to Geneva?"

"No." She smiled. "The great affair is to move. And Xavier was going to Geneva. So he drove me up. He gave me a good talking to. I'll tell you about it some time."

Actually she had pacified him by saying—and meaning it at that moment—that she only meant to keep the diamonds a short while and then let me have them back. In order to avoid trouble at the douane over the diamonds, they had put them into the roof compartment of the Lancia and gone safely through. In Geneva they had taken rooms in the Hotel Regina on the Quai-du-Mont-Blanc, and Xavier had gone about his business of trying to realise his securities and bank holdings.

"He didn't have much luck," Sarah said. "In fact, underneath, I could tell he was quite miserable about it. The banks delayed things, and then one evening he had all his passports stolen which made it more difficult because he had his accounts under different names and there was more trouble about establishing his identity."

I could imagine it and knew that there must have been times when his misery (not that that could ever be long-lived) must have been streaked with fear (not that that was unknown to him) because he knew that the great consortium of underground powers had issued orders for him to be blocked off from all channels of escape until they caught up with him.

Sarah tossed the pine cone from her, and explained. "He was attacked one night on the lakeside and just escaped. He came back around ten o'clock and told me that Switzerland had nothing for him and that he had to leave. He just packed a few things and went, and he gave me this."

From the pocket of her dress she pulled a folded foolscap envelope.

She said, "You needn't read it. It's for La Guicha. It's a document drawn up by his lawyer here transferring the whole of his estate in Switzerland, under all his different names, to La Guicha. He said he knew that he was never going to get it, but that he had an idea that so long as it was legal the authorities would gladly acknowledge it in La Guicha's favour."

"If they don't I wouldn't like to be the President of the Confederation or a member of the Bundesrat. It may take time but she'll work it. But why should he do that?"

"Because he went off with your diamonds. He left me his car and I'd been keeping the diamonds in it because I felt it was a safe place. Something made me check the next morning and they were gone. He'd left a note in their place."

She put her hand into her pocket again and handed me the note. It read:

> *Tell Charles that the gift to La Guicha has nothing to do with the diamonds. I can never touch the Swiss money so she can have it if she can get it. I need the diamonds for collateral in a project I have in mind to free me from this present money problem. Will return them as soon as I can. One day I shall achieve the calm of a forgotten backwater.*
>
> *Love. Xavier.*

I knew that La Guicha would see it that way, too. A gift from Xavier in no way invalidated the gift I had promised her from the sale of my mother's diamonds.

I said, "When did he go?"

"Three days ago."

"He gave you no idea where?"

"No."

"Why didn't you come to me before this?"

"I had to work up my courage. After all, it was my fault, Nelo. And although you never have been angry with me I knew that once you were it would be something I would never forget. You're not angry, are you?"

"I should be, but I'm not. Don't ask me why."

"You're very nice to me, Nelo. I know I'm a hopeless type, but you really are nice about it." She leaned across and kissed me on the cheek, a moth passing, the touch of a child's finger,

129

the breath of a sigh of relief, and I thought I ought to be angry with her, angry enough to beat her, but I wasn't so there was nothing to be done.

I said, "Well, we'd better go and tell La Guicha about this." I held up Xavier's document.

"Oh, she knows about that."

"How?"

"Well I went to her first to check that you were here, and I told her. Actually she sent me out to find you because she wants to see you urgently. It seems that the Swiss police are after you, and you can't stay here. We've got to go away."

"We?"

"Oh, yes. I thought that one over when I decided to bring back the diamonds. I was being cowardly. I'm in love with you. I admit it now. But I don't want to be for—"

"For reasons you've tried to explain."

"Yes. But it's no good trying to fight a battle from a distance. You have to be face to face with the enemy. So I've got to be with you either until I don't love you any longer, or until you send me away, really send me away."

"You're mad, Sarah."

"No, I'm being very logical. Anyway, we can argue it later. At the moment you've got to get away from the police."

* * * *

And I did have to get away from the police. La Guicha explained it to me some minutes later in her office. The police in Geneva had telephoned her that morning saying they understood that I was visiting or would shortly be visiting her and they wished to question me. La Guicha had told them that she'd had a letter from me saying that I was arriving late in the afternoon. But when they had rung off she had got through to a personal friend of hers in the Ministry of the Interior at Berne and he had told her that through Interpol my brother was making nasty noises about the diamonds and was preferring

130

a charge of theft against me, so that I was likely to be held, interrogated, and—if the law and the evidence warranted it— extradited.

I said, "Leno is not a vindictive man. He just thinks it's a sin to sell a family heirloom and give the proceeds to charity."

"Your brother's a fool. However, his interference is timely. I had a call from Monsieur Crozette this morning and he has found a buyer for the Monet in Florence—a Signor Calieri. I understand from Sarah here that there is a secret roof compartment in her car and I want you both to take the picture to Florence for me."

"But I'll never get past the frontier post."

"You will, Nelo. You think I have friends in high places out of vanity? If they don't help they are no longer worth knowing. No one will question you on the Swiss side provided you go out by the Simplon Pass, and the Italians at the moment couldn't care less about you, my dear boy. Besides, they will only have eyes for Sarah here. She is the one you are in love with, is that right?"

Sarah said, "He doesn't know. And I don't want him to know."

La Guicha came and put a long arm across my shoulder and hugged me. "That is a good situation. It gives room for manoeuvre. Tell Signor Calieri to credit the purchase money to my account with the Banque Nationale Suisse at Zurich. And when you've done that you must try and find this Xavier and get the diamonds back. The man has behaved most unscrupulously."

"But, La Guicha, he's given you all his estate in Switzerland."

"Only because he couldn't touch it himself. Naturally, I'm grateful. But he still has our diamonds. I have a special project earmarked for the money from them—so the sooner you find them the better. After all, Nelo, you're not doing anything else with your life. Do you want me to think that prison has made you idle? Your father always said you had a tendency that way. A day-dreamer."

131

Sarah said, "Don't worry—he'll find them. I'll keep him up to it."

I understood then something of what my father used to feel when he felt the house was overpopulated with female relations and guests, and would stump off to the stables muttering about the "monstrous regiment of women" and sit for a few hours cleaning tack and talking to the horses who couldn't answer back.

A little weary, I said, "If the combined Intelligence services of Europe and elsewhere can't find Xavier how can I hope to?"

O, ye of little faith! I knew at once I was wrong to have said it.

La Guicha said, "The good Lord wants me to have the diamonds. The good Lord will show the way." Then to Sarah she ordered, "Take him away. Men are like mastodons. They adapt very slowly to changing circumstances."

So, I was taken away, and the picture was packed into the secret roof compartment of the Lancia and we drove off with Sarah at the wheel and I didn't even ask how it had come about that her case was already packed and in the rear of the car because I knew that women had something akin to the instincts of birds and sense the coming time of migration. And as we drove round the lake and up the valley of the Rhône, through Martigny and on towards Visp and Brig, with the river on our left still holding a milkiness from late melting snows of the Alps, I told myself that while I had a deep affection for Sarah, and a better understanding now of her moods and mind changes, and could enjoy her company by day and by night, and could praise and enjoy the beauty of her body by day and by night—though some residual echo of sin whispering back from my study of St. Paul still persisted occasionally—if the day should come when I knew I loved her (and surely I would know when it happened?) then I would be entering a service which would call for and demand of me more than I could ever give or understand. My mother and father had lived and loved with a pastoral simplicity, because they were simple people. But Sarah was like La Guicha. There was nothing simple about either of them. They harboured daemons, La Guicha's obvious and firmly in her control; but Sarah's led and whipped her and even she, I suspected, could not put a name to it. I began to see how true it was (and would be with us) that the wrong people fall in love with each other. What I didn't see, at that moment, was that I almost had my hand on the real truth and nature of loving.

At my side Sarah said, "We'll have to stay the night somewhere. Do we take a double room or singles?"

"Singles."

Actually, we arrived late, almost midnight, at Lake Maggiore, and since the first hotel—the Hotel Royal—we went into only had a double room left and we were too tired to search around for another hotel, we took the double room, had a meal, and then fell into bed and sound uncomplicated sleep from which the maid woke us at eight-thirty with coffee, and I left Sarah in bed with hers and took mine by the window.

* * * *

Signor Calieri had a villa on the slope of the hills running up from Florence to Fiesole. It stood on a little mound of terraced garden, sentinelled by tall cypresses and presented black and white lozenged shutters to the city southwards. I went up by myself, having left Sarah at the hotel where she had announced that she meant to spend some of the morning shopping. I didn't think she needed anything in particular but I guessed that she used shopping sometimes as a therapeutic exercise. We had taken rooms at the Hotel Excelsior in the Piazza Ognissanti alongside the Arno. Sarah had decided that she needed a few days of *grande luxe*. I hoped it would only be a few days because I didn't have a great deal of money. In fact all I had was the accumulation of rents from my villa in France which I had drawn from the bank at St. Raphael. It would never have occurred to La Guicha even to think about travelling expenses for her emissaries.

Signor Calieri was a charming, white-haired man of about sixty wearing a thick navy-blue serge suit which must have been very hot, and a stiff collar that kept his head raised questioningly so that he had the air of an expectant thrush waiting for the sound of the turn of a worm somewhere close. It was a large, tiled room, the walls hung with red silk, completely bare, not a picture or decoration on them, and in the centre of the room was a shallow marble basin from the centre of which water fountained without much pressure from the mouths of a bronze tangle of entwined dolphins. We sat in a large bay window and a servant brought us iced drinks and I unwrapped the Monet and he propped it on the window-seat, studied it from a distance for a moment or two and then turned to me and ignored it for the rest of our interview. He made polite enquiries about Monsieur Crozette and also of La Guicha whom he seemed to know fairly well, and then said, "Tell me, monsieur, does a green Citroën car mean anything to you?"

I said, "No. Should it?"

"Possibly not, possibly yes. As you walked up the drive one slowed a little outside the gate and is now parked a short way up the hill."

"You think I could have been followed?"

"In this business one should always entertain the probability."

"I'm sorry, I should have been more circumspect, perhaps." I had openly unshipped the picture from the roof compartment at the roadside.

"Please don't worry I have plenty of protection. It's probably some tourist. They often stop on the hill for the view of the city."

I said, "You are buying the picture for yourself?"

He smiled and shook his head. "No. I am simply an agent—for many things. Although I am an expert, and could tell from one end of this room to the other whether the Monet was genuine, I am no connoisseur, or more properly perhaps, amateur. No, it will be passed on to my client and he will hide it away in some secret gallery where once a week he will closet himself with a glass of wine and a cigar and enjoy himself. Strange, no?"

"It wouldn't give me much pleasure."

"When you have all the money in the world your pleasures cease to be ordinary ones. Your vices also. I understand from Monsieur Crozette that you have a diamond necklace you want to sell."

"I'm afraid not. A friend of mine has gone off with it."

He waved one open-fingered hand through the air. "What are friends for but to take advantage of one?"

"I'm not over angry with him. He's in trouble and needs it. He's a secret agent who has outlived his usefulness."

I told him briefly about Xavier and he listened sympathetically, and when I had finished said, "It happens sooner or later to all of us. We outlive our usefulness."

"But you're not that kind of agent."

"I am every kind of agent, monsieur. And I am very tired of it. Oh, it's been an interesting life and I've made a lot of money, but the trouble is that one can never retire gracefully."

"Why not?"

"Because they won't let you. No matter what kind of client it is. They are always demanding. Sometimes the most odd and embarrassing things. And when one client dies another takes his place. The happiest thing to be is, say, a clerk who works for fifty years for the same company and then retires with a pension and a gold watch and everyone forgets him within a month and he has found peace. But a man like me or like your Xavier makes the one, original mistake of committing himself to employers or clients who are self-perpetuating and they will never let him go so long as he has the smallest scrap of usefulness for them—and when he hasn't he must be killed off because he knows too much and is a danger to them. Do I paint a black picture?"

"Indeed."

"Believe me, it is true. The moment you sin, the moment you step outside normal society, you are doomed for the rest of your life. Pleasures you will have, wealth, too, but never peace as Voltaire, I think, said, to work your own garden and grow potatoes. Even you, monsieur, though you may not appreciate it yet, are probably doomed in the same way."

"How can I be?"

"Because you do this for La Guicha. Oh, you have your own good, charitable reasons, but fundamentally you must know that you are conniving at theft. La Guicha may never ask you to do more for her, but other people will know of it eventually, and then you will be asked to do other things and there will be no way you can refuse. My advice to you is to go away and hide for a few years and hope people will forget. They do sometimes but it is not true forgetfulness—simply one dossier in a thousand that slips from a file and gets lost at the back of a drawer."

"You're depressing me."

"I know. When I like people I find I have that effect on them."

"All I've done is for La Guicha's children."

"Quite. But a wrong done from the best of motives is the commonest way to destruction."

Let destruction come upon him unawares; and let his net that he hath hid catch himself; into that very destruction let him fall. For the first time since I had come out of prison I was feeling uncomfortable with myself. I thought about it on the way back to Florence. There was no green Citroën parked on the hill and I certainly wasn't followed by one because even as I considered Signor Calieri's words I kept an eye on the rear mirror.

Just before lunch Sarah came into my room, smiling and holding out her wrist on which was a silver Florentine bracelet made up of the linked escutcheons of the Medici arms.

"Isn't it super? What every tourist should have. I knocked them down a thousand lire."

"Beautiful," I said, and added, "I am considering how big a sinner I am."

"What?"

"And what I should do about it."

"But you haven't sinned, Nelo. What on earth's got into you?"

"I defrauded a bank."

"But you served a sentence for that—so you're quits."

"Maybe to some extent. But I have committed adultery—"

"Not knowingly. That was my fault."

"Been incontinent."

"Again my fault . . . partly."

"And I have been arrogant in my thinking."

"Who isn't?"

"And compounded a theft of a painting."

"For God's sake, Nelo—even Monet would be glad to know where the money's going. Sorry, didn't mean the pun. Isn't a mother entitled to steal bread and milk for her starving children? Beat out the ethics of that one before you call yourself a sinner."

"I have many things to work out. Chiefly I have to decide whether it is the consequences which may result from my sins that have made me consider myself in a clear light, or whether it is the fact of sin itself. Should a sinner repent out of fear? Is that true repentance?"

"Oh, come, Nelo—you're putting me on. Let's go and have a drink before lunch. You'll feel better."

She came over to me, put her arms around my neck and kissed me, and said, "I love you. There, right to your face for the first time in our lives."

I said, "That's another problem, too."

It was, of course, but a long-term one and others were to intervene before it was settled, and the first of them came up just as we were finishing lunch. I was in the middle of a Neapolitan ice when the waiter said I was wanted on the telephone. It was Signor Calieri who said that he would like Sarah and me to come to tea that day as a matter of some importance had arisen which he wished to discuss.

When we arrived there was a green Citroën car parked on the road outside the driveway. The driver was slumped back in his seat, sleeping.

CHAPTER NINE

THE WOMAN SITTING in a chair by the dolphin fountain
reminded me of the governess we had had after the departure
of the French governess who had made disparaging remarks
about Lord Nelson. She had jet black hair, parted dead down
the middle and tied in a tight bun at the back. It was so smooth
and immaculately dressed that it could have been made out of
black japanned metal. She had high cheekbones, and flat,
sucked-in cheeks as though there were a permanently sour
taste in her mouth. She wore a plain grey skirt, black lisle
stockings, and a white blouse, plain except, unexpectedly, for
a ruching of lace at her cuffs and high neck. She looked a
sensible, no nonsense type. She was extraordinarily like our
old governess of whom my father used to say that when
feminine graces and charms were handed out she'd been last
in the queue. Not that this meant he didn't like her. He had
the highest respect for her—Miss Amberley was her name—
from the time she had walked into my mother's bedroom one
evening when the family were at dinner and surprised a burglar
after my mother's jewels. He had made for the open window
but as he jumped Miss Amberley had caught him by one ankle
and hung on to him, shouting for help, while he dangled fifteen
feet above ground. She did it one-handed and the glory of this
feat was not diminished for my father or us boys when the man
turned out to be an ex-jockey, a shrimp of only eight and a half
stone. Leno and I adored her and my father respected her and
my mother wept when she left. Looking at this woman I felt
that she would have to travel far for adoration and that few

would weep for her departure. But respect she engendered, not healthy but cautious, by just sitting there and watching us as Signor Calieri, without even the pretence of tea being served, talked to Sarah and myself. (I should add that at one point in Signor Calieri's opening remarks, she fished into a shabby leather handbag she nursed on her lap for cigarettes and a lighter and I was almost certain that I saw the butt of a small automatic protruding from one of the inner pockets.)

Signor Calieri was clearly unhappy. He kept jerking his head from side to side as though his stiff collar irked him and he moved up and down the room with an elegant yet aged restlessness which would have made our Miss Amberley tell him to sit down and stop fidgeting about. The woman in the chair said nothing. Perhaps for her his manner was normal.

He said, "Monsieur, events sometimes have a habit of overtaking the shadows they cast before them. No, that's not very clear. But then it's awfully difficult to know how to start this."

"What you mean is perhaps that sometimes a cloud passes over us before its shadow does?" suggested Sarah.

The woman on the chair said in a flat, unaccented, unnationalised, neutral, antiseptic voice, "I must ask no one to interrupt Signor Calieri unnecessarily." And to Calieri she said, "Dispense with the metaphors and just give the facts."

"I am," said Calieri, "the spokesman for certain people. . . . Oh, dear, well the point is . . ." His voice trailed away while he took a half turn up the room, then came back to face us. "You see, monsieur, what I was telling you this morning has happened. I mean in your case. Events have caught up with you as I warned you they might. It distresses me very much . . . not so much because I have to feel that I am the cause of it. Though I suppose in a way I have . . ." He turned away, his voice dying as though the batteries had gone flat inside him, all power lost for speech.

To my surprise Sarah said directly and with a touch of belligerence to the woman, "You'd better take over. It won't

140

be any strain on you, and there won't be any waffling about. You're not that kind."

To my further surprise, the woman smiled. "Promising," she said. "Very promising." Then to Calieri, she said, "Leave this to me. I had no idea you were such a sentimental fool."

I said to her, "Wouldn't it be a politeness—if you're going to address us—if we knew your name?"

"You can choose any name for me you like." It was said not with asperity but with indifference.

I said, "Would you mind if I called you Miss Amberley?"

"That will do very well." The primness of her voice was remarkably like the real Miss Amberley's, who was now dead.

"Who was the real Miss Amberley?" asked Sarah.

"An old governess we had. She used to take us to tea with her mother in Southampton. The old lady was ninety and very spry. She used to pinch our bottoms and give us sponge fingers, and we used to do jigsaw puzzles with her. An enormous one I remember of the coronation of Edward the Seventh—"

Miss Amberley with an impatient tap of one sensible shoe on the tiled floor, said, "This is no time for reminiscences. You are Charles Nelo Sangster?"

"Yes."

"Then listen. You were formerly a minister of religion and were defrocked when you were sentenced for fraud for which you served a prison sentence?"

"It was in all the papers."

"But some things still await publication. You have stolen a valuable diamond necklace from your brother. For this you are wanted by the police. You helped one François Xavier Mabluto, wanted by the authorities in various countries, to escape from England to Lisbon and, since then, have comforted and assisted him in his so far successful attempts to avoid apprehension by those authorities and—"

"I understood they wanted to murder him quietly. Every man is entitled to an open trial."

141

"Don't interrupt and don't be naïve. To continue. You have become an accessory after the fact to the theft of a valuable Monet and have acted as an agent in its illegal sale which has involved smuggling it from Switzerland to Italy—in itself a considerable offence. Among minor offences I could mention are, one, an assault on an employee of the Hotel Atlantico, Estoril, Portugal, a heating engineer to be exact; two, smuggling stolen diamonds from Portugal, through Spain and into France—"

"Xavier has the diamonds now."

"I know. We shall come to that, but so that you won't be too alarmed by all this, I can promise you that when we find him the diamonds will be returned to you."

"In exchange for what?"

"We are coming to that. Three, to go back to our points— the French police are at this moment considering whether they should institute action against you for complicity in the illegal importation of a prohibited animal to their country, and also for contravening the exchange currency regulations by passing a British cheque through unauthorised sources, the cheque being made out in the name of Sylvia Dupont, a well-known London prostitute so that there is the strong possibility, too, that there might be a further charge against you for living on the immoral earnings of a woman. Am I painting a black picture?"

"It has that appearance."

"So you will see that, one way and another, there is enough against you to send you to prison again for quite a long time."

Sarah said, "My goodness, you really have ferreted around, haven't you?"

"So far we have concentrated on Mr. Sangster. Only the briefest enquiries have been made about you, Miss Doreen Minihane."

"But her name's Sarah," I said.

"Don't let's get sidetracked with stupid details," said Sarah. "I was christened Doreen and couldn't stand the name. So I made myself Sarah. Why shouldn't we be able to choose our own names?"

Miss Amberley, as though there had been no interruption, went on, "Miss Minihane, I understand that there is quite a large tax matter still outstanding against you in England, and also the matter of various debts to certain large London stores, and I've no doubt that if we really went into your past thoroughly other embarrassing facts would emerge."

"Awkward facts will always emerge from anyone's past," said Sarah. "Why don't you come to the point? You have us both over a barrel—and clearly you want something from us, or else."

I said, "How did you know we were in Italy? I'm sure Signor Calieri wouldn't—"

"I didn't," said Calieri.

Miss Amberley said, "The Lancia car of Senhor Prades, or François Xavier Mabluto, is well known to us. When he disappeared from Geneva, after successfully resisting arrest, we simply followed it knowing that you and Miss Minihane here were associated with him."

"And now, through a form of blackmail, you want us to help you find him?"

She shook her head, tossing aside the absurd suggestion it seemed, and said, "Not at all. You would be useless to us. No, no—you are, as it were, by-products of a larger process. We always need people—not professionals like ourselves—for certain assignments. We are always on the look-out for them, and you have conveniently, shall we say, presented yourselves above the horizon."

Calieri, staring gloomily down at the goldfish in the marble basin, said, "I told you, monsieur, how the process would begin. I am so sorry."

Miss Amberley with a smile she no doubt meant as warming, said, "Nobody need feel sorry. In return for a reasonable forgetfulness of past sins, Mr. Sangster and Miss Minihane are being asked to help us."

143

"And who," I asked, "are us?"

Like the real Miss Amberley when asked a difficult question, she was silent while she considered her reply, not wishing to give an ill-conceived answer nor yet wishing to stifle abruptly a genuine and, in the circumstances, inevitable enquiry. The real Miss Amberley's policy had been to answer with a circumlocution that in itself raised such a string of other questions and wonders that the original question was lost sight of. My brother had once asked her how babies were born and Miss Amberley had, after thought, said that God gave a present of the seed of life to every man and that every man handed the present on to his wife who planted it in herself so that it would grow into a baby in her tummy until the baby got too big to be comfortable and then came out, and I remember that the main question for us after that had been when and where had God given our father the seed (and how was it wrapped up, like a Christmas present?) and also wonder at the thought that a man like my father could have had a direct present from God and never told us about it because he wasn't a man to miss a chance of name-dropping. This Miss Amberley did the same.

She said, "Us is us. You can break it down into departments and countries, or you can build it up into, some people say, a dark freemasonry. We are above the police and yet often with them. We can be a State or a combination of States, or we can be a state of mind. We can work legally or illegally which means that we can call on help, demand or force it from the law or from the lawless. Mostly we conceive that we are working for good, but often we are forced to employ evil to achieve good. And sometimes we enlist virtue to create a vice. We are ruthless and Godless, but know how to use mercy and charity. We are, I should say overall, the agents of policy; of a policy that can change from week to week or remain constant for years. We are a gaseous little universe, constantly whirling and flaring, and a long way yet from hardening into any definite shape. We are dangerous and benign, subtle and stupid, devious and degenerate, and the creation of a world that has lost its way but goes on thinking there is salvation in movement and action because it has lost the habit and grace of true self-examination." She paused, took her cigarettes again from her bag, and added, "I hope I have made myself clear?"

"Perfectly," I said, "and I am sorry for you."

"You should," she answered, "be sorry for yourselves, too." She stood up, lit her cigarette and before moving to the door said, "Both of you will continue to stay at the Hotel Excelsior. Your expenses will be paid—but watch the bar bills because we have a bureaucratic element which is convinced that the whole organisation is just a device constructed to enable us to enjoy high living. May I add personally, too, that I would have been happier not to have had this duty to perform and that, in any case, no trouble will accrue to Signor Calieri or to Madame La Guicha and her establishment. You will be contacted. I cannot say when."

She went, and with a deep sigh Signor Calieri moved from the spouting dolphins and said, "I will ring for some brandy." Moving to a bell push, he shook his head and said, "An extraordinary woman, Miss Amberley. Ten years ago she had one ambition, to be a concert pianist. Brilliant she was, but something went wrong."

I stood at the window and looked at Florence below, at the narrow strip of the Arno, at the churches, palaces and towers, at the tall cypresses and the distant umber coloured hills and the sky bluer than any cinquecento painting and I saw the green Citroën turn a corner far below and Miss Amberley was back in the room, explaining Us, and revealing for a few moments some of her own sadness. Destroy them, O God; let them fall by their own counsels; cast them out in the multitude of their transgressions; for they have rebelled against thee. And now I was far from sure that I too had not rebelled and, if I had, what on earth I could do about it because whether I wished it or not there was no real sense of sin in me.

*   *   *   *

Back in my room at the hotel, Sarah lay on the bed with her shoes off, and I sat by the window watching the summer-thinned flow of the Arno below, the movement of traffic and people over the Ponte Santo Spirito, and the slate-winged wheeling of a flock of pigeons above the red roofs of the houses across the river.

Sarah said, "Since they are paying the expenses, and we have two very cheap rooms, we ought to ask to be moved to a suite."

"We shall stay as we are."

"The careful servant. You don't have to do as she says, you know. Most of it could be bluff."

"I never got that impression from Xavier. Unquenchably gay his heart may have been, but he never tried to minimise their power. They want to kill him. Signor Calieri warned me. Once you do one thing for them you are shackled to them for life if they wish it."

"Then we've got to get unshackled."

"Or forgotten at the back of a drawer?"

"What?"

"Never mind. I suppose the Minihane is correct—not like the Sarah?"

"It is correct."

"Doreen is not so bad. We had a maid called Doreen. She married one of the gamekeepers and she used to make corn dollies to go on the ricks after harvesting."

"I prefer Sarah."

"What about the bad debts with London stores?"

"When I was younger and more trusting a man I knew told me I could open charge accounts at Harrods and so on. He died of pneumonia on a business trip to Finland before he could settle them up for me. What do you think Miss Amberley will want us to do?"

"Probably she doesn't know. She was just an emissary. But whatever it is I'm not sure that I shall do it. I don't like the idea of being told what I shall do."

"Or what you should think or believe."

146

"My father used to say the last thing we were given minds for was to have other people make them up. He used to say something too about many of the coins of life being counterfeit but I forget now the point he made. I don't think he would have liked this Miss Amberley."

"Do you?"

"Curiously enough, yes. She is as deprived as some of La Guicha's children. And so may we be unless we pray."

"Pray? Oh, Nelo, you don't really believe that?"

"I most certainly do. The only problem at the moment is the form the prayer must take. Prayers should not only be sincere but well-constructed. A whining beggar is not more sincere or successful than a happy one, and if you wish for divine intercession you should pay the Good Lord the compliment of washing your face, putting on your best suit and speaking up without mumbling."

Sarah laughed. "Nelo, really. I never know when to believe you are sincere."

"Never mind, the Lord will have no doubts on that score."

At that moment the telephone rang, and the hotel switchboard asked me if I could take a call. I did.

A voice, female, said, "Mr. Sangster?"

"Yes."

"Our Mr. Harcourt will be calling on you at six o'clock—in your room. Thank you."

Polite and friendly, as though they were trying to sell me assurance. In a way, of course, that was probably what it was. Also it was very short notice because it was now ten minutes to six.

When I told Sarah she sat up on the bed, reached for her handbag and began to do her lips. As she sat there in a green dress, the pillows piled high behind her, the sun through the window touching her tawny red hair I had a swift, and to some extent deeper, feeling of affection for her than I had known before. The danger of our situation still didn't worry me too much because I was having trouble in convincing myself that

147

it was real, but I did have to concede that so far she had made no complaint at all.

I said, "I'm sorry I've dragged you into all this."

"You're wrong, Nelo. We did it together."

"You could skip out of it now—before Mr. Harcourt comes. I'd just say I didn't know what had happened to you."

"And miss the fun?"

"Will it be that?"

"You heard Miss Amberley. These people have created a crazy world of their own. It's always fun to go into a different world. And anyway, if they wanted me they could find me. And, anyway again, I've decided to stay with you until I'm cured or convinced."

"Convinced of what?"

She didn't answer because at that moment there was a knock on the door. Mr. Harcourt had arrived a few minutes early.

I opened the door to him.

From the threshold he gave me a deep bow and then came into the room in two robust pirouettes which brought him to the end of the bed where he stood beaming at Sarah. It was a music hall entrance and I almost expected him to say, "I say, I say, I say—funny thing happened to me on the way over here."

Actually he said, "Here we are then, Jimmy Harcourt. Bearer of gifts—liquid. And tidings, good, bad and indifferent, but never desperate. Isn't it the thing then to keep cheerful and the wolf of melancholy from the door? Well, we can discuss that later."

He looked around the room, searching for something, found it, a small table by the window, and went to it and dumped on it a largish attaché case he was carrying. He set it up edgeways and began to open it.

"Looks like a picnic case did you say, love?" He jerked his head towards Sarah. "Well, so it is and more. The complete agent's operating kit as advertised in all the underground papers." He opened it, letting the front down, to reveal a row

148

of bottles and glasses, one of which held a small lemon and another a small orange. "Here we are then. On view the makings for dry martini"—he held up a warning finger at Sarah and winked—"don't think I haven't got ice. Battery operated fridge-pack, fits any lady's handbag. Dry martini, gin and campari—slice of lemon or orange to choice, whisky and soda, and for those watching the calories, teetotallers or other-ways afflicted, old Heffer's barley water. What do you fancy, love, sitting there like a redheaded queen from the days of Niall himself, of the Nine Hostages? And don't think that all that's on view is all that's to be had. Stowed, here and yon, there's invisible ink for writing invisible letters to invisible people, poisons that leave no trace except death, stilettos for the well-heeled, gas gun for those who can't stand noise, ordinary job for those who can, code book—out of date—and assorted mikes and induction coils for line-tapping, eaves-dropping and bugging up people's lives. Bugging, I said, my dear. What do you fancy?"

Sarah said, "Whisky and soda."

I said, "It has to be an act, of course. You should get your-self some bookings."

He winked at me as he started to prepare the whisky and soda, and said, "Always overdo it when I first meet people. That's because I'm fundamentally a nervous man, boyo. Come in on a wave of euphoria, go out like a gurgle of dirty water down a sink. In between get the job done. Glad to meet both of you. It's the happy married couple you are to be off to Greece for your honeymoon. Sit in the moonlight and listen to old men singing plaintive *bouzoukias*, sit in Syntagma Square and watch the *evzones* parading round like a lot of lost queers from *Coppélia*, eat cinnamon and honey cakes and get your back teeth all fouled up with sesame seeds. However, silence for the moment, me darlings, while the real work is done. You take the same as the lady, sir? And right you are, and you'll note 'tis Irish whiskey flavoured with the purest bog water."

It was true that his voice held an Irish accent, but I couldn't believe that it was a true one. He was a very fat man, a Humpty-Dumpty of a man, with a red, high-blood pressure varnished face and he had short, awkward arms that reminded me of a penguin. He wore highly polished brown brogue shoes, a baggy blue linen suit, a blue shirt with button down collar points, a red tie with a silver, leaping salmon on it and his grey-brown hair sat on his head like a worn rabbit skin and was—he said so later—a toupee, since he had lost all hair in an illness at the age of twenty. He had had twenty years, he said, of living under thatch. However, these revelations came later.

He fixed the drinks and handed them round with a flow of patter. Himself, he drank his whiskey neat.

Sarah raised her glass to him and said, "I've always wanted to go to Greece."

I said, "We're not married."

Jimmy—it was impossible to think of him as Harcourt—said, "Both will be arranged."

I said, "You don't mean all that about the things in your case, do you?"

"Indeed I do, then."

"You've actually used a gas gun?" asked Sarah.

"Me? Sweet saints, no. They wouldn't let me out into the field proper. I'm a desk man, a contact man, the one me Lord gives a golden guinea to to hold his horse's head while he goes in to have his armour patched up. No, no—I just have to deliver it to someone after I've finished my business with you. And tell me now, between ourselves and these four walls, how was my friend Xavier the last time you saw him?"

"You know him?" asked Sarah.

"Would I call him my friend if I didn't, dear lady? Ah, it's a fine complexion you have there. Reminds me of the girls in Killarney . . . the soft rain and the wind and the good Irish air and a diet of potatoes does it."

I said, "You're not really Irish, are you?"

"I am on this mission. They said it would suit. You're lucky.

You might have got the German touch—that's nasty and no whiskey. Or the Russian—that's nastier, but you get vodka. Ah, dear mother of mine, I've travelled far and got nothing except a bundle of personalities that wouldn't last two minutes at the Palladium without the air being red with tomatoes. Now, tell me how was Xavier?"

"Happy," I said, "but looking for a haven of rest and some money to furnish it with."

"Aren't we all."

"You've worked with him?" asked Sarah.

"Who hasn't, sweet child, from Chungking to Crewe? He was too independent, too ambitious for them. They wanted him to sell his soul. Instead he sold them. They'll get him, and he knows it but that won't dry the laugh in his throat."

He took off his toupee and mopped his bald head. (It was here that he told us about his illness.)

I said, "Why are we going to Greece?"

"Because, boyo, you have the physique for it and somebody spotted it. Six foot tall and more, big like the side of a mountain and the same hair and eyes."

"What has that to do with it?"

"Because that's how he is too—and about the same age."

"Who's he?" asked Sarah.

"This Greek poet you're going to liberate from protective custody. Now, there's a mission to warm a liberal heart. No bird sings in captivity, no heart springs behind bars."

I said, "Do you think you could give it to us in detail and consecutively?"

"No need. You'll get the real stuff from Harry. He runs a tavern and hotel on this island you're going to. You'll find it all in here . . . all the details with your passports, man and wife, false names, travel documents and tickets. From Rome you go by air to Athens, and you'll be landing in daylight which is a fine way to see for the first time the cradle of civilisation. . . . The Parthenon, the Acropolis, the hills around the Piraeus, Mount Hymettus with the pass between it and the Pantelicon that leads to the plain of Marathon and don't think it's snow you'll be seeing on the blue slopes of the Pentelicon—that'll be the scars where they took the marble for the Parthenon when the world was a simpler place but, God help us, just as wicked." He pulled a thick manila envelope from his pocket and tossed it on the bed at Sarah's feet. "Everything's there. Read it when I've gone. No problems."

I said, "Somebody must have worked fast over this?"

"Myself in person. From the time they spotted you in Switzerland."

"Before you even knew that we would do it?"

"A formality."

"You know, we haven't yet definitely decided to do this."

The red, Humpty-Dumpty face was suddenly lugubrious and he put up a hand and tipped his toupee back a little for comfort.

"Did I hear you aright, boyo?"

"Not definitely," I said, "were my words."

"That's what I thought. Well, now, let's consider that. You're a big, strong man—handsome I cannot say. You have a conscience and principles and a way of doing things that is highly original, not to say unorthodox, and you have a beautiful girl here who has been kindness itself to you. Health, happiness and felicity—splendid things. Go on enjoying them, lad. You're a long time dead. Why rush the experience?"

"Are you telling me that they'd—"

"I'm telling you that there isn't anything they mightn't do if you cross them up on a simple detail like this one. Look at the fix Xavier's in. Look at meself now, wasn't I just ordinary awkward with them once at the beginning and they had me away to one of their training schools where every time you crossed the drive you had to duck the gunfire, where a simple thing like getting into bed each night you had to watch or you'd find yourself bitten in the rear end by an asp, or falling straight through some hole forty feet into ice-cold water? Man, I tell you, it's like going to type a note of resignation and having the typewriter explode in your face. . . . Do what they say, lads

152

and lassies, and pray that they'll only have need of you once. Pray to every saint in the calendar and make it powerful."

"Nonsense," said Sarah. "You're just trying to frighten us."

"Ay, and by the tail of every donkey in Connemara I hope I'm succeeding because every word I say is the truth. Now is it a top up of your glasses you'd like before I'm going? No? Then I'll just pack 'em away and who cares if they're dirty because the one who gets the outfit is no friend of mine. In fact, I doubt he has a friend in the world which at least means he's saved some of the surprises of disloyalty which most of us get."

He gathered up the glasses and put them back in his case.

I said, "How did they get you, Jimmy?"

He closed the case, straightened his toupee, and said, "I am a young fellow, just twenty-one and only a year over me illness and fishing peaceful on the banks of the Blackwater near Bally-duff when another young fellow comes along and starts talking which is irritating in the first place because I am fishing, and doubly so in the second because I am a biologist and so is this other I learn, but only in an amateur way, and we get to talking about Darwin and I am saying he had it all wrong for it is from the bears we come not apes. So from talking we get to arguing and shouting and then, both of us being good Irishmen, to fighting and finally it is either he knocks me in the river or I knock him. So I knock him in and there's a spring spate going and me without the precious gift of natation so he drowns and what can I do but walk away and tell myself it never happened—and anyway it is to his good because now he can ask at headquarters about the whole thing and learn he is wrong about apes. And four months later they came for me, some wee little runt of a chap had been watching through binoculars from two miles away, and there I am forced to take up a position in the ranks. Which is handy for them because I am a research biologist working on chemical warfare for the French, happy in my work and coming home once a year for a fishing holiday. My sweet friends, never knock a man in the

153

river unless it's dead dark. They have these lads with binoculars everywhere."

He grinned, picked up his case and began to walk to the door. Sarah said, "Do your German bit, Jimmy."

He opened the door and turned back to us, his fat face suddenly grim and a monocle miraculously in his right eye. In a gravelly, grating voice and with a sharp click of his heels, he said severely, "Fräulein, Herr Sangster—you have your orders. Read them, burn them, execute them! But, remember, you are in a service now which does not know the meaning of the word failure. *Auf Wiedersehen!*" He clicked his heels, bowed and was gone.

I said, "It's damned ridiculous."

Sarah shook her head. "I don't think so. I think it's so awful for them that now and then they have to let themselves go." She picked up the envelope that Jimmy had left and pulled out a passport, flipping it open and studying a page.

I said, "I want to find Xavier and my diamonds. Not liberate some Greek poet."

Sarah held up the passport. "You've got no choice. You're now Mr. Charles Graham and it says here, under special peculiarities, long scar under left ribs. Jimmy and none of the others are fools, only fooling around to make us seem at home." She looked at the other passport. "Oh, that's nice—they made me Mrs. Sarah Graham."

"Man and wife."

"That's right. Oughtn't you to look pleased about it?"

I said nothing. Whoso findeth a wife findeth a good thing, and obtaineth favour of the Lord. But not this way, I told myself, and knew that I was far from the Lord's favour.

* * * *

As Jimmy had said, it was all in the envelope; our tickets, our passports as man and wife, and a typed sheet of instructions. We were to go to Rome the next day and fly the following morning to Athens. We would stay a night there and then get a small passenger-cargo boat from the Piraeus to the island of Mios which (the instructions were very full) lay some way to the east of the islands of Seriphos and Siphnos in the Cyclades. On Mios rooms had been booked for us at a small hotel run by one Harry Sleitz. From Harry we should get details of our mission. The facts of our marriage and past life were set out in a joint biography which we were advised to learn by heart and then destroy with the instructions. We were on our honeymoon and I was a farmer from Wiltshire, the farm part of the Longford estate south of Salisbury. Sarah's maiden name was still left as Minihane and she had been private secretary to a company director of a sheet steel firm on a new industrial estate near Andover. We had been married at the parish church of Downton, which was near my farm. There were a few other details. For instance I was supposed to be a keen botanist.

So we went to Rome and we flew to Athens, and it was just as Jimmy had said, for we arrived in brilliant sunshine, and that evening we sat in the Syntagma Square and watched the *evzones* and I drank *ouzo* and so did Sarah, but she laced hers with something called *vyssinade* (which was a kind of cherry syrup) and we had *kebab* for dinner that night. It had been many years since I was last in Athens on my European tour which my father had insisted on out of eighteenth-century nostalgia, and nothing had really changed, least of all the fact that the people who were the bones and flesh of the country had no great love for their Government. Since time immemorial there had been poets, philosophers and politicians in prison, and rich men and opportunist men who changed their coats and their cries according to the seasons of power, and the memory of persecution abided more enduringly than the marble of palaces and temples, and in the middle of the night from her single bed Sarah said quietly, "Are you awake?" and I said, "Yes. Why?" and she said, "I've never had a honeymoon before," and I said, "Not for your first marriage?" and she said, "No. We left the Registrar's office and drove off for Edinburgh. We crashed at the Hendon roundabout and he was killed." I said, "You've had too much *ouzo* and there is only fancy in you, but even so it is no good thing to fabricate tragedies for the creatures of your imagination," and she said, "It is the truth, but if it weren't how else would we dispose of them and have a clear mind for the next set?" I laughed and said, "Would you like me to come over and keep you company?" and she said, "No. Let's save it for Mios."

And I lay in the dark and thought, who is this woman who forms and re-forms in my affection like quicksilver held in the palm of the hand, moving, as the palm tips imperceptibly, between the lines of head, heart and fortune, never constant?

And the next morning we took the boat from the Piraeus and on deck at the stern were penned six black goats with lyre-shaped horns, and an old woman in a black dress and black headscarf sat near them and talked to them and in the lee of a port deck boat two old men squatted on the boards and played backgammon with a wine flask at their side and bunches of small sweet grapes laid out on a sheet of greased paper, and I leaned over the rail with my arm around Sarah, and I was happy, but whether it was because of Sarah or the boat I didn't know because ever since a small boy boats had been a mild delirium with me, the first movement of lifting water under the keel always liberating me with the whispered promise of grace waiting somewhere out there on the face of the waters, for out there since man's time began there has always been a spirit moving, but I knew too that within a couple of hours, no matter how mild the ocean, I would be seasick, always had been and always would be, and I would end up retching and cursing the thing I loved.

And it was the next afternoon that we sailed into the only port of Mios. The pale cliffs came up over the horizon like a small cloud at first and then as we moved in the colours developed and formed, the tilled soil, tawny like a lion's pelt, the greens of olives, cypresses and pines and the faded, summer-scorched grasses, the bright yellow of the reed screens of the quayside taverns, the browns and blacks and greys of the strung nets, drying in the sun, and the blue, red and white of the painted fishing boats, and the tans of boys' bodies as they dived from rowing boats; and I thought that in a place like this a man could sit in the sun and invite peace to come to him until I saw, at the back of the little town, the Greek flag flying from a barracks and I remembered that I was under the ridiculous duress of having to liberate a poet from the island, which was nonsense in itself for if he were a true poet he would carry liberty within him, and could not be truly constrained by the yoke of bondage.

CHAPTER TEN

WE HAD A large room overlooking the quayside. Directly below the window was the reed-thatched terrace of the hotel's restaurant. Not that it was any grand affair. There were six letting rooms in the place and the bar and restaurant were very small. The bed in the room was a very large one, iron-framed with long oval brass panels at head and foot, embossed at the head with allegorical figures of Summer and at the foot with allegorical figures of Winter. Over the bed was a small icon of St. Theodore Stratilates, so that we had a saint to watch over us. There was a sandalwood wardrobe, a few chairs, and a small wash basin in a recess with a framed photograph of a view of Klagenfurt over it. Harry Sleitz was Austrian, and ran the hotel with his wife, Elena, a woman of robust proportions, a dark moustache and piercing, disapproving eyes, but she was a magnificent cook and never flagged in her war against dirt and saw that her minions did not either. The place was spotless and gleaming with the friction of cloth and polish, mop and water. Harry was a little man, around fifty, whose squat body had a permanent list to the left as though he had been brought up on the side of a mountain. He had tight, black, curly hair and a moustache like his wife, except that his was larger and he waxed it at the ends like an old-fashioned sergeant-major. From what we could see he did little about the hotel, except empty the ash trays in the bar and restaurant and in between sit on the edge of the quayside with a fishing pole and talk to whoever was around and, if no one was around, as we discovered from our bedroom window, he would talk quite loudly to himself in German and sometimes sing a little. Not that he was a melancholy man. He had an eager bright look in his eye save when he was anywhere near his wife, and then he seemed to withdraw politely into himself, sometimes looking at her and gently shaking his head as a painter might on reviewing a portrait he had done and finding it far from the work he had conceived in his mind at the start. His wife ignored him completely except for matters of hotel policy.

The two of them received us courteously and then left us to our own devices for the first day. My instructions had been that I would make no approach to Harry about my mission. He would contact me. And he did on the evening of the second day as we were both in the bedroom, tidying ourselves for dinner.

He knocked on the door and came in to my call. He shut the door behind him and stood there lop-sided and beaming at us. Then he said, "Demetrius says that if you walk in his garden, you must taste the little grapes on the top terrace." His English was good but heavily accented.

I said, "That's nice of him. Who is Demetrius?"

He gave me a little frown, but said nothing.

"Who," I asked again, "is Demetrius?"

Sarah, who was doing her lips at the wash basin mirror, said, "Obviously someone who wants us to have some grapes."

Harry pulled a piece of paper from his pocket, consulted it, put it back, and repeated, "Demetrius says that if you walk in his garden, you must taste the little grapes on the top terrace."

"Well, thank him. Perhaps you'd tell us where the garden is."

With a weak burst of almost childish irritation, he said, "Oh, God. Don't tell me they've forgotten something again? Don't you understand what this is about?" Then he smiled, "Ah, maybe you've forgotten. When one begins there is always nervousness and one forgets. Please, Mr. Graham, you must say your piece before we can talk business."

"But I haven't got any piece. But you must know why I'm here."

"Of course I do! But how can we begin until we have established our credentials? You may not be who you are."

"I'm not. My name is Sangster, not Graham, and my wife here is—"

"Sssssssh!" He held up a warning hand, opened the door and looked out, closed it and turned back to us.

Sarah said, "What's that for?"

"Security. Oh dear, they always leave something out. The last time in Athens it caused real trouble . . . jail trouble. Fortunately not for me. Mr. Graham—don't you know what you have to say? Wasn't it in your instructions?"

"What, from Jimmy Harcourt?"

"Sssssssh!" He smacked one hand sharply against his tight black curly head. "Never mention names. No . . . you are supposed to say something to me and then I know you are a bona fide one of us."

Sarah said, "There's that us again."

I said, "How could we ever be anything else but bona fide? You were expecting us and here we are. Don't tell me they didn't give you a description of us. After all I understand I was picked because of my appearance."

"Of course they gave me a description. But the real you and your wife might have been apprehended and someone else taken your place. I've got to be sure."

"Show him your scar," said Sarah.

As I was wearing only shirt and trousers I did and he came forward and ran a warm finger along it, and I said, "My brother did it when I was a boy. Now, you can't really believe we aren't the two you were expecting. How would they, who-ever they are, have been able to find two other people so like us so quickly—and one with a scar like this."

He considered this and then nodded his head reluctantly. "I suppose so. But it is irregular. Are you sure your instructions didn't specify an answer to my introductory sentence?"

"Absolutely."

He then threw his hands up and cried loud enough to be

160

heard on the quayside, "One day they will really land me in the soup. Strictly speaking, according to *my* instructions, I don't have anything to do with you *unless* you give me the answering sentence."

Sarah said, "What is it?"

Harry said, "You are supposed to say, 'Tell Demetrius we will gather them when we come to repair the stable door.'"

I said, "Tell Demetrius we will gather them when we come to repair the stable door."

Harry gave a little sigh of relief.

Sarah said, "Who is Demetrius, anyway?"

Harry said crossly, "There is no Demetrius. It is just to establish the bona fides."

I said, "Well, now they're established tell us what to do."

"Later, later. Just to cover me, will you say you were joking when you pretended not to know the answering sentence? Just say you were joking. Although I know you weren't, I will believe you were and I shall be covered."

"We were joking," said Sarah.

"Ah, good." He smiled at her and then said unexpectedly, "You are very beautiful. I cannot help making the comparison between you and my wife. The best I can say for her is that she is a good Hausfrau and makes the hotel show a profit, but if I had known how she would develop physically I would never have robbed a bank for her."

"You robbed a bank for her?" cried Sarah. "How romantic!"

Harry straightened himself somewhat, proudly, and said, "We Austrians are even more romantic than the Germans. I was second cashier and she was an assistant in a leather goods shop, and we both dreamt of the Greek isles and the wine dark sea and of love in a small paradise so I robbed the bank and came here with her. Astonishingly, for I was young then and more romantic than cunning and I did not do it very cleverly— the authorities never traced us. But *They* did."

"*They*," said Sarah. "The ones who have us?"

161

He nodded, and then said, "Later we will talk about this drunken poet Pericli who comes here every lunchtime to eat fish and vegetables and black bread and olives and borrows the hotel stationery and pens to write his verses. My wife, you know, was beautiful when she was your age, though I must admit there was always the shadow of a promised moustache. The years play grotesque jokes on us all. A week ago he walked straight out of the door after lunch and over the edge of the quay into the water so much had he drunk, and when they pulled him out he walked home laughing all the way. Except that your teeth are better you are very much like him, Mr. Graham. Enough anyway. Forgive me, if I jump from one thing to another, but I am always a little nervous at the beginning of these affairs. Thank God they happen seldom enough and I am well known and trusted by all the garrison. Later, I will tell you the plan when my wife has worked it out."

"Your wife is one of us?" I asked.

"Without my wife, I would be nothing," said Harry. "Each day I give a prayer of thanks for her. It is only her appearance which disappoints me for I would like everything around me to be beautiful since I am so ordinary myself."

He gave us a little bow and then left, and Sarah said, "When I grow thick around the waist, have arms like a coalheaver and a moustache, will you still love and cherish me, Nelo?"

I said, "Not if the moustache comes out ginger."

"I'm not ginger."

"I didn't say you were. I was talking about a possible moustache. And anyway, I don't love you now."

"You do," Sarah said. "But God has written it on your heart in some of Jimmy's invisible ink and it will take time for it to come out. What will I do then?"

I said, "Pray for a catastrophe to deliver you."

She said sharply, her whole mood changing, "Your belief in prayer is pathetic. He was a pianist, too, like Miss Amberley, and he *was* killed on the Hendon roundabout, and his name was Alexis Winter and his dog was in the car with us, a King Charles's spaniel, and it ran away up the Great North Road and was never seen again by me. And this is the truth."

Which I knew it was not and wondered how her life somewhere in the past could have been starved of love and colour so that she had to invent a new past for herself in order to forget the desperation or dullness of the real one, and because I knew this now there was a sudden fierce tenderness in me for her and I would have liked to put my arms around her and hold her, but I didn't because at that moment Harry without knocking put his head round the door and said, "My wife is delighted about the bona fides. She always is worried until they are established. To celebrate she cooks for you tonight a special shish-kebab."

*　　*　　*　　*

The next morning, sitting on the quayside, Harry explained how the poet, Pericli Mykanis, was to be rescued from house arrest. Pericli lived in a house by himself four miles away down the coast on the cliff top. The house was guarded twenty-four hours a day by a military guard of two soldiers at night and one by day and the guard was changed every four hours. The only time that Pericli was allowed free of the house was between the hours of ten in the morning and two in the afternoon. During that time he was free to walk into the port of Mios, chat with a few friends (though he was a moody man and sometimes never spoke to anyone), take a few drinks and have his lunch at the hotel. He did this now—though not during the first six months of his custody—by himself. The guard at his house could watch the whole of his walk into Mios through binoculars (except for one small stretch of ground where the road dipped sharply along the cliffs) and his arrival in Mios was always checked by the soldier on duty as a quayside guard. He had been doing this for months and his movements now were accepted without question. I was, for the next few days, to wander about the cliffs collecting flower and plant specimens so that the guards and the island people got used to me. On the day of his rescue I was to go to the dip in the cliff road, taking with me a set of clothes of the kind Pericli wore—sandals, linen trousers, shirt and a broad brimmed straw hat. When Pericli made his walk back after lunch, he would meet me in the dip (both of us out of sight of the guards) and I would change into my Pericli clothes, hiding my others behind shrubs, and walk on to the house, nod at the guard at the gate and go indoors for my siesta. Nobody bothered Pericli once he was in the house. He looked after himself simply. At night when the two guards came on duty, one of them locked the house doors and the window shutters from the outside and they were only unlocked when the day guard came on duty at six o'clock. Pericli, when I left him in the dip, would make his way down the cliffside and keep in hiding until nightfall when a motor launch would come in and pick him up and take him off. At ten o'clock the next morning—when the guard changed—I would walk out of the house and back to Mios, go into the hotel, change my clothes and Sarah and I would leave on the one o'clock boat for Piraeus. Harry would wait until the boat went and then he would go out to the quay guard and say that Pericli—after taking lunch in the kitchen with his wife—had gone to the lavatory and not returned. Anxious, Harry had forced the door and found the window open and Pericli gone. An island search would be set up for him, and the boat to Athens would possibly be checked on arrival, but no one could connect Sarah and myself with his disappearance.

"It is beautifully simple," said Harry. "Like all good plans."

I didn't altogether share his view, but there was nothing I could do about it. One point, however, in its favour was that everyone was used to Pericli and his movements, to his moods and his eccentricities like walking into the sea when drunk, so the fact that he should escape from a lavatory would be no great surprise and the military people would expect to find him in drunken sleep under a myrtle bush somewhere.

"We have planned this for months," said Harry. "Even to

164

the lavatory window. We had it put in two months ago and I must say it has made a pleasanter place of it."

"What does Pericli think of this?" I asked.

"You shall talk to him in my private room after lunch today. You understand you must not be seen together and, in public, you must show no interest in him."

I did talk to him after lunch, and I saw that the resemblance between us was good enough, under a broad brimmed hat, to rouse no comment from a bored guard sitting in his little hut, sleepily watching me go by.

In Harry's room, a little tight from his lunchtime drinking, Pericli—who spoke good English—was not over enthusiastic. One big hand warming a glass of wine, he said, "The thing is disastrous, but one's compatriots expect it. Here I am comfortably situated . . . free to think and free to write my verse which good friends smuggle out. For two years one would say I have suffered under this regime for my ideas. But is that true? Consider—before I was martyred not a soul bought my poems. Now they sell like wildfire in Greece and all over the world. Suddenly I am a minor Byron, and I enjoy it, and my royalties are mounting up. In time this regime will pass or be modified and I can return to a pleasant fortune. In the London and the New York *Times* I have articles written about me. I am famous. And now they want to free me. For what? A six-line poem smuggled from here is an event, a message, a call to resistance. But free—my speeches and manifestos and forced verse will bore everyone after the first few weeks and I shall sit in some foreign country living on charity because all my royalties are in the homeland. Why can't they leave me alone?"

I said, "All you've got to do is to refuse to go."

He shook his head, tossed back his wine, and said, "Oh, no —then they would brand me either coward or collaborator, and the sales of my poems would drop. No—they don't care for me, even though I care for Greece. They care only to make a score against the regime. It is a game, a power game, and I am a pawn. Harry—some more wine." As Harry went to fetch

165

it, Pericli looked at me and smiled, a friendly, indulgent smile, and said, "You, too, I'm sure, don't care a damn for Greece or for me. You do it because you have to. Strange, they say you look like me. And so you might. How does any man know what he looks like? He has only the mirror to tell him and every time I look in the mirror I see something different. All I want to do is to sit on Mios at peace. Poets should sing their love of country but not meddle in politics. It kills the spirit. However, the ways of God are strange and not to be questioned."

I said, "'Which maketh Arcturus, Orion, and Pleiades, and the chambers of the south. Which doeth great things past finding out; yea, and wonders without number.' There is no contending with God."

He said, "You talk like a priest."

I said, "I was one once."

He stood up, a little unsteadily. "The priest shall take the place of the poet, and the poet shall become a politician and in all the world there is not enough purity to weight the scales against a handful of dust." He made for the door, saying, "I'll take my wine outside. Be good to my cat while you're in the house. He's called Silenus and eats sardines for his supper. You will find the tins in the kitchen cupboard."

So it was all arranged, and I spent the next two days wandering about the cliffs and countryside, sometimes with and sometimes without Sarah, and Harry in his hotel waited for the word—from wherever it would come—that the day was fixed and the launch on its way, and each lunchtime Pericli came down the cliff road to Mios and drank under the reed awning and had his lunch and then walked back again, always swaying, sometimes more and sometimes less, under the blazing early afternoon sun to his house and his siesta, and later as the sun dropped Sarah and I would take our towels and walk away from the port along the white sands under the cliffs to a small cove where few people ever came and we would bathe like Adam and Eve in the freshness of early creation and I would float on the marbled waters sometimes and worry at the way Sarah would climb some high spur of rock and dive like a strange brown bird, arms wide only to close an instant before she struck the sluicing, coiling backwash of waves from the rocks, and the white foam would spout high and often she would stay under-water to the limit of bursting breath in order to worry me, and then would be intolerant of my anger at the fright when we lay on the beach together and let the sun dry us, scaling our bodies with salt. Sometimes when I was out on my botanical farce I used to think it would be restful to come back and find her gone, but when I got back I was glad to have her waiting for me and at night when we lay in the enormous double bed I would sometimes reach out my hand and touch her while she slept in the darkness as though somewhere in me, unbidden, was a real fear that one day she would be gone even though I didn't love her as she loved me. Not that love with our bodies, the passion of the flesh that will stir at any simulacrum of love, was with us either to make me stretch out and touch her, not here, nor had been in Italy, or waited on any promise made in the past days. We lay in shared nakedness but each with a close cloistered freedom to give that waited now, not on our will, but on some destined moment of time and rightness which we both knew might well pass us, unknown, a horizon's distance away. Might even have passed us for all we knew.

On our sixth day there when Harry brought us our coffee and biscuits in the morning he told us that the message had come through. How he did not say but he probably had a secret radio transmitter and receiver somewhere—and more than likely its batteries went flat at awkward times—or it had come in with some man on the fishing boats or even as a cryptic message over the public telephone because the island was connected to the mainland (chiefly for the garrison's convenience) by underwater cable. Anyway, the next day was the day. The Piraeus boat would dock tomorrow evening and by afternoon the following day we would be away . . . to what? To no more instructions and pantomimes set up by *Them*. This I had firmly promised myself. So we had this day to go, to pass with the pretence that there was no anxiety in us, to collect moss and lichens and wild thyme and to swim. And from the bar calendar that morning I saw that apart from the next day being nearly a full moon, which anyone with eyes in his head or a calendar on his desk would have known and so hesitated to choose to send an illicit launch close to shore, it was also the third of September and the anniversary of Britain's entry into the war. Though I had only been nine years old at the time, with the summer holidays coming to a close and school waiting, I remembered my father —already a Major in the Home Guard, and heartily disliked by his local troops for his badgering and hare-brained schemes and exercises—driving to Salisbury and, although it was Sunday, knocking up the manager of Greenfield's so that he could buy up an extra supply of shotgun ammunition to repel the paratroopers who would be dropping from the sky that evening, and then coming back and rounding up every one of his troops and every able-bodied and less man and boy on the estate to set pointed tripods of chestnut stakes in each field and garden (there was bitter argument because the rector refused to allow him to trap the churchyard as well) so that if any falling Hun escaped the welcoming barrage there would always be the chance, he said, that he would get six inches of true British timber where the monkey kept his nuts. And when this was done (for a good commander must always have an alternative plan to slot into action if success should unjustly elude him) he set to with Rodmer to dig a secret pit in the middle of Mother's asparagus bed so that they could salt away safely as much of the vintage port as possible. There had been times when I had thought my father was mad, but for many years now I had known that he was merely single-minded and knew that any chimera of his brain could become fact and he was determined to be ready for any such eventuality. If ever Lucifer tries a come back heaven will not lack for advice and action from my father. No one could ever have said of him, or say, that his strength was so small that he was likely to faint in the day of adversity. He was a man diligent in his business and able to stand before kings.

*　　*　　*　　*

We went bathing late that afternoon as usual and within an hour the way which I would have to take with Sarah became clear to me. I lay floating on my back some yards out from the shore and I watched her swim back and begin to climb a rock pinnacle she had never used before for diving. She climbed up higher, too, than usual so that I had to crick my neck to watch her and saw above the cliffs a kite wheeling in the sky like a floating asterisk. She dived and hit the water like a plunging blade and the sea fountained high, so high that the sun caught it and shot the spray with all the colours of the spectrum. I waited for her to come up but she stayed below and I felt a touch of anger burn slowly through my mind so that I began to swim closer to the point of her dive ready to chide her when she surfaced. But she did not come to the surface and already she had been down longer than I had known her to be before. Anger shaped itself to panic and I porpoised and went down to look for her, forcing myself low into the green world, pebbles and sand patches, rocks and seaweed and small schools of fish clear before me. But there was no sign of Sarah. I surfaced for breath, gulping the air greedily wanting no second wasted, and went down again and stayed there, swimming until my lungs ached for relief and my body slowly seemed to turn to lead and then I came up to air again and saw her. She was lying on the surface some fifty yards from me and I swam to her and caught her hand just as she started to sink and her face swung towards me, her eyes shut, and there was a trickle of blood from a livid graze mark on her left temple.

I slipped my hands under her armpits and towed her to the beach. There was no thought in me, only a cold desperation. I dragged her out of the water on to the hot sand, threw her over on her stomach and jerked her head sideways so that it rested on one of her forearms and then I straddled her and

169

began to pump with my hands at her waist and ribs, unskilled, instinctively, and without prayer or thought for prayer for God knows that there are times when a man must act first and mourn or give thanks afterwards, and water spouted from her thinly and I pumped her as though she were a reluctant well and suddenly she jerked under my hands and vomited—and then I prayed, for with the vomit came a moan from her.

Within minutes she was sitting up, supported by me, cradled to me, held by me until—I wouldn't know how long it was— she shook her head, looked down at her sand and vomit smeared breasts and said, "Oh, Nelo . . . what a mess. Do something."

I took a towel to the sea, sluiced it and brought it dripping back to her, and as I cleaned her she said, "I'm sorry, Nelo. I went too deep and hit my head."

She sat there for a while and then she got up and walked steadily, recovering fast, into the sea until the water lapped her chin and she cleaned herself, and after that we dressed and walked back to Mios where Frau Sleitz fussed over the graze on her forehead and washed it clean with antiseptic and put a plaster on it, and by the time we had had our drinks before dinner she was Sarah again, the incident already comfortably lodged in her past; no doubt to be brought out from time to time, to be distorted and embroidered so that it would become part of the legend of her memories which were all compounds of the true and the false.

And that night as we lay in bed—since God had now clearly charged me with her care—I reached across the gulf between us and drew her to me and we made love and I took her, not only as a woman, but as my wife for, while I still did not love her as she knew love for me or as I wished love to be for me, I had known in the moments of search for her that the thought that she should be gone from me for ever—not just a running away from which she could always come back or I could go in search of her—but gone from life to live only in memory would be a loss that would make an unhealing misery of the rest of my days. I knew then that there was seldom any pure balance between man and woman. Always there was one who was lifted up and sometimes tortured by the ecstasy of love, and one who was granted the burden of anxiety and the duty of service; one to cherish and the other to be cherished, and that in this knowledge and in its acceptance there was a holiness and a comfort that demanded the union of body and spirit and made clear that it was neither better to give than to receive for the two acts were made one and indivisible. It was this that God had written in invisible ink on my heart and was now to be plainly read.

Holding her in my arms after our lovemaking, I said, "When we get away from this island I shall marry you and we shall make of our life whatever is to be made of it. There is no arguing with this."

After a moment or two she said, "Nelo, you have fallen in love with a woman you thought was dead and now lives. My head bumps on a rock and the scales fall from your eyes. I don't know that I'm flattered, but I want to marry you too, but if I'm honest I should advise you against it. And myself."

I said, "You're the last person I would take advice from."

She rubbed her face against my shoulder and I heard her say quietly, "Good. Oh, good."

* * * *

The exchange with Pericli went smoothly. I had an early lunch and then walked by myself along the foot of the cliffs to a point where I had already left a set of clothes similar to the poet's. I changed and then made the long climb up the cliff path to come out into the dip of the clifftop road. Out of sight of the port or the poet's house I sat and smoked and waited for Pericli while around me seed pods cracked on the shrubs under the hot sun, the lizards hunted among the boulders and the cicadas filled the air with a frenzied fiddling. In Italy or Athens we would be married, and then I would go after Xavier and get my diamonds and after that . . . I didn't know, but it didn't matter because I would be with Sarah.

Pericli arrived, more sober than usual, carrying a straw-covered flask of wine.

He smiled and said, "I should walk right by you. Ignore you."

I said, "Give me the flask. I've left another for you on the beach. And good luck for this evening."

He shrugged his shoulders and then said, "Just walk straight by the guard's hut. He's usually dozing and will only open half an eye. No need to talk. Just raise a hand. There are only one or two of them that I ever have any conversation with."

I began to walk away up the slope and he called, "Be good to Silenus."

It was a small white house which I had seen before in my wanderings; thick white walls with narrow, fortress-like windows, a flat roof except for one end where there was a small, rudely tiled cupola with the larger windows of Pericli's study. A small area around the house had been enclosed with a high wire fence. The entrance was through a wooden gate, a few yards to one side of which stood a wooden prefabricated guard hut. The door was open and the guard sat just inside on a chair, dozing, his carbine propped against the door and a newspaper spread over his knees. As I moved to the gate, shuffling a little, head down in imitation of Pericli, I raised a hand in greeting which also shaded my face and he nodded back sleepily. I went down the path and into the house. Silenus ran to meet me across the tiled hallway, but stopped a few feet from me knowing with a surer instinct than any guard's that I was no Pericli. He was black and white, lean and ear-torn from fights and dissipation. Abruptly he turned away from me and stalked out of the hall and I didn't see him again until sardine time that evening.

The afternoon I spent in siesta on a *chaise-longue* in Pericli's study, reading one of his books, and outside nothing stirred except the guard who went round the hut twice to urinate behind a sacking screen which had been erected there, and, of course, the guard change which took place at four o'clock. The relief was driven up in an army jeep and I stood close to the cupola window so that he should have a good view of me and be satisfied that I was safely caged. He would be on duty, I knew, until eight o'clock that evening when the two night guards would come on to lock up the house and watch over it until six the next morning. At seven o'clock I made myself a meal in the kitchen and enjoyed myself for I liked cooking. Silenus appeared and I gave him a tin of sardines which he reluctantly accepted, and I approved of his reticence for I have never had much time for people or animals that make rapid friendships, sensing that behind the eagerness there is always a motive that overrides friendship.

At eight the night guards came on and both came down the path to lock up the house doors—all the windows were grilled with ornamental iron work—and I waved distantly back to them from the study. One of them opened the front door and I had a moment of apprehension that he might be coming in, but he called to Silenus who at once emerged on to the pathway, hoisted his thin tail, stretched, and then stalked away in search of his night revels.

The soldiers went back to their guard hut and I was on my own and, as the sun went down and a great rolling brume of dusk began to shadow the distant sea, I wondered how Pericli was doing. By now certainly his wine flask would be empty and great verse would be cartwheeling in his drunken head and they would have trouble getting him into the launch for, drunk or sober, in his heart he did not want to go. Can two walk together, except they be agreed? He would have to walk in new company. Just as I walked. Just as Sarah and I walked because we were all held by a power beyond any true logic.

I went to bed and slept soundly, beyond the changing of the six o'clock guard, but that they had unlocked the house I knew because when I rose and went to the kitchen to make coffee and breakfast Silenus was there, curled in a turban on a chair, and he gave me a sleepy, satisfied wink from one eye.

From the cupola window I watched the guard change again at ten o'clock and now there was a mounting impatience in me

173

for from the change of this guard I was free to leave and return to the port and by one o'clock Sarah and I would be away on the boat to the Piraeus, and to be married. And I thought it would have been a good thing if my father and mother were still alive and at Stonebridge for I would have taken her there and they would have loved her and my father would have growled happily over the possession of her as a daughter-in-law and given her the best horse in the stable and taken her down below Salisbury to his salmon water and cursed the heavy spring-run fish until one took her fly or spinner and ran away from her so that he could curse more and shout instructions and then gaff her catch with pride. And, in the middle of these impossibly nostalgic thoughts, I saw the young man who had just been left on guard at the gate leave the hut and come down the house path with his carbine slung over his shoulder.

He came with a jaunty, happy step, his cap pushed to the back of his head and, as he saw me by the window, he waved a hand and even at a distance I could see that he was square shouldered and narrow hipped like a young hoplite, brown skinned, and smiling on the threshold of manhood, and before I could wonder why he was coming—since I had been told that none of the guards ever entered the house—he had opened the front door and I heard his heavy boots clank across the tiles and the study door was flung open and he stood beaming in the doorway and with a welcome outflinging of his arms, cried, "Pericli!"

I moved to him quickly as the pleasure of his face began to turn to a frown, to suspicion as he saw me, and grabbed his arm. I pulled him in, swung him round and held him from behind and, before he could thwart me, slipped the carbine from his shoulder. I gave him a push that sent him down on to the *chaise-longue* awkwardly and then held the carbine on him.

He sat there looking up at me open mouthed, his cap fallen from his head to show his dark, slightly waved hair with a bloom of pomade on it. Then he recovered himself and said something in Greek.

174

I shook my head and asked, "Do you speak English?"

He shook his head, and said, "Pericli?"

I said, "Italian? . . . French?"

He said, "*Français . . . un peu . . .*"

So, with a few misunderstandings now and again, we spoke. Keeping him covered all the time, I said, "Why do you come into the house?"

"To see Pericli. Where is he?"

"He's gone. For good."

"For always?" There was no mistaking the distress in his voice. "Without saying goodbye? No word to me?"

"Why should he say goodbye to you?"

He looked up at me and his eyes blinked with emotion and I realised that he was near to tears.

"Why? Because he is my friend. My only friend. You mean he has escaped?"

"Yes. Last night. He's well away by now."

He dropped his head into his hands, hiding his face from me and briefly I saw his shoulders shake, but he pulled himself together quickly, and looked up and said, "He should have told me. I would have helped. For Pericli I would do anything." The soft red lips in the young face trembled and there was no need for explanations or condemnation even though St. Paul had thundered to the sanctified of Corinth announcing the rules for entry into the Kingdom. . . . Be not deceived: neither fornicators, nor idolators, nor adulterers, nor effeminate, nor abusers of themselves with mankind.

I lowered the gun, and said, "Maybe he didn't want to cause you trouble."

He shook his head. "No, he would have told me. I have been away for a month on special training. I only got back yesterday. He would not know I was coming today. I took a sick man's place on the guard and I came . . . so happy . . . and now."

I said, "And now—you've got to help me."

To my surprise he said, "Why should I help you?"

"Because I helped Pericli to his freedom."

"Which he did not want. He was happy and at peace here. He often said so. We talked often here in this room. Pericli I would help. Anything he demanded. But you are nothing to me."

The open beauty of his face was clouded with sullenness and I knew that he would not help me. All he had to do was to go back to his guard hut, watch me depart and then be free of all trouble since he could swear that it was Pericli who had walked out as usual. He loved Pericli, the bird in the cage, and he should have had happiness now that the bird had its freedom to face the harshness of the outside world, but he had no love for the man whose hand had opened the cage. And even as I thought this, he came at me, rising from the *chaise-longue* with youth's swiftness and grabbing for the carbine in my hand, but I was favoured by the fact that I knew what he must do. I swung my left fist and hit him with all my strength on the jaw and he went back to the *chaise-longue* in a heap and struck his head on the window-sill beyond it. When he had recovered a little I marched him at gun point to the kitchen where there was rope and I bound his ankles, and then his hands behind him and I left him there with Silenus for company. It was now a quarter past ten and he would not be relieved until two o'clock and our boat left at one. If the boat had radio we might have trouble, and certainly at the Piraeus but that was a day away and I had no time to think of it.

I left him and walked back to the port and, once I was in view of the quayside guard as I came down the hill, I had to force myself to keep the leisurely pace of the true Pericli.

I went straight up to my room. It was now just gone eleven o'clock. After a few moments Harry came in, just as I was beginning to change out of Pericli's costume.

Harry gave a worried shake of his head, and said, "Mr. Sangster, something has happened down here."

"And, Herr Sleitz," I said, "something has happened up there."

"One cannot," he said, "command the movements of the

sea and the tides and ships and the orders of captains. Your boat left just after ten. There is always a large notice on board, you know, warning passengers that the company is not responsible for any inconvenience or delay caused by alterations to the timetables."

I said, "Well, we're in a pretty fix then, because up at Pericli's place I've got a guard tied up who was a boy friend of the poet, and when the guard is changed at two this island will erupt. For God's sake, what kind of organisation do your people run? You've got to get Sarah and myself out of here."

Harry stared gloomily at the icon of St. Theodore, and said, "Your wife left on the ten o'clock boat—against her will. But I insisted. At that time—without knowing of the complication at the house—there was a simple answer to any awkward question. You wanted to stay and do more botanising and she preferred to go back to Athens to see more of the noble antiquities of this land. That you should stay on for the next boat held some risk, but I did not think she should be asked to share it. And now, how right I am."

I was angry but there was no point in indulging it. I said, "The whole thing is a mess. She may have to face the authorities alone in Athens, and I'm stuck here and every soldier on the island will be after me in a few hours. If they catch me they may just stand me up against a wall and shoot me."

"Oh, no. They will give you the formality of a trial. This regime is very punctilious about that."

I said, "How am I going to get off this island?"

At that he gave a slow smile. "Ah, now is the moment when a man should be thankful that his wife has brains if not beauty. I will consult Frau Sleitz. But in the meantime you will keep those clothes on. I fancy they will be useful—all except the hat. That means Pericli to too many people."

He left me, and I sat there thinking of Sarah, nearly two hours away at sea, gone from me again, but not at her wish or mine, and with God knew what trouble waiting for her at Athens, and I thought with unrepentant lack of charity of the

177

young guard trussed up in the poet's house. The love he bore Pericli was too parochial. All he had had to do was to play a simple charade and there would have been no trouble.

When Harry came back he was in a more cheerful mood. "My wife," he said, "is wonderful and I should have known it. Always before when the organisation faltered she was ready. Come with me. But please leave the hat, and no luggage. Just your money and passport . . . small pocket things."

As I gathered up my stuff, I said, "Where are we going?"

He said, "There is a cargo boat in the port that leaves soon —for Egypt, I think."

"Egypt!"

"Mr. Sangster, you are in no position to choose a destination. The steward was here this morning to order wine and fresh fruit. We take it aboard. We smoke a cigarette and chat and you wander around and you find the hold and you hide yourself. There is so much bustle that when I go ashore no one will notice. She will be clear of here long before two o'clock. It will be very easy. And please not to worry about the safety of my wife and myself. We are not responsible for the activities of our guests. That you and Pericli planned this together is nothing known to me. Besides, we are good friends with the garrison. The Commandant eats here each weekend—free."

If it is a truism that the best plans are the simple ones it is none the less surprising when you find them working. As Harry had promised, it was easy. I went down to the berthed cargo ship with him, carrying a cluster of wine flasks on each arm while he carried a pannier of tomatoes and we went aboard and down to the galley where the cook offered us wine and he and Harry chatted in German and I eventually wandered away up to the deck where the midships hold had one of the covers still to be put in place. I sat on the edge and smoked a cigarette. The crew were working on the after hold and there seemed no one on the bridge. Before going aboard I had seen her name and port—*Larnika*, Amsterdam. She was a battered, untidy looking ship. I sat for a while and then, when the

178

moment seemed right, I swung my legs over the hold and dropped, further than I thought I was going to, on top of a pile of sacks that rattled as though they were full of pebbles but which later, impelled by hunger, I discovered held walnuts. I moved away into the darkest part of the hold and found a hiding place behind two packing cases. It was half past twelve. At a quarter to one the remaining hatch cover was slid into place, and a little later the engines began to pulse and then came a blast on the ship's hooter.

Suddenly the boards under me had movement and I knew that we were drawing away from the quayside, so I made a small prayer of thanksgiving for myself and a longer one of supplication for Sarah and realised that I was very hungry. It was then in the darkness that I groped and found the sacks of walnuts and like Agur, who knew the way of a ship in the midst of the sea, I fed me with food convenient to me.

CHAPTER ELEVEN

IT WAS DARK in the hold and in darkness I had found that one's anxieties tended to become magnified as though one needed a visual dimension against which to put them into perspective. I was worried, not for myself so much, but for Sarah. It was more than likely that when Sarah reached the Piraeus a reception committee would be awaiting her. She would be unaware that things had gone wrong at Pericli's and walk blithely into trouble, and then on to prison for certain. It was hard to imagine Sarah in prison, but not so hard in the darkness as it would have been in daylight. So I sat there, eating walnuts and worrying, and listening to the ship noises, the slow groan of timbers and steel plates and the small noises of cargo moving. In the end, to escape from an anxiety I was in no position to relieve, I went to sleep, slotted between two walnut sacks. Nobody in our family had ever had any trouble about sleeping at will. My brother Edward had told me that in the House the moment business became boring he would go to sleep and wake by some instinct when the tedium was passed, and my father in church would often go to sleep at the beginning of a sermon and wake promptly as it ended and was never betrayed except once when he awoke on time but misplaced his surroundings and from some trick of memory started to clap loudly.

I don't know how long I slept but it must have been a very long time because when I awoke one of the hold covers had been taken off and I could look up to an oblong of night sky with Orion's belt trailing across it. It was the cover being removed which had awakened me. As I watched another cover was lifted off and I heard men's voices and saw their silhouettes against the edge of the hold top. Deck lights came on and the boom of a derrick swung slowly across the hold. At the same moment a door at the far side of the hold was opened, the lights came on dimly and three men threaded their way through packing cases to the centre of the hold. I lay quietly between my walnut sacks and watched them and for a little while wondered. We were not in port for the ship was riding easily to the movement of the sea and neither were we at anchor because Orion's belt very slowly slid from the sky above and new stars winked down at me.

From the derrick boom a cable with a net at its end was lowered into the hold. The three men spread the net, rolled a packing case into it, hooked up the sides of the net and gave the signal for hoisting. The crate swung a little from the movement of the ship and it was quite a delicate manoeuvre to pass it safely out of the hold. Free of the hold, I saw it swing away outboard and I realised that it was being lowered over the side obviously to some smaller craft that lay alongside us. In this way five crates were lifted out of the hold without trouble. But as the sixth crate went up the ship swung and lifted to some bigger waves or swell and the edge of the crate smashed against the hold coaming and part of its side was broken away. Simultaneously there were shouts and curses from the men in the hold and from the gang on deck, and with their cries something fell free from the crate and smashed to the floor of the hold—it was a small box I discovered later—where it burst and there was a heavy rain of small metal objects all over the place. One of them rattled and slid across the boards to my corner and lay convenient to my right hand. I picked it up and examined it. Firearms and their ammunition have never held any great interest for me, but no one could have been born and raised at Stonebridge Park without acquiring some knowledge of them. My father would collect and read gun catalogues as other people do pornographic works and the gun talk between him and the General had an exoticism which had lodged in my young mind in disconnected phrases, like a broken litany . . . Mauser action . . . standard and two-leaf back-sight and silver bead foresight with protector . . . ·458 Winchester Magnum cartridge with recoil so heavy a recoil bar is essential. . . . Can be used on Elephant, Rhino, Buffalo, Eland and Gaur with complete confidence . . . which was no comfort at all to the animal concerned. Anyway, the thing I held in my hand was a ·404 Express rifle cartridge, whose merits I had heard often debated between the two men. But at that moment I was far from concerned with any nostalgic memories. It was quite clear to me that a mid-ocean transfer of arms and ammunition was now taking place between the *Larnika* and some other probably smaller craft.

The damaged crate was now clear of the hold and was the last to go because almost immediately the men on deck began to replace the hold covers. At the same time one of the three men in the hold began to collect up the spilt cartridges and replace them in the broken box. Following the trail of the cartridges brought him to the side of my sacks and to the dis-covery of me. He looked straight down at me where I was lodged between the sacks and for a moment he showed no surprise at all.

I handed him the cartridge I held and said, "You'd better have this one."

He took it mechanically and dropped it into his box and then, almost with the manner of a host who has been scant on courtesy, said, "Just don't move, please."

He turned and called in some language I didn't understand to the other two men and they came over, stood above me, eyed me with almost gentle concern, and then began to talk in a language which I later learned was Dutch. Then the two men moved out of the hold, taking the broken box of cartridges with them, and I was left with the first man.

He said again, "Just don't move, please." Then he sat down on a small crate and began to roll himself a cigarette.

I said, "What language were you speaking?"

"Dutch."

"Why did you speak to me in English then?"

"Natural. Always do if I get a shock. I'm English, married a Dutch girl. Live in Rotterdam. You're in a fix, mate. The skipper's a smooth-tongued ice-cold bastard—but fair if you work for him."

He was a slim man of about forty, wearing blue working overalls, and he had a pale, long face, and dusty, yellowish hair.

He said, "What were you after doing then?"

"I just wanted to get off Mios."

"You should have stayed there, mate. The best the skipper'll do for you is drop you over without a weight. He's hot on . . . well, you know, keeping his business quiet. Got a nice place in the Ardennes. Going to retire there in a few years."

"On the profits from gun-running?"

"Something like that." He looked at the broken walnut shells on the floor. "Been having a go at them, have you?"

"I was hungry."

"You'll never be hungry or thirsty again. I'm dead sorry for you."

"Where are we?"

"Right now?"

"Yes."

"No secret. Four hundred miles from Malta, two hundred from Greece and about two hundred and fifty from Africa. You'll never make any of them swimming, even without a weight. If you're a praying man you want to start sending out an S.O.S."

I said, to cheer myself up a little, "I'm sure the captain is a reasonable man."

"Oh, yes. And I know the way he'll reason—but I won't tell you because you'll hear for yourself." He picked up a loose walnut and cracked it between his teeth, examined it and then tossed it away because it was bad. "French," he said. "Kiln dried."

At that moment the two men returned. There was a conversation between the three, almost a debate, in Dutch and then my friend turned to me and said, "We're taking you to the skipper. Got a stretch of deck to go across. If you want to—and we won't make it difficult—you can go over the side. No weight. That gives you a swimming chance. Light in two hours. Water's warm. Could be a boat or two around. Gives you a chance, anyway. What do you say?"

I didn't say anything immediately for I couldn't really believe that they were serious. No man, surely, could be so callous as they were painting the captain? I had a perfectly reasonable story for being aboard, and I was quite prepared to give my word that I would say nothing about the transshipment of arms. Also I had never been a defeatist, but a great believer in providence provided that one was not faint-hearted and walked boldly into the shadow of adversity and peril. To every thing there is a season, and a time to every purpose under the heaven and although we must all eventually go unto one place; all are of dust, and all turn to dust again, it did not strike me that this moment was upon me. So, before answering, I made a short prayer for protection to be granted me if it were God's will, and then said, "You're all very kind, but I'd like to see the captain."

They shrugged their shoulders and led me through alleyways and up companionways to the deck, where it was a balmy September night and the stars were like a hoar frost in the sky and the wind was soft and warm and a crewman, sitting on a hold top, was playing a mouth-organ either against insomnia or the longueurs of his watch.

They took me into the captain's cabin which was just abaft the bridge and he dismissed the other two men so that I was left with him and the one who had discovered me.

The captain was a very small, squat man of about thirty-five. He was compact, broad shouldered, wearing a blue jacket with

184

silver buttons and a white shirt with a black tie. He looked clean and hard. Although it was long past midnight, there wasn't a trace of stubble on his broad, sea-tanned face. He had a face like an amiable ape and very soft, deep-brown eyes. He said to the seaman, "Turn out his pockets." Then to me, "Would you like a drink?" There was a bottle and several glasses on a tray on his table.

Wanting a drink and feeling a refusal to a courteous opening would be impolitic, I said, "Thank you."

"Help yourself."

He sat back as the seaman went through my pockets and I waited again politely for him to be finished before I helped myself to a drink.

All my belongings were placed before the captain and he began to go slowly through them, taking no interest in me. When he had examined everything he pushed the stuff across the table to the seaman and said, "Put them back."

The seaman refilled my pockets while the captain stared at me thoughtfully for a while and then said, "How do you come to be on my boat?"

"I had to leave Mios hurriedly. I was in trouble."

In a slow, evenly paced voice devoid of emotion, curiosity or concern, he asked, "Women, police or army?"

"Army."

He nodded as though he approved of the category, and said, "You have two passports. Which is the genuine one—if either is genuine? Not that I propose to believe any answer you give me."

"The one in the name of Sangster."

"Why the other one then?" The enquiry was detached and cool.

"It's a long story."

"Then you haven't time for it, Mr. Sangster. You know, of course, what we were transferring at sea?"

"I've a general idea. But I am well prepared to keep the information to myself if you put me ashore somewhere."

"I've no doubt you are. I've no doubt you firmly believe it at this moment. But a man at sea with two passports, a stowaway and a fugitive from justice, would be a fool not to swear to anything that would help him out of trouble. The danger comes when he steps ashore. Relief invades him, well-being returns and with it the power of speech . . . indiscreet speech."

"I don't accept that, Captain. But if I did, don't you run the same danger from your crew. Any one of them could say the wrong thing in drink or anger."

He shook his head slowly. "They're all handpicked, and they are all shareholders in this concern. Why should they incriminate themselves? Would you like another drink?"

"No thank you."

"Well, that's up to you. But it is all I can offer as a last gesture of regret."

"Regret for what, Captain?"

"For disposing of you."

"You really mean that?"

He took a long black cheroot from a box and began to light it and between puffs said, "I do."

I said, "But that would be murder."

"Speaking plainly, yes. But it's not a word that stirs me. All killing is murder some way or another. War is murder, and law and order means murder. I know, Mr. Sangster. I deal in the raw materials. Arms. One way and another I must be responsible for almost as many murders as any army commander. So, am I likely to be emotionally disturbed by the word? I do not approve of the way the world is run, Mr. Sangster—but that is a private reservation of my own. However, I accept the world's logic and have made part of it my business. I have a seven-bedroomed, white stone house in the Ardennes with a blue-slated roof, two hundred hectares of forest, a small section of river to fish in, a wife considerably younger than myself and three children. I don't list them in order of preference, but their protection is my only concern. You are an educated man?"

186

"I like to think so."

"A religious one?"

"More now than I once was."

"Meaning?" For the first time there was a slight note of real curiosity in his voice.

"I was once a priest but was defrocked. Now I have to serve God in a less formal way and, I must admit, it is often more difficult and for this, as a penitent, I am thankful."

"Interesting. So far as I know I have never murdered even indirectly an ex-priest. But it could have happened. In fact the odds are that it has. Well, at least, I imagine you will have the grace and courage to accept your end with some dignity."

"When it comes . . . yes, I hope."

"You will soon know, Mr. Sangster."

I said, "You can't really be serious, Captain."

"Have I acted or spoken in any other than a serious way, Mr. Sangster? Perhaps the truth will be more apparent if I put it quite bluntly. Your hands and legs are going to be tied, Mr. Sangster, and a weight attached to your ankles, and then you will be dropped over the side. Don't think it will be done surreptitiously. The whole crew will be assembled, as they have been on two previous occasions, and if you wish—though it has never been requested before—I am prepared to read the burial service when you go overboard. In your case, as an ex-priest, I would regard it as a reasonable request."

And because, even now, there was a strong element of disbelief in me which perhaps sought some hold or some entry to the real nature of the captain's intentions, I said, "Do you know it?"

He nodded and said, " 'We therefore commit his body to the deep, to be turned into corruption, looking for the resurrection of the body when the Sea shall give up her dead. . . .' You can have the whole thing if you feel a rehearsal is necessary."

"No thank you."

"Very well, then." He turned to the seaman and said, "Find

the mate and tell him to muster all hands. And get some ropes and a weight."

I must say to the seaman's credit, he did his best for me. Without hesitation he said to the captain, "Captain, with all respect, sir."

"Yes."

"None of the crew like this kind of thing, Captain."

The captain nodded. "I'm glad they don't. Neither do I. But it has to be done. Off you go. It's all right. I shall be quite safe with him."

As the seaman turned and began to open the cabin door the captain reached for the handle of his table drawer to pull it open and I knew that he would take out a gun of some kind to keep me covered until ropes and weight arrived, but even as it came half open I knew what I must do. There was no mercy in the man and, while I didn't approve of the morality of his logic, I could see its force for him. A young wife and three children in a blue-slated country house . . . men have found ruthlessness in themselves over less worthy objects, and, although I was naturally somewhat shocked with a natural fear, I knew it was no good dwelling on the symptoms the situation aroused. It was a time to be positive; a time not to break down but to build up, and most certainly a time to cast oneself on the mercy of the Lord since there was nothing to be looked for from the captain. And there was, of course, the simple practicality of going overboard free to swim or weighted and bound, a choice which allowed of only one answer. So, even as the captain was reaching for his gun and the door of the cabin was half open, I swung away from the table towards the door and, in so doing, I grabbed at a life jacket that hung on a chair nearby. The seaman, in the doorway, had his back to me. I pushed him aside and ran down a small alleyway and out on to the deck as they shouted after me. I reached the rail and jumped overboard. It was a much longer fall than I had anticipated and I struck the water, spread-eagled, and nearly lost the life-jacket. I went under, but not very far, and when I surfaced the wake of the *Larnika* was streaking by me in a great spume of phosphorescence.

I trod water for a while as the ship steamed away from me and, with some difficulty, got into the life-jacket, tied the strings and tapes and then inflated it. I floated, rather high and uncomfortably and—almost as though a great danger always hosted a small one—I was worried for a minute or two about my shoes. They were heavy brogues and I could feel their weight dragging at me but it took me some time to decide to jettison them. They were an expensive handmade pair which I had had for over ten years and as they sank I recalled that they had been a present made to me by my father and that with them he had given me a tin of the brown shoe polish which he concocted himself, for his own shoes and boots, from a recipe, secret, but so repellent in the preparation that he had always been banished to the stables to make it, which was handy in the sense that the only known of the many ingredients was stallion's urine.

As I briefly mourned the loss of the shoes I saw that the *Larnika*, a bulky, light-pricked silhouette against the pale September night sky, was swinging round in a circle to come back, I had no doubt, to search for me, but not I was certain because the captain had suffered a change of heart. Keeping as low in the water as I could I began to swim in a direction which would help me to avoid being found.

They searched for me for nearly an hour, and once came very close to me. After a while I gave up swimming for it became apparent that I was in some drift of current that was taking me away from their area of search. I just floated, keeping my head low while the lights of the *Larnika* grew dimmer and more distant and finally winked into oblivion over the horizon.

*   *   *   *

Although the water was warm and I was not unduly uncomfortable, except for a certain chafing of my clothes against my body, it would be idle to say that I was not without fear and, indeed, I looked on it as a healthy sign. A man who is past fear is a man who is past hope for himself. Fear, properly handled, concentrates the mind and stimulates the will to survive. I knew that my chances of being picked up were small. But at least the chance existed and justified my choice of going overboard freely rather than with a weight around my feet. However, I did not feel content just to rely on human chance. For the first fifteen minutes of complete loneliness in the darkness, I floated and composed a long prayer, the major and forward part mostly confessional and interesting, too, for the sudden remembrance of sins long forgotten, and the ending concise and sincere, putting myself in the Lord's hands. There wasn't any immediate response. Not that I would have been surprised had there been for there are many well-authenticated cases of very prompt divine intervention. So, while I waited for my plea to be cleared and forwarded for action or otherwise, I was left to my own devices which were, naturally, somewhat limited. After an hour I found with some pleasure that the watch I was wearing really was waterproof for it was still going. It was an expensive gold Omega automatic which had been given to me on the day I was ordained by my father who—being a very punctual man himself—had for years complained of my poor sense of time. He had said, "Since you're now in the service of the Lord at least have the courtesy to be punctual for all church occasions. There's nothing more irritating than fidgeting in a pew while a parson overruns his sermon time. Any message that can't be put over in twenty minutes needs editing." Which, of course, is true when one considers that the real meat of the Sermon on the Mount can be said in forty-five seconds, though after nearly two thousand years man is still struggling to put it into effect. But the thing that pleased me most about the watch—and I had only small things to concentrate on—was that this particular model was one known as a Seamaster. From that moment I had no doubt that I would be rescued for the master of the universe, heaven and earth and sea had laid his mark on me. So quite happily I waited for the tender mercy, as St. Luke long before had said, of the miracle of dayspring from on high to visit me.

And when the dawn came, it came with all the royalty and jewelled pageantry of a coronation. The grey outriders of light cantered up from the east in extended order, and soon their pennons and flags were unfurling, red, blue and silver, over the dark sea turning it to moving cobalt and serpentine marble, and churning the wave tops to white froths of spume and wind-spray under their heels, and against the royal sky the gulls and terns flew like birds of peace, screaming and dipping, and the few clouds caught the rainbow reflections of the new morning and then blazed suddenly with gold fire as the domed roof of the sun's coach lipped above the waterline, and I was so filled with childish delight at the spectacle that I added my voice to the gulls' and sang "Brightest and best of the sons of the morning" and then, though I didn't care for it much, but as a tribute to my father (whose answer it was to anti-blood sports cranks for whom he nourished a most un-Christianlike contempt), I sang:

> "The fish in wave, the bird on wing,
> God bade the waters bear;
> Each for our mortal body's food
> His gracious hands prepare."

And then, as the sun rose higher, half-circled, throwing indigo shadows in the wave troughs, I saw silhouetted in black against it a ship, heading straight for me.

It took about twenty minutes to come up to me, steaming slowly, and I saw that it was a white-painted steam yacht with a high bow and long low lines and in gold letters on its port bow the name, *Albatross*.

I shouted and waved my arms and, although I knew that my prayer had been answered, I had a moment of panic when it looked as though it was going to pass by me. Then I clearly heard its ship's telegraph ring and it slowed, turned, and came round and lay to windward of me.

191

So, I was picked up by the *Albatross*: owner, Angus Neil Campbell, Christmas and greetings card manufacturer, aged sixty-five, white-haired and white-bearded, blue-eyed, tall, spare, tanned face, tender-hearted, clear-sighted, and incurably pelagic. But I didn't see him until I had been aboard for two hours.

A steward and a seaman took me to a spare cabin where I stripped and was given some clothes. I was brought hot coffee, oatmeal porridge, eggs and bacon and a tunny steak, and half-way through it Angus Campbell's daughter came to see me, and to make sure that I was being well looked after. She was, I guessed (and later it was confirmed) a few years younger than myself, and she was a plumpish, well-rounded, reasonably dumplingish, pleasant looking woman of medium height with pigeon's wing greyish-blue eyes and warm, brown, curly hair cut very short, and she wore thick lensed glasses that made her eyes look larger and softer, and she was both shy and friendly and a little restless in her movements as though she felt that no one would welcome her company for long and she wanted it to be known that she was already going. I liked her at once but sensed that this was something that she would find hard to believe. Somewhere in her was a quiet anguish to like and to be liked—though I have to admit I only learned that later.

"My father," she said, "sends his regards, Mr. Sangster. He would have come himself but the first four hours of daylight are his working hours and he never breaks his rule. Please don't think him impolite." She had a slight trace of Scots accent and that nice, distinctive rise and fall to her voice. It made a kind of gentle music out of speech.

"Tell your father not to disturb himself for me. I'm just happy to be aboard, thanks to God."

"You're a religious man?"

"Particularly at this moment."

"Well, I'll not stay, Mr. Sangster. You'll need to have time to settle down."

I said, "My name is Charles Nelo Sangster. You get a choice of the first two, Miss Campbell."

She smiled then with her eyes and the glasses magnified it. "Thank you. If it's the same to you, could I use Nelo? The world is full of Charleses. You sure you have everything you wish?" She was already at the door, her fingers on the handle.

"Everything except your first name, Miss Campbell."

She flushed a little, then smiled and said, "You'll not like it."

"Try me."

"Hortense."

I said, "I like it. It is the name of a queen who had an empress for a mother. She wrote a famous song, too—*Partant pour la Syrie*. If it were my father sitting here you wouldn't get a word in edgeways for the next half hour."

"Thank you . . . Nelo. That shirt they've given you is a little tight. I'll find another for you."

She went and I turned back to the tunny steak, but was interrupted by the door opening and her head coming round it to say, "I should warn you, Nelo, that my father is a plain, not to say, frank speaking man with other men. He calls a spade a spade and there's nothing the family could ever do to break him." She went.

At mid-morning I met Angus Campbell. He came into my cabin wearing shorts, a beret and canvas shoes, his body as brown and lean as a beanpole, and although I had warned his daughter that my father would have talked her head off on the subject of Hortense there was little need for her father was the same. Even when he asked one a question the reply seemed to be swallowed up and made part of his own speech. He introduced himself, called me by name, asked if I had any family I would like notified of my safety by radio, took my no in his stride, explained that he had three sons and one daughter, Hortense, and that the sons ran his business for him in Edinburgh while he kept a millionaire's eye on them from the *Albatross* from all the seas of the world, digressed to tell me where she had been constructed and where her engine had been made (all in Scotland, of course), and every sentence carried a *bloody*, or other adjectives and nouns which were all made innocent by the happy smile on his face and the dancing light in his fresh blue eyes and, in fact, so frequent was this habit that after the first five minutes one took it for granted and only noticed it when he slowly and deliberately emphasised one of these words to make some special point.

Picking up my life jacket which hung at the bottom of my bunk, he said (and the modified form is used), "And how the bloody hell do you come to be in the sea wearing this sodding thing hundreds of miles from the nearest stinking land?"

I said, "I didn't like the company I was in so I jumped overboard."

"Meaning mind my own bloody business and why the flaming hell not? It's a good Scots answer to any nosey bugger of a stranger."

"Not at all. Normally I'd be very happy to tell you, but I don't want to risk getting other people into trouble, even though they deserve it, because although they forced a great wrong on me the outcome was an event which I shall remember all my life and for which every day of my life I shall praise God."

"You're a parson. I bloody well knew it. There's something about your eyes. Ay, lad, there damned well is."

"I was," I said.

"They would not keep you?"

"No."

"My bet is they made a bloody mistake. You'd fill the kirk with the lassies and the old biddies. They all like big, ugly looking men with red hair, and the men would have come to hear a little honesty about the world and the Word and there's plenty need to hear it, particularly about the world and how these same sods are spoiling and polluting it so that every damned river runs like a sewer, every lake is a cesspool, and every damned whichway you look the eye is tortured with wires on poles and pylons, great trunk roads that are black

194

highways to hell and bloody destruction, so there isn't a city or village now where what they call a glass of fresh water isn't man's own piss refined three times over and not an acre of once good ground isn't covered by his own crap and chemical rubbish, and even the blessed sea is mired and fouled here and there with oil and poisons so that the fish gape for oxygen and the birds break their hearts trying to take to the air with their wings clogged with man's filthiness. Did you know, for instance, that my own home town of Edinburgh, that runs a great festival of the arts, hasn't any sewage disposal plant and tips all its muck into the Firth of Forth where the tides just shuttle in back and forth each day? Civilisation you call it? It's a pig stye with the accumulation of man's muck slowly oozing out over the land under its own weight like lava. And plastic now. Take plastic. Once you could pick up man's decent litter on a beach and make a fire to warm yourself or cook a meal. But now—a dirty, indestructible mess of plastic containers, not an honest tin among them that will quietly and decently rust back to its natural elements. Man, I tell you, is the most bloody disgusting of all traitors for he is slowly but surely destroying not only God's gift to him but God's bounty to the birds and beasts that swim and fly and wriggle in their original innocence. Preach that one for a sermon one day, laddie, and they will all have your sodding guts for garters because they can't bear the truth of it. Well, now you know why I spend my time mostly at sea and have done for the last five years. At least out here you only see men occasionally—but the sea's marked too, up for sale and development. They're beginning on it now, but when they've really finished with the land they'll step the bloody pace up. Ay, there's only one person happy for it all and that's Old bloody Nick himself, the bugger who next to heaven hates this world most and longs for its destruction. Praise the Lord for his creation of man, he's shouting right now, praise the Lord and praise man for his phosphates and nitrates, for his detergents and chemicals, for his piss and nightsoil, for his stupid, greedy mind and his despoiling habits. And,

195

Hallelujah! for the slow but sure death of all oxygen that in a few hundred years will turn this world into a big spinning ball of sewage covered in slimy flannel weed. Ay, laddie, I tell you it will be so. And I'll tell you something else. God's given man up. He had this bloody great wonderful idea and created us— but He nodded somewhere, and we've gone wrong along the road and are heading for extinction and, make no mistake, when man goes he'll take every other living creature with him. Am I right?"

I said, "No, I don't think you are. Man is still learning— but for all his clever technical tricks he's a poor student of his own affairs. Nothing is ever lost unless God intends it to be."

"Man, you're a bloody optimist."

"That's just what I've been saying."

Wait on the Lord; be of good courage, and he shall strengthen thine heart; wait, I say, on the Lord. But I didn't say it to him because he was away already on another topic. This time organised charities and the waste and bungling involved in most of them, but as he talked it became clear that, much as he condemned men and to avoid them for the most part lived at sea, he welcomed a new face, a visitor even if dragged from the sea so that he could relieve himself of some loneliness of spirit and mind that would never have troubled a true hermit.

He was an odd bird which, since his name was Campbell would be no surprise to any Scot, but he was a likeable one, and so was Hortense who spent a fair amount of her time at sea with him. The *Albatross* was heading leisurely for Malta where Angus Campbell wanted to mail business papers and instructions to Edinburgh to his sons so I had two days aboard. Malta seemed to me as convenient a place as any other for me to go. I had only three matters of importance to deal with, one was to find Xavier and my diamonds, another to find Sarah, and the last to disappear from the files of *Them* and *Us* so that I could live my life unhampered by their stupidities.

On the second day towards evening I was sitting in a deck chair watching a pack of porpoises keeping station with us just

196

off the starboard bow when Hortense came and sat beside me. During my time aboard she had adopted me much in the way that a shy and lonely woman will take in a stray cat or dog and pamper it. She consulted me on what I would like to eat; she fitted me out with clothes, and she'd opened up the best guest cabin for me and furnished it with cigarettes, drinks and books, but never once had she asked me any personal questions about myself. When her father was around she was quietly self-effacing, but alone with me she had begun to lose her shyness, and her way of breaking through it was always to take a deep breath and plunge in with some direct question of a household nature like, "Would you like a mushroom omelette tonight?"

Now she fidgeted for a moment or two and then said, "Nelo, did you ever think of marriage?"

Off the bow three porpoises leapt high as I considered this and then said, "I have thought of it. Why?"

"Well, because you strike me as the kind of man that needs to be married. Why did you leave the church?"

"I had trouble with the law and went to prison."

With what I guessed was a considerable effort for her, she said, "I am not surprised. You have a wayward way of thinking, I fancy—but I doubt there's any real vice in you."

"Thank you."

"Would you consider marrying me? No, no, before you answer I'll tell you why I ask. It's not as you might think that I haven't had offers enough. With the money in our family there have been plenty but I fancied none of them because I knew what was behind it and I liked none of them. But I fancy you fine—and you need someone like me."

"You think so?"

"Ay. You need a woman to keep you out of trouble. I'd be glad to do it. Father would fix you up in the firm if you felt so inclined. He likes you well."

I said, not surprised now by her frankness for I had long found that shy people are strong swimmers once they have taken the plunge, "What makes you think I'm in trouble?"

197

"It's self evident. You sit in that chair thinking and it's in your eyes. On your own admission you've been in prison and the good Lord knows what other trouble, and you come to us out of a sea of troubles and you bring your trouble with you. I need marriage and a man. I've no liking for the thought to be a spinster all my life. And you need a wife, Nelo Sangster, to bring you a good dowry and set you up in the right way of living."

"What about love, Hortense?"

"By itself it's no a good basis for marriage. You've only to look around to see. I'll settle for liking and a strong and rewarding companionship. Mind you, I'm not ruling out sex and children because it's those that are important, too. I've got a good body as you can see. Beautiful of face I may not be, but then you're no oil painting yourself."

"That's true."

"Then would you like to think it over? You don't mind me talking like this?"

"Not at all—even though it isn't a leap year. And you're quite right. I have troubles. But all men are born to them."

"Ay, but not your kind though, and there are some you can finish with right away. Mind you I'm not over blaming you because a man that's been in prison—though I can tell you're from a good family—picks up bad habits and makes even worse associates and when he comes out the world's somewhat against him and so he's against the world. But together we can put an end to that if you've the will to do it, which I don't doubt, and the liking for me which I fancy you have, though I'll permit no extreme liberties before marriage because I think permissiveness is a bad form of impatience, like opening your Christmas stocking before dawn."

I sat forward now and looked at her in surprise. The ugly duckling had become a swan. The shy woman had broken the barriers of her own reserve. I said, "I always opened my Christmas stocking before dawn. My brother did, too. And he's a member of Parliament."

198

"Is he now? Well that's not saying much, but it's a good thing if you'll marry me because my brothers will count it a point in your favour. They are very materialistically minded. Of course, my loyalty to you would never permit me to tell the full story about you. Particularly for instance why you came to be floating in the sea like a long hank of seaweed."

"And how did I?"

"Oh, Nelo, you ask it with such innocence. It'll be a pleasure to deal with the trouble I could have with you at the beginning. For instance, we want no more of this kind of thing."

She reached over the side of her chair and picked up something and dropped it in my lap. It was the life-jacket which I had taken from the *Larnika*.

I said, "I don't know what you're talking about."

She shook her head. "Nelo—even if you decide you don't want to marry me you must speak the truth with me. You know I don't let the steward do your cabin. I do it myself and it's a pleasure. I was going to tidy that thing away this morning when I found out what you're up to now and why you had to jump overboard. Nelo, you're not only wayward in your thoughts, you're careless, too. I felt the wee things under my hand."

"What wee things?"

She shook her head in amiable exasperation and reached for the life-jacket. She laid it flat on her lap with the inside uppermost. Four inches of the seaming had been picked open.

"Hold out your hand, Nelo."

I put out my hand and she lifted the jacket, gathering it neatly about the open seam and tipped the contents of a hidden pocket into my palm. In my hand I held a small pile of what looked like large uneven grains of browny white sugar.

"Are you telling me, Nelo Sangster, that you didn't have to jump because you were smuggling that, or that you make a habit of going overboard with a life-jacket conveniently provided with nourishing sugar to sustain you through the night, and the pocket seam tightly sewed up at that where you'd have

199

fine trouble getting at it? Those are industrial diamonds, Nelo, and fine you know it."

And fine I did when she said it; and finer still I could understand the whole thing. The captain of the *Larnika* didn't confine his dealing to arms. He carried a wide range of commodities, including smuggled industrial diamonds, and fine I knew that when the *Larnika* had turned back to look for me there must have been no one more anxious than the captain to fish me out of the sea—though I would have gone back again, properly weighted the second time.

I said, "You don't want to marry me, you want to reform me."

"Both, Nelo. And maybe we should begin by throwing those things overboard."

"But we can't do that. They don't belong to us."

"Who do they belong to?"

"I couldn't be certain. You could say they were in the public domain and, that being so, I can find a use for them—or rather for the money they will fetch."

"Nelo, I hope prison has not made you permanently incorrigible."

"Indeed not. Would you be content if I gave the money to charity?"

She considered this, and said, "Well, it would be a wicked waste just to throw them over. You'd promise me to do that?"

"The money shall go to charity. I promise. A children's charity."

"Very well then. And now what about the other matter?"

"Marriage?"

"Yes."

"Well . . ."

"Are you married already, is that it?"

"Well, in a way, yes, I am."

"You don't sound too sure. Is it a proper marriage? I mean have you been properly churched?"

"In the eyes of God but not of man."

She shook her head disapprovingly. "It's a loose arrangement, Nelo—and I'd say a mite too convenient for a type like yourself. I'm not saying that if two people of the opposite sex were cast away on a desert island that there'd be any wrong in them offering up simple vows to God—though in most cases I would suspect that it was a marriage of convenience. But where the thing can be done according to the laws of one's church and country then it should be, otherwise there's bound to be trouble over such important things as legitimacy, family trusts and inheritances and social benefits. Where is your wife now then?"

"I fancy she may well be in prison."

She looked at me in silence for a while. Then she stood up, stared at the leaping porpoises for a moment, and said, "Nelo, I should despair of you. But I do not."

I said, "That's a very nice thing to say, Hortense. If I were really free, I would give your offer the most serious consideration."

"Well, I'm not going to say that I hope the time will come when you could consider it because I would not want any happiness of mine to come from the unhappiness of another. But if the time ever does come, Nelo, you just send a radiogram to the *Albatross*."

She walked away up the deck and I was left sitting there, holding a little pile of industrial diamonds in my hand which, although I was no expert, I felt must be worth quite a few thousands of pounds which I knew La Guicha would be happy to receive.

CHAPTER TWELVE

So, when the *Albatross* reached Malta I went ashore, showing my sea-stained Sangster passport, carrying the diamonds resewn in the life-jacket, and in my pocket were two hundred pounds in English notes which Hortense had insisted on lending me. "It's not a gift, Nelo," she said. "Though I debated making it so, but you're a man who needs to be shaken out of an easy attitude to money. So you'll pay it back when and where you can, and I'll not be charging interest. And I should warn you that when you were picked up the captain of the *Albatross*, with due regard for the customs of the sea, sent a signal to Malta reporting the fact and giving your name. Maybe there has been or will be a little in the paper about it which will bring some of your bad associates around, so find yourself a wee hotel and keep out of their way. My blessing go with you and I hope you'll not consider I've been over forward in my manner to you." And Angus Campbell gave me a copy of a little book which he had written and had printed privately entitled, *Where Only Man is Vile, a study of Pollution and Wild Life Conservation.* Dipping into it I saw that his literary style was much the same as his verbal.

So, I found a quiet, small hotel in Sliema and registered in the name of my second passport—just in case anyone should come looking for Charles Nelo Sangster. From the window of my room I could look out over the crowded waters of the bay to the distant sea from which, a little higher up the coast, St. Paul and St. Luke, travelling as prisoners of the centurion Julius to Rome, had been shipwrecked in A.D. 58. I took up residence on the anniversary of the battle of Malplaquet, that "very murdering battle" as Marlborough described it and "a senseless shambles that achieved nothing" as my father called it. His severest stricture was for the rash move of the Prince of Orange's contingent—largely because he couldn't stand Dutchmen. And, having met and survived the captain of the *Larnika*, I was inclined a little to agree with him for the time being.

For a few days I mixed with the thinning holiday crowds along the quaysides and on the beaches, and tried to decide what the best steps were for me to take to discover what had happened to Sarah, and also how I could possibly get on the trail of Xavier. For all I knew he might be in Abyssinia. My worry about Sarah was, I must confess, conditioned by the knowledge that she was a woman of considerable resource and the possessor of a remarkable facility for survival. However, since I had now decided that her love for me required in return my abiding concern and cherishing of her, a responsibility with the seal of a vow made, I was far from happy to let time take its way in the hope that it would bring some solution, so I made a long-distance call to Harry Sleitz on the island of Mios—to my surprise meeting no difficulty in doing this—and asked if he had had any news of her. He took my call as though it were the most normal thing in the world, expressed pleasure at my safety, gave me his and his wife's compliments and the news that they were well and completely untouched by recent events, and informed me that the last he had heard of Sarah—from *Their* sources in Athens—was that she had stayed for two nights at the Athénée Palace Hotel and had then disappeared. She had gone ashore from the island boat untroubled because the young guard I had left roped in Pericli's house had, for reasons of his own, not made public that it was anyone else but Pericli who had disarmed him and the island was still being searched for the poet despite the fact that the world's Press—with the exception of all Greek newspapers—had announced his safe arrival in Rome. Where Sarah had gone he did not know and his sources in Athens had no information either, or at least—which was his opinion—said they hadn't.

So, there I was stuck among the light-hearted holiday people and the repining English tax exiles and the busy, bustling, working Maltese, without an idea in my head as to what I should do next. At least, not entirely without an idea. I knew there was no point in my staying in Malta. Nothing would come to me there—but, of course, I was wrong. Many things came to me there. The first was Xavier.

I spent an evening at the Dragonara Palace Casino, first having dinner by myself and then going into the gambling rooms where I changed a hundred pounds into counters and played roulette in the hope that I would win enough to pay off my debt to Hortense. Also because I was very fond of gambling at which usually I was very lucky. In fact, both my father and brother used to say that I had the luck of the devil, which wasn't altogether a phrase that pleased me. I know, too, that the Church does not look kindly on gambling, but then the Church does not look kindly on a lot of things which it hasn't properly rationalised. The lot is cast into the lap, but the whole disposing thereof is of the Lord. And everything is from the Lord; and there is no more harm in gambling than in eating, drinking and praying—only in carrying any of these to excess. But if a man abstains from or lays a sanction against any of these for fear of excess he is a man who fears his own natural appetites and is already standing on the step below the one from which he will say let us not be joyful for fear of being too joyful and finally mad. My father, my whole family, would bet joyfully on the crawl of a snail, rain before eleven, an outsider at a point-to-point, whether the vicar would announce the wrong hymn tune, the turn of an ace, and the result of a cricket, football or any other match, and gladly leave the decisions to providence. So I played roulette and picked the numbers and colours and combinations I fancied and lost a hundred pounds all but five and went back to my room happy because I knew that for the moment God did not want me to repay Hortense (Hortense, anyway, would have been surprised and probably suspicious of such promptness) but would regulate it in His own good time.

Waiting for me in my room was Xavier. He was lying on my bed reading a book. He sat up and beamed at me with his round, Pickwickian face and his eyes shone with the pleasure of seeing me again and for a moment I didn't recognise him because, grown or false, he had acquired a moustache, neat and well trimmed to match his neat, dark business suit. On the bed lay a brief case, a walking stick, and a Homburg hat.

I said, "How did you get in here?"

"My dear Nelo," he said, "I have keys to pick all locks, words to charm all hotel receptionists—though there was no one at your desk—and only joy to see you again."

"How did you know I was here?"

He fished out his wallet and handed me a cutting from a newspaper. The headline read—M.P.'s BROTHER PICKED FROM SEA BY MILLIONAIRE. I didn't read any more. Hortense had warned me.

"That," he said, "was in the overseas edition of *The Times* three days ago. The rest was easy. I came to Malta. I have a friend in the police here. I have friends in the police everywhere. You had a taxi here from the docks. Over six foot, red-headed, and with the face of a boxer, probably registered under a false name—*They* are bothering you of course. It was simply a matter of canvassing the taxi drivers. Yours also remembered you for a reason which I will explain later. So, here I am. And delighted to see you."

I said, "And I'm delighted to see you and I presume that you're here because you have had a change of heart and have brought my diamonds back."

"Alas, Nelo, no." He bounced his bottom on the bed and added, "This is a very hard bed."

"You should lie on it for a long time. You know what those diamonds mean to me and what I want to do with them."

"Indeed I do, and thoroughly approve."

205

"Then how could you steal them?"

He shook his head and then, perhaps because the movement gave him a little anxiety for its safety, patted his moustache gently. "Nelo," he chided, "you are too naïve—particularly with valuables, and I think I have cautioned you about this before. *They* stole your diamonds. Not me."

"*They?* But they couldn't have done. You left a note, explaining—"

"*They* left a note. My dear Nelo, do you think they haven't enough examples of my handwriting to be able to forge it? Do you think after trying to kill me and failing they wouldn't take the elementary step of searching my car? They found the roof compartment and the diamonds and they took them—to have an additional hold over you—and left a note that would lead Sarah to you so that they could put both of you in the bag and then feed you a fine—and easily performed—promise to let you have them back when you had helped them. Is that not so?"

"More or less."

"I know it is. I still have one or two good friends in the service. And when I say that, of course, I now include you. However, there is no need for despair. If you are prepared to help me I think I can arrange for your diamonds to be returned —under the counter. But do not question me too closely on that at the moment. High security is involved. Our concern is at this moment entirely for the immediate problem. I need at least twenty thousand pounds."

"Then why you should come to me I can't think. I have exactly one hundred and five pounds. No, eighty-five pounds because I have already—"

"Spare me the housekeeping details, Nelo. And anyway, you have twenty thousand pounds. Have you forgotten you own a villa in the South of France? That's worth at least—"

"I sold it right after you left."

"Oh, no." His face wrinkled with sadness like a russet apple. "But no one sells a villa so quickly."

"I did. Anyway, what do you want the money for?"

"To buy myself an invulnerable position and peace in my old age and time to extract eventually my scattered assets throughout the world. Could you borrow it from your brother?"

"Don't be ridiculous."

"From La Guicha?"

"Don't be even more ridiculous."

"I am desperate."

"So am I. I want to get my diamonds and give the money to La Guicha. I want to find Sarah and marry her legally and try and look after her for the rest of my life, and I want that life to be settled and a useful one. I have, I confess, quite a liking for movement and the eventful. I even enjoy the unexpected and a certain amount of unorthodox living and dangerous vagabondage; but basically I am a simple, peace-loving, even a dull person. But nobody except me seems at all concerned about that. And, anyway, what is this position you wish to buy?"

"You remember the Bakata of Bakata?"

"Of course I do."

"The question was rhetorical. Well, he is mounting a *coup d'état*—and, Nelo, I have stage-managed so many in my time—which will take him back to his country. But he needs funds. For twenty thousand pounds he will take me with him and I shall become the Head of his Secret Service, with special powers over the police and a department, too, for military espionage. Don't you see—the only way I can make myself invulnerable to *Them* is to be appointed, as it were, to the Board. As an ordinary agent I am expendable and will be spent—but between the very top men in all countries there is an agreeable and sensible understanding that top dog does not eat top dog. It is the chance of a lifetime—and you are denying it to me."

"I'm not denying you anything. I just haven't got the money. I suppose that was how you meant to get my diamonds back for me? As top dog you would ask some other top dog to hand them back?"

"But of course. A simple trading matter. You are sure you can think of no way of raising twenty thousand pounds?"

"No."

"Nothing at all?"

"Nothing at all."

"But if you did have a way, you'd do it for me wouldn't you?"

"Of course I would. I think the Bakata should go back to his country and if you go with him—then I'd get my diamonds. But I've nothing to raise money on, Xavier."

He stood up, put on his Homburg and carefully adjusted its angle, touched his moustache gently, adjusted his stick over the crook of his elbow and picked up his brief case.

"I am," he said, "a desperate man—but not undaunted. You must forgive me if I point out that it is a combination of states which sometimes leads one to abuse old friends."

"You haven't abused me."

"Yes I have. I have been importunate and embarrassed you by asking for help which you can't give. However, in return, let me give you some advice. You see how easy it was for me to find you? Leave this island quickly—otherwise you will have them about your neck."

I said, "I want them about my neck, because I damned well mean to get my diamonds from them."

A shade of alarm swept like a cloud across his face. "Maybe so, Nelo—but there is one favour I must ask you. They will want to know how you know they have the diamonds. Please don't tell them I told you, or that you have had any contact with me, and above all—don't say anything about the Bakata of Bakata planning to return to his country. At the moment none of the big powers want this to happen. There is enough going on in Africa without their encouraging another upset. Would you do me this favour?"

"Of course."

"It will mean a few white lies and maybe stoical fortitude."

"When the moment comes I shall have to consult my conscience."

"I am happy to leave it that way. Well, I must go."

"Where?"

"It depends when I get to the airport on the direction in which the first plane out is flying. I am at home in all countries though welcome in none—except Bakata if the regime is ever changed. Goodbye, Nelo."

After he had gone I sat thinking about him and feeling sorry for him. He was determined to survive, which was entirely creditable, but I thought I had detected a slight note of resignation in his talk as though the effort of continual evasion was beginning to wear him down. If I had had the money to spare I would gladly have helped him, particularly as it would also have been helping the Bakata of Bakata. However, the immediate problem was for me to make contact with *Them*, now that I knew they had my diamonds. The easiest way to have this happen was to sit where I was and let them find me just as Xavier had found me. What he could do they were probably already in train of doing. And then, thinking about this, I suddenly remembered something Xavier had said about the taxi driver who had driven me to the hotel. He had remembered me for a special reason. Suddenly I realised what it was.

I went to my wardrobe and took my life-jacket down from the hook. The interior pocket had been slit open and the diamonds were gone. It was obvious. Xavier had them. His police friend had reported that I had been carrying a life-jacket. The taxi driver had commented on it—and Xavier had been made curious.

In confirmation my room telephone rang. It was Xavier.

"Nelo," he said, "you have now—unless I am mistaken about the way your mind works, which is a trifle slow as always where valuables are concerned—discovered that I have taken your industrial diamonds. They're quite nice ones and should fetch about twenty-five thousand pounds. I'll send the odd five thousand to La Guicha for you."

"Xavier," I said, "I made a solemn promise to someone that the money from the diamonds should be given to a children's charity. That's why I didn't tell you about them."

"I understand perfectly. I found them while I was waiting for you and I knew that if they were in your free gift you would have offered them to me. When you didn't, I knew that it was not from unwillingness to help a friend. I'm not angry about it, Nelo. You always have good reasons for your actions. I apologise for borrowing them."

"Borrowing?"

"When I get to Bakata I promise you that the twenty thousand will be paid back. A first call on all levies and bribes that I raise. Console yourself while you wait, Nelo, with the thought that not only are you helping me, but you are helping the Bakata, too. His country needs him—and me. And by the way, don't come out to the airport looking for me. I have already made other arrangements. Goodbye, Nelo. Though perhaps I should say *au revoir*."

He rang off.

I sat on the bed and poured myself a stiff whisky from a bottle which I had had the good sense to provision myself with. Someone like Hortense would have seen through Xavier right from the moment he had mentioned the taxi-driver remembering me for a special reason. And, to be charitable, perhaps that was why he had mentioned it, to give me a chance perhaps —even though he was *in extremis*—to stop him from robbing a friend. One thing, however, was more than true. I really did tend to be careless about valuables. I decided in future not to be guilty of that. I would guard my treasure when I got it where neither moth nor rust could corrupt and where thieves could not break through or steal. For where your treasure is, there will your heart be also. And my heart was set on letting La Guicha have all the help in her work I could.

That night—though I know the telling of dreams is tedium

to others, and a fault to be found even in the Holy Writ (and a reason why I have only mentioned dreaming of my mother-cum-Sarah once before, though it had become quite a frequent event with me)—I dreamed of my mother, Sarah, and this time Hortense and, while they were all grown up and clearly on good terms with one another, I was a small boy in shorts and with a nettle rash over my knees from plunging through the high growth of the river bank, and they were all scolding me for something I had done but which was never mentioned in words either because it was unmentionable or because I was presumed to know it and eventually I was sent off to bed as a punishment with a glass of milk although it was high summer afternoon and I sat staring out of the window wondering why Hortense had appeared on the scene and concentrating my childish anger on her, particularly for the way she had said, "Ay, the lad's totally incorrigible. And look at the state of his breeks. Filthy!" And my father put his head round the door briefly and said smiling, "A good farmer shuts gates and mends his fences and knows that a good bull is wasted on a poor cow."

I woke, totally confused, to daylight. Outside the air was full of sunlight and quayside sounds and a ship's hooter blasted away as she made for the open sea and a chorus of motor horns began to blow in anger at some road block, and there was a man standing at the foot of my bed holding my life-jacket in his hand and flipping through the pages of *Where Only Man is Vile*. A cigarette stuck out of the corner of his mouth and his head was cocked a little to one side to keep the smoke from his eyes, and he was nodding his head approvingly. He was tall, with wavy fair hair, elegant in a blue blazer and red linen trousers, and his face was fine drawn, big-boned and aesthetic, though not at all epicene, a youngish man, in his middle twenties, and very presentable. He flipped a page over and I was curious at the ease with which people seemed to come into my room whenever they wanted to. He glanced up from the page and saw that I was awake.

211

"Robinson," he said, and added, "Philip. It's a great morning." He tossed the book on to the bed, and went on, "He should have had a chapter about the way the dirty Danes are slaughtering the salmon on their feeding grounds off Greenland and them without a single salmon river of their own to send their fair share of smolts off to sea. The little silver darlings that go down the river in May and June. My father, dead now, bless his soul, once had fifteen thousand acres of deer forest and two miles of the Tay and a castle with a perpetual gale blowing through it, and here I am on casual work. You want it and I fix it. Cablegram yesterday from Cairo. A certain captain of a certain ship wants his industrial diamonds back. Any need for further explanations?"

"None," I said, sitting up. "Except that I haven't got them."

"Not in this, that's true." He dropped the life-jacket on to the bed.

"Not anywhere."

"Not in this room, that's true. I've been through everything while you slept. Bad dreams? You were restless."

"Someone stole them yesterday. I just found the pocket seam ripped and they were gone."

"True or false?"

"True."

"It has the ring. But it won't satisfy them."

"Them?"

"The people the captain works for. Branches everywhere, same say Mafia, some even say the Yellow Hand. Personally I think it's a vertical combine or a horizontal cartel. But standing or lying, you're in trouble and likely to lose your no claim bonus. For two hundred pounds I'll report I got here and you'd left. Skipped. Done the genie and bottle act. You got two hundred?"

"No."

"A hundred?"

"No."

"Sorry that's my limit for the risk involved. Don't mention

212

the suggestion though when I take you along to their representative here."

"I'm not going anywhere."

"You are. If you won't come with me they'll fetch you. If you run it's a small island. You could hit a golf ball across it with the wind and break a hundred, and they get nasty when they have to chase people, and I don't care for nastiness unless it's very highly paid. I'm saving up."

"What for?"

"Three acres and a pig behind a pub that has a bar sign saying, 'We have an arrangement with the bank; they don't sell drinks and we don't give credit'. Already got my eye on the ideal bar girl and bedmate. She's the daughter of a cavalry colonel who retired out here to live the life of O'Reilly on a small pension and a share portfolio that brings him seven hundred a year net. He's dying of drink and going crazy hacking round and round the scrubby little patch they call a golf course here. He's going to come too and run the public bar. They like a bit of class in there. You'd better get dressed and come along. They turned the castle into a hotel and there's a ski-lift at the back. My father was an unimaginative man. I tend to be a bit like him. A pub is my idea of heaven."

I said, "I'm not coming."

He ran a hand over his wavy hair and whistled gently through his teeth. "Do me a favour. Save yourself trouble. If you ran into a church for sanctuary they'd get you. Some nice churches here, but all a bit too ornate for my taste."

I got out of bed and began to dress, but not because I was going with him. I wanted coffee and breakfast. He watched as I got out the razor I'd bought and in the mirror I could see him studying the way I shaved.

"Wonderful barber-shops here. Nothing like a cut-throat. Lie back and be lathered, hot towels, warm scented air and all the gossip. That's a civilisation that's dying. Everything's do-it-your-damned-self, and that's what I suppose I'll have to do."

He put his hand into his pocket and pulled out a gun. I

213

was vaguely aware in the mirror that it was an odd sort of gun.

I said, "You can't use that here."

"Why not? Makes no noise. Just a puff of gas and the next thing you see, if you're lucky, is St. Peter."

"But what good will that do them?"

"A good question. Deserves a truthful answer. My instructions are: if he has them, get them. If he hasn't got them but knows where they are invite him along or leave him for us to collect if he won't come. If he hasn't got them and doesn't know where they are or who has them, wipe him off as a bad debt and a warning to others. You did say you'd given a truthful answer? 'Someone stole them. I just found the pocket seam ripped open.' Correct?"

Lie not to one another, St. Paul said, and wisely. But there was no exhortation about putting off the truth. And I didn't want the chase to switch to Xavier.

I said, "You offered to forget about me for two hundred pounds. Now you're prepared to kill me——"

"Ergo, I must be getting certainly no more than two hundred for it?"

"Quite."

"Absolutely true. But I'd rather have you alive and the two hundred. But if I kill you I get two hundred plus disappearance money. That means three months all expenses paid in Portofino. They have an hotel there. And there's the ensuing goodwill which puts my fees up for future jobs. Don't think there's any sentiment in me. The RAF buttons on the blazer I'm not now strictly entitled to wear. No old boy stuff. If you know where the diamonds might be, say so and no killing. If you don't . . . well, you'll get two inches in the *Times of Malta* and give the Colonel and his friends something to talk about at the next cocktail party which they'll be glad of because they're running out of topics. So, what's it to be?"

"I don't know where they are." I ran fresh water into the basin.

"Pity. My father was a laird and I'm trying to avoid being a layabout and life is hard but not entirely unmalleable and my dream of paradise is a row of shining optics under the whisky and gin bottles, the RAF collecting box on the bar counter, and the chunk of darts going into the board, and some ass who isn't driving saying to some ass who is 'Oh, come on, have another one!' and so many things keep getting in the way. Like you for instance and me, for instance, standing here, not struggling with scruples, not working up my courage, but just trying to make the occasion as civilised as possible and wishing that my father before he put his last thousand quid on an outsider in the 1960 Gold Cup at Cheltenham had had the idea of turning the castle into an hotel. . . ."

And as he talked so truthfully years of prep and public school training at communal washbasins stood me in good stead for there are some things that do not stale from lack of practice, like swimming and riding a bicycle and making love and offering up a prayer. The prayer I offered and at the same time jammed one thumb under the fast running cold tap, fined the tap mouth to a mere slit and sent a high pressure jet of water back behind me, sighting at his reflection in the mirror, and was overjoyed by the instant return of an old skill as the water streamed into his face and burst over him.

I turned, took the gun from him and then handed him a towel so that he could wipe his face.

I said, "If it comes to a trial of strength I think I have the edge on you."

He lowered the towel, nodded and said, "A thick edge, old boy." He smiled, "Damn neat trick that, with the water. Remember doing it at school. They'll laugh when I tell them. Don't think they haven't got a sense of humour. But it won't make any difference. They'll send someone else after you. By the way, be bloody careful with that gun. They haven't ironed all the bugs out of it yet and it's inclined to be temperamental."

A voice from the doorway said, and before I turned there was instant recognition in me at the sound, "It's handing the darling thing over to me you should be, Nelo, for haven't I all the understanding in the world about them, though no love."

We both turned. Just inside the doorway was Jimmy Harcourt, and just behind him, not quite in the room, was Miss Amberley.

I said, "Something ought to be done about this room. People keep coming into it unbidden." But because I was uncomfortable with the thing, I handed the gun over to Jimmy.

"That's my discretionary boyo. And who's your friend?"

Well able to speak for himself, Robinson said, "Ex-pilot officer Robinson, cashiered for fiddling the mess funds at the Army Aviation Centre, Middle Wallop, and now variously employed."

Jimmy said, "It's a pleasure to meet another man with a ready tongue but not silver though, I fancy. Just plated. And why would you be after wearing a Gunners' tie?"

"Camouflage," said Robinson.

Miss Amberley came into the room. She was wearing a prim light-weight navy-blue suit and a little straw hat that perched on her head like a forgotten fantasy. She said severely, "Can we presume that you've finished your business with Mr. Sangster, Mr. Robinson?"

"You can indeed, ma'am," said Robinson. "Though more properly put, he's finished my business for me. However, others will take it up where we have left off so you'd better consult him now on any particular fancy he has in wreaths."

"Do I hear the angel of death beating his wings above this poor red-headed broth of a boy, so young and so much promise ahead of him? Nelo, what mischief have you mixed for yourself now?"

"It's a small matter," said Robinson, "of the theft of industrial diamonds from my employers. I am a sort of recovery agent."

Jimmy said, "We are all agents of some sort. So Nelo—you still have this money fixation? The hard, scintillating carbon,

216

the blue bird, the Holy Grail, the crock of gold at the foot of the rainbow where the mountains come down to the sea. It's the damndest persistent boyo you are, and not that I'm after condemning it because the world needs men who dream dreams and go after them like a greyhound after a hare and a finer sight than that to stir the blood you'd have to travel far to see and—"

"For God's sake shut up, Jimmy," said Miss Amberley.

"I second that," I said.

"Women," said Jimmy with great good humour, but he shut up. Only Robinson said, "I was rather enjoying it even at this early hour." Jimmy made him a little bow.

Miss Amberley said to Robinson stiffly, "Your employers send you collecting with a Mark Four, Nitishka chemical pistol?"

Robinson said, "They've just been issued to us. We took a training course on them in an old cinema in Valletta behind St. John's Co-Cathedral. We had one casualty, fatal. The staff doctor certified death as pneumonia."

"Who are your employers?" she asked in her no-nonsense voice and I thought back to our own dear Miss Amberley. She could be just as peremptory.

I said, "They're a mixture of the Mafia and—"

"Say no more, boyo," said Jimmy, and addressed Miss Amberley. "Take the flying gunner outside and have a word with him. Bend his ear to your silver tones and give him a message to our poor cousins so that they'll stay put on their cabbage patch and till their own tatties and not, though famine rots them, come poaching on the grounds of gentlefolk. Oh, Nelo, my boyo, 'tis a genius you have for riding more than one horse at a time and neither a one of them pedigree beasts."

Robinson said, "You mean you can talk dutch to the Mafia? Who are you?"

"Go with her, you till-fiddler, and she'll reveal to you the mystery behind the curtains of the tabernacle and your masters will bless the day you took a spout of water in the eye and so stayed your murdering hand from this poor innocent. Rich treasure they will be heaping on you for their deliverance."

Looking a shade bemused Robinson went out into the corridor with Miss Amberley who closed my room door after them.

I said, "His ambition is to have a pub."

"'Tis no surprise," said Jimmy. "It's been the dream of every cashiered officer since the time of Agincourt. Now, I'm suggesting you get your trousers on while Miss Briggs is out of the room."

"Briggs? I call her Miss Amberley."

"The connotations are the same. Harry Sleitz calls her Fraulein Granz. Actually—since you're one of the family and entitled to small confidences—she's really called Emily Howarth-Guttenheim and comes from a well-known Anglo-German family which is a good thing to come from as far as possible, though possibly there's a tinge of Irish prejudice in that."

"Miss Amberley," I said.

"As you will, Nelo."

Pulling on my trousers, I said, "I want my diamonds back."

"You have a habit of rushing things which is endearing, lad. But do you not think you should take your pyjama trousers off before you put the others on?"

As I began to correct the mistake, I said, "And I'm not having any nonsense about it. Don't forget I have a brother who is a Member of Parliament."

"And a great comfort I hope that will be to you in your old age. Sure, and it reminds me of an old aunt of mine who was housekeeper to a priest in Sligo for thirty years, and she worrying all her life that she might die before him and he not gone ahead to put in the good word for her which, I tell you, was more than necessary since they'd been bedding together for years and every soul in the parish knew it and even the bishop had his suspicions, but she knew it would be all right if he went

218

ahead for he could make a lie sound like the tinkle of a silver altar bell, and he could string you evasions of the strict truth like a pianist fingering arpeggios, and after all that they both died together in a car accident, him driving, and rumour said drunk at that. Man, I wonder what St. Peter made of it all?"

Miss Amberley came back into the room and said, "There will be no trouble from Mr. Robinson's employers." She looked at her wrist-watch, and said to me, "Don't be long packing. We have a plane to catch."

I asked, "Where are we going?"

Jimmy shook his head and said, "It's the great lad you are for questions. Do you never feel that sometimes you'd like to have events come up on their own like dark horses to surprise you? Oh, by the way, because of your good work with our friend Pericli, they've advanced you a category."

"What does that mean?"

"Mean? Why, man, it means you've made a jump it takes some people years to make. As from today you're admitted to the benefits of the superannuation scheme."

Miss Amberley, over her shoulder, said, "Everyone is pleased with you." She said it over her shoulder because she was leaning over my open suitcase on the bed and packing for me, neatly and swiftly, and it was no surprise to me that the suitcase was there, even though I didn't possess one, because they must have brought it with them which showed how extensive their information about me had been.

I said, "I'm not standing any more nonsense. I want my diamonds, and I want to see whoever really runs your outfit. The man at the top."

They both looked at me in surprise, Miss Amberley pausing in her packing, and then suddenly Jimmy laughed and—much more surprising—even Miss Amberley gave a prim giggle, and then Jimmy said, "Boyo, your innocence is disarming, refreshing, dewed with the spunky bravura of a young David. So it's the man at the top you want to see? Did no one ever tell you that he's so invisible that he can't even see himself? And damned awkward it is at times for him for he has to feel for his own mouth, the poor creature, when he wants a drop of the hard stuff. Come on, comb that red thatch of yours, put your tie on and let's get to the plane. You can have breakfast aboard and all yesterday morning's papers."

Miss Amberley picked up my pyjamas from the floor, folded them and put them in the case, and Jimmy looked at me, winked and said, "Diamond Charley Sangster, you're like a breath of fresh air now in a stale world. Long life to you, though I doubt it. Such innocence cannot last, even the angels must be weeping for the beauty and the pity of it."

*　　*　　*　　*

Jimmy carried my case down and Miss Amberley paid my hotel bill and there was a car waiting outside and they drove me to the airport at Luqa where, to my surprise, there was a private executive plane—a Cessna—waiting for us, and where I learned that, although Miss Amberley was coming with me, Jimmy was not.

He handed my case over to me and said, "Enjoy the great miracle of flight, Nelo."

I said, "Why aren't you coming?"

"Because I've still a few things to do here concerning one Xavier Mabluto—who of course has made no contact with you so far. Correct, boyo?"

"Why would he want to?"

Grinning, he said, "Your footwork is nice, boyo, and who am I to press a friend? That's for another department."

So I went aboard with Miss Amberley and except for the crew and a stewardess we had the plane to ourselves which was a luxury I would have enjoyed under different circumstances. The plane took off into the smoky blue and tiny little curls of cirrus cloud and the stewardess served breakfast and the previous day's London newspapers, and Miss Amberley took off her little straw hat, touched her bun into place and gave me a thin smile which had the smallest hint of friendliness in it so that I was prompted to say, "What has happened to Sarah?"

She said, "I don't know." And it was like the old Miss Amberley saying, "Ask no questions hear no lies." But to prove her humanity, she went on, "Are you very fond of her?"

"So much so that I have decided to marry her."

"In the service it is better to remain single and abandon all hope of a private life of any consequence."

"I'm not in the service."

"All beginners say that from time to time."

"Did you?"

"I am not disposed to discuss myself, Mr. Sangster."

"Then you're different from most people. Perhaps you will tell me why you and Jimmy came and collected me? Not that I wasn't going to go looking for you myself."

"I understand that you are wanted for interrogation and reassignment."

"Where, and by whom?"

"You will see."

I said, "Is Jimmy really Irish?"

"I don't know because I've never seen his dossier. Personally I think he adopts his manner to make the more gullible assume he's a harmless fool, and occasionally he overdoes it to annoy his colleagues. Please get on with your breakfast and don't let the coffee get cold."

Shades of my Miss Amberley who would say, "Finish that up, Master Nelo. There's thousands of starving little boys and girls all over the world who would be glad to have it."

So I finished up my breakfast and my coffee and the stewardess came smilingly and cleared it away, her long, slender legs carrying her with poise and balance, and the legs reminded me of Sarah, for she had beautiful legs, too, and I wondered where she was and how she was faring and I was pretty sure that Miss Amberley could have answered both questions. And from thinking of Sarah I went on thinking of how difficult it was proving to carry out a simple act of charity like stealing my diamonds from my brother and giving the proceeds from them to La Guicha and how, in a sense, it had become with me a kind of crusade, or perhaps search, as Jimmy had said, for the Holy Grail whereas in the beginning it had only been conceived by me as a simple act of kindness, soon to be done, so that I could return to the everyday world of ordinary people and find myself something useful to do, though quite what it was I would have settled to do I was far from sure. So we sat there in the plane's lounge—and for such an unimportant person as myself I thought it was an extravagant mode of travel—and Miss Amberley read an Everyman edition of *The Travels of Marco Polo* she had taken from her handbag and I thought it a reasonable choice maybe for someone without a private life to live another's vicariously, and below us the cobalt spread of the Mediterranean was marked with cloud shadows and the arrowing, frayed wakes of a fleet of fishing boats from Sicily, and I wondered with not too great a curiosity where we were going and then, when out of boredom I picked up the nearest newspaper, I read that my brother had made a controversial speech in Manchester about the immigrant problem and a body of students and protesters had plastered him and his car with eggs and other missiles as he left the meeting, and I could imagine how pompous and self-righteous he would be about the whole thing, but honest at least because he always said what he thought and spared no man so that he had never a hope of getting even the smallest cabinet appointment.

We came down at Rome's Michelangelo Airport for refuelling and then flew on up the long leg of Italy and over the Appennines and then the great plain of the River Po and then on, north-eastwards, over part of the Alps with the Dolomites away to our right hand and finally, in the dark, landed at a small airport near Klagenfurt in Austria where a car met us and drove us away in the direction of Villach, an itinerary which was not entirely clear to myself at the time but which was subsequently easily reconstructed.

We drove up a steep mountainside in a series of spirals to a large, Schloss-like building which I had no time to see properly in the circumstances and I was led by Miss Amberley up a succession of marble stairways with badly illuminated oil paintings looking down at me, and on a top landing Miss Amberley said goodnight to me and handed me over to a servant, a man, wearing a green baize apron, blue and white striped shirt and an expression of deep melancholy, who took my bag and led me into a suite of private rooms: bedroom, lounge and bathroom. As he shut the main door of the suite he said, "It's self-locking, guv. Electric. When I want to go out I have to use this thing 'ere." He held up a small hand transmitter that hung on a cord round his neck. "Then they opens up. And the suite's bugged so they can 'ear every bliddy word we say so watch your language during the day 'cos the girls is on then. Not that they're any better than they should be so far as morals is concerned—"

He was interrupted by a slightly nasal, public-school voice coming reedily out of some hidden speaker in the room, saying, "For God's sake, Dusty, cut the cackle and let the man get to his bed."

Dusty thumbed his nose in the direction of the voice, winked at me, and led the way into the bedroom. He dumped my case on a chair and then went to the window and slid it up quietly about a foot and beckoned to me to come over.

I went to him and he pushed his head and shoulders out of the window and signalled to me to do the same. With our heads hanging over what, the next day, I realised was a two hundred foot sheer drop into a valley, he whispered, "Only place you can speak, guv. For reasons to come later, remember this. When I winks wiv me left eye, it's serious. When I winks wiv me right, take it wiv a pinch of salt. When I don't wink I don't bliddy well know."

He drew back into the room and said loudly, "Well, there we are, me old cock. Get your head down and 'ave a good night. Breakfast at eight sharp. And if you're took poorly during the night press the red button by the bed."

He left me before I could say thank you and from the outer room I heard him say into his hand mike, "All right. Open up bloody Sesame."

Almost immediately there was a click from the main door and I moved into the lounge just in time to see it closing after him.

CHAPTER THIRTEEN

DUSTY, WHOSE SURNAME it didn't surprise me to learn was Miller, was a man in his fifties and in all the time I was at the Schloss I never saw his face express anything but melancholy, or melancholy contempt. He was a small man with a tough worn body, tanned and trimmed and gnarled by many campaigns through most of which he had served as a batman to various officers. Although my apartment was bugged it in no way inhibited him from general conversation. He had joined the army as a boy soldier and been invalided out at forty with a chronic gastric ulcer, and the only reticence he had in speech was about his subsequent career, the exact details that is, though he referred to it in general terms often. He brought me my breakfast the next morning, laid it out on a table by the window and then, from the wardrobe, produced a dressing-gown and slippers for me, and took away my own shoes. I sat by the window and made a good breakfast of poached eggs on toast, and hot rolls with butter and marmalade, and the coffee was excellent and strong enough—as the good Proverbs say—to make a man forget his poverty and remember his misery no more.

From the window I had a monotonous view of pine-clad forests covering steep mountain sides and not a sign of another house or a road. Immediately below the window the grey stone face of the Schloss fell sheer, unbroken by windowsills, ledges or cornices to the top of a cliffside that dropped, pine-clad, at a sharp angle to a valley and the broken glimpse of a stream. To the left of the window I could get a view of another wing of the Schloss running up with a studding of windows and balconies to a grey slate roof and one high, pinnacled tower on and over which moved a colony of black and white pigeons.

At nine Dusty returned with my shoes and said, "On parade, guv, in five minutes. And don't be saucy with the boss. He's a fair man but not 'is own master same as all of us 'ere."

I said, "If someone hears all this, do you think you ought to make remarks like that?"

"Don't worry, guv. I've known him man and boy for thirty years and there ain't a thing I'd say to anyone else about him that I 'aven't already said to his face. Brutal frank we all is with one another 'ere. Frankness and rows and arguments every day, but like a good family we keep it in the family which you, according to the bliddy bulletin, is now one of." He gave me a solemn wink with his right eye, and went on, "You're the careless type with clothes I can see. I'll have to get some pressin' and launderin' done."

He began to make the bed while I put on my shoes and a few minutes later a girl's voice said over the hidden speaker, "Dusty, Mr. Sangster for the Chief."

"All right, Trudi, love. Open up the gates."

The door duly clicked free and Dusty led me out and down some of the same marble stairway, angled rectangularly round a deep central well. Halfway down Dusty led me along a side passage and stopped before a mahogany door which had a brass knob that shone like a small sun in the gloom. He knocked, then opened the door and stepped inside, came smartly to attention and announced gloomily, "Mr. Charles Nelo Sangster, sir, reportin'."

A pleasant voice said, "Thank you, Dusty." I was ushered in and Dusty retired leaving me facing a great spread of stained glass window on the far side of the room depicting St. George slaying the dragon. Below it was a large desk, mottled in colour by the sunlight coming through the window, and sitting behind the desk was a white-haired man with a moustache of the same

226

colour, and of a military bearing which made it clear that he had not retired below the rank of Lieutenant-General. He was wearing a Hawks tie (recognised by me because my brother was a member) and a grey flannel suit with a small white stripe in it.

He rose and said, crisply but with friendliness, "Nice to see you, Sangster. Come and take a seat."

I went across highly polished boards to a chair by the desk, and as I sat down he said, "I hope you're being looked after well?"

"Thank you, yes."

"Good. Sorry I can't introduce myself. It's a damned stupid departmental ruling for people in your category. But just refer to me as Chief. Now then, I want to thank you for the splendid job you did with Pericli. First class, and no lack of initiative when things went a little wrong. Just our type. You'll be pleased to hear you won't have to kick your heels around the centre here long. Got another job for you. Trickier—but you're the man for it."

I said very evenly, because I knew that it would not take much to make me angry unless I controlled myself, "I think before you say any more, sir, I must make a few things clear."

"Of course, Sangster, of course."

"Well, first of all, I wish you and all the others would stop regarding me as one of you. I have no wish to be and no intention of becoming. I was forced to do a job for you, and it is finished. To a considerable extent I disapprove of the things you do. Furthermore I allowed myself to be brought here because there are two things I must demand of you and if I don't get them I shall, to be a little vulgar, raise hell's own delight in every way I can."

He looked at me, fingered his moustache, tugged the knot of his tie, and showed no emotion whatever. Then slowly, almost with a trace of humour, he said, "Well, that's quite a big pitcher to bring to the well, isn't it? But never mind. Just go on."

227

I said, "First of all I want my mother's diamond necklace back which you are holding illegally. And secondly I wish to be informed of the whereabouts of Sarah Minihane."

"Who?"

"Sarah Minihane—the girl who was with me in Greece."

"Ah, yes. Well, I can answer that. No news since she left the Athénée Palace Hotel which was of her own accord. For your comfort—though, I'm sure you appreciate we don't encourage close or prolonged personal relationships—we are doing our best to find her. Next point, the diamonds?"

"Yes."

"How do you know we've got them?"

"Because—well, anyway I do. I have my own sources of information."

"I can assure you, Sangster, that I know nothing about the diamonds. You must understand that there are a lot of things I don't know and a lot of people I just call Chief as you call me Chief. But since you clearly feel strongly about this I will make enquiries and let you know the position."

"Very good."

"And now what is all this about not wanting to work for us? You have, and you've been promoted into category Wild Goose. That's high for a beginner." He gave a light laugh. "It really wouldn't do, you know, Sangster, to have soldiers suddenly in the heat of battle handing in their resignations."

I stood up then, and I was angry. With all of them there was this obtuseness of vision which prevented them from looking at things under their noses. I was sick and tired of them. I wanted my diamonds and I wanted to find Sarah, and that was all, and I meant to make it clear to this man.

I said, "Please get this straight. I never wanted to work for you in the first place. I was blackmailed. And now I have no intention of working for you—and there's nothing you can do to make me. Personally, if you really want my philosophical summing up of the matter, I think you all live in a dangerous world of fantasy which you have created amongst yourselves

228

because you are incompetent and ill-fitted to live in the real world. And if you think you can drag me inside your international asylum you are wrong. Have I made myself clear?"

"Admirably."

"Then I suggest you find out about my diamonds as quickly as you can, and also about Sarah Minihane. I'm sorry to be forceful about this but that is the way I feel and to speak any less frankly would be dishonest."

He sat there, looking at me calmly and digesting what I had said, and then he nodded his head either because he agreed with me or more probably because he had come to some private decision of his own about me, and he said, "I like the bit about fantasy. Of course, it does appear like that and maybe we foster it as a form of self-protection. But there is no more fantasy in our world than in any other, Sangster. I have a brother who is a farmer in England and he lives in a world of fantasy. In ten years the price of his wheat has dropped two per cent and the price of bread has risen one hundred and eight per cent. Last year he left his plums unpicked on his trees while the government allowed our home market to be flooded by plums exported and subsidised by the East German government. Fantasy, Sangster, walks with everyone no matter what world he inhabits. Pardon me if I sound pompous but it is only natural that I should defend my profession, which is a necessary but devious one."

"Of course, I understand your point of view. But I am not coming into your profession. On this point I am quite adamant."

At this moment a telephone on his desk rang. He picked it up and said, "Yes?" and listened for a few minutes and then put it down. He looked across at me and said, "You'll be glad to hear that Miss Minihane has been located and arrives here tomorrow evening. In the meantime, since you've used the word adamant I feel it's only fair to give you twenty-four hours to think over your decision. And, Sangster, if on reflection you still stick to your decision I won't pretend that it will be very pleasant for you. We need you—not desperately—but enough to persevere with you."

He pressed a bellpush on his desk and Dusty soon came in to take me back to my suite.

* * * *

Going up the stairs Dusty said, "You 'ad a bit of an up-and-downer wiv 'im?" and when I didn't answer because I was still angry, he went on, "It's all right, you can say what you like on the stairs. They ain't bugged. Only the rooms on your floor."

I said, "Did you serve with him in the army?"

"That's right. He's a nice gentleman so long as he gets his own way, which he does mostly."

"Well, he's not getting it with me."

He said, "Pity I ain't a betting man."

I said, "There's a Miss Sarah Minihane arriving here to-morrow. Have you any idea which room they will put her in?"

"Friend of yours?"

"Yes."

"Only free visitor's suite is the one next to yours." He hesitated for a moment, gave me a melancholy sideways look as we crossed a landing turn, and then said, "You been giving old Xavier a 'elping hand now and then, 'aven't you?"

"I suppose you could say that."

"Fair enough, then. Very fond of Xavier I am. One good turn deserves another so long as you're prepared to keep the information to yourself."

"What information?"

"Swear? Cross your throat and so on? I'm ready to take your word even though you're an ex-padre."

I said, "I swear."

He said, "She's been in the next suite to yours for the last five days."

Astonished, I said, "The man's a liar!"

230

Dusty said, "Who isn't in this outfit? But don't you say nothin' or they'll crucify me. How was Xavier when you last saw him?"

"In good form."

We stopped outside my door. There was no lock to open. You just turned the handle and went in, but once inside the door had to be unlocked electrically to let you out.

Before opening the door to usher me in Dusty said, "I'm beginning to think old Xavier might get away with it. If he does, he'll be the first. You want my advice, sir, you'll settle down and work for 'em. It ain't a bad life so long as you don't 'ave no family ties."

I said, "The days of the press gang are over, Dusty; and what's more I have family ties."

Except for Sarah, of course, not very strong ones. The moment I was left alone I pushed up my bedroom window and looked out. Three yards away on my left was a window on the same level as my own. If the suite Sarah was in had a similar layout to my own it should be her sitting-room window. Between the two windows was a smooth run of wall with no possible hand-hold for a crossing. However, necessity being the mother of invention and my desire to see and talk to her strong, I went into my sitting-room and studied the large curtained window there. The long curtains were pulled across and opened by two long draw-cords and on the end of the cords were small brass weights. I climbed on a chair and with a blade from my razor cut off one of the cords near the top of the curtains so that I had a nicely weighted piece of cord about fourteen feet long.

From my open bedroom window I dropped the weighted end of the cord and began to swing it pendulum fashion, gradually increasing the arc of its swing until the brass weight was coming up level with Sarah's window. I swung it up and inwards at a slight angle so that it cracked against the glass, fell to the sill with some noise and then rolled off to dangle below me. I did this three or four times but there could have been no one in the room, otherwise they must have heard the noise and come

231

to investigate. I repeated the process at half hourly intervals during the rest of the morning and then, just before Dusty was due to arrive with my lunch, I went to the sitting-room and tied the cord back into place so that Dusty would not miss it when he came into the room.

I did this at intervals for the rest of the day and as the afternoon began to wane and the shadows of the pine trees on the mountains lengthened, I was rewarded. The far window opened and Sarah looked out. It was a wonderful sight for the lowering sun caught her hair and it flamed like a burnished halo of copper, and the smile of welcome on her face was warmth in a cold place. I raised my fingers to my lips to caution her not to speak or shout and then I hauled in my weight and went to the sitting-room where I wrote her a note at the small desk which was provided with stationery, though none of it bore any address and it was of a very inferior quality.

I wrote:

Darling Sarah, I am overjoyed to find you. They are still trying to coerce me to work for them, but this I shall refuse to do. I shall now apply myself to working out some method of escape for us which should not be difficult for they are all very incompetent. Would you arrange to be at your window tomorrow at every even hour in case I wish to communicate.

Love, Nelo.

P.S. Burn this.

I folded the letter into a thin slip and attached it just above the weight with a couple of rubber bands of which there was a supply in the desk, and then worked up the pendulum movement and swung it across to Sarah. She caught it, and withdrew with the weighted end to her room. I waited, holding my end of the cord and in due course her reply came back:

It read:

Darling Nelo, I still love you and have given up hope that it will pass. It is a pity I have not long golden hair for I could lower it and we could both escape down it; but no doubt you will think of a more practical scheme. I am having dinner with the Chief tonight and then playing bridge with him and two of his staff. I am allowed a certain amount of freedom and will find out all I can which might help us to get away.

All my love, darling. Sarah.

P.S. If you burn this you will be burning the first love letter I have ever sent you.

Nevertheless I did burn it, and I spent the rest of the evening considering ways of escaping from our captivity, to escape as birds from the snare of fowlers; and we would have to be birds, I thought, with a two-hundred-foot drop below us which made me giddy just looking down.

* * * *

I was taken to the Chief early the next morning and the interview was a brief one. When I said that I was adamant still about not working for him he shrugged his shoulders and said, "Well, Sangster, it's out of my hands. I'm only concerned with fully integrated operators. You're now the responsibility of the Department for Discipline and Disintegration. When they've brought you to your senses I'll be glad to welcome you back. But you'll have to drop a category, of course, and start again."

I said, "Discipline I can understand, but what's disintegration got to do with it?"

"The disintegration of your moral, ethical or personal block against working for us. In a way, it's like redeeming a sinner."

So Dusty led me off to the Department of D. and D. as he called it, and he ushered me into a small room on the next floor down and his melancholy face did not permit itself a wink of either eye.

The room was bare except for a table and two chairs. The

233

walls were covered with brown leather held in place by a geometrical studding of copper-headed, domed nails. There was one small window high from the floor so that nothing could be seen from it except the sky, and it was barred on the inside and outside. In the wall behind the table was a recess which was covered by drawn curtains of yellow silk, bordered in black with a Greek key pattern. I sat on the chair in front of the table and across it sat a small, middle-aged man in a dusty navy-blue suit, blue and white striped shirt and hard white collar and a stringy black woollen tie. He was bald except for little terminal moraines of hair above his ears, and he had a sleepy, dormouse look and a gentle, tired smile as though years of disciplining and disintegrating had worn him down. On the table in front of him was a pile of clean white foolscap paper, a yellow pencil, an intercom set, and a row of push buttons set in a piece of highly polished mahogany.

He said a little huskily as though dust had got into his throat, "For purposes of reference, I am Jessop. Before we get to work there are certain preliminaries to be established. They're not important, but I need them for the forms that have to be filled out eventually. Name?"

I told him, and then he went on through a string of questions: age, education, family—living and deceased—religion, and so on, and, since he was polite and we clearly both had time on our hands and my thoughts were still nibbling away like a squirrel at a nut with the problem of how I could engineer an escape, I answered them and he wrote down the answers in a very slow hand, and eventually he said, "Married?"

I said, "No," though I considered myself to be.

"When was the last time you had sexual congress?"

I said sharply, "That's my business."

"It's mine now. When?"

I said, "I'm not answering."

Rather wearily he said, "I wish you would. It's only to go on the form."

I said, "No."

234

With a shrug he reached out a hand and pressed one of the buttons set in his mahogany plaque. An electric shock hit me —I presumed through the chromium handles of my chair— and I jumped to my feet and swore.

He said, "I don't want to call the guard and have you strapped in the chair. I prefer a personal, relaxed note in the first stages. Please sit down, the current is off."

I sat down and he said, "When?"

I said, quite untruthfully, but then I had no intention of making my emotions and love-life with Sarah part of any form, "With the chambermaid of my hotel in Malta three or four days ago."

He nodded and wrote it down and said, "For payment?" Then seeing me stir he added, "It's important from a personality assessment angle. Either you are a man who has to pay for his pleasure or you have a gift—not enjoyed by many —of stirring genuine reciprocity in the other sex."

"For payment," I said. "Five pounds."

He asked a few more questions of an ordinary nature and then said, "What is a dugong?"

I said, "Why do you want to know that?"

He straightened his black tie a little and shot his cuffs, which were stiffly starched and a little frayed.

"It is the general knowledge section. I have to have some broad idea of your mental range in the field of unimportant miscellanea. Dugong?"

I said, "It's a large herbivorous mammal found, I think, in the Indian seas. A sea-cow."

"And a petalon?"

"I have no idea?"

"Nor might you have even if you were of the right faith. Look it up some time. All right, now let's tackle the current problems section." He reached into his table drawer and pulled out a small parcel wrapped in white tissue paper. He opened it and laid out my mother's diamonds on the table.

"Those are mine," I said.

235

"I'm not concerned with the legal aspect. How did you know we had them?"

"Through a process of rationalisation, and a belief in human nature."

"Explain."

"A note was left in the car by Xavier saying he was taking them in order to raise money. Xavier would never have taken them. He knew how much they meant to me and what I wanted to do with them. Even more, in the note he refers to me as Charles. This, on reflection, convinced me it was a forgery. He always calls me Nelo."

"A good point—on reflection. Did anything help your reflection? I mean, is it perhaps of recent origin, this reflection of yours?"

"Sometimes the truth comes slowly."

"Ah, how heartily I agree. Did Xavier visit you in Malta?"

"Yes, he did."

"Why?"

"To borrow money. I had none."

"So he stole your industrial diamonds."

"They weren't mine. Yes, he took them."

"How much were they worth?"

"Some thousands. I wouldn't know exactly."

"And what would he want a large sum of money for?"

I said, "What heading does this come under? Discipline or disintegration?"

"Disintegration. How can we discipline you until we have established your prejudices against working for us? Would you say your antagonism is based on a personal sympathy for Xavier or more on an ethical revulsion from the services we perform?"

"Both, equally."

"And what did Xavier want the money for?"

"To escape from you and to provide him with some peace in his old age."

Mr. Jessop smiled and nodded his head. "Xavier is a dear

236

friend of mine, and I would gladly see him achieve those ends
—but he never will, and professionally it is my duty to foster
that conclusion. Just what plan had he got in mind?"

I said, "How would I know?"

Mr. Jessop smiled. "Because he will have told you. Xavier
is remarkably frank with his friends when they have helped
him. It is a weakness that was often pointed out to him. What
does Xavier plan to do?"

"He talked of getting to Abyssinia."

"Frequently, I know. But what did he talk about in Malta?"

"I am more than reluctant to say."

"A pity." He put out his hand and pressed the current
button for my chair. But I got no shock. He pressed the button
once or twice, but still nothing happened. He frowned and
pressed another button. The door of the room opened and
Dusty came in.

Jessop said with a shade of irritation, "Dusty, this damn
chair has gone wrong again. Get the electrician."

"Very good, sir."

When Dusty had gone, I said, "Does it happen often?"

"Frequently. It's an old model. I've been trying to get them
to replace it for ages." He pressed the button again experi-
mentally but nothing happened. He sat back and sighed,
smoothed a hand over his bald head, and said, "Xavier is up
to something and we want to know what. It would be a great
help if you assisted us without the need of all this grand
inquisition stuff. You will in the end, so why not save yourself
a lot of trouble?"

I said, "Why don't you just give me my diamonds and let
me go?"

He said, "Your mother was a good and beautiful woman?"

I said, "She walked like a queen, and the birds flew to her
hand and the flowers shed their petals to make a path for
her."

He said, "You sound a bit like Jimmy Harcourt. But I take
your point." He reached down to a bottom side drawer of the

237

table and began to put bottles and glasses on the top of the table, saying, "They'll be ages getting the electrician and it's nearly lunchtime. I can offer you pink gin or brandy."

"Brandy would be nice."

"It should be, it's Hine. I can't stomach this awful Austrian stuff."

He poured two neat brandies and we sat there drinking.

He said, "I understand you have a certain strong regard for a Miss Sarah Minihane."

I said, "That's true."

He said, "Would you mind describing her in something of the same terms you used for your mother?"

"Not at all. She walks in a cave lit by changing coloured lights and no one sees her real face for she is always masked, now Tragedy, now Farce, and when she speaks her words are full of hidden truths."

He nodded and said, "We could do a lot with you, and you could rise high in the service. Would you mind shutting your eyes?"

"Not at all." I shut them.

"Give me," he said, "three small peculiarities of my appearance."

I said, "You are wearing odd cufflinks. The second mother-of-pearl button of your shirt is missing and your wrist watch is either broken or wants winding for it has been showing six o'clock ever since I came in."

"Very, very good," he said, and added, "you may open your eyes."

I did so and immediately said, "You've also while I had my eyes shut substituted your brandy glass for mine."

"Quite true." He beamed. "But not for any nefarious purpose." He changed the glasses back. He had drunk rather more of his than mine. He went on, "A most interesting morning. When we've overcome your prejudices, would you, if I could arrange it, and I think I could, consider the Department of D. and D.? You are just the material we want."

238

I said, "I am not joining any of the Departments."

He said, "We would assign Miss Minihane as your personal assistant as often as possible."

"No."

He held up the diamonds, fingering them as though they were prayer beads and said, "As an earnest of our good will you can have these now and no obstacles will be put in your way of disposing of them as you wish."

I said, "I am not joining."

He said, "I didn't make that a condition. I said you could have them now." He handed them over to me and when I looked puzzled he smiled a fatigued little smile and said, "You are now considering the subtlety behind the gesture. Don't strain yourself. They are yours legally—almost. When you join us we would now—because of your potential which I shall make the subject of an interim report—wish it to be almost entirely of your free will." He topped up both the brandy glasses, and said, "And now a few moments of free association."

I said, "What on earth is that?"

"A word game. I say a word and then I would like you to respond with the first word or phrase that comes into your head. An old-fashioned game which is the foundation of many new truths. For instance—Greek?"

"Meets Greek."

He shook his head. "Try to be instinctively responsive. Fish?"

"Pie."

"That's better. We'll follow that one to establish confidence. Walewska?"

"Sole."

"Splendid. Mountain?"

"Molehill."

"Maori?"

"Xavier."

"Ham omelette?"

"Journey."

239

He said, puzzled, "I don't follow that one."

I thought he did for all that, and said, "It would take too long to explain."

He nodded and said, "Purely subjective link. Elephant?"

"Pink."

"Villa?"

"Aston." He was puzzled again so I added, "A football team." It was quite clear to me now where he was leading and maybe he meant it to be. They were so devious that it was impossible to tell. He fired a few more words at me and I gave him my replies. Then he said, "Overthrow?" and because I knew clearly what he was after I said, " 'Evil shall hunt the violent man to overthrow him'." And to my surprise he said gravely, " 'I know that the Lord will maintain the cause of the afflicted, and the right of the poor'. But often, Sangster, he is inclined to be dilatory."

At this moment Dusty came into the room and said, "Can't get the electrician, sir. They're having their Autumn Goose Fair in the village and he's playin' in the band."

"Never mind," said Jessop. "Take Mr. Sangster away and bring him back the same time tomorrow." He stood and smiled at me. "A most interesting session. I think we can dispense with the chair anyway in future."

So, Dusty took me back to my room and I took my mother's diamonds with me and I examined them closely to check whether they had palmed me off with paste substitutes but they seemed to be genuine since I could easily write my initials on the sitting-room window with one of the string.

I spent most of the afternoon in thought and then just before it became dark I had a brief interchange of letters with Sarah. I wrote:

Darling, I have got my mother's diamonds, and have almost worked out a way for us to escape. Will pass you full instructions tomorrow.

Love, Nelo.

Sarah replied:

Darling Nelo, Be careful—you have cracked the glass of the window, but I will make some excuse to Dusty. I have every confidence in you. I once escaped from a police guard room in Tangier which is why I can never go back there since I was convicted in absentia.

Love, Sarah.

The next morning at the same time Dusty took me back to Jessop, who looked as though he had been sitting in the same position ever since I had left him.

He asked, "No change of heart?"

"None."

"Good. I would not have believed it if you had said 'Yes'." He leaned back in his chair and put the tips of his fingers together, and went on, "I have now a very clear picture of the problem facing us and it is plain to me that with a man of your firmly held convictions we can dispense with all the graduated disintegration devices and come to the final one. A pity, because I think they would have amused and interested you, even while conditioning you. There is one where we fit eye clamps to you so that you can't shut your eyelids and then you are strapped in the chair and made to face a battery of differently coloured spinning discs while a jet of alternately hot and cold water is projected at the base of the skull. It rapidly produces a state of hypnosis in which the subject talks freely and answers frankly. Unfortunately it has a side issue with some subjects, caused by the drumming of water on the skull, of promoting permanent deafness after a time so that there is only a comparatively short period of hypnotic clarity during which he can be questioned and one often misses it. Between ourselves we have an agreement with all other nations' services not to use it above a certain category because it frequently permanently injures the brain so that a man becomes useless and an early burden on the pension fund." He pressed the button on his desk and I jumped with shock. "My apologies. I just wanted to check that that damned electrician had fixed this. He was rather drunk from the fair when he came in this morning."

He got up and drew the yellow, key-patterned curtains behind him to reveal a little recess, big enough to take two or three people, lined with thick plate-glass windows on its three sides.

"The observation gallery. No, no, stay where you are for a moment. I just want to make one point clear. It has become obvious to me that you have a high degree of stoicism in the face of most compulsions. In a mild way it is a character trait which produces martyrs. But emotionally and sentimentally you are as weak as clay. Faith, hope and charity are your poorest weapons, and a sense of responsibility to the more unfortunate than yourself makes you very vulnerable. So, I want you to remember three things when you come up here. One, I am armed." He patted his jacket pocket. "Two, you can stop the whole process by agreeing to join us and telling us all you know about Xavier; and, three, if you do so, you will be taken back—and this is quite exceptional—in the category of Swan-Flight. That's three above Wild Goose and entitles you, not only to an increased pension when you retire, but to a knighthood. Wild Goose never ranks more than an M.B.E. at the most." He drew an automatic pistol from his pocket and, stepping to one side of the observation gallery, beckoned me up. I went and looked through the centre pane of glass.

I was looking down into a stone-walled, stone-floored, windowless room. It was lit by ceiling floodlights in each corner of the room and the lights were red, green, yellow and blue. In the centre of the room was a raised stone platform and resting on the platform was a glass tank about six feet long and four feet wide with sides about three feet high. I could look straight down into it. Over one corner the end of a length of green hose had been fixed, the hose trailing away across the stone floor to disappear through the wall by way of a small grille. It was a cave of coloured lights and truly a place of Tragedy and Farce. Lying in the tank on her back, arms and legs spread as though for crucifixion, completely naked except

242

for a brief bikini slip about her loins, was Sarah. Her eyes were closed, her face on its side, facing me.

Jessop said, "She was heavily drugged before breakfast. She will be aware of nothing. We like to keep a very low level of sadism. However—unless you agree to join us and tell us what you know about Xavier—and it must be both—she will die." He pressed a switch in the wall of the recess and water began to spout through the hose pipe into the glass tank.

I made an instinctive move towards the switch but he said, "That won't help. It works a time mechanism which keeps the water running until the tank is full. The water I may say is at body surface heat. If you wish to stop it running all I have to do is to speak over the intercom on my desk. But please don't leave the timing too fine. Accidents have happened."

So, I stood there and watched the water splashing into the tank and slowly filling it, my eyes on Sarah and my mind heavy with disbelief. The world I was in was peopled with sadistic, clumsy clowns, and the world outside was at their mercy too. I said a quick, silent prayer for both worlds as I watched the first inch of water rise about the beloved, spread body of Sarah, water which began to lift and seep into the tangle of her spread hair, and there was a deep anger in me as the evil farce began its slow performance. But God is not to be mocked, nor are His gifts to be shabbily valued, and I was grateful for the ones he had endowed me with so that I could stand there and watch the water rise over the rounded limbs, lap into a small lake over the shallow bowl of the sweet navel and rise like a reservoir filling to drown the rounded hillocks and the long, clean slopes of thighs and shoulders and then creep centimetre by centimetre up the lovely curves and planes of a cheek towards the red-lipped half parted mouth. As it touched the creased corner of Sarah's mouth I turned away and went down into the room and sat on my chair and said to Jessop, "One day you and your kind will stage a farce so obscene that the only charity God will be able to find for you will be a million years of penitence."

243

And he came down from the gallery, sat at his desk, flicked the intercom and said, "Switch the water off." And then he reached down and brought the brandy bottle and a glass to the table and poured himself a drink without even a shadow of a gesture of invitation to me for he knew I would have refused, and he said, "I have come a long way from innocence and there is no road back. It happens to us all in lesser or greater degree."

I said, "The real Miss Minihane has a birthmark shaped somewhat like the Isle of Wight two inches below her left breast."

He said, "The eyes of love are not to be deceived. Our Art Division here should have been more thorough in their research, but they have the anachronistic belief that Art should not mirror Nature but only generally suggest it and while they have to be very careful in the wax modelling of the different heads—and I must say make a first class job—they carelessly often use the most appropriate female body they have in stock. Oh, dear, what a pity that the thing has gone wrong. It now means that I have to devise a whole new programme for you. However, could I ask you a question?"

I said, "Why don't you just give up and let me go?"

"There is no provision for it. Tell me, had it really been Miss Minihane and not a wax model, would you have saved her?"

"Of course."

"I'm glad to hear you say that because I've argued for a long time that we shouldn't use models but the true thing. No real danger could possibly be involved, but for some reason we can't get a clearance on it from Archangel."

"Archangel?"

"The town. There is a secret Soviet institute there for the investigation of compulsive practices and devices. Their findings are highly regarded by all intelligence services and there is an international congress of all interested parties there once every two years. We, of course, strictly adhere to them."

244

"Why should you if you're British?"

Jessop looked surprised, but then what he looked and what he felt were not always the same, and said, "Why should you assume we're a British service?"

"But—?"

"Because we mostly speak English? My dear Sangster, that's rather a naïve assumption, isn't it?"

"So you're not a British service?"

"I didn't say so. Nor did I say we were Russian. I am not saying anything and let me add you would have to be in a much higher category than Swan-Flight before you would be told. It is a security procedure which is of the highest importance."

I said, "It is a madness of which I want no part."

He said, "Perhaps you'd better go back to your suite until I have devised a new procedure. I'll have some books sent up from the library. Do you like fiction or non-fiction?"

I said, "Thank you, but I don't need any books. I have a great deal to think about."

"As you wish."

He rang for Dusty and I was taken back to my suite and Dusty said on the way, "They give you the old tank treatment, guv?"

"Yes."

"That's a good sign."

"Why?"

"Never bother wiv it wiv ordinary people. Just bash 'em about a bit and they soon come round. You must be very special."

I was left alone for the rest of the day except for the visits of Dusty with my lunch and dinner and his last visit to turn down my bed. During the afternoon I passed a message to Sarah explaining the preliminary moves for our escape and there was an argument between us over the small detail of whether I should transfer to her room or she to mine and in the end—not without some relief to myself for I had no head for heights—she won on the grounds that she was lighter than

I was and that she had learned that Dusty always brought me my breakfast before he served her. It would never do for him to come in and find my room empty.

As soon as Dusty had bid me goodnight and gone I took some sheets and blankets off my bed and with my razor blade cut them lengthways in strips about two feet wide and then sat on the floor and began to plait the strips into a substantial rope about thirty feet long. The only time I had ever done it before was with my brother when for some transgression we had been sent to our room and locked in on an evening when we had both wanted very much to go to Salisbury to see a showing of Noël Coward's film *In Which We Serve* and we had bound our sheets together and slid down them into the blacked out night of the fading war years, and when we had returned and we were about to climb up the sheet rope, someone—clearly our father—had tipped two buckets of water down from the window on us, though when we got up to our room there was no sign of him or the buckets and he never mentioned the affair.

When I was ready I opened my window and swung my weighted cord and raised Sarah. She caught the weight and held it and then to my end of the cord I tied the end of the sheet rope and she pulled it across. It was a dark night, the stars blanketed by clouds and nothing to be seen below but a great blackness from which now and then came a faint war-whoop of an owl. I tied my end of the rope to the leg of the bed and then hung out of the window holding the slack of the rope in my hands and waited for Sarah who, twelve feet away, I knew, would be knotting the rope round her waist. I wondered how good she was at knots for it is easy to tie a granny instead of a reef knot, or a slip knot to slide agonisingly tight instead of a bowline and, although I had well tested the rope, I was full of anxiety for the moment when she would hang from the window ledge, rope about her waist and let herself drop on the slack to the jerking point when I would have to hold her and then pull her up. Pulling was no problem but the moment of jerk as the slack tautened worried me. Below us was a black pit and I did not want Sarah to fall into it even though in the falling, as St. Paul said of the Gentiles, salvation could come, because Sarah was in no need of such extreme redemption. She had a life to finish, the warmth of children and cherishings to know and a marriage to make and a place to find which she could call her own, and the gentle peace of this world to enjoy before the angels lifted her to glory. So I spat on my hands like a tug-of-war man and gripped the rope and waited and saw the bulk of her form climb out of the window and hang and then fall. As the point of jerk came I let six inches of rope slide through my hands to ease the jolt and then held her and felt the rope spin in my hands as her body twisted round and then I hauled her up and her weight was nothing against the strength of my arms and the gladness in my heart as I consigned a brief prayer of thanks into the dark night.

She came through the window and into my arms and I kissed her mouth and stopped it before she could say anything that the hidden microphones could pick up and I felt her body tremble against mine.

Then, in silence, we hid the rope in the wardrobe, and in darkness we undressed, hearing each other's movements and finding pleasure in their familiarity and so moved to the bed and lay on the mattress, under a large patchwork eiderdown which would have served no use as a rope, and found one another and the recurrent joys of being at once man and woman and husband and wife; and we made love to welcome each other, and then again to worship each other and again, finally, to salute love itself which is the true token of man's kinship with God and then we slept, cocooned in each other's arms, against the coming of the morning and I was happy knowing that sin had no dominion over us for we were not under the law, but under grace.

CHAPTER FOURTEEN

WE WERE UP early the next morning, but there could be, of course, no talk between us. I scribbled a list of instructions on paper for Sarah and she read it and kissed me and hid herself in the large wardrobe a few minutes before Dusty was due with my breakfast. He always left me with my breakfast and then came back a little later to tidy the bedroom. I met him in the sitting-room and he gave me a melancholy good-morning. Outside autumn had laid a green and gold wash over mountains and trees and the sky was a thin, scrubbed out blue and there was a slight shading of frost in the shadowed lee of rocks and cliffs. Just by looking at it I could tell it was the kind of autumn morning which I had welcomed as a boy, when for the first time the air's nip frosted one's breath and the first leaves of the willows would drop silently, spinning through the air. St. Luke's little summer was still to come, but winter had sent a note for his arrival to be expected.

Dusty set out my tray, examined it and said, "Got all you want, guv?"

I nodded and he turned away to the main door and said into his hand speaker, "Open up, Trudi."

The door lock clicked and he pushed his way into the corridor and in four steps I was with him, passing through the door, locking one hand and arm round his neck and over his mouth and with the other holding the door open until Sarah had come through. The door shut behind the three of us and, hand over Dusty's mouth still, I said, "You give one shout and I'll knock you out. All right?"

248

He nodded against my hand and I released him. He surveyed us, pursed his lips and frowned and then shrugged his shoulders and said, "For the record, guv, what you just said is you'd break me bleedin' neck and drop me over the banisters. All right?"

I nodded and said, "Just take us down the stairs and outside. Look as though you're escorting us normally. Where's everybody?"

"Them what's up is 'aving their breakfast in the mess. You're a right little number, aren't you?" He looked at Sarah. "And you, miss. Never 'ave believed it. Ah, well, come on." He began to lead us downstairs, and it was all very simple as things are sometimes when you have the initial advantage.

We met no one all the way down. In the hallway there was a small reception cubicle with a telephone switchboard and a girl was busy at it with her back to us. We went out to the circular gravelled drive in front of the Schloss. It was the first time I'd seen it in daylight and there was a splendid granite-bowled fountain in the middle with a group of four rearing bronze horses springing from the water, and fat golden orfe moving in its depth like lazy zeppelins.

Half a dozen cars were parked on the gravel and one of them was a well-polished saloon with the ignition keys in it. I drove off with Dusty and Sarah in the back.

Dusty said, "How far you takin' me, guv?"

I said, "We'll drop you in the country somewhere, and don't hurry to find a telephone."

Glumly he said, "I don't 'urry for no one. Miss Trudi's car, this is. Boy friend keeps a garage. Looks after it like a baby."

Sarah said, "Thank her for the loan of it when you get back."

"There ain't going to be any thanks from anyone. Still, I'm used to that."

We went down the mountainside in the fresh of the morning, a silver, spear-bright morning, and if I'd been by myself I knew that I would have begun to sing, but to do so I thought would have been a little unkind to Dusty. After a little while

249

we reached the bottom of the valley and a main road which was signposted Villach and a river running to our right which was the Drau bringing back memories of my geography lessons with Miss Amberley—the real one. The Drau into the Drava, and the Drava into the Danube. We took Dusty through Villach and dropped him halfway along the road to Klagenfurt. I was rather surprised as he stood by the car door, waiting for Sarah to move up alongside me, when he put out his hand to shake mine and said, "Good luck, guv. You'll need it." Then he smiled at Sarah and said, "You're a right one. Ain't often you find a woman with a good 'ead for heights. Regular little Miss Tarzan."

We left him standing there and drove on. Sarah leaned over and kissed my ear and said, "You're very clever, Nelo. Where are we going?"

"Vienna and then a plane out of this country."

"You know the way?"

"Roughly. My mother had Austrian relations near Vienna. There was a period when Teddie and I spent holidays here when Mother made her yearly visit. My father would never come because it was right in the pheasant shooting season. If we don't get to Vienna in time to get a plane out tonight, I know a hotel where we can stay. How much money have you got? I'm down to about sixty pounds."

She said, "Haven't they paid you?"

"What do you mean?"

"*Them*. They gave me my first month's salary when I arrived at the Schloss. Four hundred pounds. That's four thousand eight hundred pounds a year. It's the best paid job I've ever had."

"You haven't got it any longer. What happened in Greece?"

"I just got off the boat and went to the hotel. After a few days a man came for me and took me to the Schloss. What happened to you?"

As I drove I told her, but from some delicate scruple which I didn't bother to rationalise I made no mention of Hortense's offer to marry me. Seeing that I was now married to Sarah it seemed an irrelevance.

We reached Vienna about six o'clock in the evening and in order to be respectable bought ourselves a suitcase, some night clothes and a few odds and ends. Then, abandoning the car in a side turning off the Philharmonikastrasse, we took a taxi to the hotel in the Stephansplatz where I had often stayed with my mother. It was a solidly built place and, except for new paint, untouched by the years. We registered under our false passports as Mr. and Mrs. Graham (none of our passports had been taken from us) and found from the desk clerk that there was no plane out for the South of France until eleven o'clock the next morning. I asked the clerk to get us a booking on that.

In our room Sarah said, "Why the South of France?"

I said, "I've got to see Monsieur Crozette. I want to sell the diamonds as quickly as possible and give the money to La Guicha. After that we can think about our own future."

Sarah said, "One can think about it, but not often arrange it. Remember Xavier? The great affair is to move."

"Xavier is a special case."

"Every human being is a special case, only some are more special than others." She came and put her arms around me and, before she kissed me, said, "Dear Nelo, please try to make me a good wife to you. Also, I should tell you that I never was married before."

So, there we were, man and wife in the eyes of God but not the law—although I intended to do something about that as soon as possible—staying in an hotel where I had often stayed as a boy. As we lay on the bed together, not making love but just lying together, I wondered, too, about the great affair of moving and whether for all her love for me and my loving concern and responsibility for her there could be a future which would bring us both happiness for happiness is a will-o'-the-wisp, the dancing *ignis fatuus* that dazzles the eyes and blinds one's steps to the boggy ground it leads one over. And I kissed her eyes and lips and she lay back on the pillow and stared at the moulded ceiling and, as though something of what I was thinking had started some cognate sentiment in her own mind, she said, "And all that stuff about my mother and father was wrong. I never knew a mother and father. I was abandoned to an orphanage at nine months and the only clue to my identity was odd woollen bootees, a pink shawl and a nightie that had seen better days. I didn't even have a name. I came from nothing and everything had to be made up. I had nothing familiar to lean on, nothing apart from myself to remember. I was wild and wilful and resentful and I ran away when I was fifteen and learned very quickly that too many people are just simply too bloody concerned with themselves. You know your family back through great-great-great-grandfathers and -mothers on the distaff and spear sides and I don't even know for sure on what day the waters broke and where I first saw the light of day. So who's to blame me if I say the great affair is to move? I never truly loved another human being until I met you. I knew it as I stood up to my knees in that pond— and it frightened me and still does because I'm so used to being underprivileged that I feel there must be a catch in it when life presents me with anything really good. Do you believe me, Nelo?"

And I said, "Of course I do." But that was for her comfort. What I really believed was that the truth about her past was always a shadow of the words she used for it, and sometimes the shadow was thrown ahead of her and sometimes behind.

She said, "You are a VERY GOOD AND TRUSTING person, Nelo."

I laughed because she said the emphasised words in the way Miss Amberley had sometimes spoken to me as a boy, though Miss Amberley's words were more often condemnatory, and I said, "Where did you learn to ride a horse so well?"

"For a while I was a stable girl. It came naturally to me. Many things do, or did, like knowing how to set a table and which knife and fork to use and how to peel a peach properly. I think I must have come from an aristocratic family, though clearly the wrong side of the blanket. They gave me the shawl back when I was much older and in one corner something had been picked away from the material, fraying it. I think possibly a coronet could have been embroidered on it."

"Or a laundry mark."

"Never."

She rolled over on top of me and held me by the ears, looking into my eyes and said, "Treat me well, you ugly, solid, single-minded man or I'll disappear on the stroke of twelve."

I kissed her and reached up for the bellpull over the bed and tugged it, and said, "You go and have a bath and change. I'll order some drinks."

She slid off the bed and performed the minor miracle which I had seen before of seeming to strip her clothes from her in one long easy movement of hands from the neck down to the feet, and I wondered from the great depth of my joy in her whether perhaps she wasn't after all a strangeling abandoned in this world by the little people but liable to be whipped away in a cloud of stardust some midnight if I did or said some clumsy thing, like the unhappy sailors who marry mermaids and forget to keep their scales wet, or leave a window open on a moonlit night of flood tide.

*　　*　　*　　*

The next morning, while Sarah still slept, I had my breakfast in the hotel dining-room as I knew she would only want a cup of coffee when she woke. On my way upstairs I picked up a day-old London newspaper, and I had just settled down with this in our small sitting-room when I was interrupted by a knock on the room door, and when I called "Come in" in walked my brother Teddie, dear Leno, whose house I had robbed and who with me, once in this very hotel, had smuggled half a bottle of Schnapps to our bedroom where we had got boisterously drunk and then been very sick and ashamed.

He shut the door behind him and stood with his back to it, a big man, a little bigger than myself, a couple of years older, my brother with the same coloured hair, though a shade thinner

253

than mine, and the same craggy boxer's face but no gleam of warm greeting in his blue eyes. He was wearing pin-striped trousers, a well-brushed black jacket, a stiff collar with a dove-grey silk tie, and he carried a bowler hat and a tightly rolled umbrella.

I stood up and cried, "Leno!"

At once he frowned and said, "For God's sake, Nelo, don't call me that."

"Teddie, then. Sorry. But what on earth are you doing here? My goodness, you look very smart in that outfit, but a bit out of place."

He sighed, the sigh of an elder brother which I was well used to, and said, "All right Nelo—we'll get the incidentals out of the way first or we'll never get anywhere. I'm wearing this because I'm going to see the Minister this morning. In fact I'm having lunch with him."

"What Minister?"

He sighed again, and said, "You'd never be any good with Parliamentary papers. The thing is to pick out the meat at once. Leave the details until last. The Minister is the Minister of the Interior, Dr. Hans Hoener. Our uncle Professor Wolfgang Hoener's son."

I said, "I'd forgotten he was in the government."

"No doubt. A fugitive has other things on his mind."

"But how did you know I was here, Teddie?"

He came forward into the room, sat down, pulled a gold case from his waistcoat pocket and lit a cigarette. "I didn't know you were here. I knew you were in Austria and I came over to find you because I'm damned well fed up with the inefficiency of the police and all these Interpol people. They couldn't find a needle in a haystack."

"Then how did you?"

"Because I had a cable addressed to the House from someone signing himself Xavier Mabluto saying you were in trouble at the Schloss Marberg near Villach and in danger of losing Mother's diamonds. You haven't lost them, have you?"

"No."

"Good. Then I'll take them back with me. This morning just by the merest chance I saw you coming out of the breakfast room. Why in God's name are you calling yourself Graham?"

"It's a long story. But why are you going to see the Minister?"

"Because I wanted some information about the Schloss Marberg before I went barging in there. Old Hoener would know the form if there was any. Anyway, I'm saved that trouble."

"You were worried about my safety?"

"Of course I was. You're my brother—even if you are a thief. And, by God, a home-wrecker. Do you know what it's cost me to put that study right? And the fireplace! Damn it, Nelo— you really did go too far."

"There was a slight over-calculation. I wonder why Xavier sent that cable?"

"For me to get you out of trouble of course and for me to get the diamonds back. Sounds like a sensible, straightforward bloke."

"He's sensible. I don't know about straightforward."

"Well, I'm not really interested in his character. And I must say, Nelo, yours seems to be going from bad to worse. Mr. and Mrs. Graham. The old man would turn in his grave."

"Father would have liked her very much. He would have welcomed her into the family."

"Into the family? Are you married?"

"In the eyes of God, yes."

He stubbed out a half smoked cigarette and rolled his eyes. "What does that mean exactly?"

"We're just waiting for the opportunity to have a civil or religious ceremony. But we have made our vows to each other."

"Why bother, my dear chap, with such a formality. Just forge a marriage certificate."

I said stiffly, "Teddie, do you want me to smack you on the ear."

"Try it. It'll be twenty years since you did and the result

255

will be the same. However, I apologise. I can see you have some feeling for her. I only hope she knows what she's landed herself with."

From the bedroom behind us Sarah's voice came clearly. "I know very well, and I'm very happy about it." I turned and saw her standing in the doorway, dressed in a plain green frock which we had bought the previous day, slim and beautiful, and wearing around her neck my mother's diamonds which I had left hidden under my pillow. She went on, "Is this your brother, Leno?"

"He likes to be called Teddie."

"Teddie," she said. "How nice to meet you." She walked to him and my brother rose—good manners had been beaten into us through our bottoms years ago by my father—and took her hand.

"It's a pleasure to meet you, Mrs. Graham," he said. "Though why you should be called Mrs. Graham I don't know. The family name—in case you don't know—is Sangster and we're all very proud of it."

"The Graham is a temporary expedient," said Sarah. "You must call me Sarah."

"As you wish," he said, a little gruffly, but I knew the gruffness. It was the lowering of register which meant he liked her.

Sarah said, "I overheard some of your conversation. It was good of you to be so concerned about Nelo's safety, though I've a feeling that Xavier cabled you because he wanted to embarrass certain people if he could. And don't fuss that Nelo has made a bad marriage. I love him and I come from a good family. My father was the Colonel of the Seventeenth-Twentyfirst Lancers and my mother was the daughter of an Irish peer. Perhaps you've heard of my brother, John Minihane? He's in the Foreign Service and is just going as Defence Attaché to—"

"Sarah," I interrupted her. "You can give my brother your credentials some other time."

I must say Teddie knew when to be gallant. He said, "You

don't need any credentials, my dear. Anyone with half an eye could see you came from the right stable. But I should warn you, you've tied yourself up with a ne'er-do-well. However, that's your business. Well, I've got a heavy morning ahead of me. I'll just take my diamonds and leave you two in bliss."

Sarah put her hand to the diamonds at her throat and looked surprised. "You mean these?"

"But of course," said Teddie. "Nelo damned well stole them from me and wrecked half my house doing it. Though I must say my wife didn't seem as upset as I expected about the marble fireplace going."

"But these are my diamonds," said Sarah. "Nelo gave them to me as a wedding present. It was his mother's dearest wish that they should go to his wife."

Teddie said to me, "You told her that, Nelo?"

"No, of course not."

"I didn't say he did," said Sarah. "I said it was your mother's dearest wish. She left you the emeralds, Teddie. What did you do with them?"

"Gave them to my wife, of course."

"And that's what she knew Nelo would do with the diamonds. It's what any mother would expect, what any mother's wish would be. Why, my own mother left my brother John a most fabulous—"

I didn't have to interrupt her. Teddie did it for me. He said, "Sarah—if any woman merited diamonds and a better husband, you do. But it so happens that those diamonds were left to me, legally, with due regard to the law. And I'm here to recover them. And let's face it, if I were fool enough to waive my claim he'd only have them off you at some time to help someone like La Guicha or some charity. Now be reasonable, please, and hand them over."

I said to Sarah, "You leave them where they are."

Teddie gave an angry grunt and said, "I only have to go down and get the police. They probably need you for other things, too."

"That's uncharitable," said Sarah.

I said, "You make a move for that door, Teddie, and I'll have another go at you, no matter what happened twenty years ago."

"You're not in such good shape as Nelo," said Sarah.

Teddie said stiffly, "Don't think that my Parliamentary duties have made me neglect my physical fitness. I could still take Nelo and break him in half, but naturally I would prefer not to do so in front of a lady and that lady my quasi-sister-in-law. Now, do I get the diamonds or do I go down and call the police?"

I said, " 'And the brother shall deliver up the brother'— even though the diamonds are morally mine?"

"And legally mine? And don't give me any of that Biblical stuff, Nelo Sangster!" He stepped forward and pushed an angry face towards me, and I knew he was really angry because—as in all our fights—he had called me Nelo Sangster.

So I pushed my face towards his as we had done as boys, two fighting cocks in a pit, and said in due form, "You need a great deal of Biblical stuff before the bowels of the saints are refreshed by thee, brother Leno Sangster."

"Right, that does it," said Teddie.

"It certainly does," I said and began to move back because I knew he was a great believer in getting the first blow in and making it tell since his fighting was a wild but effective form of brawling while mine was more classical and rule-bound, not that it had ever prevailed over his. But before he could make the first strike and before I was out of his reach a key clicked loudly in a lock. The door opened and two men stepped smartly into the room and slammed the door behind them. Teddie and I swung round and faced them.

One was short and powerfully built and dressed in a chauffeur's green livery, his high black leather boots brightly polished. He kept his peaked cap on. The other, much taller, with a thin, aquiline face, wore a deerstalker cap and a long tweed coat with a small cloak or cape over the shoulders which

258

made him look like an illustration from an old copy of the *Strand* magazine of Sherlock Holmes. My father had had a copy of every *Strand* which had carried a Sherlock Holmes story and on the day the copy had arrived in which Dr. Moriarty had pushed Holmes over the cliff to his death, he had raised the Union Jack to half mast and decanted two bottles of his best port to share with the General in the evening that they might drown their sorrows.

As the two men stood inside the door, the abruptness and discourtesy of their entry carrying a clear threat, Teddie—who was never one to beat about the bush when due formalities had been contravened—said, "Who the devil are you and what do you mean by barging in here like this?"

Sherlock Holmes in a heavily accented voice said, "You do not speak German?"

Teddie said, "No, I damned well don't!" Teddie would have rather died than speak German; lesser races and breeds without the law had to speak English or put up with it.

Sherlock Holmes said something in German to his chauffeur, and the chauffeur put his hand in his pocket and took out a piece of paper which he handed over to him. With the same movement he also brought out a short, squat looking truncheon.

Teddie said, "What the hell do you want?"

I didn't attempt to say anything because I knew my place in matters like this. Teddie was always the leader.

Sherlock Holmes consulted his paper and then looked rather puzzled at us. He said, "I want Mr. Sangster."

"What for?" asked Teddie.

"I have to take him back to the Schloss Marberg. You are perhaps Mr. Sangster?"

"There's no damned perhaps about it. I am Mr. Sangster."

Sherlock Holmes allowed himself a faint smile of approval. "Good. You fit the description given here." He consulted his paper again. "A little over six feet—"

"Six one and a half," said Teddie. (He was always proud of his height.)

"Ginger hair—"

"Red," said Teddie, and added to appease his obvious bad temper, "Damn you."

"Blue eyes and weighing about two hundred pounds." Sherlock Holmes nodded with pleasure, and went on, "Yes, it is you. Please to come with us quietly. If trouble is given, we deal with it. Hans." Hans, the chauffeur, stepped forward a little in order to be able to deal with trouble. To Sarah and myself, Sherlock Holmes made a little bow and gentle click of his ankles and said, "Apologies for any inconvenience, and please to remain in this room for fifteen minutes after our departure otherwise we are not responsible for what happens to your friend."

I said, "He's not my friend. He's my brother. I am Mr. Sangster, too. And as you will see I have red hair, blue eyes, weigh two hundred pounds and stand something over six feet tall."

"That I had noticed. But you cannot both be Mr. Sangster. Not my Mr. Sangster."

I said, "Which Mr. Sangster do you—"

"Leave this to me." Teddie interrupted me. He did not like matters taken out of his hands. To Sherlock Holmes, he said, "Are you the police, or officials of any sort?"

"Unofficially, yes, Mr. Sangster."

"Unofficially, my ass," said Teddie, and then quickly to Sarah, "I apologise my dear."

"It's all right," said Sarah. "Anyway, I agree with you."

Teddie turned back to Sherlock Holmes and said, "Produce some properly constituted warrant or authority for your presence here. If you can't—I'll give you twenty seconds to get out or be kicked out."

Sherlock Holmes consulted his paper and said, "The man I want is Mr. Charles Nelo Sangster."

"Twenty seconds," said my brother.

"It would be better if one or other identified himself," said Sherlock Holmes. "My instructions are if there is extreme

260

opposition to eliminate it." He reached into his pocket and pulled out a gun which I recognised immediately from my meeting with Robinson as a Mark Four, Nitishka chemical pistol.

Teddie said, "You mean you'd damn well shoot us? What is that peculiar thing?"

I said, "It's a chemical gun. Most lethal."

"My God," said Teddie, "you do mix in some odd circles to know that."

Sherlock Holmes said to him, "You are Mr. Charles Nelo Sangster?"

"Of course I am," said Teddie, which surprised me because I would have thought after all these years he would have lost the habit of protecting me when in trouble. It was warming to realise that the blood ties were still as strong as ever.

"Then please come with us," said Sherlock Holmes.

"All right," said Teddie. "But put that damned thing away first. It worries me."

Obligingly Sherlock Holmes pocketed the gun, which was very stupid of him because as he did so Teddie said very loudly, "Victoria Regina." (Now, there had been a period at Stonebridge Park when the village boys had given us a lot of trouble. Chiefly because Teddie had been particularly favoured by Ethel, the butcher's daughter, whom most of the village boys were courting. To walk through the village or its environs in those days had been a hazard. We were constantly being waylaid by Ethel-hungry youths, usually hunting us in pairs. Teddie who was always the master of tactics had quickly developed a set of signals for us. If there were more than two youths, he would say "Prestonpans"—though whether because he was an admirer of the Bonnie Prince Charlie or a sympathiser with Sir John Cope, I never knew—and we would run. On the other hand if there were only a couple of youths, no matter how much bigger, it would be either "Victoria Regina"—meaning I should take the right-hand one—or "Edward Rex" for me to take the left-hand one, and the moment the call was given action had to follow immediately.)

261

It did now, because instinct could not be held back and I was strong for battle. Yet also pleased that Teddie had selected the chauffeur because he looked as though he would give more trouble than Sherlock Holmes since he still had a truncheon in his hand. I threw myself forward at Sherlock Holmes in a low flying rugby tackle and took him with my right shoulder just below his left ribs and he went down in a great gasp of lost breath with me on top of him, and I held him with one hand while I pulled the gun from his pocket and skidded it across the floor to Sarah who picked it up quickly and then stepped back to watch Teddie who—Sarah informed me later—after taking a crack on the head from the truncheon had bowled the chauffeur over and was now sitting on his back on the floor holding him with a painful half nelson and a one-leg lock which I knew from experience could be very painful. Under me Sherlock Holmes showed signs of recovering so with as much charity as I felt wise I cracked his head against the floor boards and cautioned him to remain still.

After that it was very simple, largely due to the masterful way in which Teddie handled things. He was a very practical, precise man in the moment of triumph, and there was no standing against him. He ordered Sarah to rip a bedsheet into four lengths and the ankles and wrists of the two men were bound. Teddie picked up the chauffeur, carried him to the bathroom and dumped him in the bath and locked the door on him. Sherlock Holmes was carried into the bedroom and bundled into the wardrobe and the door locked on him, and then Teddie came back into the sitting-room, adjusting his tie and clothing and beamed at us both.

"I don't know where you're going or how you're going to get there. But get out of this place. I'll keep an eye on these two incompetents for an hour and then I'll go and see old Hoener and report the matter and whoever the people are at Schloss Marberg they'll have a bad time coming to them."

"Which," said Sarah, "is just what Xavier intended. Teddie, you were wonderful." She went forward and kissed him and he pretended to be embarrassed but I knew he was pleased because kissing and pretty girls had always been a passion with him.

I said, "What ever did happen to Ethel the butcher's daughter?"

He said, "She married a G.I. after the war and sends me a card every Christmas from a place called Owensboro in Kentucky." He looked at me, flapped the back of his hand against my stomach and said, "You're getting a bit slow. Want some of that off. And, for God's sake, what kind of life are you living, getting mixed up in all this sort of thing? Sarah, my dear, can't you do something about it?"

Sarah said, "It's only temporary. Until we settle down."

"Well, do that soon. And, for God's sake, get married properly. We don't want any damned permissive stuff in the Sangster family. Your children won't grow up to thank you. Oh, yes, and about the diamonds. I've been thinking—Mother would have liked you to have them, and no damned nonsense about Nelo's moral claim. They're mine, legally, and I'm giving them to you. They're yours absolutely. I'll have my lawyer draw up a deed of gift—but the gift will only operate as from the date of your legal marriage to Nelo. Sorry about that, but I wouldn't want them to leave the family . . . you know, if things didn't turn out the way you see them now."

Sarah put her arms around his neck and really kissed him and when she had finished he stepped back and said, "By God, Nelo—you've got something there. Damn good job I'm a married man. Now get packed and get off."

Which we did; taking a taxi to the airport and arriving at Nice late that afternoon and hiring a car to drive us to Monsieur Crozette's house at Beauvallon where he greeted us warmly, since I had sent him a telegram to announce our coming, and would not hear of our going to a hotel but put us in separate rooms in his house, said business could wait until the next day, and then cooked us a splendid dinner of *homard en chemise* with a *ravigote* sauce. Afterwards we sat in his conservatory with our brandy and coffee and the Arizona coral snake came out and looped itself obligingly into a colourful multibanded necklace over a shrub branch. When it was time to go to bed I went up to Sarah's room with her to say goodnight. Perhaps a little unworthily, the thought had occurred to me during the day—though I had kept pushing it away (telling myself that although I was now poor there would be no need for entreaties, or that the rich would answer roughly)—that she was Sarah and there were certain inconstancies in her of behaviour and thought, a peacock marbling of oil on the crystal waters of her true nature, which might have become more marked by the generosity of my brother in his gift to her of my mother's diamonds which were morally mine and dedicated to La Guicha. So, before I left her, I said, "Teddie's gift to you of the diamonds was very generous, noble in fact, for at heart he's a fine if quick-tempered man—but, of course, I know you will want me to sell them and give the money to La Guicha as was originally intended by me."

She considered this while taking off her dress, and then turned to me in her brassiere and pants which was a sight disturbing enough to make the matter of diamonds seem temporarily irrelevant (I had noticed lately that my love for her was acquiring a strong physical content), and said, "My darling Nelo—you've got nothing at all to worry about. . . . Remember the diamonds are not legally mine until we are legally married," and she came and put her arms around me.

Which was all I wanted to hear her say, though later in my own bed, I did wonder uncharitably whether her first sentence did not carry the implication that I had nothing to worry about *until we were legally married and the diamonds legally hers*, but then I was ashamed of myself.

* * * *

The next morning after breakfast, while Monsieur Crozette was feeding his serpents and reptiles a mixed diet of mice, alive and dead, ants, grubs, chrysalises, worms and beetles and, for a few, raw eggs still in their shells, I explained about the diamonds,

gave him a rough idea of why they were still in my possession
—a synopsis which seemed to cause him no surprise—and told
him that I wanted now to realise them speedily in order to let
La Guicha (his friend as well as mine) have the money. He
said that since *They* were so clearly interested in me it would be
necessary to keep any negotiations by him with third or fourth
parties as discreet as possible which meant that he would trust
nothing to letters, telephone calls or telegrams. He knew at
least three people who would buy them but he would have to
visit them personally to arrange it. In the meantime it would
be better if Sarah and I stayed in the villa and showed ourselves
as little as possible. Any food or supplies we needed could be
ordered by telephone from Beauvallon and, since it was a
semi-skilled job not to be trusted to us, he would have a friend
of his, a widow, who lived down the road, come in and feed
his reptiles each morning as she often did when he was away.

He left later that morning in his car and when he was gone
Sarah said, "How long will he be away?"

I said, "He's not sure. It may be a couple of days or a week
or more."

"In that case, Nelo, mightn't there be time for you to get a
special permit, a residential qualification, or whatever is
necessary so that we could be married? After all, I imagine
that to be married in the eyes of God is only all right by him
just so long as we simply can't do it any other way. You know,
like being on a desert island."

I said, dismissing the thought I immediately had that it might
be Mammon and not God she wished to pacify, "I'll make
enquiries. I'll phone *la mairie*."

"Why not go down personally now?"

"Because Monsieur Crozette says we mustn't leave the house.
You never know who might see us, and we don't want *Them*
on our tracks again."

"Well, I suppose so," she said a little grudgingly which might
have been because she was now truly longing to be a duly
certified bride and able openly to adorn herself with her jewels

and to have the unquestionable right of their disposal. But it was only a passing thought. I did ring *la mairie* and had a most unsatisfactory talk with a clerk who took umbrage because I would not give my name or any details of myself except that I wanted to be married in France, an Englishman to an English woman, though I was not sure of this last because Sarah often claimed Irish nationality even though she carried a United Kingdom passport. The clerk proceeded to be as oblique and obtuse as only clerks can when they sense they are not being accorded the trust and frankness their positions demand. Anyway, the matter had to be shelved because on the third day of his absence Monsieur Crozette phoned and asked us to take a train to Avignon and meet him there the next day and to bring the diamonds with us. He had found a customer.

So, the next day, just after noon, Monsieur Crozette met us at Avignon, enquired after our health and the well-being of his reptiles, and drove us off in a north-westerly direction, refusing to say where he was taking us, as he wanted it to be a surprise, and assuring us that it would be a happy one.

That evening just before the light went we drove down a long valley with walnut and chestnut trees fringing the meadows and here and there on the river banks the blues, yellows and reds of the tents of camping French families still reluctant to acknowledge the autumn, and then up a winding road along the sides of a great cliff bluff where we came to a château enclosed with a high wall pierced by double wrought-iron gates, flanked by Judas trees still clinging to their purple blooms, and surrounded by a parterre of small, box-hedged flower beds leading to the flighted stone steps of the château. Standing at the top of the steps were two figures I knew well: Alfy, the Bakata of Bakata, a slim, boyish, wiry figure in well-cut white trousers, dark blue blazer with the Bakata elephant crest on its pocket, and a big cigar in his mouth which he took out to shout laughing orders at three Jack Russell terriers which came yapping towards us, and with him the Archbishop of Bakata, Dr. Watsa Bomokandi, his big face beaming, teak-coloured, the evening breeze ballooning out his blue silk shirt, a straw hat on his head, and a large glass of brandy in his hand. They came down to us in a galaxy of bouncing terriers, and shouted welcomes and, when I introduced Sarah, they both shook hands with her and then Dr. Bomokandi thought better of it, kissed her on the cheek and raised his glass-free hand and pronounced a blessing on her and then on me and finally on Monsieur Crozette. We were swept into the château in the vortex of the small whirlwind which these two always seemed to create about them and when I was finally left stranded in a guest room, that was a high eyrie in a battlement overlooking the river and miles of the dusk-touched countryside, Monsieur Crozette came in to me and said, "Are you happy? I have found the best buyer in the world for your diamonds. The Bakata will give you three hundred thousand pounds for them. Think of La Guicha's joy."

Sitting on the bed, I said, "How can he? He has no money—and, anyway, you yourself previously valued them at one hundred thousand pounds."

"Don't worry. Tomorrow we will go into conference and it will all be arranged." He smiled happily, and left me and a few moments later Sarah came into the room and crossed to the window and looking out said, "You never mentioned these people before."

"It went out of my mind with other things popping in."

She said, "Why is there a man leading a small elephant round the garden?"

I said, "That is Bakatsi, the symbol of Bakata sovereignty. Wherever Bakatsi is there is Bakata."

She said, "He's very small."

I said, "He's very young."

She looked at me, smiling, and it was a warm but secret smile as though behind its open joy there lay other joys, and she said, "These are all your friends?"

"Yes."

"And is Dr. Bomokandi a real Archbishop?"

"Yes. Why?"

"Oh, I don't know. I suppose the straw hat makes it hard to believe."

* * * *

The next day there was no conference, at least not about the diamonds. While I was shaving Monsieur Crozette came in to me and said that Alfy had been called away to Paris on urgent business, but would be back the following day. Monsieur Crozette I noticed with some interest was quite a different man when he was away from his villa and his beloved serpents; no longer untidy and easy going, no longer, it seemed, affected by the heat. He was portly but crisp and favoured a neat grey suit and a blue shirt and cream-coloured tie and his unruly hair was firmly pomaded down, giving off the unmistakable orange scent of eau-de-Portugal.

After he had gone, looking out of my window I saw Dr. Bomokandi and Sarah standing on a small, hibiscus bordered lawn chatting together and feeding Bakatsi with his morning bananas. They seemed to be in good spirits and there was a deal of laughter between them and, as they turned away from the royal elephant, I saw Dr. Bomokandi, in response no doubt to some flirtatious remark of Sarah's, for she naturally fell into that manner with she liked, give her bottom a beneficent pat while still keeping his cigar in his hand.

But as I said, although there was no conference that day about the diamonds, there was one concerning another subject of almost equal importance. Indeed, no, of greater importance. I was summoned by one of the servants, they were all Bakatans, a strong young man whose gleaming teeth were white as a flock of sheep that go up from the washing as the Song says, and who wore a royal blue apron with the silver-grey elephant symbol on it, who requested me to attend upon the Archbishop in his study.

It was a small room, richly carpeted, lined with books and sporting prints. (The château—which was called La Verna— I knew by now was rented furnished by the Bakata of Bakata.)

268

There was a large morocco-leather-topped desk, a sideboard with a tantalus of spirit decanters on it, and the Archbishop sitting in a high-backed wooden armchair. He was dressed in his full vestments—the first time I had ever seen him so arrayed —and it was a splendid sight, though I am not sure that the Archbishop of Canterbury would fully have approved since there has long been argument over the ornaments of the Church and its Ministers. (My father used to make a great fuss at Stonebridge St. Mary's Church if he detected the least sign of Popery creeping in.) Personally my own views were very liberal. The good Lord's job has inevitable tediums for Him and I could never see why He should not be worshipped with every richness of song, prayer, ceremony and vestment to gladden His ear and eye. And clearly Dr. Bomokandi agreed with me as he sat there arrayed in all the liturgical colours, white, red, green, violet and black, looking like an illustration I had seen once of Cranley, the Archbishop of Dublin (died 1417), sporting mitre, amice, chasuble, maniple, dalmatic tunicle, stole, alb, gloves and caligae, and wearing the pallium over the chasuble. He gave me a big grin and said, "Not to be overcome, son. I've got a christening in half hour in the château chapel. First born of Landa the cook and Tombo Thompson, my chauffeur. First born in wedlock that is. How are you this morning?"

"I'm very well, thank you, Archbishop."

"Good, but Dr. Bomokandi not so well. His heart is heavy for you."

"Why?"

"You listen to me, man." He tapped the end of his pastoral staff on the floor and frowned. "You've got a good woman there in Miss Sarah. She's good on the eye, good on the ear, good everywhere, I guess, but her heart is not so good. Her heart's heavy with sorrow for you don't marry her yet in the eyes of God—that's okay when circumstances can't be fought —but you know as well as me every woman wants to make it legal, to make it stick, and so does the church. So why so dilatory?"

"But I'm not, Archbishop."

"You sure are. The good Lord's going to put another mark in His book against you, if you don't look out. Why you not tell me last night to arrange things? For me that is simple as Archbishop First Church of Bakata. All marriages in our church, no matter nationalities, accepted legal by all civil authorities, and canonical by all branches of Christian churches everywhere. You got racist feeling about it, man? because if you have your heart's not pure."

I said, "You know I haven't, Archbishop."

"I'm right away glad to hear it." He reached out to a box on the desk, took a cigar, propped his staff between his knees, and lit his cigar. Then he went on, "You love her?"

I said, "I want to marry her."

"Not always same thing. You love her?"

"Yes, I suppose you would call it that. Personally, I think it's more a compound of—"

He tapped his staff hard, and said, "Son, are you one of those who like to eat the fruit and then walk away from the tree?"

"I want to marry her, to make her my wife and to cherish and protect her for the rest of my life."

He nodded. "That's good. Any woman with sense will settle for that. Tomorrow morning eleven o'clock in the chapel. I make a special dispensation. You want the word *obey* in the service?"

"Only if she does."

"She doesn't. Marriage is no slavery with the man top cock giving orders. Well, that's fine. His Royal Highness the Bakata of Bakata will give her away since she has no parents, and you pay him fifty pounds."

"What for?"

"Bride money. Equal two cows. You're getting her cheap, man, seeing she has no parents. Also we find best man for you somewhere. Not to worry about that. Also you fast"—he looked at the study wall clock which showed eleven—"for twenty-four hours."

270

I said, "Is that necessary?"

"Under rules of First Church of Bakata, yes. Bride and bridegroom come clean, inside and out, to ceremony. Man, I am happy for you both." He stood up, put the head of his staff on my left shoulder, raised his hand and blessed me briefly and then said, "Must get to the christening. If we keep Landa waiting we don't get any lunch today."

He went, and as I wasn't going to have any lunch anyway, I helped myself to one of his cigars, which I saw were large Bolivar Coronas, specially rolled from the finest Havana leaf for His Royal Highness the Bakata of Bakata, a label on the box said, and then poured myself a large neat whisky from a tantalus decanter, smoked and drank, and stood staring out of the window at a heron that was stiffly poaching gold fish from a lily pond in a far lawn and wondered why—although I wanted to marry Sarah, had vowed to and in no way regretted my vow—I had the feeling that there was the meagre, flitting shadow of a conviction in me that the whole thing was a little too precipitate. We belonged to each other in the eyes of God, making now a legal contract in the eyes of the Church and the State seemed no occasion for indecent haste. However, I had no time to follow this line of thought for Sarah came running into the room and into my arms before I could put down cigar or drink, held me and kissed me and then swung me round so that I sprayed whisky over the carpet, and cried, "Darling, Dr. Bomokandi's just told me the marvellous news. Oh, it was clever of you to think of it, and don't think I'll let you down. The maid I've got here is wonderful with her hands and says she's got some white organdy or satin or something so you'll have a proper bride and there's even some orange blossom still out in the garden. And doesn't he look splendid in all his get-up? It'll be just the kind of marriage I've always wanted."

I said, "I will do everything in my power to be the kind of husband you want. But you'll have to lend me fifty pounds for the bride money."

"Of course I will."

"Also we have to fast for twenty-four hours."

"Darling, I know. That's why I had an enormous breakfast." She smiled. "Some instinct told me that you might think of this, so I had a little chat with the Archbishop about it in the garden this morning." She kissed me, and went on, "Now I must go and phone Teddie and tell him the good news. Will he be at the Houses of Parliament?"

I said, "It's Saturday and the partridge shooting season. You'll get him at six o'clock this evening at his home. Why do you want to tell him?"

She looked at me with surprised, green and amber, pool-shadowed eyes and said, "But he's your brother. We've got to let your family know."

CHAPTER FIFTEEN

So, THE NEXT morning at eleven o'clock we were married in the small chapel of the château, and the day was the 16th Sunday after Trinity, the day of St. Michael and all Angels, and the day before the one on which Calais was reoccupied in 1944 which was a day I remembered well—I was about fourteen at the time and still on holiday from school. My father had come back from partridge shooting with the General and they had lit a bonfire in the stableyard to celebrate the event and a strong north-easterly wind had taken it out of hand and one of the lofts with a store of that year's hay had caught fire and burned down and it had taken my father a year of wrangling with the insurance company to get his compensation from them.

My best man was Xavier Mabluto, who had returned from Paris with the Bakata of Bakata, bringing with him a hired morning suit for the occasion, alerted, he said, by a telephone call from the Archbishop. He came into my room before the ceremony to have his cravat adjusted and for me to approve his outfit.

I said, "What happened about the industrial diamonds?"

He said, "Nelo, on this happiest of days for you I am happy to tell you that my troubles are receding. I got twenty-two thousand pounds for them, sent two thousand to La Guicha and have bought myself into the Royal Kingdom of Bakata as head of all the Secret Services and Internal Security."

I said, "All you lack now is the kingdom in which to operate."

"That," he said, "will come eventually. Did your brother come to the Schloss Marberg?"

"No—we escaped. But we met him in Vienna. However, he knows the Austrian Minister for Home Affairs and there could be trouble at the Schloss."

"Some, but I have no doubt they will come to an arrangement. Some Austrian quid which will be bargained for their quo." He gave me a long look, and then went on, "You know, I have come to the conclusion that you are the kind of man who needs to be married. You need someone to control your impulsive habits, to temper your rose-coloured innocence, and to manage your affairs. Sarah is just the girl."

I said, "I thought it was the other way around."

"Oh, no. That girl has her feet firmly on the ground and her head well screwed on. Nelo, you have found a treasure."

I didn't argue further, and I pushed from me the growing gaggle of uncharitable thoughts and doubts which had arisen in the last two days, and I went to the altar with him to await Sarah and our nuptials, clean inside and out, and with happiness in my heart because I knew that my kind of love for her was the rock she needed beneath her feet and there was now an eagerness in me that this solid foundation should be acknowledged openly and lawfully by all.

The chapel was filled with the servants and all the members of the exiled Royal household, all dressed in their finery and uniforms so that the narrow, grey walled building rioted with colour and the women's hats waved and stirred in a gentle breeze of expectancy and pleasure. And finally Sarah came in leaning on the arm of the Bakata of Bakata who wore the uniform of a Field Marshal in the Bakatan army, pale blue with gold epaulettes and a high red shako from which sprang a bursting plume of ostrich feathers; and Sarah, herself, was dressed in a sheath of white silk, sewn about her body like a skin (and caught under the armpits as she showed me later with safety pins), her hair wreathed and entwined with orange blossom and white geraniums, a veil framing her lovely face and falling over her shoulders, her jade and amber eyes shining, her hands holding a bouquet of small-budded white roses fringed with a feathering of yellow-centred horse daisies while from her left shoulder, and diagonally across her breast, fell a wide purple sash terminating in a silver tassel. This was I learned a little later, the Order of the Purple Bakati, one of the highest civil orders a Bakatan woman, or friend of Bakata, could be awarded. In the centre of the sash between her breasts, hung on a gold chain, was a silver miniature of the Royal elephant. Alfy had awarded her with it that morning. They came in, first to a blast of trumpets and a roll of drums from four Bakatan musicians who were in a small minstrels' gallery at the back of the chapel and, as the noise of their fanfare died, Monsieur Crozette (a man of many and mostly hidden talents) at a small organ to one side of the altar began to play "Here Comes the Bride" in quite a lively fashion. As pages, holding the rather short train of Sarah's gown, came the two, born-out-of-wedlock, children of Landa and Tombo Thompson, a boy of eight and a girl of seven, dressed in miniature uniforms of the Bakatan army, while for bridesmaid she had her own dress-making maid in traditional Bakatan costume—I was told afterwards—of a high, gaily coloured turban and a flowing cotton red gown printed all over with replicas of the labels of world famous hotels.

So we stood before the splendid figure of the Archbishop and made our vows and bowed our obeisance, and the ring was blessed and I put it on the fourth finger of Sarah's left hand and then the whole chapel sang the *Beati omnes*. . . . Thy wife shall be as the fruitful vine; upon the walls of thy house; Thy children like the olive branches; round about thy table . . . and so on through the ceremony with the powerful voice of the Archbishop pouring over us. . . . For this cause shall a man leave his father and mother, and shall be joined unto his wife; and they two shall be one flesh . . . until with drums and trumpets and organ hammering away in a great paean of sound I led Sarah, my wife, out of the chapel to the Wedding March. We were showered with Bakatan rice all the way to the wedding feast which was set on tables in the mellow autumn sunlight

275

and there were toasts and speeches, a cake to cut, and food and drink to be taken and a telegram of congratulations from Teddie and his wife to be read, and also one from the General whom Teddie must have informed; and a small Bakatan band played for us and their dancers danced and the Royal elephant wandered free amongst us, reaching a slim trunk over our shoulders to help himself from the table and was made to return the largesse later by giving the children rides on his back, and the Archbishop, divested of his robes, wandered amongst us, cigar and brandy glass in hand, and scattered blessings and laughter from the richness of his store, and Alfy, the Bakata, screwing his monocle more tightly in his left eye, joined the dancers for the one dance he was by tradition allowed to join, the Royal Dance of the Elephant, and he pirouetted, stamped, charged and leaped until the battered plumes of his shako began to droop and one fluttered to the ground like a large, limp snowflake.

At the end of the day we were led to a fine double suite in a wing of the château and as the sound of drums and trumpets rolled away down the corridor to rejoin the dancing and singing that still went on outside, we both fell exhausted on the large bed while outside the bats cut through the purple night air and I wondered how my father would have taken it all and knew that to begin with he would have been critical of certain procedures but his criticisms would have evaporated before the explosive joy of the Bakatans and the champagne and nothing would have stopped him joining the Elephant Dance (for he had a peculiar, almost mystical reverence for these animals), and he would have been happy that I was married because, despite his friendship with the General, he was condemnatory of bachelorhood; and as for my mother, the day would have held no flaw because her love for people was simple and true and no matter how strange a custom or behaviour that sprang from joy and celebration she embraced it gladly knowing that virtue and truth wear many guises.

So Sarah and I lay together that night, in happy tiredness

and gentle love, and woke early in the morning to a passion like the sun breaking the horizon and when we were spent we lay in harmony, our fingers just touching, and from outside a thrush in a poplar began a long, sobbing glorious song of delight in the never failing miracle of morning.

But harmony is not a constant state for even the most blessed of mortals.

Over breakfast in our room, one of the servants said that the Bakata would like to have a conference with us at ten o'clock that morning.

I said to Sarah, "I can't think how he can pay three hundred thousand for the diamonds. I know for a fact that he is short of funds, and the French government only make him a small grant for household expenses."

"A king," said Sarah, "can always find ways."

"But why does he want them? I mean, it savours of the imprudent. The diamonds are no use to him."

"Darling, why ask me these questions? He'll explain later this morning." She put apricot preserve on a buttered croissant and handed it to me. "Just coffee isn't good for you. You must eat to keep up your strength." For a moment she sounded just like the real Miss Amberley.

*   *   *   *

The conference took place in the château's library. We sat on hard, gilt-legged tapestried chairs around a long table. From above the marble fireplace, in much better taste than Teddie's, a gentleman in a seventeenth-century peruke eyed us darkly from his golden frame. At the head of the table in a striped, double-breasted grey suit and Guards' tie sat Alfy, looking very businesslike. At the bottom of the table in gaiters and black habit sat Dr. Bomokandi wrapped, I thought, in the gloom of a hangover (a state that should have been mentioned in that verse of the Psalms that says "And wine that maketh glad the heart of man"). Sarah sat on Alfy's right hand and, as a compliment to him, was wearing her Order of the Purple

Bakati, and I sat on his left hand and below us, one on each side, were Monsieur Crozette, neat and crisp and gently glowing with quiet importance, and Xavier still in his wedding morning dress to which he had taken so much a fancy that I doubted whether the Paris hire firm would ever see it back. Dead in the centre of the table laid out on a piece of black velvet were my mother's diamonds.

Alfy called the meeting to order, took out his monocle, polished it and forgot to put it back and said to Xavier, "Be damned good of you, Colonel, if you'd kindly take the minutes of the meeting and all that sort of thing."

I said, "When did Xavier become a Colonel?"

Alfy said, "Courtesy rank always held by the Head of the Secret Service in Bakata. Now then, the first item on the agenda is the matter of the purchase of Mr. Charles Nelo Sangster's diamonds."

"And the only item, I hope, Alfy," said Dr. Bomokandi, coming to life a little.

"Correction," said Sarah. "They are the diamonds of Mrs. Charles Nelo Sangster. It's important to be legally precise. The deed of gift is already in the post to me."

"My apologies, Sarah," said Alfy.

I said, "What's the point of bothering with these quibbles, Alfy? I don't see how you can possibly afford to buy the diamonds. And far less can I see why you want them."

Monsieur Crozette said, "Don't rush things, Nelo."

"He always did and he always will," said Xavier.

Alfy said to Sarah, "Just to avoid confusion, old dear, do you mind if we address ourselves direct to your husband in this matter as though he were the owner of the diamonds legally?"

"But of course," said Sarah. "But I'll have to sign any contract."

Dr. Bomokandi nodded and said, "Good girl," and put a cigar in his mouth but did not light it.

Alfy screwed his monocle back and smiled at me. "Nelo," he said, "you want to sell the diamonds?"

278

"Yes, I do—to give the money to La Guicha."

"Charity can be overdone," said Dr. Bomokandi.

"Not to La Guicha," I said.

"Come to order," said Xavier.

Alfy said, "Steady on, Colonel. I'm the one running the meeting."

"My apologies, Your Highness," said Xavier.

Sarah said, "I am entirely in agreement with my dear husband about La Guicha."

"Harmony," said Dr. Bomokandi. "Marriage was ordained for the mutual society, help and comfort that the one ought to have of the other. Yes, sir. And it's good to see it working so soon." He lit his cigar and allowed himself a half glance at a far sideboard on which decanters, bottles and glasses were arrayed.

I said to Monsieur Crozette, "You're the expert. How much are the diamonds worth?"

Monsieur Crozette fingered his chin delicately and said, "Give or take a bit, around one hundred thousand pounds."

"Then that is all I want for them," I said. "There is no joy in making an exorbitant profit out of friends."

Alfy said, "Jolly decent of you. But we wouldn't dream of it. We will give you three hundred thousand."

"We insist," said the Archbishop.

"But why?" I asked.

Xavier gave a little cough to draw Alfy's attention, and said to him, "With your permission, Your Highness, perhaps you would allow me to explain things to Nelo?"

"Go ahead," said Alfy.

Xavier stood up, gave a little double tug to the lapels of his coat, cleared his throat and beamed at me and said, "My dear Nelo, all of us here are men of the world—with the exception of Sarah, of course, who is one of the most beautiful, worthy, generous and capable ladies it has been my pleasure to meet for a very long time . . ." He paused, no doubt for us all to appreciate how the mantle of office so well fitted him,

279

and then went on, "You, Nelo, have raised some pertinent points and of course they must be answered before any contract of sale can be drawn up. One, it is true of course that His Highness—"

"Strictly, old chap, Royal Highness, but don't fuss over it," said Alfy.

"His Royal Highness, of course," corrected Xavier. "One, then; it is true that the Royal purse at this moment is hard put to meet normal demands. Inter alia, I may say, the wedding feast and etceteras will be a big additional strain on it. Nevertheless, His Royal Highness wishes to buy the diamonds and certainly wouldn't consider only giving one hundred thousand pounds for them—even if he had it."

"Then how the devil can he give three hundred thousand pounds for them?" I asked.

Monsieur Crozette gave a gentle sigh and the Archbishop said, "You almost too naïve, man."

I said, "Naïvety is one thing, but arithmetic is another. How can he pay that money for them?"

Sarah smiled at me and said, "Don't get impatient, darling. Listen to what Xavier has to say."

Xavier went on, "Nelo—in the world of business you are a child. Do you think that all men of position, financiers, manufacturers and so on always have the ready money to buy the things they need in order to survive, to keep their businesses running? No. What they have to have is assets, assets of goodwill, brains, financial foresight and privy information about good things coming in the near future. They are men ready to throw their miserable crusts on the turbulent waters of life knowing that in the fullness of time whole bakeries, flour mills and grain loading wharfs will come floating back to them. Do you think any man temporarily out of funds has ever held back from buying ten thousand shares in a tipped-off company when he well knows that he can sell at a profit before settling day?"

"Good simile," said Alfy.

"Metaphor," corrected the Archbishop.

"Neither," I said. "And anyway, don't talk to me about company shares. I've had some experience."

"I was talking, son," said the Archbishop, "about Xavier's penultimate remark. It's a metaphor." He got up and wandered to the far sideboard.

I said, "I wish someone would come straight to the point."

To my surprise Sarah did. "It's simple, Nelo. We hand the diamonds over to Alfy . . . I mean His—"

"Don't bother, old girl," said Alfy.

"We hand the diamonds over to Alfy," said Sarah. "And he sells them for one hundred thousand pounds."

"And then what?"

"And then he uses that money for political purposes which within a few months, maybe even weeks, will result in his triumphant return to Bakata where he will be reinstated as king."

"Not reinstated," said Alfy. "Wherever Bakatsi is, there is the Kingdom and the King of Bakata. But I know what you mean."

"And," said Sarah, "when he's back in Bakata he will pay us three hundred thousand pounds."

Monsieur Crozette said, "One hundred and fifty thousand pounds in cash, and the rest in trading concessions and the allocation of mineral and development rights which will be as good as cash because you can sell them to the companies which will be lining up to buy them."

"That way," said Xavier, "you will end up by having one hundred thousand to give to La Guicha, and two hundred thousand for yourself and Sarah to begin married life on."

I said, "The whole thing is highly speculative."

"Man," said the Archbishop, a full brandy glass now in his hand, "you don't speculate none, you don't accumulate none. Even the good book says—"

I said crossly, "For every one thing the good book says there is almost always another that contradicts it."

"My son," said the Archbishop, "as a debating point that

281

interests me, but as a fact, why it's damned heresy. However, let's make nothing of it."

I stood up and addressed myself to Alfy, "May I have the floor."

"Anything you want," said Alfy.

I said, "As I understand it, what you want me to do is to make a loan of the diamonds to you, so that you can cash them and use the cash to finance a return to Bakata. If this is successful you will then make available for me a sum, variously constituted, of three hundred thousand pounds?"

"In a coconutshell," said the Archbishop.

"Precise. Succinct," said Xavier.

"So it may be," I said. "But there are other aspects. I don't know what arrangements you would make for the return to Bakata, or what the political and military position is there—but I do know that in a venture of that kind no man can possibly guarantee success."

"In any business venture that offers big profits, Nelo," said Xavier, "there is always risk. But in this one very little indeed."

"A cloud, my son," said Dr. Bomokandi, "not as big as a monkey's paw."

"Nevertheless," I said, "there is risk. And I do not feel at liberty to take it. I want to be sure that La Guicha gets her money. She needs it for her work."

"You could make your ultimate contribution to her two hundred thousand if you wished," said Monsieur Crozette.

"Two birds in the pot feed more than one," said the Archbishop. "La Guicha will bless you for ever more."

"But she may end up getting nothing."

Alfy said, "There's no chance of a slip up over the return to Bakata, old man. Later, I'll go into the details of the set up over there. For the moment let me say that as soon as I turn up with Bakatsi and a few odds and ends the place will be mine again. The real crunch at the moment is to agree in principle to the arrangement. Think, too, of your slice of the cake. You and Sarah will be set up for life. You can buy a farm or a business or just live the life of O'Reilly."

I said, "My own future is of no importance against the risk of La Guicha's not getting her money. I don't think it would be moral to take such a gamble when the lives, welfare and futures of hundreds of needy, distressed children are in the balance. And I'm sure that Sarah would agree with that. Wouldn't you, Sarah?" I looked across at her.

She smiled back at me and said, "Not entirely."

"Why on earth not?"

"For two reasons, Nelo. One, in this life everything is at risk, and La Guicha well knows this. She takes risks every day to get what she wants for the children. She gambles her own skills and resources against their happiness every day. You know that. I'm certain that if I telephoned her and explained the proposition she would accept it at once. Would you like me to do that?"

"No. Anyway, what is the second point?"

"Son," said the Archbishop, "you got a good wife there. St. Paul would be proud of her."

"The second point," I said.

"It's purely legal, darling," said Sarah. "The diamonds are mine and utterly at my disposal and I have to think, also, for both of us. You're my husband, but you have a certain, well . . . indifference to the facts of life, like a house to live in, groceries to buy, and insurance premiums to meet so . . . well, a good wife takes up the slack left by her husband. You're my husband and my lover, and I love you deeply, but you are also, in many ways, a small, irresponsible boy that I have to look after. La Guicha needs money and we need money to start our married life properly. My father always said that true bliss is a large share portfolio and an eye for a good horse and—"

I said, interrupting her, "You want us to agree to this?"

"Yes, Nelo, I do."

"Well, I don't."

"Nelo, we are having our first quarrel—and in public?"

"I'm sorry. But I must say you're the last person I would

have expected to care about money for the future."

She said gently, almost modestly, "For myself alone I would have no care, Nelo. Nor would you for yourself alone. But we are married, and when a woman marries she changes and has a new vision of life."

"Damn right," said Dr. Bomokandi. "But it always takes a man longer to get used to keeping his feet under the table."

I said to her, "You really want to do this and you genuinely feel it's the right thing to do?"

"I do, Nelo. And though I don't like to overstress it, the diamonds are mine and I think we should make the contract with His Royal Highness."

I said, "Would you make it even if I disagreed?"

She said, "Yes, Nelo. For your good, for our good, and for the good of La Guicha—to whom by the way I think we should give one hundred and twenty-five thousand eventually because after all she is taking part of the risk and should have some reasonable profit. But there's no need for us to disagree, is there? I'm sure you see it my way, darling."

I said, "I understand your concern for us and our future and that legally you can go over my head and sign the contract, but I wouldn't like that to happen. But this is what will have to happen, unless I get one assurance, and if I do then I'll agree."

"And what's that, old chap?" asked Alfy.

"You can have the diamonds if La Guicha is prepared to take the risk. I couldn't agree without that."

Xavier stood up and beamed. "I always said you would stick on that point, Nelo. But don't worry. I've seen La Guicha and she agrees. Here. Read this." He pulled a letter from his pocket and handed it across to me.

It was from La Guicha, written in green ink, and read:

Nelo, your nice friend Xavier has been to see me with the B——a proposition (I'm already well on the way to realising my claim to his estate here in Switzerland, but what a tangle!) and I entirely agree about the diamond arrangement. God will keep an eye on things for

His little ones, just as He always has done. But it has to be one hundred and fifty thousand pounds to me, and we will call our new place the Sangster Clinic, and also I must have an annual contribution from the new government of two thousand pounds a year and the right to put our collection boxes in all banks, post offices and public buildings in perpetuity. I thought that Sarah girl would make an honest man of you. Mille baisers. La Guicha.

I said to Sarah, "Have you seen this letter?"

"No."

I handed it to her.

Xavier said, "I kept it by me as a form of insurance. The rest of us have seen it, and His Royal Highness agrees to the conditions."

"Absolutely," said Alfy.

The Archbishop said, "There are many distressed and parentless children in Bakata; she can have her pick of them. You can come with us in charge of medical supplies and relief food and select a few for her."

Sarah handed the letter back to me and said, "Well, you must be satisfied now, Nelo. And as far as I'm concerned she can have one hundred and fifty thousand pounds. . . ."

I said to Alfy, "Very well, Your Royal Highness, I agree."

"First class, old man," said Alfy, and then added, "No more business on the agenda this morning. Conference in the War Room, ten-thirty tomorrow. Put you right in the picture, Nelo. But remember, from now on all our plans are top security. Officially the French don't want us to go—though they'll shut an eye to anything we do. But there are quite a few other interested parties who'd like to queer our pitch. Now then, what about a few drinks, eh?"

I said, "Thank you, no, Your Royal Highness. I think I'll take a little walk."

Which is what I did, through the grounds and along the top of the great bluff that overhung the river and the road where the swallows were gathering on the telephone wires in small

285

cohorts waiting for the signal to migrate southwards, just as the Bakatans in the château were waiting no doubt; and I wasn't very happy because I was a little confused and unable to see my way clearly to the truth of things. Sarah was taking the business of marriage quite seriously, and had changed, and I was worried that the change was concerned less with being married than of becoming a rich married woman. I had married her basically because her love for me, simply, directly and passionately declared, increased her volatility and her disorientation and I had felt, over and above my passion and deep, tender affection for her, that I was the kind of man who could truly dedicate himself to her welfare and comfort and protection. But in a few hours the brilliant rainbow shift of her nature had steadied to the glowing maturity of capable wifehood. In a sense, by marrying her, I had made the job of marriage redundant, for it had changed her in the moment (or maybe a little before) of its celebration. She would have signed the contract had I disagreed and inevitably this would have made some emotional and intellectual change in me. But for the moment, I decided, no hasty judgments should be made. She was my Sarah, and my cherishing and care for her still were unbounded, my joy in her now merely slanted along a different bias and her love for me no longer solely the mystical and physical passion of a woman for a man but growthy now with a merging maternalism. And this was made clear when I got back to our room, for the first thing she said after embracing and kissing me was, "You didn't go off sulking, did you?" reminding me of the real Miss Amberley, for as a boy I was a great one for sulking if I didn't get my own way and had my own special sulking place—unlike Teddie who used to lock himself in the lavatory—in the crook of an old oak that overhung the river where I used to huddle and watch the caterpillars spin down to the water on their silk life lines while the trout and grayling patrolled below.

I said, "No, I haven't been sulking. I've just been adjusting. And I'm sorry if I've been obtuse or stubborn."

286

"Darling, you never could be. We both know what we want and there's never going to be any quarrel between us." She put her arms around me and so spontaneous was the gesture and so loving the warmth of her lightly clad body against mine that passion, provoked a little perhaps by a desire for true reconciliation through the body which is the ultimate channel of love, stirred strongly in me and I lifted her to carry her to the bed, but she shook her head and said, "Oh, no, darling, not now. There's no time before lunch."

I said firmly, "The bed can be our table and we can feast on love, and anyway there's a good half hour yet before the gong goes."

*   *   *   *

They had turned the billiard room into the War Room, taking down the cue racks and the marker so that one wall was free for a large run of detailed maps of Bakata which were studded with little coloured flags and pinned-down stretches of red tape outlining various strategic areas and offensive lines. The billiard table itself—without any protection for the green baize cloth, which would have sent my father up in the air at the sacrilege—was covered with a relief model of Bakata in multi-coloured clays with tiny model trees and woods, and bridges and airports and main towns. The room was in the charge of an aide-de-camp in full army uniform and a Bakatan young girl in a green silk blouse and black mini-skirt who kept the flags and tapes up to date on the wall maps as information came in from Bakata by whatever ways it did come in. Colonel Xavier Mabluto already had the information network firmly in hand, and it was he—at the request of the others—who briefed me about the past and present position in Bakata, though in the end I retained only a very general idea as I am not very good with maps and had never—to my father's despair —quite mastered the difference between a battalion and a brigade or a corps and a company.

Broadly, so far as the past history was concerned, I under-

287

stood that owing to a certain intransigence on Alfy's part over some aspect of Bakata's joining the Central African Federation, certain great powers (annoyed by this and for political and commercial reasons—Great Britain being one of them) had engineered a palace revolution—headed by one of his nephews, now the recognised (by the interested powers) ruler of Bakata, and Alfy had had to flee the country with a handful of supporters but leaving behind a considerable element of faithful army and civilian supporters to carry on a guerrilla and commando struggle against the new ruler's forces. Alfy's supporters lately had been achieving a few limited successes, and controlled about a third of the country. That part, I may say, which was mostly composed of mountains and jungle so that the commercial and economic life of the rest of the country was little affected. But they did hold one town of minimum importance—since it had on its outskirts a small airstrip—called Sokota.

France, again for her own good political and power reasons, had offered Alfy asylum and a small grant for the upkeep of his establishment on the understanding (not to be taken too seriously so long as he was discreet about it) that he conducted no active moves while on her soil that could be construed as prejudicial to the new regime in Bakata.

"Actually," said Xavier, "so long as she can show a clean pair of hands, France would welcome His Royal Highness back on the throne."

That, sketchily, was the history of the affair. As for the present position it was even sketchier. Alfy, through an organisation known as the Friends of Bakata, had raised quite a lot of money for the purchase of arms and equipment to supply his loyal supporters in the homeland, and they had made some small progress, culminating in the capture of Sokota. But now the funds had run out and the Friends of Bakata had no more money to offer. However, secretly conducted opinion polls throughout the country, carried out, Xavier hinted, by the American C.I.A. for reasons they were more than reluctant to reveal, had shown that the whole country was ripe for Alfy's return (so long as he brought the Royal elephant Bakatsi with him) because ever since the elephant had left the country there had occurred a series of catastrophes which could only be ascribed to the direct intervention of some angry power. A plague of locusts had devastated the crops in one section, a river dam supplying hydro-electric power had collapsed two weeks ago, an earthquake had destroyed a small town and, more seriously, had caused the collapse of a viaduct over which ran the main railway line from the capital to the coast, a virulent epidemic of skin boils was defying the meagrest of medical resources in the north and there had been other signs and portents which had made the populace ripe for Alfy's return. The only impediment so far had been that his supporters, running short of ammunition, insisted that his return would be fruitless unless he brought ammunition for them and also a good supply of medicines and food as a goodwill gesture in view of the crop failure and the plague of skin boils. To do all this, to hire two large transport planes and buy the ammunition and other supplies Alfy had needed two hundred thousand pounds. He had already raised—Xavier did not state how—eighty thousand pounds here and there, another twenty thousand from Xavier, and now would have a hundred thousand pounds from my diamonds. In fact, I—or Sarah and I—would be listed among the saviours of Bakata. (Thinking it over, later, although I have no personal love for orders and decorations, I thought that with any lesser man than myself it might have been a diplomatic mistake to have given Sarah so promptly the Order of the Purple Bakati and ignored me since she had me to thank for the diamonds.)

"So you see, Nelo, old man," said Alfy, "with the money from the diamonds we shall soon be all ready to go. We land at Sokota with ammunition and supplies, and, of course, the Royal elephant Bakatsi and the country will rise. Most of it, anyway. That part which does not we shall deal with."

"And when does all this happen?" I asked.

"Say two weeks," said Xavier. "The orders for ammunition and supplies and the planes went out some days ago."

"Before you knew we were going to let you have the diamonds?"

"Intelligent anticipation," said the Archbishop, "is a rare gift with some folks, but every Bakatan is born with it."

So it might be, but it was so also with Xavier and Monsieur Crozette. I was not deceived. I understood now that long before I knew it I was being gathered into their hands and controlled and manipulated and, no doubt, it was they who had raised and nurtured the mild shoot of cupidity and wifely foresight in Sarah without my knowledge. However, I decided to make no point of it.

I said, "Well, I wish your project every success. But now that Sarah and I have made our contribution, I think we shall go to La Guicha and offer our services to her. She can always do with help."

Xavier said, "You mean leave the château?"

"Of course."

Xavier shook his head. "You can't do that, Nelo."

"Why on earth not?"

"For two reasons. The first, security. And as Head of Bakatan security I have to give that priority. A few loose words from you or Sarah anywhere near a stewpot of intelligence like Geneva could wreck the whole scheme. Think, the news would leak—if openly, the French would have to deny all knowledge and then clamp down on us to show their solidarity with the other powers. If the leak were passed secretly to Bakata—well, we might find a reception committee waiting for us and the whole scheme would go sky high, including my future career and the laudable aspirations of His Royal Highness for his unfortunate country."

"Bakata," said Alfy, "needs me."

"And the second reason," I asked Xavier.

"Well, Nelo, don't disappoint us. We all naturally assumed that you and Sarah would be coming with us."

"I really can't think why. We have our own life to make elsewhere."

"Where better," said Dr. Bomokandi, "than in Bakata?" Absently he fiddled with his finger in the loose sand of a river bed on the contour map. "Particularly," he went on, "since your wife can't wait."

"Can't wait to go to Bakata?"

"Absolutely," said Alfy. "I've offered her the post of Minister of Arts and Culture and she's very keen."

"But she doesn't know anything about Art or Culture."

"Irrelevant," said the Archbishop. "Seven-eighths of the population in Bakata don't either."

"The position, Nelo," said Xavier, "carries a salary of five thousand a year and an official residence."

"You can't let her go alone, old fellow," said Alfy.

"But what would I do there? I mean . . ."

They all looked at me and smiled, Alfy tapping his teeth with the edge of his monocle and the Archbishop showing his with a cigar clenched in them. Then he slowly withdrew the cigar and said to the others. "Shall I tell him?"

"Do that," said Alfy. "After all it is your province."

The Archbishop flexed his shoulders and then reached out and grasped my shoulder in a manly fashion, giving me a firm shake. He said, "My son . . . you're a man of fine character. Maybe in the past you pursued the Lord's work in an un-orthodox way, but your heart is right there. You think after all my years in the Ministry—starting altar boy in a Roman Catholic mission is true, but I soon changed to the true Church—that I don't read human nature like any Bakatan reads a lion track? No sir. Last day or so you been saying perhaps 'Why they lay net for my innocent feet? Why they give honour to wife before husband? Why turn wife into weapon against husband?' But also—because you're a fine, Christian man—you been saying, 'The Lord's will be done. He will make all things clear.' And, my son, He does—through His servant Dr. Bomokandi, Archbishop of First Church of

Bakata. Through your diamonds you make Bakata great again, put Alfy—His Royal Highness here—back where he belongs, but also the good Lord will reward you too, for He knows your heart is sad since you been kicked out of His service. Me, also I am sad about this. I pray for you, ever since we first met. Mighty prayer, sometimes right down on my knees, and the good Lord He gave me the sign and the go-ahead word at last. Welcome back the prodigal, He says, in my name, in my service, to fight the good fight once more under His banner. My son, I am going to reordain you into the Church, into the First Church of Bakata, and you're going to have a big parish in our finest seaport where there is less malaria almost than in the capital. You are coming back to your true vocation, cleansed of sin. Tomorrow we do it in the chapel. Eleven-thirty sharp."

I said, "But you can't do that." I couldn't think why, but it sounded like a cry of despair. But possibly it was just confusion or shock.

"Why not?"

"Well, to begin with I don't think, in fact I know, you won't find any service for the reordaining of priests in the Prayer Book."

"A quibble. We just rejig the existing ordaining service. My chaplain can do that in two shakes. And if I got the good Lord's message wrong and He objects while we're fixing you up . . . well, that in His gracious and loving hands. Amen."

"And you and Sarah can fly in to Sokota with us, old chap," said Alfy. "Right on the spot, ready to take up your duties." He turned to the Archbishop and said, "Bomo, my dear man, you must excuse me from the reordaining service, but Colonel Xavier and I have to go to Paris tomorrow on business. But I'll see Bakatsi is there to stand in for me."

"Certainly, Your Royal Highness, but that royal elephant's got to be held. Can't have him wandering around everywhere."

His Royal Highness, the King of Bakata, came up to me, his

thin, aristocratic face shining like oiled ebony and grasped my hand. "Nelo," he said, "this must be one of the happiest moments of your life."

I gave him a polite, but vapid smile and moved out of the room, dazed, and feeling that I was the plaything of forces too great for my handling, stormwrack rising and falling to every wave and at the mercy of every undertow and eddy of life's ineluctable currents. But who was I even to give houseroom to the arrogant and impious thought that God in His goodness might not be working His will, for where God is least felt or seen, there He must certainly be for God is everywhere.

When I got back to my room, Sarah came to me and said, "Did they tell you?"

"Yes."

"Oh, Nelo, isn't it splendid? Just what you must have longed for. And I can't wait to see you in a dog-collar. They always suit big, burly men like you."

293

CHAPTER SIXTEEN

IN ACTUAL FACT it took only two weeks to organise the
return to Bakata, a speediness which I felt owed much to the
fact that a large part of it had already been put in train long
before Sarah and I had agreed to hand over the diamonds, and
that this had been done by Xavier I had no doubt. He was
the kind of man who was used to planning well ahead, knowing
that resources and finance would eventually be forthcoming.
I had very little part in the organisation, but I was briefed
from time to time on its progress. There were to be two planes
and in one would go Alfy, and his staff, headed by Xavier,
and Bakatsi, and a full cargo of ammunition and war supplies;
in the other would be myself and Sarah and the Archbishop
with a cargo of food and medical supplies. The planes were
lodged in the hangars of an old NATO airfield—now re-
possessed by the French authorities and for all normal purposes
non-operative—which lay off the main Route N89 between
Bordeaux and Perigueux. Since, I had discovered, Château
La Verna stood overlooking the River Lot, the airfield was a
little less than a hundred kilometres from us. We were to take
off at dusk and make one stop for refuelling at some point in
Africa not disclosed to me for delicate political reasons (a
manoeuvre that reduced the planes' fuel load overall and
allowed more cargo to be carried), and land at Sokota just
before dawn where lorries for offloading would be waiting and
also a body of troops to welcome His Royal Highness back.

In the meantime I became the Reverend Charles Nelo
Sangster once more and I cannot pretend that any small

doubts I had about the authenticity of my reordination marred for very long my pleasure at being back in the Lord's service properly accoutred and legally—at least in Bakata—on the strength. Sarah, after only brief demur from me, found a small tailor in Cahors (which was not far from the château) who made me a sober, well-fitting dark suit and also supplied me with a dog collar and black vest and also a cleric's hat which was a little over continental in style for me to take to immediately, but Sarah said it suited me and the Archbishop took a Polaroid colour print of me for his album, and two or three of Sarah, one of which he gave me.

The Archbishop conducted the reordaining and his chaplain, who had rejigged the service and also considerably shortened it, presented me as a person apt and meet, for his learning and godly conversation, to exercise his ministry duly to the honour of God and the edifying of His Church, though I was momentarily put out after the Collect and Epistle when the Gospel reading came from the tenth chapter of St. John and began, *Verily, verily, I say unto you, He that entereth not by the door into the sheepfold, but climbeth up some other way, the same is a thief and a robber.* But it was not for long and was soon lost in my joy at being rededicated in the Lord's service. Nor was I offended when we all took refreshment and drinks after the service with the Archbishop and he said to me, "Son, you keep your nose clean and you will pretty soon end up first white bishop in Bakata." I was already thinking ahead to Sokota and the work which awaited me there, for through Xavier's intelligence service I knew that it now held quite a large refugee population brought there by famine and war which was desperately in need of food supplies, and also a hospital which badly needed medical supplies. When the planes landed, Alfy would go off and into battle with his troops while Sarah and I would take over the distribution of relief in Sokota. What the Archbishop intended to do he had not made clear as yet, but I had a feeling that he would not stray far from the King. I should mention—though probably it had no significance, yet I like to think it did—that towards the end of the service when I was kneeling before the Archbishop and the congregation were singing *Veni, Creator Spiritus*, Bakatsi, the elephant, who had been standing, docile, between two attendants in the aisle, came forward, dragging his purple guide ropes and lowered his trunk and tapped me two or three times gently on the head as though awarding me an accolade.

And in bed that night Sarah for the first time I had known her was shy and hesitant, even a little coy and somewhat indirect in her response to the happiness in me which I wished to share with her as a husband and wife should, and when, eventually, I asked why, she said, "Well, somehow I feel . . . well, you're a priest now, and it's different."

I said, "I've taken no vows of celibacy, and a priest is not proscribed from being a man, a husband or a lover. You'll soon get used to it."

Which she did, of course, and clearly took great pride in my new status. In fact, at times, I thought a little too much pride.

Anyway, there we were with a handful of days to pass under the October skies until the planes left and I gave thanks morning and evening that I was truly blessed with a loving wife and a place back in the ranks of those who serve the Lord. Through the post on one of the days came wedding presents from Teddie and his wife—an expensive travelling case complete with crystal and silver fittings for Sarah, and a silver whisky flask for myself, each one monogrammed with the appropriate initials.

Two days before we were due to leave Monsieur Crozette came to wish me goodbye.

I said, "But aren't you coming with us?"

He said, "Why no, Nelo. I am not a man of action. I just arrange things for people. Besides my widow friend doesn't like to be left with the snakes too long. Emergencies arise."

I said, "Well, I hope sincerely the day will come when we can pay you your commission."

He smiled. "Don't worry. I have already forgotten it. Just

now and then it is healthy for a man to do something for a cause and not for cash. Good luck, and goodbye Nelo."

"God bless you," I said and then, feeling that that was rather pompous, added, "and thank you for everything."

And so, two days later, in mid-afternoon, we left the Château La Verna for the ride to the airfield, in two private cars and a small hired bus from Cahors. Alfy and his entourage travelled in one car, the Archbishop, Sarah and myself in the other, and various attendants, staff and servants in the small bus, and it was 21 October, which—as every schoolboy ought to know, and my father never gave me opportunity to forget—is the anniversary of the battle of Trafalgar, when the flag was hoisted, not only with a slow roll on the drums but with a salute fired from a small brass cannon which my father had acquired and which, on the occasion of its first use, when he had not accustomed himself to its vagaries, recoiled on its small carriage and went backwards across the house terrace and smashed into the conservatory which was my mother's pride and joy, causing havoc amongst the pot plants and vines.

*   *   *   *

At the airfield both planes, still in the large hangar, had been loaded with their supplies under the able supervision of Xavier who in his new post radiated efficiency and optimism and looked forward cheerfully to the paradise of security which was soon to be his. When we arrived he was sharing a few bottles of wine with the two pilots and their first officers and a civilian member of the French customs who—I learned later—had cleared the cargo and authorised the manifests as medical and relief supplies—which was a typical example of Gallic logic since, I suppose, a siege howitzer could be termed a relief supply. All the Bakatans, I should say, were dressed in civilian clothes, though those who held military posts had their uniforms with them in suitcases. When the wine was done and just before the light went, the Archbishop, in black habit and gaiters, held a short service of blessing for the enterprise and took as his text

297

a simple compression of 1 Kings 8, 44 and 45—*If thy people go out to battle against their enemy, whithersoever thou shalt send them; then hear thou in heaven their prayer, and their supplication, and maintain their cause.* And a fine, short stirring address it was, marked most appropriately by Bakatsi (caged in an open-barred crate), who seemed to have a well developed sense of drama, for as the Archbishop said *Amen* he thrust his small trunk through the bars and trumpeted, in a juvenile soprano, a thin battle cry welcomed by all.

And when the service was done and the planes were being towed out onto the taxiing strip, I walked across the grass which was studded with purple-headed thistles over which hovered humming-bird hawk moths with Sarah, her arm in mine, and the smoky, darkening sky of France above us, ruddy on the western horizon, and I said to her, "You are sure this is what you want us to do?"

She said without looking at me, staring straight ahead of her at the long vista of the airfield and maybe farther into her future, "For me now there is for the first time purpose in my life; to go with you, to be with you, and to serve you wherever you are called upon to minister. And, anyway, we can't stay in Europe for *They* would be bound to catch up with us some day. And also I've always wanted to see Africa, ever since my father was posted to the Sudan for a term of duty and I had to stay behind at boarding school."

And I sighed to myself and knew that with her the dream and the reality would never meet, no matter her new-found maturity as a wife; and perhaps she guessed something of what was in my mind, for she went on, "You must be patient with me, Nelo. Everything I do is for you, for us. I'm not very good at it at the moment, so if sometimes I seem to go behind your back, or to manoeuvre you, or to be not quite such a nice person as you would wish—just put it down to clumsiness in a new way of life. I know now that the great affair is not simply to move, but to move in the right direction towards great affairs."

And I sighed again to myself for I knew clearly that she had thrown away a whole cast of outworn roles and was hard at work learning a new set of parts and, since instinct told me that she would have as much trouble with the new as with the old, I knew I was right to have married her and that she was always going to need me; and I prayed briefly that the full flowering of our love might not come like a laggard, trailing always just out of sight of the parade ahead.

So we went back to the planes which were warming up and we said our *au revoirs* to Alfy and his company, and then we boarded our own plane and Sarah and I were given improvised seats behind the two pilots in the cockpit which was open to the cargo-stacked fuselage run, and the Archbishop settled himself comfortably on a sack of flour between some crates of dried milk, lit a cigar, checked that his brandy bottle was within reach and then prepared to ignore the fact that he was going to be dangerously divorced from earth for many hours and abandoned to the hazards of an almost obsolete aircraft and God's grace.

We rumbled down the runway, the engines were run up until every nut and bolt and plate shook wildly, and then we sped forward and rose into the dark, cloud-littered sky and France and Europe began to slide away beneath us, and the co-pilot, who wore a blue, large peaked golf cap and a leather jacket with a coloured stencil of a bikini-clad girl on the back, turned and said, "An Archbishop and a priest—first time I ever carried such insurance. With apologies to the lady, hope you all did a leak before you left because we ain't got no facilities aboard." Which reminded me of the real Miss Amberley who never took Teddie and me on any excursion without supervising a bowel drill and was not to be deceived by the sound of a running tap. And after that there was just the monotony of flying at night, distance being eaten up with the roar and rattle of the plane, and then some time after midnight we came down, circling over a faint stipple of light from some African town, to another airfield where we got out to stretch

299

our legs in the warm, odour-filled night air and the planes were refuelled by a laughing, shouting gang of native boys and men while overhead there shone now a great copper-coloured moon and Sarah said, "We're in Africa. It smells different . . . good and thick and rich. Like gravy." And she laughed and held my arm so that the excitement in her ran through to me like a current, and the bikini-symbol pilot, stretching his legs also, came up to us and said, "I worked out of this dump once for three months, ferrying rich pilgrims to Red Sea ports on their way to Mecca. That was really the bottom."

An hour later we took off, flying straight towards the heart of the great moon while the forests, jungles, mountains and plains of Africa peeled away beneath us and the moonlight plated the convoluted rivers below with silver, and the plane of the Bakata kept station with us a half a mile away on our starboard and the hours droned by and the level of the brandy in the Archbishop's bottle dropped lower and lower.

Finally in the dark hour before dawn there were the meagre lights of Sokota below us and beyond it, clear to be seen as we dipped lower and circled while Alfy's plane went in to land, a row of brush fires flaring to mark the limits and length of the landing strip. We landed badly with a bump and a leap as though the plane had no wish for reunion with earth and then taxied to the far end of the strip and stopped just behind Alfy's plane. From then on there was only the noisy, laughing, shouting bustle and confusion of greetings and off-loading around the planes as a dozen lorries of all kinds drove forward and began to take aboard the supplies. All of them were manned by loyalist Bakatan troops in grey and green battle dress, wearing combat helmets—some psychedelically painted (which reminded me of Horace Dorsmo, who, in a way, had made all this possible)—and all of them were armed with rifles or automatic weapons and some of them strung with hand grenades in bunches about their persons like French onion sellers. And the first thing unloaded was, of course, the royal elephant Bakatsi, stepping out of his crate onto his native soil,

300

conscious that he had the centre of the stage and acknowledging his and the occasion's importance with another thin trumpeting which set the handful of troops cheering; and where I thought —looking at the dark perimeter of forest around us—there should have been quiet and swift loading and an urgent need to get the job done in case of unseen dangers, the whole procedure was delayed while first Alfy made a royal speech to mark his return and conferred a majority on the captain in charge of the welcoming troops, and then the Archbishop, a little unsteady but in good voice, added the Church's portion of oratory to that of the State and then was driven away in a private car which had awaited him—no doubt stocked, as Sarah said, with a fresh supply of brandy and cigars.

We had three lorries allocated to our plane and I did my best to supervise their loading without clashing with the military, but it was hard work, for officers and men were elevated by a euphoria which it was impossible to curb and every now and then an officer would pull out his revolver and fire a couple of rounds in joyous salute.

And, of course, disaster did strike, but not from the Bakatans' lack of military caution, but as it so often does in warfare out of treachery long planned and deviously contrived. The lorries were all loaded, and the first one, with Bakatsi aboard and the Bakata of Bakata, was just moving away down the strip when from the forest beyond the planes, the tall trees just beginning to catch the first light of dawn, the coming of morning waking the monkeys and jungle birds to screeching and calling, there came, sharp and staccato above the sound of the animals, the ugly rattle of automatic and machine-gun fire. The air was filled with a whistling of bullets like a swarm of hornets passing and there was the thick, brutal smack of lead into lorries and planes. I reached for Sarah, pulled her down, and together we rolled under the nearest of our medical and food relief lorries. Pandemonium swept down the strip like a whirlwind. The weapons from the forest chattered again and this time were punctuated by the short-range blast of field guns and the slow give away any vital information. Name, rank and number, that's what my father used to say was all they could ask for."

I said nothing, for there is seldom anything to be said against naïvety, but I was worried because I knew that troops on this continent could execute a very rough justice and be extremely unpleasant to women captives.

The party stopped a few yards from us and then the officer came forward alone. He carried a revolver, was dressed in combat overalls with three silver stars on his shoulder and his helmet was covered with camouflage netting in which, with some artistry, had been stuck a millinery of leaves and wild flowers, the flowers I noticed remarkably fresh.

He was a man of about thirty, tall, with an easy yet wary catlike walk, and his face was long, well-formed and intelligent, a pleasant looking man who came up to us, a long length of grass stalk held between his teeth in the way my father would hold one sometimes when he walked thoughtfully through his acres. Oddly, I had the curious impression that I had seen him somewhere before.

He said, politely removing the grass stalk first, "I am Captain Felaka, First Leopard Commando Group."

I said, "And I'm the Reverend Charles Nelo Sangster, a minister of the First Church of Bakata—"

"Ordained by the Archbishop himself," said Sarah.

"And this is my wife, Mrs. Sarah Sangster," I said. "We have with us food and medical supplies which I understand are urgently needed here in Sokota."

"Which Archbishop?" asked Captain Felaka.

"Dr. Bomokandi," said Sarah.

"Not recognised, ma'am," said the captain. "But I presume he arrived also with the ex-Bakata?"

"We are under no obligation to tell you anything except who we are," said Sarah.

The captain smiled pleasantly. "Don't worry, Mrs. Sangster. We know all about you both. All about everything. So, personally, you have come on an errand of mercy."

"Yes," I said.

"Well, I can't pretend there isn't need for supplies, particularly medical ones. The hospital here is shouting for them." He turned and said something in his own language to his soldiers. They moved at once round to the tail of the lorry and began to unload some of the supplies.

I said, "Wouldn't it be better to leave them on the truck and get them to the hospital quickly?"

"I'm a trained nurse," said Sarah.

"Darling—"

"Semi-trained," she corrected.

"All help will be welcomed," said the captain. "Also you will both be treated with every courtesy. We are not savages. I was at the Sorbonne and then a cadet at St. Cyr. However, you will understand that at the moment you are my prisoners."

One of the soldiers from the back of the lorry called to him. He beckoned us to follow him and we went to the party of soldiers. They had unloaded two of the crates of dried milk and ripped the plywood tops off and removed some of the large tins. A soldier tipped one of the crates forward so that we could look into it. Packed at the bottom half of the case where they had been hidden by the milk tins was a stack of grease-wrapped parcels.

Captain Felaka took one out and unwrapped it. From the paper he took a new, oily looking automatic pistol. Without a word he unwrapped another parcel, a much larger one. That held a new, short-barrelled automatic rifle.

The Captain shook his head sadly, and said, "I should say that you have brought probably only half the genuine supplies you thought you had, Reverend. In war the deceit of man is infinite. I am sorry for you."

"But we didn't know," said Sarah.

"I am glad to hear it," said the Captain, "but it makes no difference. You will both come with me."

* * * *

304

We were put into a jeep, sitting at the back while the captain drove, and alongside him sat an armed lieutenant of the Commando force. My lorry was driven after us.

We went off the strip and down a narrow rutted road towards Sokota.

I said to Captain Felaka, "When did you take Sokota?"

He said, "We didn't. It was not defended. We walked in an hour ago. All the garrison were out on the airstrip to welcome their rebel companions. We arrived a little too late."

I said, "Is that how you think of them, as rebels?"

"Naturally. They have been declared such in Army Orders. If it's in orders then it is so. I'm a professional soldier. Army regulations and orders are my bible."

Sarah said, "Now that the Bakata is back with Bakatsi the whole country will rise for him. Why don't you just turn round and join him. The Bakata would be glad and I would personally guarantee that he will make you a major on the spot."

"You have influence with him, Mrs. Sangster?" he asked, smiling.

"Of course. I am to be the new Minister for Arts and Culture."

Captain Felaka said, "For your own sake, I haven't heard that remark, neither has my lieutenant."

"Why not?"

"Because, Mrs. Sangster, I do not wish to change your category. At the moment you are just a misguided relief worker."

We drove on in the brightening morning to Sokota, and women and children waved to us as they worked in the maize patches, and finally we rumbled over a low wooden bridge that spanned the river and into the town. We stopped before a two-storey white plaster building with four or five corrugated roofed huts to one side of it.

Captain Felaka said to his lieutenant, "Unload the lorry of its food and medical supplies here. Take Mrs. Sangster in to the

305

hospital superintendent and explain to him the position and that she is a trained nurse who will help him and his staff. Then bring the rest of the stuff into headquarters."

As the lieutenant got out and waited for Sarah to follow, I said to the Captain, "You're separating us? I could help, too."

"Unfortunately," he said, "you come in a different category which will be explained later."

Sarah, now out of the jeep, said, "Don't worry, darling. Everything will be all right, I'm sure, and I'll come and see you as soon as I can."

She leaned over and kissed me, and her lips were fresh and cool, and as she stepped back I knew that all this for her was less a dangerous reality than an unusual dream in which she was adopting a new role with smooth assurance and optimism. Life to her was a succession of absorbing games whose variety was never ending.

I said, "Look after yourself, darling, and God bless you."

And then we drove away and left her there. We drove down a street lined with palms and single-storey flat-roofed houses and huts and into the main square of Sokota which was lined with false pepper trees and bright with the canopies and displays of a morning market and noisy with the chatter of men, women and children who all looked remarkably well fed and healthy; and finally, around the corner from the square, we stopped at a tall wooden-framed three-storey building which had a board across the front announcing "Hotel Livingstone" and two armed sentries on the door.

In the hallways I was booked into a charge book at the reception desk by Captain Felaka, who gave a sergeant with a beaming, coal black face my name, age, religion and nationality without reference to me; and I thought it odd that he knew my age, not just in years, but accurate also as to the exact day and month of birth. And then I was led up to the top floor and given room No. 33 and locked in, but informed that a sentry would be on duty outside at all hours and told not to try to jump from the window because it was a long drop and the hotel main door sentries would be waiting below, and that breakfast would be served in half an hour.

Which it was by a young, plump, good looking native girl in a red dress, her hair wrapped in a yellow turban and a row of Pepsi Cola bottle tops strung round her fine throat as a necklace. She gave me a warm smile, teeth flashing, laid a tray with, surprisingly, eggs and bacon, toast and coffee on it, before me and said, "Good morning, Reberend. You eat good now. And anything else you want just press the bell."

"You work here?" I asked.

"Days, yes, Reberend. Nights I work for my own account. Dey eggs is fresh. Same as officers have."

She went and I ate my breakfast, but not with much relish because I was worrying about Sarah. But I was not over-concerned about the Bakata and his supporters. Hiding extra war weapons under my relief supplies had been a treachery which was hard to forgive, and I meant to say so in no uncertain terms when he had control of the country and we met again.

After breakfast I sat at the window and smoked a cigarette. Through some tall trees opposite the hotel I could see the wide run of a muddy river, dotted with sandbars on which a few crocodiles lay like rotting logs.

At mid-morning Captain Felaka came to my room where I was reading for comfort a Gideon Bible which I had found in the bedside cupboard.

He said, "Your court martial is set for two o'clock this afternoon, Reverend."

I said, "Court martial? But you can't court martial me I'm not a military person."

He shrugged his shoulders. "Any person giving comfort and aid to the enemy is a military person. I have been appointed your defending officer. You want to brief me on the line of your defence?"

"Against what charge?"

"That I don't know until we get in court. But maybe you've some idea?"

I said, "All I know is that I came here at the invitation of the lawful head of this State and as a duly constituted member of its Church, in order to carry on God's work."

"That sounds very good, but it isn't a defence against anything. It's just an affirmation of intent."

I said, "How did you know the Bakata was coming this morning?"

He smiled. "We have our intelligence services, you know. Just as the ex-Bakata has. I take it then you have no briefing to give me?"

"That's correct—until I know the charges."

"Very well, Reverend. In court I just play it by ear."

Which is what he eventually did, but with no success at all. At two o'clock I was led down to the American bar of the hotel which had been turned into a court room. The President of the court and his two members sat on stools behind the bar, all of them full colonels in blue and red dress uniform, an ample supply of spirit bottles and glasses arrayed behind them at the back of the bar. The prosecuting officer was on one side of the room, his few papers spread out on the top of a pin-table machine, Captain Felaka used the top of a piano on the other side, and I stood more or less to attention in the middle of the room which was decorated around three of its sides with a crudely painted mural of African scenes and wildlife. There was one of a mild-looking hippopotamus which someone had decorated with a pair of spectacles and a pipe.

The President rattled an ashtray on the bar to call the court to attention and then the charge, or rather charges, were read out against me; to wit, that I, the Reverend Charles Nelo Sangster (there was an interruption here while the prosecuting officer protested the "Reverend" as being incorrect and unrecognisable and so on, but this was overruled by the President affably as of no importance) had (1) given comfort and aid to the ex-Bakata during his exile abroad, (2) made available to him the sum of one hundred thousand pounds—by a gift of diamonds—to enable him to buy arms and ammunition, hire planes and recruit disaffected rebel elements in order to mount an armed assault against Bakata, (3) been instrumental in, and given assistance towards, the abduction from Bakata of the Royal Elephant, Bakatsi, (4) had accepted in return, or would accept, bribes, offers of concessions and places of honour and importance for myself and my wife, and (5) had taken part in the armed return of the ex-Bakata to the country and had been party to the smuggling of arms and ammunition in the guise of relief food and medical supplies.

"How does the prisoner plead?" asked the President.

"Well, I don't really know," I said, because it did need some thought.

"That's fair enough," said the President. "Write him down as mute but not necessarily of malice."

Then, ignoring me, the prosecuting officer began to go through the charges, substantiating them with a wealth of detail which was really surprising and from which I could draw one conclusion only, that there had been some traitor at the Château La Verna who had compiled a most comprehensive dossier of events and conversations, and that person—by a process of deduction and the fact that he was the only one not to take part in the return to Bakata—I felt had to be Monsieur Crozette, which, remembering his fondness for snakes, did not now seem to me out of character.

When the prosecuting officer had finished, Captain Felaka spoke up on my behalf, but there was not a great deal he could pertinently say, though he said a great deal mostly in defence of my character, for which I was grateful and really quite touched, and then an argument developed between him and the prosecuting officer as to whether I was wrongly charged since the diamonds were not legally mine but my wife's and that she too should be standing trial with me, but the President would have none of this and gallantly said, "A wife might think she owns a few things, but under Bakatan law all belongs to husband. There's nothing in army regulations about court martialling a woman. Women in Bakata are not recognised as military personnel—only as military comforts." And then, since it was very hot in the bar and I had been standing a long time, he said, "Reverend, you look hot and tired. Take a seat—and have a drink." He reached under the bar, selected a bitter lemon for me, flipped the top off expertly with the bar key and poured the drink, which Captain Felaka brought to me and for which I was grateful.

And so the affair went on for another half hour and then Captain Felaka, the prosecuting officer and myself marched out of the bar to leave the President and the court to make their findings. Melana, the girl who had brought me breakfast, arrived with a tray of drinks, this time Scotch and soda, and we all refreshed ourselves while waiting and the prosecuting officer complained of the President to Captain Felaka. "He over-rides protocol and regulations too much."

"He's a good man," said the captain. "Live long enough he'll make general. King Alfy had him lined up for it before he was kicked out."

Then the prosecuting officer with a burst of friendliness asked me, "How are Alfy and Bakatsi?"

"They're in very good health."

"Splendid. Things never the same since they went. My mother-in-law, she's covered in boils, and the train to the coast don't run no more."

It took the court ten minutes to reach their findings. I was marched back, brought to attention before the President, told to take off my clerical hat, which I did, and then he read the findings and the sentence.

I was found Not Guilty of charges (1) and (3) and Guilty of all the other charges without leave to appeal. I was sentenced to be shot in the main Sokota square one hour after dusk on the following day, but since I was a British subject, a person of standing and good family, the firing squad would—as a mark of respect—not be composed of non-commissioned troops but of two officers. Captain Felaka and the prosecuting officer were detailed to compose themselves as the firing squad, and when

310

the President asked me if I had anything to say, I said, completely at a loss, "But this is nonsense."

He said, "You wrong, Reberend. This is war."

* * * *

So there I was, sitting at my window looking out at the African night, the moon turning the river to black and silver flood, and a brass band playing out of sight in the town square. The night was so hot that I stripped off my shirt, sitting naked to the waist.

Melana brought me my dinner, a plate of curried chicken and with it a bottle of wine (though I had not asked for it) of which I drank a little. It was a Yugoslav Riesling and lukewarm. Seeing the scar under my ribs, Melana asked me how I had got it and, when I told her, she laughed and said, "Brothers, dey ain't got no respect for family. My brother always wanting me to let his friends sleep with me half-price," and I laughed with her and gave her a glass of the Riesling. Well, it was better to take wine together and to laugh rather than be gloomy.

When she came back to collect the tray, she said, "Captain Felaka says your wife comes tomorrow morning to see you, Reberend."

I said, "Does she know what is going to happen to me?"

She nodded. "She knows, Reberend. She's been to see President of court martial already and made big fuss about some kind of thing called Geneva collection. Everyone hear her bawlin' him out in the office. Is true her daddy is general in British Army and mother head of British Red Cross?"

"Not quite, Melana."

"Also she makes speech at hospital saying you come to help people of Sokota and Bakata with supplies. She says army goin' to martyr you 'cos they missed putting King Alfy in the bag. I tell you, she's real top-grade fireworks. Like I tell Captain Felaka, too, only right he let her be with you tonight. Man with one night to go got a right to enjoy his wife for last time. But he say no, dat not covered in Army regulations, but he say if I want to stay and you want me that's O.K. 'cos workin' at Headquarters I reckoned as army comforts. So it's up to you, Reberend, if you want me to be like your wife for tonight. You fancy that?"

I said, "It's very kind of you, Melana, but I shall be happier just on my own."

"Well, Reberend, you change your mind, just ring bell. I'll be around 'cos I don't go to work on my own tonight, just in case you change your mind. I don't ever sleep with white man before so be pleasure for me and education, too. You feel like it, you just ring."

But I didn't feel like it. I went to bed and read the Bible and tried not to worry too much about Sarah, and finally I fell asleep and slept dreamlessly.

The next morning a little before noon they brought Sarah to me and we were left alone. She was wearing a snow-white nurse's uniform with a red cross on her breast and a little white cap with a smaller red cross on its front and her red copper hair was tied severely back. There was a capped clinical thermometer sticking out of her uniform breast pocket, and her eyes were soft, sad shadings of green, grey and amber and somewhere at the back of her mind I knew she was touched by noble thoughts probably of Edith Cavell and Florence Nightingale and I loved her for it because there is a wonderful merit—even when it disconcerts and discomforts others—in people who love life and its pageantry and perplexities so much that they respond with a protean shift of personality to meet it. And she came into my arms and we kissed and held each other, and then she sat down and wept a little, but not in any extreme way because the occasion was too severe to be vulgarised by ugly sobs and lamentations. This I knew, too, was largely for my sake because she understood that I would want to face the last few hours and the final moment with dignity and she wanted in no way to undermine that resolution by any weakness of hers. And neither did she suggest that she should give me any physical comfort because we both knew that this was a time and a place when the solacing of our bodies would be no more than a hasty, puerile snatching of a meretricious joy.

She said, "Nelo, I can make no headway with the military authorities here. But the telegraph office is working and I've sent telegrams and cables on your behalf. I've made a plea to Alfy's nephew, the upstart, for mercy. I've sent a statement to the Reuter office in the capital, and to the United Nations and a few other places. And you mustn't be cross with me if I've exaggerated my own background, but I'm your wife and it is my duty to fight for you with every weapon I can lay a hand on."

I said, "Of course, darling. But they'll probably block your cables. Let's face it, I was in many ways foolish to get involved in all this and, clearly, somewhere in Alfy's camp there has been a traitor. But if I have to die, then it is God's will and it is no good trying to discover His reasons, or, if one knew, arguing with them. All I'm concerned with now is your happiness and comfort when I'm gone. I wouldn't want you to make your life grievous for me."

She said, "I shall fight for you. I am not going to believe that this will happen. I am not going to give in. You are my life and my love and I won't let you go."

I said, raising her and kissing her, "And you mine."

She leaned back from me, and said, "You could try to escape."

I said, "The only way is through the window which means landing up with a broken neck at the feet of the guards."

She said, "It's a pity you're so big. You could put on my uniform and go out as me. Your hair would pass and I've got dark glasses."

I smiled, kissed her again, and said, "If there is anything to be done, God will do it."

She stayed with me for over an hour and then went because she had thought of other cables to send, one principally to the Archbishop of Canterbury about the persecution of priests engaged in foreign mission work. Before she went I said a short prayer for us both, and from the door she said, "Darling Nelo, don't be a sheep, don't lie down and die. If you get the slightest chance to, try and get away. Remember God helps those who help themselves. I refuse to believe that this is going to happen."

During the afternoon Captain Felaka came to see me and said, "I'm sorry to tell you this, Reverend, but we have had to take your wife into protective custody because she is making such a nuisance of herself and jamming our communication systems with cables."

"None of which, I imagine, will ever be delivered?"

"That is so. But you need not worry about your wife's future here. *Our* Bakata has sent a message that she is to be released as soon as you are shot, and that she will remain working at the hospital until the military situation is clearer and then she will be free to leave Bakata."

I said, "Thank you." Then I added, "Why do I have the odd feeling that I have seen you before?"

He said, "Probably because if you are an observant person you have."

"Where?"

He said, "You are soon going to have the answer to a big mystery. Take a little earthly one with you."

He left me and the day wore on and from the window I watched the little white egrets flirting across the sandbars of the river and now and again the slow slide of a crocodile into the waters. The monkeys punctured the air with frequent screams and flocks of bright coloured parakeets drifted among the trees like slow showers of confetti and somewhere very distant I heard the occasional *thump, thump* of a field piece firing. And so dusk came, at first a smoky, transparent veil settling over the land and then, with fuller darkness, the neon sign outside the hotel was switched on and the roadway was marked with red and blue colours of destiny, the red of hell and the blue of heaven from which at this moment I knew my mother watched and, I hoped, approved of the way I was bearing myself for in our family the greatest misdemeanour was not to behave like a gentleman, no matter the circumstances.

And then Captain Felaka came for me and with him was the prosecutor who, I had learned, was called Captain Umlala which I thought was a nice name, and he looked very nervous and he said to me, "Reverend, I just want you to know that I am a bad shot so I probably don't hit you at all which is good for my conscience. Kill in battle one thing. Execution another, and strictly for non-commissioned ranks."

"That's true," said Captain Felaka, "but of no importance. I am a first-class marksman and can shoot the eye out of a crocodile at a hundred paces. You would like to be blindfolded, Reverend?"

"No thank you." Which was not bravado, but the truth because I saw no reason why I should shut my eyes to the world for my last few moments in it, a world which I had enjoyed and delighted in, and sinned in.

So, I was marched to the square, which was only a short distance away, with an escort of four soldiers and the two captains, and the air was warm and full-bodied with earth and river and growth scents, and the square had been cleared of all civilians except on one side where men and women stood in silence and watched us come a little raggedly into the place because I could not accommodate my steps to those of my escorts, and then the silence was broken by a little murmuring from the crowd as I was halted with my back to the tall trees fringing the far river and Captain Felaka went behind me and began to tie my wrists together and said quietly, "The blindfold, Reverend, is at the prisoner's option, but tied wrists is obligatory under Army regulations."

So I made no objection and saw a few yards away a small open army truck parked with a driver leaning against the tailboard and I knew that it was waiting to take me away when the firing was done, and knew, too, that it would not take me, Charles Nelo Sangster, but only the limp shell that had held me for a few years, that shell which is of so much concern to so many people who in their vanity forget that the Lord seeth not as man seeth; for man looketh on the outward appearance, but the Lord looketh on the heart.

And Captain Felaka walked away and joined Captain Umlala and a soldier handed them their rifles, and the murmur from the crowd grew a little louder, like the sound a river makes in the peace of a night when the floods begin to take it and it comes grumbling down the valley, spate-angry and tearing at its banks; and this made me think of Stonebridge and the river and I thought it was good to remember the place where I had begun my pilgrimage through life on this its last day. And then I put the thought from me and made my silent private prayer to the Lord, which was only His concern and mine, but when I had finished I looked at the two captains and the crowd beyond and knew that no man should go out without sound, without some affirmation of his belief and, since it was my last moment, there were no better words than those that are also the last of the beloved Psalms, so I said, loud and clear, " 'Let every thing that hath breath praise the Lord. Praise ye the Lord.' "

Three seconds later the two captains fired. I was briefly aware of a tremendous indignation as one bullet hit me, and then I dropped into darkness.

CHAPTER SEVENTEEN

Job asked: *If a man die, shall he live again? All the days of my appointed time will I wait, till my change come.* Well, I did and it would be idle to hide that since it was into a life I had already known there was a certain feeling of anti-climax about it. However, there was some profit to it for at least I knew that the face of death is not necessarily an unfriendly one.

And certainly the face of the man hanging over me was friendly, for it was the face of Jimmy Harcourt. I came swimming up to him out of a great, black tiredness and with a dull, persistent ache in my right shoulder just below the collar bone which, I subsequently learned, was broken. I was lying in a wide bunk with spotlessly white sheets and counterpane and the sun came slanting in through a highly polished porthole and sent water reflections dancing about the cabin. Through my supine body I could feel the gentle throb of engines and there was a clinical smell of disinfectant in the air. Beyond Jimmy stood Miss Amberley in a black dress with a tight coral necklace about her throat and a genuine look of concern in her eyes, and beyond her stood a grey-haired man in khaki shirt and slacks with a doctor's stethoscope hung about his neck.

Jimmy smiled and gave a great, whisky-tainted sigh of pleasure and said, "Welcome back, boyo, and if you bear any secrets of the Great Beyond then it is keeping them to yourself you should be and not spoil the pleasure of us common mortals in the surprise to come. And don't try to move because that's a nasty shoulder ye've got there seeing that Captain Felaka is

317

not the marksman he said he was and should only have broken your arm, but not to mind for the realism of it all was enough to convince any saint but the good Patrick himself."

I said, and was surprised at the thinness and weakness of my voice, "Where had I seen him before?"

"Sure now, that's a great question for the first day of rebirth. Would it be in a photograph in La Guicha's office where she keeps mementos of all her old boys and girls?"

"It would," I said, remembering.

Miss Amberley said, "You shouldn't make him talk much, Jimmy."

"And why not? The boy has got to learn to do it again," said Jimmy. "But as a stimulant let's give him a drop of the hard stuff if the doctor says he can have it."

The doctor nodded, and Jimmy handed me a glass from which I sipped neat whisky and then coughed a little.

"Where am I?" I asked.

"And isn't that the first question convention demanded you should ask?" said Jimmy. "But not you, Nelo. You come back from the grave wondering where you'd first seen the man who killed you and had you carted away on a lorry like old horse meat for Tom Maloney to sell in Fitzpatrick Street as best prime steak. Well, boyo, you're on a river boat, a day and a half down stream from Sokota which saw you die and staged a riot afterwards so that the troops had their hands full and then had to run for it because they didn't notice King Alfy and his boys sneaking back into town to cut their throats."

"A temporary setback," said Miss Amberley taking the whisky glass from me.

"Was Captain Felaka working for you?" I asked.

"Who else, boyo? We'd have recruited the Angel of Darkness himself if we'd needed him to get you back."

"Oh, no," I said.

"Oh, yes," said Jimmy. "We knew you'd never stick with us so long as you had that girl . . . your wife, I mean . . . at your side to worry over. But now she's a respectable widow

318

and a mature woman capable, as you have learned, of taking care of herself."

The doctor said, "Let him rest."

"He can do that and talk," said Jimmy. "I know this boyo, doctor. Sure and he has a questing mind that is like the old lady's donkey always in some other soul's patch to clear up the thistles and the beans. Am I not right, Nelo?"

I said, "You arranged it all? Right from the moment of our escape from Schloss Marberg?"

"That's so," said Miss Amberley. "Monsieur Crozette is one of us—"

"Category Wild Goose, the like to you," said Jimmy.

I said, "I thought I was Swan-Flight?"

"It's temporarily demoted you've been, lad. But never fear, there are plenty of dead men's shoes to fill in our service."

"Monsieur Crozette was a traitor," I said.

"It comes to us all," said Jimmy. "But there was a little mistiming at Sokota so your friend King Alfy is on the loose. There'll be hard words and hard drinking about that in the corridors of power, but the outcome now is in the hands of the Lord and at the moment He is not saying which side He'll favour. Personally, for Xavier's sake, and just between these four walls, I'm hoping He's got his money on King Alfy, but as far as you're concerned it's academic."

"Why?" I asked.

"You're due for hospitalisation and then convalescence, say four months in all," said Miss Amberley, "and then you'll start a reindoctrination course."

"I'll submit to no such thing," I said.

"You will, boyo," said Jimmy. "We'll have your obituary notice in *The Times* tomorrow for the world to know you're good and dead, and that makes you the precious little jewel in our crown. 'Tis walking in glory you will be in the service and no back answers taken because now if you kick back against the pull of the reins they can wipe you out without a single question being asked. You have to learn, Nelo, you red-haired, innocent, overgrown choirboy, that in this hard life it is not permitted to live and to die twice for that only plays hell with the records."

I shut my eyes and then felt Miss Amberley put her hand on my brow and say in tones that had often come from the real Miss Amberley, "He's got a temperature. Let him sleep."

And I drifted off to sleep. When I woke again it was night and Miss Amberley was sitting by the bed reading a book and I saw that it was still *The Travels of Marco Polo*, who too believed that the great affair was to move; and when she saw that I was awake she smiled like a kind aunt and said, "Is there anything you want, Nelo?"

I was touched by the Nelo, for it was the first time she'd used it to me, and I said, "Perhaps you could in very plain language, as relief from Jimmy, outline something of what is going to happen to me?"

"So far as I can, yes, Nelo."

And she did, and subsequent events proved her more or less correct. To begin with she explained why I was of so much importance to them. In the past they had recruited in a rather random fashion and then submitted their recruits to training and the testing and trials of actual experience in the field. This had, of course, resulted in a frequent wastage of time, training and money on people who subsequently proved fallible at some point. But recently they had gone over to a computerised system which had been programmed by an international board of consultant psychologists, brain specialists, lawyers, high ranking criminals, outstanding explorers and eminent divines and demonologists. All putative agents were programmed, every known detail of them fed into the machine which turned out a detailed classification of the candidates' potential. This had been done for me and I had come out, broadly speaking, Alpha plus, which was something that only happened about once with every thousand candidates. I was too good to lose.

I said, "The computer must be wrong."

A little shocked Miss Amberley said, "Nelo, don't ever let anyone hear you say that."

She then went on to outline the immediate future. We were on our way to the coast, and from there I would be flown to a hospital and convalescent home on the shores of the Caspian Sea. (I didn't at this stage raise the question of the nationality of the service which coveted me and, to tell the truth, in my subsequent work I never really knew because national loyalties seemed to have disappeared and the whole thing was of an international complexity which only the faceless, nameless men at the top were presumed to understand.) From the Caspian, when fit, I would go to Patagonia for reindoctrination and training and after that be assigned to an Occidental or Oriental area according to suitability and need.

I said, "But they can't hold me like this? Some time or other I could escape or get in touch with my wife or my family."

Miss Amberley shook her head, "I'm afraid not, Nelo. You see, when you married you made your own prison. If you even attempt to do any of these things the hostage you have given them through your love will be destroyed."

"What on earth do you mean?"

"They will kill your wife."

I said, "You're joking, and it's a bad joke."

"I have never been more serious, Nelo. So just resign yourself."

"But she'll know I'm alive, particularly if King Alfy recovers his kingdom because Captain Felaka would tell that my death was faked."

Miss Amberley shook her head. "He can't do that, Nelo. He was the only man that knew it was faked and I'm afraid he will have been killed in the Bakata's assault on Sokota. We left someone behind to make sure it happened."

"Good God, the poor fellow." And then, another thought striking me, I said, "Do you mean that Captain Umlala didn't know? That he fired in earnest?"

321

"Of course, but we relied—correctly—on his bad marksmanship. For the sake of security some risks have to be taken even with exceptional candidates like yourself."

I was silent for a while, feeling sick and disgusted and deeply depressed, but then I knew that it was no good succumbing weakly to the evils of this world for though my enemies were lively and they were strong I knew that the good Lord would not forsake me and would not be far from me, for in Him I had hope.

So I said, "Are you, as I imagine, disposed to be a good friend to me, Miss Amberley?"

She put her book on the cabin table, avoiding my eyes for a moment and then turned and said, "It is possible, Nelo."

"Then tell me what it is that I must do to free myself. There must surely be something?"

She considered this and then said, "For most people, no. But with you it is possible. There are some crude solutions they will not impose upon a man of very high rating. They try to find a civilised way. But there is only one situation I know of that will put you in such a category and your hope of reaching it is infinitesimal."

"Tell me."

"Amongst the men at the top, the nameless and faceless ones, there is a strong freemasonry which makes the Mafia look like the Boy Scouts. For one another they will arrange anything. First, you must work with us for two or three years and then— and this is up to you—you must find one of these nameless men who has a marriageable daughter and you must get her to agree to marry you, but I must warn you that the daughters of such men are not likely to be fools or easily taken in. But if she wants to marry you, then because these men do not like their close family in any way involved in their work, you will be released and never interfered with again. There are only three men who have ever done it and two of those were accidents since they did not know, nor did the girls, that their fathers were nameless ones."

322

I said, "But that's impossible. I'm married already."

"No, Nelo," she said, "you are dead."

I said, "I am not dead, and I cannot marry anyone else since I already have a wife whom I love."

"Then, Nelo," she said, "you must put a good face on things."

And in this she was right for if a thing cannot be cured it must be endured until such time as it is God's will that it shall be otherwise. So we went to the coast and I was flown to the Caspian hospital and convalescent home where we had caviar at least once every day, and then I did my training in Patagonia and while there heard that King Alfy had recovered his kingdom, but I had no news of Sarah except that I knew she had not become Minister of Arts and Culture for the Press published the names of King Alfy's new cabinet and there was a Mr. Amamba Bomokandi listed as the Minister for Arts and Culture, a nephew I learned later of the Archbishop; but just before I left Patagonia Jimmy, who had arrived to give a course of lectures on *Assimilation and Dissimulation in Undeveloped Areas*, handed me a Press cutting from a Geneva paper which recorded the opening by the Bakata of Bakata of the new Sangster Clinic for Children and I knew that, in effect, my diamonds had come to roost where I had desired and that Alfy had honoured his pledges to La Guicha at least; but of Sarah I could get no news except six months later when I made a brief visit to Schloss Marberg where the Chief, pleased with my rapid progress, told me as a kindness that Sarah had left Sokota a month after my death and no one knew where she had gone.

And so I worked for *Them* for over three years and I would not want to put any details of my tasks on record except to say that I tried to carry them out with the maximum of charity possible which was far less than I would have wished, and that all this time the memory of Sarah remained sharp and clear in my mind, and the hope of escape even sharper, and then eventually the miracle happened of which Miss Amberley had spoken, though by this time Miss Amberley had passed away in what for us were normal circumstances. She boarded a

British Railways steamer at Calais to cross to Dover and never stepped off on the other side. The only thing they ever recovered of hers was her handbag with a copy of the *Life of Benvenuto Cellini* in it, which she had left or been forced to leave in a ladies' cloakroom aboard. And because of the miracle—worked for I may say assiduously by me but with no real conception of what it would be—and a delicate pact made in frankness and faith and also secrecy, I at last found myself one night back at Sokota, standing in the square in front of a statue.

It was a very bad statue made of some cheap metal lacking the virtue to weather gracefully as bronze or copper does. The tropical atmosphere had played hell with it. The metal had been scaling and rusting away from the day it had been put up. On the top of the stone plinth a reddish sludge had dribbled down in the rains and had been baked hard by the sun. The head and left shoulder were covered in bird droppings, but there was none on the right shoulder because the right arm was raised aloft, leaving no space for roosting. There was nothing flattering about it.

There I stood, eight feet high, wearing a flat-topped, wide-brimmed hat over a face which had lost part of its nose. A tight ecclesiastical dog-collar pressed hard against my throat, the coat tails streamed out in an eternal gale, and there was a sticker for the local cinema plastered across my waistcoat. At my feet, perched on the plinth top, was a rusty can that held a bunch of dried grasses and an artificial arum lily on a short stem. The inscription on the base was easily read in the moonlight which was washing the squalid square with a rinse of pale light. The metal letters had shared in the general deterioration; a few had fallen off and the others were weeping their life away in red rust tears.

THE REVEREND   ARLES ELO ANGST

-197

ART R

Leaning back against my tree, one of the three false peppers that lined the potholed piece of road, I smiled to myself. Time's schoolboy jokes against Man and his pomposities always please me. Not knowing it they hadn't put my date of birth on the base. It should have read 1930. ART R originally had read MARTYR—which I never was or will be, not being of that stuff. I walked round to the back of the statue. It was better from that side, a dark mass silhouetted against the moonlight, the forward stance and raised right arm giving it a powerful, monolithic feeling. Perhaps we all look better from behind. Beyond the statue the moon made a coarse filigree work of the branches and trees by the river. On the mud flats the frogs were eructating irregularly and, now and again, when they fell silent, the night was stitched with the faint, neurotic whine of the mosquitoes. The same sounds that I had heard when I had been in the square before—and that had been for less than an hour. A crocodile splashed heavily in midstream and a little breeze came spurting through the trees, rustling the leaves like an aged spinster riffling through dead love letters, and bringing with it the smell of Africa, a damp, warm, ashy, sour-sweet smell of decay and growth.

Somebody shuffled round from the front of the statue and stood in the moonlight with his bare toes just touching the uneven line of shadow it threw. It was a coloured gentleman in a woman's cast-off maxi-coat.

He said, "I hear you laughing, boss?"

"Should a man hide it?"

"I hear you from clear the other side of the Reberend. You know, you look like him."

"My nose is better."

"Could be."

I nodded at the bulky back above us. "Did you ever see him?"

"No, boss. I am away fighting. But my sister knew him for a little while. She look after him for food and drink while he's here. She say, once she even make Copernicus with him. But I don't believe her. She big liar."

"Copernicus?"

"Some words I don't like, boss. So I put another in place. Everyone understand just the same."

"You know who Copernicus was?"

"Sure, he say earth go round sun, not other way. Pope is very angry, but I never see why. Mealies ripen just the same."

"That was Galileo."

"Same thing. My sister make Copernicus with some, Galileo with others. You interested in Reberend?"

"All my life."

"You best come and talk my sister. She very interested in Reberend."

I knew who she was now. I said, "How far?"

"Round the corner, boss."

It was an open-fronted garage of corrugated iron and backed by a small, flat-topped house made of concrete blocks. There was a yellow-painted, topless Chevrolet in the garage and three men sat on the ground playing cards, using a metal advertisement placard for Michelin tyres as a table. At the back was a stairway that led to a top-floor bedroom. Outside the door my friend said, "Beer or whisky, boss?"

I said, "Whisky."

He opened the door and, without going in, called, "Is gentleman here, Melana—very interested in Reberend. Maybe Copernicus, too. I fetch whisky."

He eased me politely into the room and shut the door between us. She was half-turned from an electric Singer sewing-machine where she had been doing something with a red-coloured cotton dress. The loose folds of the stuff fell over her knees and made a brilliant contrast with the yellow and green dress she wore. She had her hair knotted up and caught in a yellow turban affair and under the naked blaze of the high-powered ceiling bulb her bare arms and face gleamed like mahogany, silvered with bold light planes. She'd put on weight, but evenly.

I gave her a nod and said, "Miss Melana?"

326

She stood up. "In the flesh. None other. Who are you?"

"Don't you remember?"

"I don't try to yet, boss. I got plenty to keep my mind going without lookin' for fresh material. You don't look like you want that."

She nodded towards a bed that lay beyond the sewing-machine. It had been made into a canopied four-poster by light wood battens draped in white, blue-spotted muslin, flounced and gathered at the head and foot.

I said, "No. But you remember me, though you aren't going to let yourself admit it yet." I took a photograph from my pocket and handed it to her. "I want to know what happened to her."

She looked at the photograph and then said, "You want to do something for me?"

"If I can."

"Unbutton your vest."

I undid the buttons of my shirt front. She came over to me, took one of the loose flaps and pulled it aside to expose the long scar on my left side just below the ribs.

She said, "How did you get that?"

I said, "I told you once."

"Tell me again."

"My brother threw a dustbin lid at me when we were bathing."

She stepped back from me and I did up my buttons. Her brother came in with an enamelled tray holding two plastic glasses, a tarnished hot water jug full of water, and a bottle of whisky labelled *Highland Servant*, only Highland was spelt *Higland*. He put the tray down and said, "Other services, boss —just bang on de floor." Then he went.

As though there had been no interruption, Melana said, "Yes, that's how you tell it the first time. And you laugh a lot. Remember? You laugh still so much?"

"Now and again, but I fancy the now gets farther away from

327

the again each time." I nodded at the photograph. "What about her?"

"She left here some time after they killed you." She handed the photograph back and poured whisky for us. "If they killed you, how come you're standing there waiting for whisky?"

I am the Resurrection and the Life. In the midst of life we are in death, and somewhere between the two the strands of farce and fate are incredibly twisted. I said, "They made a mess of it. The last miracle has the dust of centuries on it. What happened to her?"

She handed me the whisky and I touched my lips with it. My father would have spat it out, but then he had had a cossetted palate. I let it run, striking fiery buffets at my throat as it went.

She said, "Who knows? She went away from this town. She the one you love?"

Over and above all others, beyond life itself.

I said, "Yes."

"That why you don't take comfort from me just them few hours before they shoot you?"

"Love isn't a reed mat on a hard floor, or a bed with pretty hangings. Love is a holiness given to all men and women to prove to them that they don't have to be alone and animals all the time."

She smiled, big, strong white teeth showing in her broad face, and then suddenly laughed. "When you finally get to be real dead, whoever they is, angels or devils, they goin' to have trouble with your tongue. Yes, you is de Reberend. What you really doin' back here?"

"Looking for her." I held up the photograph.

"She went away. More I don't know."

I said, "If she went away, then you know more. Did she go alone or with someone? Did she go on foot, on mule or by car? Just tell me one thing which will start me moving from this town towards her."

"Some things not good to hear."

I said, "Just tell me, anything, no matter how small . . . so that it will set my feet moving."

And Melana said, "O.K., Reberend, I see you is set in your mind. You come back tomorrow morning and I take you. I not free till then 'cos I got good customer comes later."

So I went back to the Hotel Livingstone and then, the next morning, I was at Melana's house by eight o'clock and the three men were still playing cards on the Michelin advertisement but they had to move to let Melana and myself get in the yellow Chevrolet which Melana drove. She went out of the town and down the new road by the old airstrip and she made no conversation, as though the passing of time and distance were enough burden for our minds, and I watched a vulture circling in the sky and the green peaks of the distant hills and the Bakatans working in the fields and the occasional road advertisements, one of which was for *Bomokandi Beer—The Drink of the Elite that All Men can Afford.*

After about an hour we turned off a side road, through neat patches of gardens of vegetables being irrigated by sprinklers and drew up in front of a long low building with low, straw-thatched huts behind it and a sign board which said—*The Mission of Our Blessed Lady.* To one side was a small playing field where children were squatted in a great circle on the grass listening to a Roman Catholic priest and shouting with laughter now and then at his words.

Melana stopped the car and said, "You go on alone, Reberend. They know everything from here."

I walked up to the front of the building where there was another priest, tall, robed, his feet in sandals, who was painting the verandah railings with blue paint which had spilled over his right hand. He turned and nodded and smiled at me, and said, "Good morning, my son."

And I said, "Good morning, Father. My name is Charles Nelo Sangster and I have come in search of my wife whose maiden name was Sarah Minihane."

He considered this for a moment, then nodded, put his paint

329

can and brush down and then wiped his hand on a handkerchief he pulled from his robe pocket, and finally said, "It is curious, but I had a feeling that one day you would come, for you know, my son, it is a strange thing but I think our Lord reserves more miracles for this country than any other. Come with me."

He led the way round the corner of the building, and then down a long path, edged with whitewashed stones, past the thatched huts and on to the edge of the forest and through a small wooden gate into a low walled enclosure which on the moment of entering was preparation enough for me so that I refused myself all bitterness.

He stopped before one of the many small, roughly carved wooden headstones and just stood there without words while I read the inscription. SARAH SANGSTER. Just that.

I shut my eyes and my being was one prayer for her while I stood there, hearing the children laughing and calling in the distance. Then after an interval the priest said, "Do you wish to be left alone, my son?"

And because I knew I would come back again to talk to her when I could find the language and the mood she would want, I said, "No thank you, Father. But tell me about her."

He said, "When Sokota was overrun, the hospital was destroyed and she came to us with such of its people that survived, and she worked here for seven months, nobly and unstintingly, and then she could work no more and she died of a fever. Malaria, in fact. We all loved her."

I said, "Thank you, Father," and turned away and went back the way we had come and he followed me without speaking until we reached the verandah and, as I paused, he said, "Wait here, my son. There is something she left you."

He moved away and I sat down in the strong sun on the steps and had no thoughts, only a numbness and coldness which I felt could never pass for now she was gone beyond my poor protecting and cherishing and I knew how poor a thing it had been.

Then I heard steps and looked up to see the priest approaching, no longer alone. And he came up to me as I rose and said, "She died a month after the child was born, and she had her christened Felicity. A happy name."

Which it was, but how could he know that it had been my mother's name, too? The child staring up at me in a plain yellow dress had Sarah's hair, red-copper fired by the sun and caught at the back in a drooping bow of white ribbon, and she had her face, and the same curve and run of the lips, but her eyes were blue like mine, and there was nothing I could say because for the moment all words were choked inside me, so I squatted down in the dust and took the four-year-old hand in mine and then I touched the warm, tanned skin of one cheek and leaned forward and kissed it gently, and the child laughed and gave me a little push with her hand.

I stood up and the priest said, "What do you want to do, my son?"

And words came now, for there was a rising liberation in me, a release from some part of numbness, and I said, "I will come again, Father. We must grow together, gently."

And he nodded and said something to the child in Bakatan, and she raced away to join the other children, and then he walked to the car with me and said, "Your wife said she was of our faith and that she wished the child to be, too."

I nodded, and got into the car and as I did, he went on, "We tried to get in touch with your wife's parents but we could never find them."

I said, "She had them everywhere, Father, and they all loved her."

He looked curiously at me, as though he would say something but I gave Melana the sign and I raised my hand to him as we drove away, back to Sokota, back to the Hotel Livingstone where my wife to be, the daughter of a nameless one without knowing it, waited for me; and for that miracle I gave thanks to God for without Sarah there was no other woman in the world who could give Felicity and myself what we needed, the

331

child her love to match mine, and to me the high blessing of her presence and strength, for if there are few Sarahs in this world and I had come to know my true love for her too late, there were few women, too, like Hortense.